BIRDENWHEEL

BIRDENWHEEL

A Novel

LINDSAY RICE

Miracle Ticket Press

Paperback ISBN 13: 979-8-218-60446-2

Miracle Ticket Press

"If I knew the way, I would take you home…"
~ Robert Hunter, "Ripple"

For all the good ones we lost
including Jerry Garcia, Robert Hunter,
and Phil Lesh

Birdenwheel Characters

Chapter 1
Devon

1991

Speed raked Devon's body like a raw flame following gasoline across wood. He could feel the hairs on his neck ruffle, pleasurable and cool. His old Indian motorcycle revved higher and higher. Water in his eyes hazed the sight of the road. It was early night. Star flecks still and shining. Somewhere between Flagstaff, Arizona, and home, somewhere through desert and over earth. Devon wanted this rush; the only thing near enough to flight. He wanted the raw slap of wind, the heat of an engine, but wanted to control it with his own boot heel on the pedal. The road was a straightaway, but he could sort of see ahead, where the pavement hugged a hill.

As the road curved, Devon wished for wings. He kept going fast, trying to break through to some other space. His mind stuck. He just wanted to leave the blank space of family behind. Devon's chest vibrated from the motion. But, in the moment just before the bend, he smelled water and met rock—the bike turned and slid out from under him. He could hear the sound of wheels rushing against air, and when his own body stopped skidding, he felt the surprise of blood.

Devon lay there on the side of a secondary road, waiting for change to take its inevitable place. In his mind, he saw Pigpen, the dead singer, shake his head, cowboy hat points waving side to side. The man in his vision just smoothed his grisly beard and walked away. Devon's body was hurt, but how bad he couldn't tell. His eyes blinked, watched the dotted sky, waited. He couldn't feel anything but numbness. He wanted to feel the rush of feathers through wind, of talons on wood.

As the day's fading light crept across the road, Devon noticed a hill covered with shrubby grass, he saw small birds fly past him, he registered the faded white lines in the middle of the road. When he heard the grumble of a truck coming up the road, Devon felt his humanness return, his stupid humanness. He sat up, brushed a hand across his lip, then his brow. A streak of rusty red smeared his skinned hands. He unhooked his helmet and stood up, willing any pain to just get the fuck gone. Devon's thick pants and leather jacket saved most of his skin, but he could tell underneath, his body was bruised. His bike was a hundred feet away, looking like a beaten tin can. As Devon pulled it up from the handles, a dirty black pick-up sped by. He could see the lines of a gun rack across the cab window, just below the rigid outline of a cowboy hat. He waited for another. Twenty minutes later, a blue pick-up slowed to a stop near him. An older man got out slowly and walked around to Devon.

"You alright, son?"

Devon nodded and stood up as the man reached for the bike's handle. The man was probably a rancher, Devon thought. He smelled like hay and motor oil, like grease and fresh laundry.

"You could have been killed on this bend of road, boy," the man said.

"Oh yeah?" Devon said half-heartedly.

"Yeah," the man said, frowning and staring Devon in the eye.

"That bike a' yours looks pretty beat up. I can take you into town. My buddy Jake's got a shop, and he'll drive ya back with his tower."

"Ok, thanks." Devon met the man's eyes for a moment. He could sense his age, the man's own weariness. He could feel the stomach punch of blue, like a cold morning blue, like the blue of his own Dad's eyes.

"Really, this stretch right here's a killer," the man said.

"Maybe that's what I wanted," Devon said quietly. The rancher kept his stare and shook his head.

"That's not what you want, son. Get in."

Devon got in the passenger side. The heavy truck doors slammed secure. Devon stared out the window as they drove. That rancher talked all about his daughters and sons and lazy ranch hands. Devon glanced at the man's face, his sun-bleached and graying hair, his skin pocked but with lines at the corners of his mouth and eyes like someone who's had a happy time of it. "That's not what you want," he heard in his head again. Devon didn't say much, just listened to the man who had enough to say about life. At Jake's Body and Tow, Devon offered to give the man some cash for the ride.

"Thanks, no. You save that money for fixing your bike," he said winking. They both stepped out of the truck and before the man went in to get his friend, he took Devon's hands like a preacher or something. Looking into his eyes, he said "You don't know what life has for you, son. Keep on and stick to it." He squeezed Devon's hands before saying goodbye.

The words made Devon feel empty. Not just because they couldn't grasp the half of what he wanted in seeking flight, but also that his own father never said anything like that to him. His dad was a silent man from beginning to end. After getting his bike to the shop, he had to wait nearly the whole week for it to get fixed.

When Devon was finally back in his shack between New Mexico hills, nothing sat right for him, not the routine of rolling thick tobacco cigarettes, or the clean fire of whisky or the starchy fill of beans in his belly. He spent hours reading the same damn articles in music and motorcycle magazines, trying to trick his mind out of the ordinary. During this time, he barely touched his bike and didn't talk to or see anyone. Days went by and he couldn't even engrave his silver buckles—his right thumb still black and blue from the fall.

No birds gathered at his back door, no caws or garbles woke him near night. It had been way too long since he'd felt the whip of wind through feather. A craving lodged itself under his skin, growing there like a bad dream. Devon spent hours lying on an old cream and color-striped wool blanket, memories screening behind his eyes. He wanted out of the projector. He didn't want to remember the cold metal of prison. He didn't want the crack and fly of beer-bottle glass before him. He didn't want to even think of the good days before, or his daughter. But as the quiet land around him repeated its perpetual patterns, light dark light dark light, he settled into his body.

After a while Devon even began running down the hill, past the old hag, Mrs. Jones', house, listening to the heavy clod-clod of his feet on gravel, in daytime or in nighttime. It didn't matter. He spent time rubbing polish over the dull red tank of his Indian bike again, reworking wires, sluicing gas into the machine.

When his bruises healed, Devon sat at a little wooden desk, scattered with files, clippers and small hammers. He bent a flat piece of silver back and forth, warming it in his fingers and catching reflections on the window. He let pictures outside dictate his designs. A stack of folded paper with pencil drawings occupied one corner of the desk. Some from a walk he'd taken—sharp pines, chipped wood paths, a starling settled on a branch. Some came from his memory—streams winding between boulders in the mountains. Devon was silent with this first piece, warming it and waiting. The large window in front of him faced the forest, a scene he watched change daily, mostly in small ways.

When he worked like this, Devon would imagine himself a nice person, a simple man and he'd want to ride a long way, out on the open road again.

Chapter 2
Hettie

One careless step and Hettie's purple-veined, thin-skinned ankle bent in ways that weren't natural. She was standing in the prairie grass when her body crumpled and a hot flash shot through to the ends of her grey black hair. Goddamnit, she mouthed to the approaching night. She surveyed the field, but her vision was fuzzy. She hadn't left any lights on at the cabin 500 yards away and the orange sun was fading. A distant dove cooed by the New Mexico highway. You'd better get up from here or you'll be eaten by coyotes, she thought to herself. You better wrap that ankle or it'll swell twice the size. So she mustered strength, forced her bones to shift, then willed herself to sit. Hettie had come to the bottom of the hill in the first place to listen to the water there. Now the cool stream bubbled like laughter. She was sweating, as pain sharper than a cactus needle, pierced the insides of her ankle. She carefully pulled back her old socks and saw the skin purpling. Dammit, what am I gonna do now? Hettie knew the question was serious as the sun started its descent below the ridge of western pines. She tried scooting her bottom towards her feet, but that pushed the pain down along the bottom of her left sole. She took a breath, blew out and shook her head. A quarter mile from her house was the Spencer property, and she thought about screaming. Marni and Jim would be tucking into their supper about now, the house doors closed shut. Shit! She hated needing other people, especially when she was laying on the ground like some ravaged carcass. No, I'll get my own self home.

Hettie focused on the porch stairs, not too far away, but up a little hill. She turned over on her right side, smashing small shrubby plants.

She pulled her sweater sleeves down. She stacked her now lame leg up on the other, stretched her arms almost a foot and dragged herself towards her hands. She let a song come to mind and hummed a tune she'd lived her whole life with: *Big train, big train, get me home.* Her hips bumped over tiny dirt mounds and rocks, but her ankle stayed stacked. She did it again, moving another half a foot. Again and again, feeling the sweat drip into her armpits and watching her sweater become a tumbleweed, gathering sticks and grasses and bits of rabbit dung. Cooing doves called in the night as she approached the wooden outhouse. Her whole body was damp with sweat and the cool air chilled her. Hettie's hands were swelling and scratched now, too. That old outhouse needs lime, she thought, trying to scooch herself quickly past the scent of decaying shit. She glanced up a rocky path that wove through manzanita bushes to her porch. It was dark now. A path that she'd walked a thousand times now felt foreign—the small ones' territory. She already heard the scurry of small feet and imagined the wriggle of centipedes and ants and beetles. Oh, stop it, she said to her thoughts, those won't hurt you and you know it! Then she thought of coming face to face with a bulbous raccoon and its sharp claws. Just get up there, she said to herself.

Her ankle was numb and kept slipping off the other as she hoisted her body up the hill. No lingering light helped her. It was that time of night in these low mountains when the lack of sun eclipsed everything, before the moon and stars took over. Hettie felt the ground with her fingers, before finding solid stones to pull herself up on. Two-thirds of the way to her snug cabin, she picked the wrong stone. It unearthed from her weight, kicking up and falling into Hettie's chest as her body slid two feet down, and her bad ankle stopped her, but sent sharp pain up to her hip. Ahhh, help me, spirit! She starting to whimper. Get me home! But she was almost there, due to her stubborn self. She straightened up, fixed her gaze through the black night, and tried again.

When she reached the cabin, and crawled up the porch stairs, she turned the doorknob and fell halfway into the cabin. She lay there for some time, so grateful to have her walls. Then she dragged herself in, and managed to pull off her clothes, tug on dry ones, and get to bed.

In the weeks that followed, Hettie's ankle healed slowly. She used a chamber pot and didn't go outside much. When she could walk again, she took to using an old mangy stick—one that her dead husband,

Wilson, used to leave right inside the front door. Her ankle was almost healed. As she sat out on her back porch, peeling a bucket of early apples, Hettie scanned the skies for that bird. For the past few weeks, a raven the size of a small vulture had started visiting her porch. As soon as Hettie would come outside, he'd fly away. She knew it was the same one visiting though, because through her window she could see, in the outline of its body, that its right wing had a section missing, like he'd gotten caught in a cage or something. He wasn't a particularly comforting presence, all sooty black, something waiting to turn to ash, and his piercing caws had woken her twice in the middle of the night.

The white flesh of all the apples exposed, Hettie picked up the bowl of scraps, and instead of carrying them down the hill, on account of her ankle, she flung the peels over the porch onto the tangled bushes. Hettie watched as the red twills rained to the ground like sprays of fresh blood. Let the ants get 'em. Hettie knew it was a risk, throwing food scraps so close to the cabin, but she also knew the feisty ones, like squirrels, raccoons, possums, and then the mice and ants were quick this time of year, and it would all be gone before night fall.

Later on, the scent of baking pies mixed with the sap smoke trailing from the logs in her wood stove. Hettie settled into her rocking chair and poured herself a little cup of whiskey. She let her eyes linger on a blue star quilt pinned to the wall—another mystery not yet stitched up in her mind. Its sharp edges were navy and teal, powder and black; the blue no color of a rainbow, blue like a dumb memory.

Rain began to hit the tin roof of Hettie's cabin like sharp bells. Then the wind picked up and Hettie could hear the slap of tree branches against the cabin. She got up, took the pies out to cool, refilled her whisky glass, and returned to her rocker. Hettie started to move in her own time, not that of the weather. Drops of rain turned to sheets, lightning cracked in the distance, and the corner with the roof leak began its drip drop drip into the red plastic bucket that lived below it.

This withered cabin, its mouse-run walls, was what she had. That and her grandson, who, these days, was traipsing around the country, trying to forget about his mother's death. Hettie's eyes were jumping to the midnight blue diamond shapes nestled in each corner of the quilt's octagonal design. Then her eyes adjusted, holding those diamonds as a ringed pattern which made an inner white square stand out then the star points became feather tips. A bird's tail, bird's wings. She gazed back to the center but the folds and creases that made up the bird's head tracing had disappeared. How'd I see that before?

Hettie reached up to move the lampshade and look for the bird in the quilt again, but thunder rolled over the top of the cabin and the light sizzled out. Damn you, bird, she cursed and slowly raised up from her rocker, felt for the table, and made her way across the room to the bureau. Her knobby fingers found some matches but knocked over the silver frame with Jessie's picture. My eyes are going like the bats, she said as the flame flared from her hand. She lit the fat candle on the dresser and then stood the picture up.

In the faint smoky glare of her dead daughter's photo, Hettie saw something move in the reflection. She whipped her eyes around and there, sitting with folded hands, in Wilson's old chair, was a spirit. He was sitting there, sure as shit with the storm raging outside. Hettie drew a sharp breath—she was not rocking, not smoking, not moving. Nothing had made him come but the wind. Hettie closed her eyes for a second and nodded. She heard the chair creak, she felt cold enter the cabin, heard the rain drip into the bucket. Cautiously, Hettie turned to the side, let her eyes slide to see him. He was a plain-looking man, in a buttoned up shirt with a jacket that was a little too big, pants, and a wool cap. Hettie felt scared, he was just too close. But he wasn't moving, just sitting still like a crumbling statue. She was afraid to look straight at him, as if he was a wolf or a horse or a deer—something that did not like to be looked in the eye. His eyes were small and kind and some part of her knew him, like the inside of her skin.

Hettie stood near the bureau, wondering if she should reach for something sharp, if he was going to hurt her. She turned her head slowly back to Jessie's picture, and felt the stab of her daughter's absence, the anger that she'd gone before. Reflecting through a bright smile and wind-blown hair, she saw the figure behind her. His thin body was agile. Hettie heard a small cough, then sensed tobacco smoke. The smoke from his pipe filled up the picture frame. But Hettie couldn't really smell it, couldn't trace the comfort of tobacco. She could barely smell the scent of pie or fire anymore either, it all seemed doused out with musty dead.

In the moments he sat there, Hettie could feel some kind of crack at her breastbone, like the opening of a walnut shell or the clunk down of one of her sewing machine parts. The storm outside had stopped, but she still felt the cold. He wasn't going to move. As if he could rip through her solitude, just like that. The chair creaked and Hettie breathed, still baffled, but willing to stand her ground. She looked down at her hands, the wrinkled folds of skin, the crooked splay of her fingers. I'm too old for this.

"No you's not," the spirit mumbled. He could read her thoughts, so she clenched her body.

"What do you want?" she managed.

"Nothing," he answered, "just visiting."

Hettie's eyes opened wider. She wanted to scream. There the devil is.

"Not like that," he said. The rocking chair stopped its creak. The spirit stood, and Hettie watched the mirror of his body rise out of the picture frame, his movement blending and disappearing in the reflection. Her mind flashed to sepia photos of her ancestors. The ones who worked the land and made music. When she knew he was gone, Hettie stumbled onto the couch, pulling the green afghan over her thinning knees. It was as if he'd brought in the whole damn galaxy, and now, in the quiet cabin, Hettie crossed her arms over her heart and wept.

Chapter 3
Devon

Devon's heavy black boots crunched small sticks and ground pointed pine needles under him. He wove through the forest path behind his house. He'd left "Workingman's Dead" playing inside his cabin and let the fading sounds of the boys' voices follow him. The heat from a high sun popped the sap in trees and smelled rich like vanilla and dust. He heard birds slicing through the air, twittering and cawing far away. The rawness of nature was nothing he took for granted. Having lived without fresh air and freedom to walk among trees in prison, changed him. The path wound up and Devon could feel his breathing stick in his chest, labored and short. He felt his body, heavy and thick. The sun behind him cast his shadow a few feet in front of him—leaner, longer, melded more with the dirt and Earth. Devon kept walking, following his other self on the ground. His vision blurred with the hazy sun, tracking his limbs and knowing the shadow was as much a part of him as raven. It was so close, and so much an extension of him, yet produced only by the right angle of light. Devon's mind went to the concert campground, nearly twenty years back, when he saw PJ's eyes tighten into black glassy beads and the next minute his body wasn't there. He'd become a sooty colored bird, circling above the dying embers of a campfire. Devon thought he'd just been tripping, but that vision stayed in him and was, in his mind, the best idea in the world. As a person, Picasso Joe was an elusive little fucker. He supposedly used to be a professional artist, and that's why he got the name, that and he loved the song, "Picasso Moon." Nobody saw him shapeshift besides Devon, at least that's what he thought, but PJ was always hard to find. He'd show up, swagging his tall frame in hippie cotton clothes, overtake Shakedown Street in the Grateful Dead's parking lot scene, then disappear. If Devon tried to look for him, or ask about him, someone would say they saw him in the Phil Zone—the band's bassist's side of the stage, up high, or with a group of Spinners in a hallway. But he'd never be there. Then he would surface three venues later, always catching a ride in some dilapidated VW bus. He was an original trickster, and Devon knew PJ loved that role, and was a good chap, but also knew way more. Devon remembered sitting on concrete steps out the back of a stadium with him, before his bust. The man was older than Devon and weathered. He'd listen though, to Devon's sad story of his broken marriage, and the daughter he couldn't see.

"You have to let it all go, brother," he'd said. Then leaned in and stared at Devon in a way that twisted his stomach, like he could see way into him, past all the pain he had. Devon could see some kind of flash in his black eyes, too, and feel a closeness or understanding.

"Uh-huh," PJ said, "You have it, too. Damn!" And then he hopped up and started dancing around the steps like the crazy hippy he was.

"What are you talking about, man? And what the heck is in that blotter?" Again, Devon had just attributed everything to the drugs. But PJ was gone again and cawing like a lunatic bird from the top of the arena. It seemed an impossible vision even. It happened like that a few more times, PJ just disappearing in the middle of their conversation. And then one day, even without giving him any acid or anything, he grabbed Devon's hand and pulled him. Devon could feel PJ's fingers gripping tighter and tighter, digging into his skin, and then he could feel his own skin toughen and contract, everything in him compact. Then a vague memory of shoulders turned to wingspan and nose turned to beak. He couldn't track much more of any change in his body, but he remembered the freedom of being up high, of swooping and moving by feathers through air.

Devon looked up to the trees, pines with swaying limbs and pinons and taller trees, three or five times his own height. He thought of climbing, of placing his skin-covered hands along bark, his lumbery boots on a branch, but it felt heavy and slow. Devon so wanted that agility, that quickness and perk—it felt miles away from his body. When he walked back down to his cabin, he used the senses he did have to listen to the snaps beneath his boots, to smell the warming sap of the trees. His heart sagged a bit heavy in his chest. He knew he couldn't make it happen. He knew he had to live his regular life and wait for it.

Chapter 4
Rowen

owen's black van entered the stream of cars piling into the lot. A big Volkswagen bus, patch-worked with stickers, sputtered forward and Rowen turned his stereo up louder. The song coaxed him to try harder. He was in his van alone for the first time since Spring Tour and he relished the space. The solitude also made him think of his mom. He flipped the car visor down, to see the back side of a folded photo. He couldn't look at it yet, just made sure it was there. "The Wheel" kept playing and Rowen thought of his mom at the restaurant. She'd worked there near 20 years, serving plates of hash browns and eggs, while he traveled around the country the last five.

Rowen left California for New Jersey two days after the funeral because he didn't want to be around anyone who knew her anymore. He didn't want to be alone either. He'd picked up riders and kept focused on tour. After it, Rowen thought he could catch a good show or two back in Cali before heading out again. These shows were home to him. He'd spent more time in the past two years in the California venues' lots than his actual family's place in the San Fernando Valley. Now it'd all changed, and he didn't want to see his brothers. They just wallowed and fought over who would get the apartment. Better to stay out.

Inching slowly into a parking spot facing Cal Expo Arena, sun poured through the windshield, and Rowen decided to rest before the show. No riders coming in and out of the van, no messes to clean up, and he had his ticket. Hippies spewed out of the van in the next spot, already clinking beer bottles. Rowen climbed to the back of his spacious van, spreading out on the folded down bed, covered with the pinwheel blue and red quilt. He covered his eyes and sighed. Fuck if I'll ever carry that many on tour again, he thought to himself. Spring Tour had been partially hell, with 11 riders crammed in the van on one driving stretch and bags, bottles and pieces of things he didn't want to think about stuck between the seats. Rowen fancied himself a clean Deadhead and riding with too many swag passengers just wouldn't do. He let his thoughts go dreamily back to Fall Tour 90' right before he turned 24: stylie hotels and inner circle parties with Penny. That was good touring, hanging with folks who were part of the band's inner circle. He was sick of this parking lot shit. But he loved the music too much and there was nowhere else to be. The lyrics were telling him to slow down and let go. Rowen realized the tape had gone around and when he turned the key off, he felt the van lurch from the side. What the hell? He glanced out the passenger window. Two guys were leaning against his van, getting ready to smoke a bowl. Rowen hopped out, shut and locked the door to his 1990 Chevy conversion van, and walked around. They had propped their beers on Rowen's hood. "No man, somewhere else," Rowen said, keeping his voice low.

"Oh, hey, brother, it's cool, it's cool," one guy with rips on his corduroy pants said. He ignored Rowen and focused on his pipe.

"It's not cool. Move on," Rowen said, keeping steady, reaching for the beers, "move on." Rowen was about to lose his temper, but he knew that was the worst way to deal. He didn't want to have to talk to these people. The dirt of the scene, just there to cause havoc. These were the heads that begged for narcs and cops. It was bullshit for the rest of the heads. They did stupid things, broke shit, fought with fists and swung deals in the open. Rowen took the guys' beers to the middle of the aisle.

"What the fuck, bro, those are our beers."

"Yeah," Rowen said, "Come and get 'em," and he set them carefully down on the pavement, away from his van.

"You're a buzzkill," they said.

Rowen didn't answer, just walked away. The dreaddies picked up their beers and moved to another aisle, another nice car to camp in front of. Rowen found Shakedown, the bustling, wide aisle at shows where folks sold sandwiches, drinks and stuff and generally hung out. Pretty quickly, he spotted one of his California taper buddies.

"Row, hey Row, man, how's it going? Welcome back, bro," the guy said when they came close. Rowen embraced the tall man who was dressed in jeans, a striped work shirt unbuttoned at the neck and cuffs and green Vans tennis shoes.

"Dean, brother, how've you been? You didn't make it to any of the East shows did you?"

"Hell no, I have a day job, remember!"

Rowen shook his head slightly. "I'm telling you, man, a lot of good shows happen out there."

"Did you do the whole thing?"

Rowen grinned wide and shrugged his shoulders.

"You're a monster, Rowen. How'd it go?" Dean asked.

"Nasty, I mean there were some good shows, a smoking 'Wang Dang' in Philly, a real sweet 'Sugaree' in Chapel Hill and 'Lazy River' is growing on me. But it was the riders. I had a whole gaggle of them. We got a lot of work done, but they were sloppy messes, every one of them," and he spat on the ground behind him. Dean chuckled and hooked his hand over Rowen's shoulder.

"What you need, brother, is one of those sweet young thangs to keep house for you," and they both watched as a tank top clad girl with flowing hair and a board of stickers walked past them.

"Huh, you mean one of those," Rowen said, jerking his head up, "they're even worse trouble."

"Did you mail order for the show, man?"

"Yeah, they're getting kinder to me these days, especially in Cali. I'm on the floor somewhere. Let's go in," he said to Dean and the two guys walked through rows of heads, past girls with open back shirts waving arms in the air hoping for a "miracle." The parking lot was full and all the folks who'd traveled the miles from the East Coast were looking weary, but happy to be back. Most of these heads could go back to a pad of some sort to rest for a few days; and let go of dragging coolers around lots and searching for spare car parts in small towns.

As they walked towards the arena, Rowen heard a sharp cawing from the top of a streetlight. He smiled slyly, flicking his head up towards a black bird. Rowen let the loud cawing circle in his head, "Cu-*caw*-caw, cu-*caw*-caw." Rowen looked back up at the pole and the sheen of the bird's feathers. It made him think of his grandmother, and he flashed on her small, hunching body as she'd climbed the bus stairs less than a month earlier. The bird lifted off, flapping its heavy wings. It was larger than Rowen would've thought, and he watched it swoop over Shakedown Street. He flashed on the stories his grandmother used to tell him when he was a boy, of the raven being a messenger. He sighed as they entered in the line. Maybe it means the show's gonna be good tonight.

Inside, Dean's clear blue eyes scanned wildly at all the girls.

"It's like you've never seen a chick before, man," Rowen said, pulling Dean's arm towards the aisles.

"These are not just any girls bro, they're the peaches," and Dean kissed the tips of his fingers winking at a redhead with freckles and green eyes. The girl giggled and Dean practically tripped on his tennis shoes. Rowen had known Dean since they were in junior high. They both got into the Grateful Dead at about the same time, although Dean's scene was comparing notes with other serious tapers and cataloguing shows in his massive computer at work in Santa Monica. Rowen respected him, and he always had good copies of Cali shows due to his taping and trading. Rowen, on the other hand, was a full tourer.

The two of them looked for plain clothes cops, then saw some empty rows to the left scattered with respectable heads. They climbed the steps and Rowen nodded his head at small groups, all discretely smoking. They sat down and Dean untied his shoe pulling out a double plastic baggie with two dense, lime green buds. Rowen produced a small glass pipe from his pocket and handed it over. When Dean broke off an edge of the bud, Rowen looked at him immediately.

"What the hell is that?" He said smiling, the air mixing with the scent of Kool-Aid and candy apples.

"Some beach shit," Dean said, showing his teeth. The two of them slid down a bit in their seats and lit up. Rowen drew in long and held it, swishing the smoke around and waiting for what he considered the "test results." When he blew out between his teeth, a guy with long black dreads a few rows down turned around, obvious as a hound to a scent. Rowen and the head exchanged nods and Rowen turned to Dean to take another toke.

"Thanks man, that's good stuff. Keep me in mind," Rowen said raising his eyebrows.

"Hey, Row," Dean said leaning towards him, "I heard about your mom, man, I'm real sorry." Rowen looked in Dean's eyes, the sincerity slicing him, and he just nodded before taking the pipe from Dean. They smoked the rest in silence, until the house lights began to flutter. The two guys left that spot to find their individual seats. They clasped hands at the hallway and walked in opposite directions, Dean towards the taper's section. Rowen pulled his ticket stub from his back pocket. He could feel his head settling as he walked onto the floor.

On stage, the carpet was laid, the mics steady, the drums stacked. He was about sixteen rows back between where Jerry and Bob would be standing and he took in his full view. Others found their seats, a middle-aged couple next to him. The woman smiled and Rowen nodded. The man was quiet and Rowen was thankful. Rowen played it cool. He just wanted a good show and he let the pot linger in his head. The couple next to him began rolling a fat joint and Rowen looked over. Shwag kind, he thought, I gotta get some of that bud Dean has. The cloud in his head was pushing the edges of his mind. He got high so often these days that it took really good bud to make him feel something beyond just a tingly hum. Rowen usually bought enough good bud for himself, unless it was super kind, which he would buy a pound of then sell off all but an ounce, to pay for itself. Four hundred bucks was not crazy to Rowen but not pocket change either. He made his money, at least tour money, on good beer and sometimes grilled cheese, when he had riders to help with the work and often he swung a small deal or two. He sold swag weed in The Valley in between tours. Rowen scanned the round arena, packed with moving figures, all there for another show. Some probably saw The Grateful Dead only that one night of the year, others for their first time ever. For Rowen it was his life.

Jerry and Bob walked on stage, picking up their instruments. The band members looked at each other and then broke into the funky low-down rhythms of "Shakedown Street." It was a good surprise, and Rowen stood up with all the others letting the guitar grooves and the piano notes bend his knees. The band sang, encouraging everybody to find the pulse of the city, by just looking around. The music enveloped Rowen. He was cool. It was fine. He watched Bobby's wrist moving like a steady metronome. The room between the seats began to widen and Rowen let his feet swivel back and forth, feeling the whole audience. It was this kind of groove that he came for and the wah-wah flavors of Jerry's guitar tempted him further. He thought about

Penny again and how much she'd loved "Shakedown." She could slip into a seventies style and hold it with such class. He could feel a tingling in his body as the bare shoulders of dancers began to appear and the woman next to him inched closer. Fuck, maybe Dean's right. Rowen couldn't remember the last time he'd slept with a woman. Penny and he broke up over a year ago. The cool spring air of California was lighting his nerves.

He took a deep breath, raised his head and focused on the boys. Rowen saw Phil smiling under his big glasses. Boing, boing, he plucked the thick strings and the song began to change. Rowen sat down again and felt his feet against the concrete as the song ended. Bobby stepped up to the mic for the first deep licks of a down home blues rift. Bill in the back was grinning wickedly and beating out a solid pattern. The boys cooed about a man going nuts for a woman in a good dress. Rowen ran his tongue along his front teeth and grinned, shaking his head. The red lights cast a glow that made him feel giddy. Bobby sang about cats scouring the night. The keys on the piano were clear and piercing his mind like skin pricks. He thought about a few babes he'd seen on Spring Tour.

Chapter 5
Devon

I'm working to fix up mine, and stay out of the slammer.
Each day I get up and think it's gonna get easier.

Back on his bike again, Devon relished the feel of wheels on road. Everything seemed fine. His bike carried him past mountains, through tunnels, over newly paved streets. His pack was filled with five buckles, all silver shined up and ready to wear. He was meeting his friend Charlie the next day in Bonner Springs. He'd convinced himself in the past weeks that life was worth living.

Still, he wished for flight, for the take-over of his body. The lure of the surrounding landscape, seen from under his helmet, produced an itch or an insatiable thirst. It was as if he was being forced to sit inside hot skin, the vibration of his bike intensifying the feeling. Devon pulled over to the side of the road, where a stand of pines huddled close together, determined not to wreck his bike again. He got off and walked between the trees, reached out and grabbed two thin trunks several feet apart. He let his arms pull and stretch the sides of his body. Devon wanted this feeling, the lifting of his chest, the straightness that pulled his human shoulders back. He closed his eyes, trying to feel freedom, trying to get outside himself—relate to those trees in another way. Flashes of flight and light came into his head. He pulled his arms harder. A memory of earth from above, treetops, distance to pavement and grass, rooftops. Devon breathed, then held his breath as he remembered soaring. His body numbing but alive, he tried to replay these good pictures in his mind.

Other scenes mixed in, though—the confinement of walls, the movement of his bike, the sluice of whisky down his throat. As mundanity took over his concentration, his arms ached. Devon let go, opened his eyes, and realized that the trees were leaning apart slightly. He dropped to his knees, letting the blood return to his limbs and his eyes scan the deserted road. It wasn't going to happen. Not this time.

Crossing the border into Kansas, Devon kicked his heels against the throttle and pulled the bike to a stop. Later, in a dingy bar outside Wichita, he sat for two hours till the slip of liquid through his body was a murky steam, and his cigarettes tasted like burning cardboard. Devon watched the chubby figures moving on a television. When he heard kids' voices from the screen, he looked down to his own calloused fingers.

✪   ✪   ✪

Devon picked up his little girl in the dirt yard, holding her stick legs close to his body. Not two seconds and the front door swung open.

"You can't be here no more, no more," Cora said, her eyes wide and dark.

"Come on baby, it's still me. I'm her daddy. I need to see her." It was like yesterday.

"Emmajean, come with Mommy," she said reaching out her hands. The little girl turned her face into Devon's shirt, defiant.

"Emma!" Cora shouted, scaring the girl, so her body became floppy and she let herself be taken into her mother's arms. "That's a girl, now let's go inside."

Cora opened the door, set Emma down and directed her back into the living room. Devon could see her face, crumpled. She quickly waved to him. A little hand movement he would see over and over and over. Cora faced Devon at the door.

"I mean it! Get out of here. This is no place for you. You'll see how it works. This is not your life anymore."

"See how it works? It's still me. I still love her."

"You can keep on loving her," Cora softened, "but from out there, not here. Not anymore."

Devon shook his head, her words, killing his will for living.

"No, I won't do it."

"Oh yeah?!" Cora screamed, and the door slammed in his face.

He would try again in weeks that followed, until he was arrested. Two months later, a metal door slammed him in, for defying a restraining order. The lies continued at a trial where Cora's four brothers dressed in button down shirts no one knew they had and said all kinds of things about their brother-in-law. He was made out to be a monster. A judge, noting his past drug arrests, signed off on the case—sending him to prison for three years. Three years, with no contact, and a promise to never see him again.

"I don't think it's supposed to be an easy path, man," he remembered his one friend, Andy, saying on a visit to prison.

❂   ❂   ❂

The sounds of kids' voices turned to rock music, and Devon slicked the last bit of scotch down his throat and stumbled towards the door of the Wichita bar. Cool air kicked his back and he hunched towards the gutter, retching the pain from his gut. Music blared from a bus parked behind his bike and the noise reeled inside his ears, not blocking, not comforting his drunk spirit. Devon walked it off, rounding the blocks of the little city, weaving on the sidewalk, trying to conjure the other part of himself. He could feel the effort he made to survey food scraps, the intoxicated glance to streetlight-lit metal objects. When the light of day peeked through the clouds, he had enough clarity to start up the bike's engine and peel away from the dirty downtown buildings.

The next day he met Charlie in the parking lot of a Grateful Dead concert. At the end of one row, a few heavy bikes were propped up and a small crowd of leather-clad men milled around. Charlie walked up to shake Devon's hand. When Devon unwrapped the velvet cover over his buckles, Charlie threw his smoke on the ground. The afternoon sun, flashed over the silver and Devon played up the revealing of its magic, tilting it to catch the rays.

"Those are beauties man," Charlie said reaching out his hands. Devon let the buckles thud onto the smaller man's palm.

"How much you want for them?"

"Same as always."

Charlie pulled out a fat wad of bills, ripped off twelve gleaming green hundreds and folded them, adding a little plastic baggie. He stepped towards Devon and placed them in his hand, money side up. Devon turned the small stack over, revealing a nice bud, then stuck it in his back pocket feeling the weight of the bills like tar. Charlie also gave Devon a ticket to the show. "Thanks man, appreciate it." This gesture lifted Devon a bit and he twirled the shiny ticket in his own fingers before tucking it into his other back pocket.

"You want to have a drink with us?" Charlie said walking back towards the rowdy bunch of bikers.

"No thanks."

"Listen, enjoy the show man!"

As Devon walked away from Shakedown, he felt lightheaded, like his blood was thin and cool. He turned a corner, passing a groundscorer and sensing the snug of bills near his ass. Even though the scene was a home of sorts to him, part of him didn't want to be around there. He wanted trees, the Southwestern sky, space.

It was the first night of the Bonner Springs shows. The seat was a good one. Devon slouched in the plastic chair and clasped his hands under his chin. He was close enough that he could see the guys like he had 25 years ago in California, when they were Haight Street hippies and played little venues and free shows in the park. This whole deal was a completely different thing. Most of the kids milling around, googled in their own sense of space, had no clue what those days were like. These kids were from rich homes, shrugging off things he never had the chance at. He studied the cool lines of Bobby's face, who'd been a young guy. He could play the guitar, but his voice was a little too high for Devon. Jerry could take him to the core. His beats and graveled voice did the same thing to him that the open sky did. The same thing his big mates had done for him in the slammer. It made him feel calm. It made him forget.

The set started with "Help on the Way," and Devon looked away from Bobby's pearly eyes. Then Jerry stepped in, plucking the chords of "Althea." Devon pulled out the little plastic bag, rolled a tight joint and sunk down, pulling the weed into his lungs to accompany Jerry's words. He heard the boys sing about finding direction. The heat of the stage lights shone on Devon. He would have liked to see the show from above.

Chapter 6
Cass

The stream was a low, cool babble. Cass listened, closing her eyes, lounging under the small stand of birch trees behind the apartment building. The sun was still warm and made a bead of sweat on her temple. Kansas City's approaching summer released a grassy smell and caused a little flutter in her chest. She was finally done. Done with papers and tests and rushing to classes. She was out of high school, and the tedium of its days. Everyone was happy, and she remembered the party the weekend before. Her sort-of friends got so drunk and then smoked pot on the roof of the party house. It was stupid, Cass thought. Really, she was terrified that her mom's boyfriend, Jack, would show up in his squad car. The embarrassment of him finding her would be too much. Why did her mom have to date a cop? It was so lame. So she hung out in the basement, sipping a beer and knowing right where she'd stash it if the party got busted. Her classmates were stupid anyway, and boring. Cass sighed, rolling onto her back, between the tree trunks. Her eyes followed the speckled pattern of light above. Cars whipped by at rush hour and she smelled the hot street. Although her mom was pushing community college, Cass liked the thought of taking it easy, at least through one more summer. Maybe she could travel with her dad, to one of his photoshoots in a foreign country. Though that would never happen. All she ever heard from him was on postcards and in sentences that weren't considerate enough for even a poem. "Wish you were here," "World's a lovely place," "So much craziness out here!" If Katmandu, El Salvador or The Nairobi Desert were so great, why wouldn't he want to share it with her? But her mom said he was under deadlines all the time, and she would never feel comfortable with Cass going around with him. She hated his free ways and worked to keep Cass and her life as steady as possible. Cass groaned, thinking about another boring Kansas City summer; working at a grocery store was her mom's suggestion.

Above, a loud, slicing sound caught Cass's ear. It increased till she saw a shadow move there. Cass tensed up when the black body of a raven came into view. The bird extended its talons and caught a higher branch. Cass didn't move a muscle or hardly breathe as she curiously watched the charcoal feathers settle. Then his thick head pointed at her, like a funny looking doll. A smile spread across Cass's face, and she drew a staggered breath in, watching the bird. He stood still, too, waiting for her to move. They entered into a stand-off, watching the smooth sheen of each other's skin and feathers. As she watched the raven, her vision blurred, forming sun rays into thin energy lines. They extended from the tops of the trees, from that bird's eyes to hers. It was mesmerizing. Then he broke it by hopping on the thin branch. Cass blinked and her eyes watered, spilled onto her face. The bird cocked his beak down, looking straight into her eyes again with his sharp beady bullets. Fear trickled into her stomach then awe picked up her heartbeat as she stared at the creature. An apartment door opened nearby, the bird let out a loud "Cah, Caw," and flew away.

The next day, Cass watched the Kansas City street from The Broadway Café window, cars and buses speeding, scruffy looking men dropping cigarettes on the ground. Then she saw a girl in a thin patterned skirt walking quickly, a white handbag slung over her shoulder, and strawberry brown hair cascading behind her. Cass noticed that she looked back over her shoulder every few steps. She pushed up glossy sunglasses and opened the café door. Cass refocused on her blueberry Italian soda and the magazine opened in front of her. The cafe was packed and she didn't want to be seen staring. Five minutes later, Cass heard, "Pardon me." She looked up to see that girl standing at her table.

"This place is really full, but you're sitting alone…mind if I join you?"

Before Cass could say anything, the girl slung her purse over the opposite chair, let her sunglasses clink onto the table, and sat down.

"I'm Hillary…call me Hill. And you are?"

"Um, Cass, Cassandra, nice to meet you," and she took Hill's hand faintly. "Are you from here?" Cass inquired, knowing that it wasn't true.

"I've been traveling for the past few months," she said, smiling.

Cass shifted in her seat. Hill looked up at the counter when she heard the faint wiz of the steam wand.

"And you," Hill said raising her eyebrows, "do you live here?"

"Yeah, I mean I live about 15 minutes away."

Hill lifted her sunglasses and twirled them in her finger. "Oh," she said flatly

"Yeah," Cass said, surprised by the defensiveness of her own voice. Hill's latte arrived, presented waveringly by a young counter boy. She gave him a curt smile and raised the drink to her pretty lips. Cass just watched her, wondering why someone as beautiful and interesting, and a traveler, would be sitting with her. No one she knew, at school or work moved with such free elegance like this girl did. Hill pulled a large notebook from her purse and set it on the table. It was leather-bound and engraved with a circular pattern. Cass stared as she flipped the gold-lined pages and began writing. She was not two sentences in when she looked up to catch Cass staring at her

"Just a little writing, got to keep my mind going," she said. Cass nodded, looking down and blushing, then went back to flipping the pages of a newspaper magazine and sipping her soda through a straw.

Hill wrote furiously and moved some photos and stickers to turn the page. Cass tried to mind her own business and finish her drink. After 10 minutes, Hill set her pen down and started to take another sip of her mocha. She gazed out the window, and Cass followed her eyes. They both saw a tall man slinking hastily down the opposite side of the street, his green silk coat flapping and stern gaze searching.

"Shit all mighty!" Hill said slamming her drink on the table and grabbing her sunglasses. She turned to the center of the room.

"What's wrong," Cass said turning from Hill back to look out the window. Hill softened, and looked at Cass smiling, but also visibly shaken.

"Do you have a car, Cassandra?" Hill said in a sweet voice.

"Um, yes, why," Cass said hesitantly.

"Will you be a dear and give me a ride?"

"Um, where do you want to go?" Cass said, wondering why the woman would want a ride from her.

"Anywhere, love, but fast," Hill said glancing out the window to see the man crossing the street.

Intrigued, Cass resisted her instinct to gather more information, and got up saying, "Sure, I'll give you a ride." Hill pulled her to the door, grabbing a newspaper to cover their faces. The man came closer to the café. He didn't look dangerous, just clean-cut and also a little goofy in the green blazer. Cass and Hill ran down the sidewalk towards a parking lot.

"Hill? Hey, Hill, is that you?" They heard shouting behind them.

"Come on," Hill said taking Cass's hand. "Where's your car."

"There," Cass said pointing at a black Nissan. "Who is that guy?" Hill swung around and saw the man coming towards them.

"Todd," Hill said scrunching her face up. "Can we go?" The man came towards Hill.

"What's up doll? Where are you going?"

Hill became very calm. "This is my friend, Cass We are just taking a ride," Hill said being sweet again.

"No you're not. We have to get going. Our car leaves in half an hour!" The man was shouting now and started to reach for Hill's wrist.

Cass watched him, her heart pounding. "Hi, I'm Cass, I…I need Hill's help. We'll only be 20 minutes," she lied just wanting to get them both safely into the car. The man looked up and released Hill's arm.

"See you later, Todd," Hill said as she got in the car and slammed the door.

They sped out and entered the stream of cars on Broadway. Cass couldn't help herself, and the rush of their escape made her join in laughing. Hill reached into her purse and pulled out a cassette tape. She popped it in the player and turned up the volume. "This set was so sweet. I was fourth row on Jerry's side," Hill said excitedly, "and I swear he winked at me during 'Sugaree'," she stared at Cass who seemed bewildered. "Oh my god, you have no idea what I'm talking about. Ok, ok, have you ever heard of the Grateful Dead?" Hill bit her lower lip.

"Yeah, some friends from school listen to them," she said slowly, then flashed on an ad she had seen in the newspaper. "Hey, aren't they coming here for a show?"

"Uh, yea, that's why I'm here. I tour," Hill said sounding like a valley girl.

"You what?"

"I tour, as in I go to Grateful Dead shows, like all the time," Hill said shaking her hands to emphasize her words. Cass turned the corner onto Ward Parkway and looked over at Hill.

"So you're a Deadhead?" It was a term Cass knew people used to categorize a kind of hippy.

"Well," Hill softened, "I prefer a traveler engaged in a particular kind of music." She flashed Cass a sly smile.

"Was that guy your boyfriend?"

"Oh, not really. I mean he's nice and all, but…" Hill reached into her purse and pulled out a cigarette, long, slim and white. She pushed in the lighter as Cass began rolling down her windows. "Oh, do you smoke?

"Um, sometimes, but my mom doesn't like it," Cass said. Hill tucked the cigarette back into her purse and let the lighter knob pop out between them.

Cass's mom was surprised when she came home with the pretty, hippy girl in tow. She was kind, though, and made a big salad and ordered a pizza before she left around seven. With the apartment to themselves, the girls blasted Grateful Dead music while Hill tried to explain the songs to Cass and what the next day's show would be like. Hill showed Cass photos and talked about the band and touring, giving Cass a glimpse into a world she didn't know existed. It seemed like a carnival and all the faces in the pictures had huge smiles.

Lying on her bed that night with the lights off, Hill sleeping on the living room couch and everything quiet again, Cass thought about her day, about Hillary, and this band called the Grateful Dead. The music was pretty cool, and traveling was something she liked hearing about, even if it was just in the US. She worried about that guy, Hill's supposed ex-boyfriend, Todd. He looked like a normal guy, but he had grabbed Hill's wrist. Every time Cass tried to ask her about him, she changed the subject. Cass didn't have a boyfriend, and never really had, so she just thought it was something she couldn't understand yet. Her heavy eyelids were just about to fall, when she remembered that raven in the tree—its black eyes—just two days ago. For a moment, it made her heart quicken as if waiting for the coming of a storm.

The next morning, Cass met her mom in the kitchen while Hill slept soundly on the couch. Joanne pulled her daughter's arm lovingly and whispered to Cass, "Who is that girl anyway?"

"Oh, Mom," Cass said moving over to start the coffeepot. "She's just a girl, traveling around. She's from Texas. I met her boyfriend, but he wasn't very nice, so I thought it would be good for her to come here for a rest." Cass watched her mom's eyebrows raise. They both sat down at the kitchen table with empty cups, waiting.

"Hey, Mom, you saw the band The Grateful Dead once didn't you?" Cass asked, looking down at her cup.

"Yeah, I guess, they were around when I was in New York."

"Did Dad like them?" she asked.

"Your father was more into jazz, but I think he took photos of them once, at a big social event."

"I'm going to go to a Grateful Dead concert with Hill," she said as casually as she could. "It's in Bonner Springs. Are you alright with that?" While she spoke, she got up and poured coffee in both their cups.

Joanne hesitated, then said, "Sure honey, if you want to see them, that's fine. Where is it?"

"At the Renaissance Festival place. I can drive, It's not too far. I know where it is," Cass said.

"Oh, ok," Joanne said.

Cass knew her mom trusted her. She changed the subject. "Are you going out with Jack?"

"I'm not sure. He's still at the station."

From the other room, music started playing, and Cass and her mom looked at each other. "Guess she's up," Cass said.

Chapter 7
Percy

The circle is moving and it's coming back around.
It's hard to know the when, but the why is always found.

1897

He sat on the edge of her bed and could feel the metal frame press in behind his legs. The bedcovers, old and threadbare, were pulled up to her neck. He watched as sweat bubbles gathered on her forehead. He held her hand in his, and the limpness of her fingers turned his stomach like a butter churn, smashing something good down, making it greasy but unrecognizable. He would offer her butter, if they had any. He would offer her new air to wipe away the sickness in her lungs. The chickens squawked, squawked in their pen 200 feet from the house. He sure as hell hoped nothing was going after them again.

"Percy," his wife wheezed, "we need something new. We gotta do something, cuz this ain't no life." Then she coughed for a solid minute, and Percy watched her thin chest heave.

"There, there, baby," he said, half lifting her body so the coughing could get out. He lay her back down and bit his lip, trying not to let her think about anything else but getting better. "I know, we'll find something."

"Play for me, will yer?" She said managing to give him a strained smile.

Percy got up from the bed and got his fiddle from the chair. He lifted it under his chin and thought of what songs she knew. What could help her sleep. His thick knuckled hands gripped the instrument and he took a deep breath, letting his hand slide the bow slowly across the metal strings. He watched her eyes perk up. She sure was lovely, even though she might really be dying. Percy pulled and pushed and angled the bow for the music. He coaxed it, like he'd coaxed a foal to be born, like he led the horse to plow, slow and patient. He found his words to a sad ballad about a sailor and a woman wanting to pass as a man. He knew his wife liked the song and always laughed a little, imagining herself on that boat, wishing she was going somewhere new to make herself a second life.

He sung, working out the lyrics he couldn't fully remember. His mind wasn't so strong these days, trying to keep the cabin, to make the children behave and to keep his wife happy and alive. She couldn't do anything these past few months. "Let's get married, you and me," he whispered, as she slid into sleep. Percy slowed his playing then set his fiddle back down on the chair and walked, trying to keep the creek of floorboards to a minimum. There was so much to do with a day half gone and the sun already drying the land.

His house was nestled in the valley of two good mountains, and as a raven swooped down over the cabin, he took unsteady steps. His crooked hands held reigns drawn to a raggedy mule, and the animal's hooves hitting the hard ground.

Chapter 8
Devon

As always, Devon wondered if PJ would be milling around the lot. He ambled slowly between parked cars, peering into the more dilapidated rides. There was nobody he really wanted to see around these shows. Charlie was ok, and his crew, but after a while, it was just the same thing. If he was in California, the tug to drive by Cora and Emma's house would be strong, but half way across the country, his mind could soften a little. He missed the conversations he used to have with PJ. Apart from his off-tour buddy, Andy, PJ was the only one he could really talk to. And after Andy died while Devon was still in prison, PJ, if he ever surfaced again, was as close to a friend, still in this world, he had left.

Devon searched the lot, but he also searched the skies. He didn't know, maybe PJ was just a bird now. Maybe he swooped the skies over the lot, or anywhere, and listened to the music from above. Or maybe the music and partying didn't mean anything anymore to him. He was such an institution in the scene though. Back in the 80s, Devon remembered PJ everywhere he went, sitting on a blanket talking to a lady, swinging his goods on Shakedown, twirling with the spinners, holding lofty conversation with Deadhead come lawyer fans. He could bridge things and people. Cora met him a few times, at shows, but she couldn't stand him, thought he was no good. Maybe just because he would look so straight into her, and she reacted. PJ was, is, prone to saying things like he sees them, things not everyone wants to hear. He once told Devon he might never see his daughter again, ever. That was shit, and he stopped talking to the guy for half the summer tour. It was after that, PJ transformed nearly in front of him.

Chapter 9
Hettie

A spider's web stretched across the North-West corner of Hettie's kitchen, like a grand announcement of Some Pig. Hettie didn't notice it until her hand got caught in one gossamer strand as she reached for the coffee canister—sending the whole bottom half recoiling into itself. The spider rushed back into her creation. "What! I didn't see you. This is my kitchen," Hettie said. The legs of that spider looked fuzzy in a way that gave it more girth, so Hettie moved to her own working space.

The wooden edges of her desk were strewn with scraps of material, pins scattered every which way and threads that flew to the floor. It's out of control, like a squirrel's nest, she thought. After she'd stacked quilt scraps into little piles and wound the thread back on its spools and found the square of quilting she'd worked on last, she went back to the kitchen. Grandmother Spider there had repaired half her web. This time, Hettie let her side of the kitchen just be. The quilts lining Hettie's cabin walls reminded her of past accomplishments. All of them except that blue one. She remembered the church table piled high with gifts and pies on the day her husband died. She remembered that apple-faced old woman, her hair covered with a handkerchief, her thick arms and hunched shoulders curving around a bundle. She didn't go to the give-away table. She walked right over to Hettie and tumbled the quilt into her lap. Then the woman turned around and walked out.

In her grief, Hettie never found out who the woman was. Months later someone came and put that quilt up on the North wall. It had been there nearly two decades now, and still Hettie never tired of looking at it—it held her mind like a just started crossword puzzle that can be continually and enjoyably ignored. Hettie stared at its folding corners, the sharp shapes and tight stitches. She tried following the pattern, tried finding that trace of bird beak in the center she'd seen before. It was as if seeing that trace, that word in the center of the puzzle, would bring some light to her mind—a place that seemed to be filling up with smoke more often these days.

It took nearly twenty minutes for Hettie to string her needle with thread. She just kept staring down at her shaky hands and the uneven line of her stitches. She just kept thinking of that spirit who'd shown up. What did he want? What did he want her to feel or do? She'd had spirits visit her before, especially the women from her family tree. Her grandmother, Betty, who'd woven rag rugs and taught her to crack tree nuts with the head of an axe. Her spirit helped Hettie a lot in being strong so no one took her property. All her grandfathers had died before she was born, and stories brought them to life some, but not enough to know them.

Hettie searched in her dresser drawer for a thin notebook, kept together with old photographs and notecards by a rubber band. In her mother's angled script on a browning page she read: Betty Ann, Gerald Pepper, Percy Gage Johnson. There were empty spaces under those names, unrecorded other generations. Hettie knew her family history got complicated with moving.

She went back to her quilt square, and as the needle finally made its way through the three-sheet stack of cloth, Hettie could feel her insides twist. She pulled the thread through. She sensed the great effort of quilt-making. But Hettie kept slowly going, pulling the white thread through cream and red material, piercing the needle through cotton one after another after another time. Late afternoon sun shone through the cabin windows and the room glittered with patterned dust. Shiny strands of the spider web. The north wall quilt brought her eyes right to the center, and there folded for her to see was a good outline of a bird's head and beak and neck.

⊛   ⊛   ⊛

She had fallen asleep on the couch, sitting up with the quilt pieces in her hand, her breath going in and out like a rattled muffler. The spirit made himself comfortable in the rocking chair again, pulling out his pipe to smoke. He watched Hettie, not knowing her in the living world when she was young, but able to track her blood line and stories over time. The world was different when he'd lived. Still, she had the trace of good ways, even in her older years. The steady creak of rocker on wood mixed with Hettie's dreaming. Creamy, steady, sure.

Percy set his head down in his hands, letting the motion of the rocker move his body. He sat there while Hettie slept.

When dust tickled her nose, Hettie woke up with a sneeze, realizing she'd dozed sitting upright. Her eyes adjusted to hazy light and she saw the rocker moving. It stabbed her, that movement so close.

"What in heaven's name," she wheezed, coughing and setting her sewing squares aside. She changed the fear to anger in a heartbeat. "Don't you come in here scaring the bejesus out of me!" she screamed. Her heart raced like a jackrabbit. "You hear me," she said looking up at the man, who lifted his head and blinked at her. She didn't care if he was her Great Grandaddy, there was no reason he couldn't be polite. The spirit looked at her wild face, smiled a sly smile, stopped the rocking chair and got up very slowly and sad-like, turning to the door. He disappeared before he had to open any doors. Hettie looked at the place where he'd walked away, head slightly down. She felt bad for a second. He seemed a gentle soul, but still, with spirits or anyone visiting her space, she was sensitive. She wanted to be the one calling him, she thought. When she was ready, in her own way.

Chapter 10
Cass

I might be shy and afraid of your ways,
But I want a stroke of Luck each of my days.

Late on Tuesday morning, Cass and Hillary set out for Bonner Springs, and the Old Renaissance Faire grounds. Hillary was anxious, because she'd missed the first night's show.

"Hurry up," Hill said, "Park on the side so you can find the car again." Cass ignored her and followed the men in yellow vests directing traffic. Hill sighed and pulled down the visor mirror to put on lip gloss. When they got out, Cass followed Hill through the rows of parked cars. Hill was holding her hand in the air and shouting, "Cash for your extra!"

"You should do this, too," she said to Cass, "so we can get tickets. It shouldn't be too hard."

Cass put her hand up in the air, her little finger pointed up like Hill's. She felt stupid shouting but did it anyway. She watched Hill's confidence, the subtle movement of her hips and the way she used her body to draw attention. Cass kept one hand firmly shoved in her pocket and the other up. "Cash for extra," she said while walking past a non-hippy looking couple. They shook their heads. Cass followed Hill closer to the entrance, and a larger crowd.

"You go over there," Hill said, pointing to the other side of the entrance. "If people ask, you're looking for one or two. Say, face value."

Cass walked where Hill told her to, keeping her hand raised but not shouting too loud. "I need a ticket," she said to people moving past her. This is stupid, Cass thought, why didn't she get a ticket before, like everyone else. She wanted to put her hand down. On the other side, Hill was shouting loudly and making up other things to say like "Be my miracle!" "I need and extra, pretty please with sugar on top."

Cass kept doing it her way, "I need a ticket," "Face value." "Do you have an extra ticket, please." It went on for a good fifteen minutes. Other people had their hands up and were shouting, too. She felt defeated and ready to go ask Hill what to do, when a middle-aged man with a trimmed beard and tie dye shirt came up to her. She dropped her hand.

"You need a ticket, doll?" he said.

Cass blushed. "Yes, face value. Do you have one?"

He nodded. Cass pulled the cash from her back pocket, but the man pushed her hand gently away.

"No need," he said handing her the Ticketmaster General Admission ticket.

"Really?" Cass said.

"Yeah, I always bring an extra. Have a good show." He winked and took off towards the entrance. Wow, Cass thought, looking at the date on the ticket, the printed numbers and words of the venue. She beamed, holding it as she walked towards Hill.

"Oh, good girl! You got one!"

"Yeah, this guy," Cass said looking towards the entrance, "just gave it to me."

"Perfect! A miracle for your first show. You lucky girl!" Hill said.

"Miracle?" Cass asked.

"Yeah, that's a free ticket!" Hill kept her hand up, shouting and jumping a little. It only took five more minutes and young guy approached her, and she paid him for her ticket.

Inside the show, Cass could feel the warmth of the sun against her too-tight tee shirt that Hill had told her to wear. The two girls found a little patch of grass near the aisle and sat down to wait for the show. By the time the steady strumming of guitars started, Hill had abandoned her again and was on the other side of the grassy area jumping around in circles, holding onto a boy's arm. Her flowing dress and flying hair made her look like pink spun sugar. Cass, left alone, was mesmerized by all the hippies in their element. The band's voices sprayed over the crowd as Cass pulled her knees up to her chest. They sang "Jack Straw," and she smiled at the name of a Kansas town in the lyrics. As the music swelled, her head began to move on its own.

When the first song slowed, the folks next to her brought their hands together at their chests, as if they were praying. Then the guitar twang rolled out from the stage again like lazy sunshine and the piano dropped notes like ice in a glass of cool lemonade. A greasy, comforting voice leaked through the speakers.

Hill walked towards Cass and grabbed her hand before she could pull it away, leading her down the aisle. Hill moved her hips to one side, then the other, loving "Sugaree" and Cass tried to follow, feeling terribly self-conscious. Cass knew this was Hill's favorite song. The melody was like a southern afternoon. Finally, Cass let her body go, twirling and brushing close to the cute boys who'd moved in to dance with them. One boy shook his head of bouncy brown curls. Cass had never seen guys dance like this before. She inhaled, marveling at the aroma that smelled like incense.

The band continued to play with a fury that Cass couldn't follow, like she was watching a movie of everything around her. When the song slowed, Cass sat down on a concrete step. The large man on the stage strummed his guitar slowly, with an underwater feel. The curly haired boy came over and sat down next to her, his tattered thin pants touched Cass's bare leg.

"How d'you like the show?" the boy said with a slight lisp as he leaned into Cass's hair.

"Oh, it's good thanks," she said, moving back a little from his strong body odor. He looked into her with eyes that sparkled like gems.

"I'm Forrest," he said sticking out his hand to Cass. She put her hand in his and he closed around her fingers, holding on tightly and intentionally. Cass liked the weight of his hands.

"I'm Cass," she said.

"You wanna toke?" Forrest asked, pulling a little pipe from his pocket and swiftly filling it with a little green bud. Cass's eyes went to the black jacketed people walking around the place, checking on things. She didn't want to get in trouble. Forrest seemed oblivious.

"I, I don't know," she said.

He chuckled, "It's ok, just be quick about it." She brought the pipe to her lips and he leaned over to light it. Cass drew the smoke in quickly, but it stung her chest and she blew out. With a sly smile, Forrest took the pipe and expertly drew one long drag followed by quick little inhales at the end, then put it back in his pocket. Cass watched as he held the smoke inside, grimacing. Her head was starting to tingle and her foot began to move.

"Come on," Forrest said standing up and reaching out his hand. They moved to the other side of the grass. She watched Forrest swivel his feet. She let the music relax her and move her own body in new ways. She closed her eyes and pictured herself in a moving canoe. The thoughts made her smile and when she opened her eyes, Forrest was waving his arms in the air. Cass shyly closed her eyes again, liking the private space in her head. The music swirled and Cass shook her head more furiously, following the momentum of the guitars, the screeching and the steadiness of the drums, and the piano notes over it all.

Later Cass found a little place on the grass. Forrest had disappeared and Hill hadn't returned. Bright colored lights were coming from the stage and Cass watched an old woman a few rows in front of her. The woman was rocking a child in her lap, back and forth, a big knitted afghan pulled around them. A few feet down, she saw a hairy man, wearing pants and a tall, stripy, cat-in-the-hat top hat. The man was waving his arms wildly in time with the drums. There were beads of sweat on his exposed skin, and it looked like he was engaged in his own marathon. His jerking movements both disturbed her and made her smile. Cass wanted to remember everybody and everything she was seeing. She wanted to print it all in her memory like one of her father's postcards. The beat slowed and Cass saw the guitarists slink back on stage. Screeching sounds came bubbling from their instruments. The crowd got quieter. Then Hillary waltzed down the aisle, stopping abruptly in front of her.

"Hey, you," she said loudly, "I wondered what happened to you." Hill sat down next to her. Hill smelled like a mixture of flowery sweat and cigarettes.

"Are you having a good time, sweet girl?" she said to Cass, her eyes twinkling and glassy.

"Yeah, this is great," she said not knowing how to explain it all. "What's going on now?"

"This is Space, honey. They just noodle away on their guitars," Hill said making a little sneer, "I could do without it."

"Is the show almost over?"

"No, there will be more songs after this," Hill said, like a patient teacher, "I also found out that there's a campground open a few miles away, and they have some bands and stuff. I think we should go there. I could go with my friend, Emily, but I'll ride with you if you want to stay?"

Cass stared at the ground, trying to get all this into her head. She had driven the two of them to the show in her little black Nissan. Her mom would be expecting her to come home after the show, but Bonner Springs was a good hour away, and she didn't really want to drive the dark highways alone. She felt let down that Hill wouldn't go back to Kansas City with her. A campground could be cool, but she knew her mom wouldn't like it. "Um," Cass started.

Hill looked at her, nodding her head up and down, and smiling before saying, "Maybe you should call Joanne, to let her know your plans." The way Hill used her mom's name made Cass feel like an adult.

"Yeah, I guess. Ok." Cass got up to go to the phones she had seen by the bathrooms. Hill bounded off to the other side of the grass again, turning and shouting to Cass, "I'll find you towards the end of the show."

Cass's stomach fluttered. She stood up straight and took a breath. She would just tell her mom, be calm, it wasn't that big of a deal. The music was screechy and chaotic behind her. She had to cup her ear to hear the phone ringing.

"Hello," Joanne answered.

"Hi. Mom, it's me," Cass said relaxing. "Everything's fine. It's fun, actually."

"Good, honey," her mom said coolly.

"So, Mom, I'm going to go to a campground, after the show, near the amphitheater," Cass said, feeling her stomach tighten as she waited.

"What was that, honey," Joanne said a little more strained.

"There's a campground where Hill and I want to go after the show… is that ok?"

"I thought you were coming home right after the show," Joanne said, "Where will you sleep?"

"I'll sleep in the car," Cass said, biting her lower lip, and leaning into the phone booth. "You know, I have that blanket in the trunk. It'll be fine."

"I don't know Cass. It doesn't sound like a good idea."

"It'll be fine, Mom," Cass said, wanting to feel herself as the high school graduate that she was. It was getting time for her to make her own decisions.

"Don't tell me what will be fine," her mom had raised her voice.

Cass waited, shifting towards the phone stall as a young man came up to make a call next to her.

"Come on, It's going to be late driving. It'll be better to do it in the morning," she said, trying to appeal to one of the very reasons her mom didn't want her to go in the first place. The music was frenetic. Really, she wanted to get off the phone though

"Cass, just come home after the show, better yet, come home now."

"No!" Cass shouted, and the boy next to her looked her way. She rolled her eyes and smiled slightly, as her face turned pink. "The show's not over yet," she said more quietly.

"I don't care," Joanne said, "and I don't like that girl, Hill."

"What? Why not? That's not very nice," Cass scolded her mom, feeling her own power return.

"Cassandra, you are really pissing me off," Joanne said.

"So sorry about that," she mocked, "So, I'll see you tomorrow then." Cass waited feeling her breath hot in her chest.

"This is not cool, and you know it!"

Cass started to worry that Jack could come find her, but she remembered he was on duty in The Ozarks for the week, and a missing person report couldn't be filed for 24 hrs. "Sorry about that," she said again. "So, see you tomorrow."

"Cass?"

Cass quickly hung up the phone before she could hear her mom say anything else. Shit, she thought. Mom's going to be really, really pissed. Cass went to the bathroom. She washed her hands next to two girls in lightweight Indian print dresses. They both had long braids and looked really happy. Cass looked at herself in the mirror, her thick ponytail and tiny hoop earrings. The t-shirt hugged her chest and made her breasts stand out. In her mom's eyes, she wouldn't seem innocent, she wouldn't seem like herself. So what, she thought, she was out of school now and everything could change.

She wandered aimlessly around the amphitheater's hallways, she could hear the band's noodling, taking the shape of a song, the singer's voice slow and clear. There was a small group of people in wheelchairs sitting near the entrance, and Cass watched them, their eyes closed, listening. She shuffled along the hallway to the other side and saw a group slowly twirling on the concrete. It seems like the music is woven into these people, Cass thought.

When the song changed, she wandered back onto the lawn. The pace of the music picked up and Cass wanted to dance again to the rhythm. She let her head bob and her feet slap, moving her arms and smiling at the folks next to her. Sweeping lights from the stage shot red arcs over the crowd, and Cass recognized the song, "Good Lovin'," from one of her mom's oldies tapes. Somehow the words made her blush. The whole place seemed to heat up as the musicians rocked on, steady, louder and hot. Cass wanted to laugh and hide at the same time. The singer jumped several octaves and began screaming and shaking his head at the microphone. Cass was offered another pipe and she took a long toke, allowing the smoke to sooth her nerves. She blew the hit out slowly. When the band brought things to an end, Cass whistled, joining the roar of voices around her. Cass could feel the beating of her heart and the pulse of her blood. In the sky, tiny bouncing stars complimented the hazy blue lights of the stage. The band members sang beautiful melodies together in the encore.

Hill skipped up, and grabbed Cass's hand, her skin soft and damp. "Come on. Let's go so we can get to the campground. I heard it's going to be a blast, but the line will be awful." Cass let herself be pulled through the crowd by Hill, who seemed to have lost a bit of her sparkle; she was focused in a way Cass had not seen. When the two of them got to the parking lot, Cass's senses were bombarded by folks shouting, "Ice cold beers!! Grilled cheese!!" Scents lingered in the air and people brushed close to her.

As they walked back to the car, Hillary gave her low-down of the night's show. "Wow, that Scarlet-Fire lit me up!" she said skipping for an instant.

"Which one was that?"

"It ended the first set."

Cass nodded, not really remembering much except smoking and dancing with Forrest, and the shitty phone call she had with her mom. Fuck, she's going to kill me.

"Oh my God, and that 'Smokestack' was really hot, too!" Then Hill got really quiet and shook her head back and forth. "And, and, 'Comes a Time', she whispered, "Is really, really special." Cass thought she knew what song she meant. It had given her chills, after she'd gotten off the phone. It was slow and sung with such meaning and beauty. The two girls made it to their car and readied for the rest of the night.

Chapter 11
Rowen

“This looks good, should be smooth, and the rest we'll sell at the campground,” Rowen said as they found a good spot on Shakedown. It was an open amphitheater, so he and Ollie could hear the last licks of “It's All Over Now.”

“Yeah, man, easy,” Ollie said, “long as they don't give us any trouble.” He looked over the lot and twirled a bottle opener in his hand. They'd loaded the coolers before the show with Bass, Heineken, and Sammy Smiths Nut Brown Ale. Now the slick glass bottles were cold as a ski slope. Selling that beer would take about 20 minutes and bring a few hundred.

When the cheering soared from inside the show, people filled the path in front of them. Rowen and Ollie popped open bottle tops and took the first wadded bills. Their customers were hippies of all ages. Then Ollie noticed a man coming towards them with a black zippered jacket.

“Ten o clock, Row,” he said dropping the lid of the cooler and bending down. Rowen turned and handed an open beer to a young guy, before following Ollie's movements.

“What you boys got in there,” the man said as he approached them. He looked like he was in his sixties, with balding hair and small eyes. Rowen could tell he was new, new at dealing with a Dead crowd.

“Nothing,” Ollie said and moved to lift the cooler, but the man put his foot on top of it and forced it back down to the ground. Ollie threw his hands in the air, “come on man, we're leaving, ok?”

“Not ok,” he shouted, obviously loving his new-found power.

The crowd was heavier and circling them, many stopping to ask

Rowen for a beer. Rowen looked around the crowd, to see if guards were harassing other sellers. It seemed like it was just them. He caught the eyes of a few people he knew and jerked his head slightly for them to see what was going on. Rowen stayed still near his cooler, watching the guy open Ollie's. Fuck, he didn't want to lose the time, he needed that quick cash. Rowen and Ollie looked at each other, also conscious of all their customers right around them. Someone knocked the guy a little bit and he stumbled. It was a girl

"Oh, I'm soooo sorry," she said reaching out to help the man up. Many other heads moved in around him, and Rowen and Ollie slowly backed out, helped by a few others to move quickly with their coolers. They both lunged behind some cars, and when they looked back, the man was turning in circles looking for them.

"Sucker!" Ollie said.

"Come on, let's put the coolers back and just sell by hand," Rowen said. They moved stealthily back to the van, and slid the coolers in. Each one grabbed four and went back to the crowd, easily selling them and gaining cash. They did this again three or four more times and emptied one cooler. Other heads were selling drinks and jewelry, brownies and stickers by hand, too.

"Kansas, man, they're not ready for a Shakedown, they just want to shake us!" Rowen said, wiping his damp hands on his shirt and pants. The parking lot was a quarter emptied and they jumped in the car to head to the campground nearby where the party in this stretch of the Midwest would continue.

Chapter 12
Devon

Devon lingered on the lawn at the end of the show. He watched the steamy mess of Heads stumble out the amphitheater and thought about the show. "Smokestack" in the second set didn't have the deep groove of Pigpen's voice he remembered from long ago. The music was all softer these days. He let the country feel of "Going Down the Road Feeling Bad" bumble in his mind. He saw himself happy, driving with Cora when she was pregnant, and he took her to a show. She never did get it and just wanted to be someplace quiet. He thought of his love for the road and imagined himself more like Jerry. Devon stood up and followed the cattle crowd. Most people walked in pairs or groups, smiling their asses off and joking. He walked by himself, watching the intermingle of hippies, bikers and men in spanking new tie dyes. It was the closest he came to community after being ousted from Cora's family. But he didn't really know anyone. Sure, people recognized him. Some knew him because of his buckles, or his bike, or just because he'd seen the Dead for a long, long time.

As Devon walked into the parking lot, a tall lanky woman sidled up next to him, hooking her arm around his waist. The touch woke him, but her breath was a storm of liquor.

"Well, well, look who's here!" she said grinning up at him.

"Hey, Carla," Devon said to the woman he'd once known close. She was a touring head, about 50 or so, but she liked to drink as much as he did and that meant trouble.

"Where you been, handsome," she said, slurring her words.

"Here and there," he said holding her up and walking towards Shakedown, "You?"

"West mostly. Hey, my son's here," she said dragging him to a row of cars, and one van with the back popped open. "Jacob, Jacob," she started yelling at a drugged-out looking kid, maybe 20 years old. Devon jerked his head at the kid who nodded under a floppy cap. Carla stumbled towards her van.

"Hey, take care gal, see ya round," Devon shouted then wove back into the crowd, getting out of her clutch. Seeing her made him want to drink, but not with other people. A tall kid passed by him holding beers. Devon reached out and grabbed his arm to stop him. The kid whipped around jerking his arm away quickly and scowling at him.

"Hey, man, watch it," he said. Devon looked at his dark eyes, then down at the two beers he cradled against his chest.

"Sorry, uh, can I have one of those?"

"Sure, man," the kid said, "two bucks."

Devon dug two bills out of his front pocket. He watched the guy flip the top with a cigarette lighter, and when he handed it to him, Devon felt a strand of the guy's black hair brush his forearm. He looked down and it reminded him of Cora's hair. He took the beer and the guy was gone. Devon swigged it back, walking towards his bike on the edge of the lot. When he climbed on his bike, the last rifts of "It's All Over Now" came into his head, urging him to get out of there, crank up the bike and start over. He knew it wasn't that easy though. What he wanted couldn't be controlled, at least not by him, not yet.

Chapter 13
Percy

Percy'd been feeling sick, probably from eating old food, but at least he'd had something in his empty belly that twisted and turned when he tried to sleep, one eye open, in the open-sided train car. Lumping his coat around his fiddle and the few other things he owned, Percy stepped to the edge of the train. They were going steady, but who knew when they'd slow and some guard or thug would try to pry him from the train. Then he'd be in the middle of nowhere, again, and that would be way too far from his goal. He needed work, he needed money to send back. He knew his sister would be taking good care of his kids, but it wasn't fair.

Percy let his legs, wrapped in baggy pants, dangle over the side of the train. He smelled the dank coal wafting from the open cars and listened to the bump and rumble of the tracks not far from his feet. The train screeched and occupied Percy's mind with notes higher and less pleasing than his fiddle music. He thought maybe he could find a place on the ground in the next few days, maybe build a fire, rest, hunt something decent to cook up and eat. That's what he wanted. Maybe life was supposed to be that simple. Life was that simple, before Molly got sick.

Percy's mind filled up with the song he'd heard someone else signing the other night, the notes he could probably figure out on his own. It was about traveling on a road and feeling sorry. Which he was right about then.

Cass wove through the crowd following lantern shadows and the hazy light from glow sticks. The compact ground under her tennis shoes felt and shined like stone. She placed her feet carefully between bits of food, cigarette butts, plastic cups, camping lights displaying t-shirts on blankets. Cute boys called to her about their wares, and she blushed, walking on. The road seemed to go on for a long time and in the distance was a big lit-up tent. Cass looked over the open coolers for something icy. It was mostly beer but she didn't want a sour taste. Up ahead she spotted a tall man backlit by the tent's glow. Cass noticed the length of his black hair. His clean clothes made her think he wasn't a hippy. He wasn't hawking, just standing in front of a full cooler, propped open, hands sunk into pockets. He seemed to be searching for someone. As Cass neared, he turned her way and their eyes met. His grey-blue gaze was strong and she let it lock, making her stomach drop. That sinking feeling made Cass want to stop and turn the other way, but her feet walked right up to him. He lowered his eyes, as did she. Cass saw the bottle tops and cans sticking out of the ice.

"Do you have any soda?" she said, daring to look up at him. He bent down so fast over the cooler that their heads knocked.

"Oh, shit, I'm sorry," he said, reaching out to touch her hair.

That really fricking hurt. Cass touched her head, then started over, kneeling down in front of the cooler. She peered up at him and her heart raced. She plunged her hand in the icy water and shifted cans and bottles 'til she found a raspberry soda, which she lifted to the top of her head. He smiled sheepishly and rubbed his own head.

"Hey, I'm really sorry," he said, not daring to reach out and touch her again.

"It's ok. How much for the soda?"

"Oh, it's on the house…or on your head," he chuckled.

"Thanks," Cass said and stood up to walk slowly away, but the guy moved quickly around the cooler, blocking her exit. Cass's head and heart thumped.

"Hey, um," he said, "did you get into the show tonight?"

"Yeah," she said cautiously, "It was my first one,"

"No shit?" he said.

"Yes," Cass said, feeling a little stupid.

"Are you serious? It was your first show?" he asked.

"Yes," she said, defensively, until he added,

"That's really great." He was almost giddy, "that's cause to celebrate!"

"Why?" she said, "what number show was it for you?"

He stepped back a little, shoving rich, olive-colored hands into his pockets as he looked up. "Oh, somewhere in the 350 range," he said.

Cass laughed out loud. "You're kidding right?" she said and popped her soda open, taking a sip.

"No, really, hey you got a good one, ya know. I mean the 'Jack Straw' was supreme and that 'Fire'…fuck!" he said waving his hand in the air. Cass smiled at his lingo, wondering where he was from. He certainly is cute, she thought.

"Hey, what's your name," he asked, becoming gentler.

"Cass," she offered, "what's yours?"

"Rowen," he said.

"That's a cool name. It sounds like a bird."

Rowen clasped his hands together and blew gently in them making the muffled hoots of an owl. They were standing near the edge of the campground Shakedown, and folks were crowding towards the big tent.

"What's happening in there?" Cass asked him.

"It's a band, Johnny's Collar. They're local, supposed to be good. You want to check it out?" Cass looked at him and automatically wanted to be dancing close to him.

"Sure," she said, then pointed at his cooler.

"Oh, I gotta take this back a few rows." He leaned down. Cass finished her soda and set it carefully among a pile of trash. She walked to the other side of his cooler.

"Here, I can help you," and she lifted the other side up. Rowen smiled at her. The two of them walked across Shakedown and towards the rows to his van. Cass felt a little nervous, walking away from the lantern light with this man she just met, this man whose head knocked hers, but this kind of thing seemed normal at a Grateful Dead show, and Hill didn't seem to care where she was. When they stopped in front of a sleek black conversion van, Cass was impressed. Rowen reached inside his pocket and unclipped a chain that was attached to his key. He opened the doors and Cass peered at the carpet, a bench and a bed towards the back. "Nice van," she said as they hoisted the cooler in.

"Thanks, it's home."

What? Did he live in his van?

"So," she said, pulling her sweatshirt closer around her body and waiting for him to lock up, "Do you see the Grateful Dead all the time?" She was still trying to understand the whole thing. It was as if there was some grand magic secret all these folks had.

"Well, not all the time," he said, "The band does three full tours a year with other shows in between, as well as Jerry," he said patiently, "He's the lead singer, the big guy. He's got another band and they play shows, too." Cass nodded as they walked down a dirt path toward the tent. She could hear her heart beating so loud, she wondered if he could hear it, too.

"So, are you from around here?"

"Yeah, I live in Kansas City." Rowen nodded and walked forward.

"Where are you from?"

"Southern California," he said blankly. The two of them were walking close when they approached the tent. He seemed serious as they joined the group of hippies crowded around. Cass spied Hill on the other side of the tent, laughing with a beer hanging from her fingers. She felt estranged from her and not fully trusting of this new man.

Chapter 15
Rowen

Three scruffy looking guys—a drummer, a guitarist and a sax player—coaxed out a strange mix of music; sultry but also chaotic. Rowen leaned against a pole and crossed his arms, watching the girl he'd just met. He remembered that he didn't want to get mixed up with anyone. He calculated the odds of just sleeping with her. She was attractive, and he let his eyes wash over her blondish brown hair and stray down to her hips. Somehow, he knew he couldn't do this. She's delicate, and too pure, he thought. She turned around to smile at him, making his chest hurt. Fuck, he thought. As she turned back around to face the stage, he thought about going back to his van, getting high, and crashing out. The band mellowed out and began a gospel groove, something like the soothing riffs Jerry often played. Then a large woman dressed in a swanky red gown sauntered onto the stage to the sounds of whistles and hisses from the Heads. Rowen smiled, assuming his cool, relaxed stance. The girl turned around to look at him again, smiling and laughing and seeming to blush. The woman on stage swayed and grabbed the microphone as the band steadied a deeper groove. She opened her mouth and let out a deep bellowing voice. Rowen snickered, recognizing the song, "He Ain't Give You None." He folded his arms, curious at this woman's rendition.

Cass began to sway a few feet in front of Rowen. The singer bellowed about caution and heartbreak. She showed her teeth under red lipstick. Rowen let his mind go into the music, as he watched Cass's stiff body sway in front of him. He watched the way her knees bent in her faded jeans, and he liked it. There was a dirty Deadhead in between them who started to dance closer to Cass, but the song ended and everyone cheered. Then the musicians began another slow rhythm, the singer snapped her fingers and shook her head. She brought her lips to the microphone, folding her arms around her body. She dropped her head and worked into it, then let out a belting vibrato. Couples were grasping each other, soothed by the melody. Rowen loved the song, "Shining Star," and although it wasn't Jerry singing, it softened him. He watched Cass stick her hands in her back pockets, unaware that she was being checked out by several guys.

The singer stepped back and winked sharply at Rowen. He blushed and said, "Fuck it" under his breath. He walked up and came close to Cass, slowly wrapping his arms around her front. He could feel her heartbeat as she laid her head back onto him and their bodies melded as if it was the most natural thing in the world.

The woman nodded her head. "That's right honey," she said softly.

Rowen placed his hand against Cass's hair and noticed his hand was shaking. He tried to control it by holding her tighter. The singer was wooing and cooing. Rowen kept this new girl locked in his embrace. He could feel his blood being stirred; he could feel her so clearly. Somehow all the Heads around them melted away and it was just a melody and the two of them.

She leaned slightly away from Rowen's chest, as he held onto her waist. She looked at him, blushing, and Rowen gave her a cool wink. This brought out her smile at the corners of her green eyes. Rowen felt a tightening in his chest. The singing slowed and the two of them moved away from each other. Then Rowen became aware of the scene in the tent and the people around them. He scanned swiftly to see if there was anyone there; he didn't want to be seen latching onto a freshie.

Rowen coolly walked out of the tent under the dark sky that was flecked by stars, and she followed him. He turned around and smiled at her, but before they could speak, another girl skipped up, wrapping her drunken arms around Cass. She stood still, covering her face a bit when Cass realized how much the other girl smelled of alcohol.

"Well, well," she said. "You having fun, Cass?"

"Sure, Hillary, how's it going?" The drunk girl didn't answer but turned to look Rowen up and down. Rowen snickered sarcastically, stepping away from her scrutiny and shooting a sharp glance at Cass.

"Rowen, this is Hillary."

"You can call me Hill, darling," Hill interrupted.

"No thanks," Rowen whispered to himself, laughing.

"Hillary, this is Rowen," Cass finished.

"I'm going to get another beer. You want something?" she said to Cass

"No thanks. I'll see ya later." Hillary skipped off and Cass shoved her hands in her pockets.

"You know her?" he said, lifting his eyebrows.

"I met her about a week ago. She brought me to the shows. She really is a sweet person," Cass said a bit defensively, "She's just a little drunk. I think something happened with her boyfriend."

"Yeah, which one?" Rowen said under his breath. Rowen tried to believe that Cass and Hillary were different types. That Southern princess shit annoyed him. He definitely didn't want to get mixed up with anyone like that. But, he had a sense that Cass was very different. Rowen shrugged the whole thing off when he looked over her pretty figure again. Maybe I could just sleep with her, he thought.

"You want to take a walk?" he said. The band was changing and mostly drunk hippies were hanging around. It was probably almost 3:00am.

"Sure," she said.

The two of them began walking away from the crowd, bordering quiet rows of cars and vans where heads were already asleep. The ground was moist and the trees had been cooled by a late evening breeze. A cricket's hum, steady and serene, soothed the two of them. They came to the edge of the campground and ducked under a wooden fence; the whole Kansas wilderness lay before them. Rowen walked up closer to her, taking her hand.

"Have you been out to these fields before?" Rowen asked.

"Not here, in particular, but I've been to the place where the concert was. Every year, in the fall, there's a Renaissance Festival I go to," she said.

Rowen watched her mouth move as she talked about the festival grounds. He noticed the width of her lips.

"Had you seen a show here before?" she asked him.

"No, I've been to plenty of shows in the Midwest," he said, "but this is the first time I made it to Kansas."

"So, what do you think?" she said, playfully swinging his arm back and forth and smiling at him.

"It's flat," he said and they both laughed, "no, I guess it's alright. I mean I like the old trees," he said gesturing to a giant oak they were walking towards, "but I also like the ocean."

There was a dim glow of light that had lingered from the campground, and the sky was filled with bright pointed stars. The twisting bark of the oak tree and its leaves produced a canopy over the ground. Rowen peered up into the branches of the trees and the broad leaves. Something felt really old there and it made Rowen uneasy.

Chapter 16
Devon

There's no place left to go or follow through.
What we cannot understand, escapes very few.

Devon got sloshing drunk at the campground. He wasn't meaning to, but he couldn't help it. The tedium of humanity plagued him, he just didn't want to feel. He'd tried to interact, tried to not view the younger folk as just himself when he was happy and not focused on what he didn't have. He was so free now, he knew, and that fact should bring him solace, bring him peace. The world on the outside, though, didn't really forgive him, didn't give him the things he wanted: to soar, or be a father to Emma. Everywhere he seemed to turn, he saw himself unfulfilled. The carefree hippies chasing freedom, the bikers taking up the road or the bottle, the birds in the sky, just doing bird things.

Devon walked away from it all, stepping out under the Kansas sky, stepping away from lights and partyers. He heard the stiff grasses crunch underfoot, even as he weaved from the campsites. He sensed the quiet of night, in someplace he'd never been before. Someplace he wished would deliver him to another way of being. He knew getting drunk was not the way there, would not leave him with anything other than headache, but it dulled his heart and numbed his pain. When he found the thick trunk of an old oak, he slumped against it, trying to call his spirit, trying not to slip too far from it all. The bottle draped in his fingers, as he rested. Devon felt calm here, in the middle of a field. Felt he could take a load off and wait for morning birds.

"These are strange places," Cass said. Rowen caught a glint of light in her eyes. She let his hand drop and brushed back her hair, resting against a tree. Rowen squared off in front of her. "Your hair is so beautiful," he said.

"My hair?" she said, stretching to touch his long black locks, "yours is gorgeous." She was feeling stupid again, until he leaned over and brought his lips to the side of her cheek. His breath was warm and she felt her heart fluttering as he worked his way to her lips. He pressed firmly, and a bright flash filled Cass's head. She drew a breath and he stepped closer, pressing his body against hers and parting her lips to receive his tongue. Overwhelmed by weight, by his breath, Cass could feel the rough edge of the tree pressing her back.

Rowen traced the map of her mouth, but the heat was too much. Cass turned her head to the side, breaking their kiss. She looked at this beautiful man, felt his body; she didn't know him, couldn't really trust him. Her eyes looked for light in the distance, back at the campground. A part of her knew she was being stupid. It was unlike her, but then again, she'd never gotten the chance to make out with a hot guy.

"You ok?" Rowen took a half step back. His voice was far away and Cass wondered briefly who in the world he was, really. But she nodded, and he leaned back in. Cass tried to match him, though her heartbeat was so fast and loud and distracting. He pressed her against the tree again and the bark dug into her back. She wanted to push him, but she also didn't. She moaned and shifted her body, then a muffled grunt and part of a loud snore filled the air.

"What the hell?" Rowen said, stepping away from the tree and pulling Cass with him. They walked around to the other side of the giant trunk. There, a big man, slumped against the tree with legs splayed and an empty bottle between. When Cass saw this, she felt a stab of fear.

"Oh, man!" Rowen said, catching a whiff of the man's alcohol stench. The man's eyes rolled open for a second, then shut back, followed by another loud snore.

"That happens," Rowen said shaking his head, "Come on let's go," and he pulled Cass back towards the parking lot. Now, Rowen seemed safe compared to that big half-dead man.

When they came to Rowen's van, he quietly unclipped his key and opened the door before Cass could protest. The campground had settled, with only a few around. Faint twinges of daylight appeared which Cass tried to ignore. The two of them crawled into the van and Rowen reached back to pull the door shut. Cass remembered they were surrounded by other people in cars, and Hill was somewhere, too. A side window was partially open, but the van was dank and dark. Once again, Cass saw the bed in the back of the van, draped in a red and blue quilt. The patterns were intricate and reminded her of a grandmother. She convinced herself it was all fine, and she should loosen up.

"You want something to drink, Cass?" He said as he propped the top of a cooler.

"Sure," she said, remembering how she'd met this man in the first place. Rowen reached in and pulled out two slim bottles. Cass didn't protest and he popped the tops using the end of a lighter, handed one to her. She took a sip and the sour taste filled her mouth. Rowen gulped his back and set it on an old wooden coaster before climbing to the front and popping in a tape. The music was slow and sounded like the Grateful Dead. Cass relaxed on the side bench, taking tiny sips from her bottle, and watching Rowen's movements. He reached inside a cabinet to find a little woven basket. He set it in front of Cass, and pulled back the corner of the sheet covering the window to let a little light in. Cass felt anxious when she glimpsed the light, knowing that a new day would be starting soon, and she'd have to leave.

"Do you like crystals?" He asked.

"Sure."

Rowen cupped the basket in his palm and presented it to her. Cass let her fingers pick up the crystal inside. It was clear and pointed at one end. The surface felt like glass and was as smooth as Rowen's hair. She looked up to meet his eyes as he leaned, kissing her again. He was gentle this time, and Cass relaxed. Rowen took her beer and placed it with the little basket on the table before coming back to her lips. Her fingers clutched the crystal as he opened her mouth wider with his tongue. His hand reached to grip her breast, sending a shiver from Cass's chest to the space between her legs. She tried to meet him, using the muscles of her mouth to grip his. When he leaned back, Cass looked down to see her white-knuckled fist still tightening the crystal. As she unfolded her hand, Rowen took the crystal and softly kissed the fading red mark on her palm. She smiled at him, not knowing what she could possibly say. The music coming from the front of the van caught her. It was folky with fewer instruments. She heard the word the music, which picked up her heartbeat. "Who's this?" Cass asked, as she watched Rowen slide to the bed in the back of the van and lie on his side.

"This is Jerry's Band. Remember I told you, the lead singer's group?"

"Yeah," Cass said. Rowen flicked his head up, gesturing her to join him. She carefully crawled to lie next to him, hanging her feet off the edge of the bed. Cass bobbed her head to the music. Rowen reached over to touch her hair, then he ran his hand over her breast, down her side and over the tightness of her jeans. She dropped her head and leaned into his chest and the woodsy smell that was now stronger and mixed with the scent of pot on his shirt. Rowen lifted her chin with his finger and began kissing her slowly, lingeringly, in a way that made her lean into him, wanting more. But when she realized that he had unhooked her bra in the back, she pulled her body away and rolled off him, laying on her back. Cass could see his face more clearly now as the light of the day seeped into the van, his eyes sleepy. Rowen crawled over her, flopping onto his back. He stared, tired and defeated. Cass sat up and reached back to hook her bra. She had the thought that she should leave. Turning to Rowen, her heart sank a little. She wished he was not a touring Deadhead, but a guy from Kansas City that she could get to know, a little more slowly. Rowen propped his elbow up, resting his head.

"You going to the next show?" he said sleepily.

"No," Cass answered, "Are you?"

"Yep, that's what I do."

"Oh," Cass was angry that she had mixed with this guy; that she'd allowed her heart to be stirred. She began to get up but Rowen stopped her.

"Hold on there," he said sitting up. "Give me another kiss," Cass leaned over, and Rowen parted her lips.

"So, you live in Kansas City," he said, "what do you do there?" He was brushing his hand over her hair.

"I just graduated high school. I live with my mom." She didn't care what he thought. She'd probably never see him again.

He nodded. "Well, can I have your number, sweet Cassidy?"

"It's Cassandra," she said smiling a little, "and sure, Rowen." He got up, found a piece of paper and a pen where she wrote her name and number. Rowen folded the piece of paper and tucked it into the little basket. Cass climbed to the doors of the van, opened them, and let the grey blue of the sky flood in. Rowen followed as she climbed out, grabbing the little crystal she'd clutched from the table.

"Don't forget this," he said, handing it to her. Cass twirled the clear crystal in her fingers then tucked it in her pocket. She looked up at Rowen, his eyes fading. He wrapped her in a big hug, and they both breathed, feeling the other's heartbeat. When Cass's arms fell to her sides, Rowen framed her face with his hands and leaned in to give one kiss on the lips, then one on her forehead.

"Can you make it home alright?"

She nodded.

"Bye Rowen," she said turning away from him.

"Bye beautiful," he said.

Cass made her way past cars and sleeping bodies, looking for the black Nissan. She found her way to an empty Shakedown Street and walked along it until she remembered her row. When she came to her car, she found a little piece of paper tucked under the windshield wiper. It was a mess of scribbled handwriting, but she saw a big "H" swirled at the bottom. It read:

Hey, Cass, Hope you had a good time with that cute guy!
I've gone on to Ohio. It was fun to meet you. Here's my number,
if you want to get in touch, or I'll try to call you next week,
Ciao, H.

The little note made her smile and she tucked it into her other pocket. Luckily, there was enough room for Cass to get her car out. She drove down dirt roads as the morning sun broke.

She felt clean, driving away with the sunrise. Hill had left a Grateful Dead tape in her player, and she listened to the music, trying to connect and make better sense. She turned onto the highway, listening to a crowd cheering on the tape when a huge bird swooped not ten feet above her car. Cass gasped noticing the black sheen of its tail feathers and watched as it swooped to a field. For a moment, she remembered the raven she'd seen by the stream the other day, but her thoughts returned to the show, the campground and especially Rowen's touch. As she pulled into the parking lot at home, she felt estranged from her life.

Chapter 18
Hettie

It was afternoon as Hettie stepped out of the cabin to walk across greening grass towards the bluff. Her muscles were achy and stiff, but she wanted to hear the trickle of water near the edge of her property. Pulling her cream-colored shawl tighter around her shoulders, she watched as yellow sunlight drove a shadow back across the field. Silica speckles lit up the dirt. Hettie tried listening for the quick movement of water, its rush she wanted to hear singing like a sparrow. From her porch, she breathed in the scent of deer dung. The sound of water grew louder in her mind. Hettie closed her eyes, whispering prayers to the water—prayers of thanks, and movement, of ease and flowing. She let the sounds softened the inside of her mouth, until they grew to song, melding with the warming breeze and the flowing stream. By the pull of her heart, Hettie faced the open field. Her eyes fluttered open, and through the reeds, on a patch of the illuminated weeds, she saw a young woman with gold-brown hair and gentle features, the air moving her thin skirt and t shirt. She squinted at the vision, tracing the fuzzy edges of the face. Hettie didn't know her. The girl turned her head, taking in the sunlight, then tucked a strand of hair behind her ear. A tickle formed in Hettie's heart, as her mind took over. "Who's that," she said to herself, cutting off the flow of her prayer. Then the vision faded. Hettie blinked a couple times and followed the beats in her chest. They were fluttery like a hummingbird, fast and light, but pleasant. Immediately, she thought the spirit had something to do with it. After waking in her cabin the other day to find the scent of pipe smoke, she knew he'd been there.

The constancy of the rushing stream returned to Hettie's ears and she stepped away from the water. She walked carefully back inside the cabin as evening's shadow descended on the Earth. She cooked herself a simple dinner of thawed stew meat, beans and bread. Then she sat in HER rocker, with a small cup of whiskey, rocking and sipping. "So," she started aloud, "this is how it'll go. You hear me?" she asked of the air inside her cabin. Hettie was sure that spirit was nearby and could hear her. "Don't know who ya are, but I've an inkling you're someone I've heard about." A smiled crept to her mouth and she sipped a little more whiskey, silently calling her great grandmothers to her side—the ones she bet could tame him. "I'll admit, you got my curiosity, but just don't go startling me, ok? When I light that candle on the dresser," she said lifting her hand towards it, "and I'm not all in the middle of something else, then you're free to visit," she said nodding her head like that was that. She would call the shots. "And this is my rocker… it helps me think," although she knew that wasn't all welcoming and he would like it, too, as he'd sat there twice before. Hettie kept steady though. It was her place, she could say when and where and how.

She went over to the dresser, turned the sticky candle. Hettie lifted it to her nose and sniffed the thick beeswax. She struck a match against a stone and lit its nubby wick. The flame was short and sputtered, dancing side to side before holding straight. "There, like so," she said. Hettie knew it might take some time, so she pushed the back door open and walked out on the porch. Streaky grey clouds laid across the sky in front of Crystal Mountain, with a quarter moon rising. There was still some dark blue above and she heard the easy rumble of tires on gravel roads. A dog barked, and the wood slats creaked as she leaned against the porch railing, scanning the field. A faint image of that girl came back in her mind, and she looked to the spot where she'd seen her. Dark grass swayed, the field empty. Hettie heard a scuttle on the roof, probably a mouse, and she thought she heard the swish of a wing. She looked back through the window and noticed the candle flame burning steady.

Later on, she was getting ready for bed, dressing in a long white nightgown with a modest robe over it and socks. The candle was still burning and had been for a good two hours. She went to the kitchen to put away the cups she'd washed and then heard creaking. She turned around and there he was sitting in her rocker. Hettie smiled and shook her head. As she stepped back into the room where he was, her heart beat picked up. She walked slowly, to sit on the couch, and looked at him carefully. This time she noticed, under his scraggly hair, a couple small gashes below his ear. They were red, and streaky, like they'd bled at some point.

He started rocking, slowly like a video playing in slow motion. Hettie squinted, watching trails of energy waft behind him, or maybe it was just dust. He looked really old. "Ok," Hettie said, "thanks for respecting my candle," she looked towards the flame which was high and flickering. He nodded. Hettie looked at the North wall and the quilt. The outline of the bird was perfect, the thread lines of its beak pointed and clear. She took a deep breath, tried to calm her mind, and the first thought went to that book of her mother's, the names there.

"Yah, I's one of them, Percy's my name" the spirit said, continuing his slow-motion rock. Hettie nodded continuing to breath. She kept her gaze away from him. A tinge of fear still in her. Seemed they could connect through thoughts, too. She thought of the stream water, of walking around her property, she thought of the coyote she'd seen when her ankle had buckled. He let out a muted grunt. Hettie tried to make her mind just blank, let him say something.

She looked up and saw his eyes close. Hettie remembered how her daughter'd got out of La Cueva as soon as she could drive, going all the way to California with some joker who would leave her in the end, with the three boys. She knew people moved all the time, for different reasons. She remembered her own move from Oklahoma to New Mexico when she met Wilson.

Her momma stood in the doorway watching her go, like she knew it would happen. But, nowadays Hettie couldn't imagine moving anywhere. That New Mexico land kept her stuck like glue, just like she liked it. She'd been tied to that patch of ground right in front of Crystal Mountain for decades. The trip to California after Jessie died wiped her out. That bus ride, streaming across highways, was too much. She knew Rowen was a traveler though, going all over the country, barely stopping for his own mother's death.

The spirit kept rocking and Hettie smelled smoke. He'd lit a small wood pipe, just letting the tobacco smoke trail against him as he moved. She watched his sunken face as the smoke moved in and out, wondering how it was possible. She saw him smile, and felt like a little kid, in the presence of an old uncle. She knew she'd never met him in her life, but there was some bond there. "Who's that girl," she finally said.

"What girl?" he said, pulling the pipe from his mouth.

"The one in the field today," she said, sweeping her arm towards the window.

"I don't know what yer talking about."

Hettie rolled her eyes and sat back on the couch. Ok, she thought. She studied him, sitting there, hunched over in her rocker and smoking his pipe. He really looked like he just wanted a rest. His clothes were dirty and looked like he'd had a hard life. Hettie felt sorry for him for a minute or two. She leaned over to lift her cup and when she sat back up, he was gone.

Chapter 19
Rowen

The tattered campground was mostly empty, scattered trash and soiled spots left from the night before. Rowen knew he was getting behind. Most folks would already be in Ohio, even though the show wasn't until the next day. The drive would be about ten hours, and he figured on doing most of it that day to snag a prime spot in the lot. Rowen was glad he was far away from California. The distance made him feel calm. Every time he thought about it, his mom's death disoriented him. Better to be half-way across the country, where she wasn't under some piece of ground.

Rowen had the back of the van loaded with enough cases of beer and figured he'd be ok. He just needed to fill the coolers with ice somewhere along the way. Rowen thought about waiting around for Picasso Joe. A sheet or two of blotter acid would be nice, but that shit was always risky in the Midwest, plus Picasso was always hard to find at the end of venues. Rowen knew he wasn't thinking straight. After Cass had left, he drank too many beers and fell asleep with thoughts of her circling his head. Now he was behind. He noticed Ollie's messy pack on the top of the van to signal he'd be coming back for a ride. Ollie was a regular rider with Rowen. He was from Indiana and knew all the Midwest highways like the back of his hand. Also he was one of the few people Rowen trusted to drive. Ollie usually had some money and was a good worker, too. Rowen could stand touring with him, and he was funny. A few minutes later Ollie sauntered up. Rowen threw out his hand, grasping Ollie's large white fingers, and shaking twice before pulling him into a side shoulder hug.

"Glad you're still here, bro. I'd been looking for ya but then ended up with these crazy chicks last night," Ollie said with a wide grin. "Mountain Jim, that Head from Cali was telling wicked stories around the fire…I thought I'd see ya."

"Nope, I was in." Rowen said, not offering any more information about his time with Cass, "You ready to go, man?"

"Yeah," Ollie said reaching up to grab his pack which he let thud to the ground. "I saw Changa. He said he was looking for you, too, and wants to ride. He just went to grab his stuff."

"Shit man, we're already late," Rowen said. Changa was most likely out cruising for ground scores. He never had money, but found most things he needed on the ground, discarded by other people. Rowen hoisted himself into the van's front seat and turned the engine over. The black van started up smoothly and Rowen put on the brake, revving it to warm up for the drive. Ollie had scored a tape of last night's show and popped it in the dash. The recording was mostly crap, but good to hear it anyway. He shook his head remembering that it was her first show

"Scan for glass man," he directed Ollie, who promptly bent down to check for any broken glass around the tires then climbed in the back of the van to clean things up. Ollie tucked the edges of the quilt under the mattress. Then he reached under the bed for a big wooden-handled bristle brush and began brushing the carpet, sending little pieces of bread and dirt out the open doors. Rowen watched him from the front seat. Ollie cleaned off the shelf above the ice box, gathered three empty beer bottles, and tucked the sheet in to cover the side windows. Ollie hopped out to take the beer bottles away.

When Changa finally showed up, he was carrying dirty plastic bags, a roll sleeping bag and a couple crumpled jackets. He looked towards the ground. Rowen smelled him first, a mixture of fire smoke, cigarettes and B.O.

"What man," Rowen said harshly, "you want a ride?"

"Yeah, if you got room," Changa said quietly. Ollie came back running to get there before Rowen took off. He moved past Changa and chucked his huge backpack on the van floor.

"Put that shit in the back. Tuck it in," Rowen said to Changa who nodded and disappeared around the back of the van. Rowen got ready to drive and Changa scouted the dirty path again before hopping in the back. Ollie took the front seat.

The first riffs of "Fire on the Mountain" came through the speakers as Rowen adjusted his sunglasses and slowly bumped the van to the entrance. The campground was well off a major highway, and the flat stretch of hard dirt road combined with the easy groove of the song seemed to slow Rowen down in a way he was itchy to shake. Ollie adjusted his legs and pulled the seat belt strap over his wide belly. He slid his glasses up and looked over at Rowen whose white knuckles clenched the steering wheel.

"You toke yet, man?" Ollie said

"No," Rowen muttered. And then it hit him. He knew how to shake this. Rowen held the wheel with his knee and carefully pulled the cover off the steering wheel. He reached in to pull out a little baggie, then lined up the Velcro strips to set the cover back into place. He threw the bag at Ollie. "You got a paper?" he said.

"I think so," Ollie answered, shifting to one side and stretching his scrunched hand into his pocket. He pulled out a lighter and a flattened package of Zig-Zag rolling papers. Then he took the road atlas from the console pouch, spread it over his lap, and pulled a choice green bud from the baggie. After a lingering sniff with eyes closed, he carefully massaged the bud with his fingers as it crumbled into the white paper, then rolled it tight and licked it closed. He gave the baggie back to Rowen, who replaced it in the steering wheel's secret compartment, and held out the large joint.

"Go ahead, man," Rowen said.

"Carpe diem, thanks bro." Ollie checked the side mirror, then lit the joint and drew it long. He shook his head, holding his hit in, and passed it to Rowen. Rowen lifted the joint briefly above his forehead before toking hard and long, while watching the road with one eye. The smoke billowed into his lungs, clearing out his throat and soothing the fiery nerves in his chest. A relaxed smile returned to his face.

Ollie noticed how hard Rowen had hit the joint and said, "Fuck, Rowen, you been depriving yourself, bro?"

Rowen nodded, still holding in his hit. They listened to the tape, going back in their minds to the show.

"Did you see Bobby during 'Smokestack'? He was shaking like a chicken again," Ollie said, offering the joint back to Changa. Rowen smiled as Ollie rambled on. "That 'Sugaree' was pretty sweet, too. I mean,

Jerry's voice was actually crisp and he went way high on those last riffs." Rowen nodded in agreement, taking another long toke and remembering the show. He had a seat on Phil's side, pretty far back, and he reviewed the set list in his mind.

"'Candyman' was certainly tripped," Rowen said, flashing on the band singing the chorus together. "And Vince's voice was good."

"The 'Scarlet-Fire' still stands," Ollie said, shaking his head.

Rowen nodded again in agreement, not taking his eyes off the small two-lane road. The beating pattern of drums pulsated out of the stereo, and with the soothing hum of pot and the cool cover of his black sunglasses, Rowen dug the expansive Kansas fields. His mind drifted back to that grove of trees from the night before, and as he shook his head bemused, he caught the quick swoop of a bird. He looked in his rearview mirror for a minute and saw what he thought was a raven diving towards the ground. He let his mind wander, protected by the hum of THC. If his mom was a bird now, she probably wouldn't be a blackbird. No, she'd be something like a dove, or pigeon. The road curved as they approached the on-ramp to the highway, and Rowen brought his mind back. "What's our stats, man?" Rowen said.

"Buckeye's pretty much 70 East the whole way." Ollie said. Rowen nodded as he looked in the rear-view mirror. Changa was asleep on the back bench. Ollie flipped through the pages of a road atlas, looking for the smaller towns that would be on the way.

"Do we have a stash?" Ollie asked.

"No more than we need."

"Do we need anything?"

"I think we have enough beer…just ice before the lot," Rowen said, "I wouldn't mind finding a spot for showers."

"Nice call," Ollie said, looking down at the smoky smudges on his hands. "What d'we have to sell?"

"About ten cases, mostly Heineken and Bass, some Sammy's," Rowen said. "But we're late, a line-up will have already started, and I wanna get in the lot early."

"Oh, we can slip by that," Ollie said, a little smirk on his cheeks.

The plastic boxed showers at the truck stop set them back $5:50 each. It was seven-thirty that evening and they had already passed Indianapolis' small tangle of highways. After showering, Rowen sat in a phone booth and dialed the number of his voicemail. There was a message from his brother, Lou, indiscreetly mentioning a stash arrival; Rowen shook his head and erased it. He half wished the other message would be from Cass but remembered he hadn't given her his number.

Instead, a crackly voice came over the receiver, "Rowen, it's your grandmother, Hettie, where are you, boy?" Rowen smiled at the tinge of sarcasm in her voice. "I'm feeling you, little black cat, give me a call sometime. Rowen felt for a minute like the little boy who used to pretend he was a cat, cuddling into his granny's lap. The memory lingered until he decided not to call her back. Then he remembered watching her get on the bus in California. His van was all packed that day and he drove away before her bus left the station. He remembered glancing up and seeing her face in one of the windows. She just watched him go. She was leaving, too, he'd told himself. No one wanted to stay in the wake of a death, except maybe his brothers who didn't have anywhere else to go. Rowen reached in the pocket of his jeans and pulled out some folded bills. He flattened them out, finding a small piece of paper tucked among the forty-five bucks. Instead of Cass's number he found a reminder to "call D.B., sweet bud" scribbled over a Southern California number for a new connection back west. He wanted to call Cass, and closing his eyes, he thought of her soft lips on his neck. But he also remembered her talk of being in school, living with her mom. Her number was still in the crystal basket, in the van, maybe. Rowen shoved the money back in his pocket and strode out of the phone booth to meet the other guys in the restaurant.

"I'll drive man, you can chill," Ollie said as they walked back to the van after eating.

"Alright, thanks," Rowen was moving slowly. It was dark, he was tired from several hours of driving. Rowen got in the passenger seat. Ollie adjusted his body in the driver's seat. He went to shift the visor, and a photograph fell to the floor. Rowen looked down to see that photo of his mom. It was taken probably 10 years ago, she was squinting in the sun and smiling. Even in the muted light from the parking lot, it was too much. He hadn't wanted to see that photo right then.

"Sorry man," Ollie said. Rowen picked it up, and quickly put it face down in the glove compartment. Ollie pushed his glasses up and looked at Rowen. "That your mom?'

"It was," Rowen said, "leaning back in his seat.

Ollie paused. "Hey, I'm really sorry man. I know she was sick."

"I don't want to talk about it," Rowen said.

"Yeah, yeah," Ollie said, then shut up and clicked his seat belt.

Rowen changed his mind, and crawled in the back, past Changa who he motioned to take the front. Rowen went to the way back and flopped on the bed, turning to face the back window. The van sped up and settled on the highway.

The more people who knew, the realer it became, Rowen thought. He just wanted to ignore it all, just keep traveling. Anyway, he didn't feel like he'd even known his mom the past few years. He hadn't wanted to end up like her either, working in an endless job, slinging dishes. Tour had much more meaning. Plus, staying away kept her life easier. She worried herself over Lou going in and out of jail, and Tate using. His absence gave her one less thing to worry about while she worked morning to night to pay for that apartment. But she was always happiest to see him when he came home. He could tell because she got up to kiss him when he walked in the door, leaving her cigarette burning in the ashtray. She never yelled at him either like she did to his brothers. If he could, he gave her money when he showed up. She always spent some of those dollars on lottery tickets that she'd scratch off while he was still around. Rowen's chest hurt, thinking about her, and he pulled the quilt over him, willing his body to sleep.

Bobby's voice was deep as it pushed out of the speakers under the dash, belting that old song Muddy Waters sang: "Same Thing." Rowen had been sleeping in the back for a few hours and Changa took up the side bed. Ollie wheeled the black van through the quiet streets of Columbus, then out to the country, a few blocks from Buckeye Lake's entrance, where a line had already begun. Ollie crept along, watching for cops out of one eye and a spot to pull into out of the other. Earlier arrivals were already pulled over, locked up and crashed, so he rolled the van up along the line and double parked next to a little Toyota. He left just enough space for the driver slumped in the back to get out. Ollie cut the engine and climbed in back with a groan. They'd traveled eleven hours. He spread his sleeping bag on the floor and joined the chorus of deep breathing in the back of the van.

Chapter 20
Cass

It wasn't until late afternoon that Cass stumbled into the kitchen. Her mom was sitting at the kitchen table, reading.

"Well, well, look who's home, and awake," Joanne said, slapping her magazine on the table.

"Oh, hi, Mom," Cass said.

"You look terrible Cass, what, did you sleep on the ground last night?"

"No! I didn't sleep there. That's why I've been sleeping in my room all day, ok.

"Not ok, young lady. You hung up on me, and if I hadn't known where you were, I would have been out searching with Jack. You know that!"

Cass leaned against the counter folding her arms. Her mom was being a drag.

Joanne continued, "What's gotten into you?"

"Nothing! I was just having fun! Aren't I allowed to have fun once in a while?"

"It's more about communication, respect and following rules. Do I really have to remind you?"

Cass went to the refrigerator, opened then closed it. She knew her mom was right, but she wanted to think about other things. Doing everything her mom had wanted seemed easy before, but now that she finally had something interesting happen to her, she just wanted to go with it, regardless. She knew fighting wouldn't work with her mom, so she softened, and sat down at the table with her.

"Look, Mom, I'm really sorry. Really. I just wanted to go along with the friends I'd met."

"Oh, you mean that stuck-up little hippie princess, Hillary?" her mom said sarcastically batting her eyebrows."

"Come on, that's not fair. Hillary was nice." Cass took a breath. Hillary seemed an easier friend for her mom to know about than Rowen. She doubted she'd be ok with her hanging out with a 23 year-old guy who traveled following a band for a living. "Ok, ok," Cass said, "You're right. I shouldn't have hung up, and I should respect your rules when I'm in your house." Cass looked up to see her mom's dropped face when she said 'your house. "I won't do it again. I promise," Cass said and went around to give her mom a hug.

"Woah, you stink!" Joanne said, hugging her daughter limply, "hit the shower!"

"Ok, sorry." Cass said walking out of the kitchen feeling like maybe she'd won the argument, or at least didn't let on about Rowen.

Cass tugged off the dirty clothes she had crashed on her bed in and slung a yellow robe over her shoulders. She thought of Hillary and where she would be by now. She thought of her and Rowen running into each other and Cass wished that she was traveling, too. Slinking into the bathroom that her mother had cleaned up when she was away, Cass locked the door and turned the old creaking knobs of the shower until it was blasting water. She stepped inside facing the spray and reached up to pull back her hair. She stood motionless under the water, focusing on the sound of its patter and rush. The steam billowed to the ceiling of the bathroom and Cass watched, musing that it was a soft cloud, something she could rest in, pull over her like a blanket. As the water beat on her body, her tired mind heard a slurred sound. She thought it was a word like "soothe" or "slip"… a word that rolls off the tongue. Cass reached for the bar of soap and slowly ran it along her legs. She saw herself in a rainforest next to a stream, the slippery skin of a papaya against her leg. The water streamed down and hit the porcelain tub like rain. The sound of it pierced Cass's ears and she listened more closely as the hushed voice of musicians came back. Cass's head started to nod to a Grateful Dead song that came into her mind, but a loud pounding on the bathroom door jerked her back to reality. The humid rainforest turned to a chilly drizzle.

"Cass, what are you doing, for God sake's, you've been in there long enough!" Joanne yelled from the other side of the locked bathroom door.

Cass realized the water was getting cold. She shut it off and quickly jumped out of the shower, wrapping herself in a blue towel.

"Cass, is everything ok?" Her mom said.

"Yeah, Mom, I'm fine. I was just taking a shower, ok!"

"Ok, I'm going to work. Let's have dinner tonight? I think we should talk."

"Sure, Mom, whatever."

"I'll cook, honey," Joanne said, her voice becoming softer.

Cass wasn't going to open the door to say goodbye. As soon as she heard the front door close, Cass walked out of the bathroom, still clutching the towel to her chest. She stumbled into her room, closed the door, and let the towel drop as she crawled into bed.

Head still spinning, she brought one finger to her lips and let the other rest on her breast. She could still feel the raw heat of Rowen's tongue and the pulse of his hand over her heart. Cass's breathing became steady and she fell back into a deep sleep.

Chapter 21
Percy

The wail of a little girl shattered Percy's sleep as he rolled over to see a woman and her child huddled on the other side of the train car. The woman looked mean, feral; the little girl just looked lost and cold. He wanted to help them, he felt their helplessness, out there in the middle of the country, without much, like him. Percy blinked at the girl, and she turned into her mother who was still asleep. She stopped crying, probably more out of fear than anything. Percy wrapped his arms around himself and rolled over to stare at the train's metal sides, bouncing and moving. He wished he was home. He wondered why he wasn't home. What did he plan to prove, leaving like he did? Percy started to shake some and hugged himself tighter. His sister probably hated him by now. Thinking about that land and the bed where Molly'd died, he couldn't be there no more, not now. It wouldn't be until he could send money back that he'd feel alright with himself. Percy wanted to tell his kids: Johnny, Marthajean, and little Mattie that their daddy had the blues. Percy tried to fill his head with string sounds, instead of rumbling train sounds. Back to music, like he always did, for soothing, for getting on.

Chapter 22
Hettie

Hettie sat on her couch with quilt squares piled around her. Determined to patch something together, she wanted to practice the skill she'd known her whole life. Hettie pinned and sewed the stacked white and red material. She thought about the quilts she'd made for Jessie, and the ones for the boys and even the one she'd given away to her community years and years ago. It was afternoon and the candle had been lit for a good hour. She'd started liking the spirit's company. As much as she liked being alone, it was good to talk to someone other than herself, even if he was dead. She'd pretty near figured out that he was the great-granddaddy of her mother. He wasn't talked about much in her youth, but Hettie knew that her ancestors had moved, from Appalachia to Oklahoma—the homeland she knew. Hettie guessed that hadn't been a good time and that's why no one wanted to talk about it. She did remember her Papa yelling at her about gratefulness one time when she was a surly teenager, and how she knew nothing of what her grandparents endured. There were old things around her family's house though, like musical instruments forgotten and gathering dust.

Hettie got up from the couch and went to the kitchen to make a sandwich. She was just bringing the plate back to the living room, when he arrived, walking through the side wall like it was made of clouds. Hettie almost dropped her lunch, seeing that. She kept her gaze down and bee-lined for the couch, not crossing his path to the rocking chair.

"Hi," he said as he plopped down.

"Hello," Hettie said, looking up to notice his change of clothes. He was wearing clean slacks and a cream-colored shirt with that ratty jacket thrown over it. He looked like he'd bathed. Hettie lifted her eyebrows.

"Got a job," he said.

"Oh," Hettie said taking a bite of her sandwich. The spirit rocked a bit, and flashed Hettie a vision of a big factory, dirty urban streets. Hettie remembered photos of a front porch, bigger than hers, and men in similar dress packed around. She guessed the photo was much later than when he was talking about. It seemed like he was at the beginning of something, not worn down by it just yet.

"It's real important," the spirit said, brushing his palms along his pants.

"I see," she said. Least he had a job. She thought about Rowen, not working at anything, as far as she could tell, and barely stopping to mark his mother's death. Hettie didn't like it and worried for him.

"Yes, yes," the spirit said, reading her mind. Hettie saw a slumped man, next to a tree, and a thick glass bottle dangling from his fingers. Hettie nodded. She knew her family had a history of alcohol abuse, but this wasn't Rowen's problem, at least she didn't think so. Her granddaddy danced his knee and clasped his hands. He turned around and peered out the window. The sun was still high, but afternoon would take it soon.

"He's always going around in that van, seeing some rock and roll band," Hettie said. "He's your kin, too, ya know," Hettie went on, but the spirit wasn't listening. He stood and turned towards the sun, leaving the way he came. "Well," Hettie said to herself, "must be in some hurry." She ate the rest of her sandwich, a little disappointed by his quick exit. She had more to say.

Chapter 23
Devon

The Indian Motorcycle's engine purred and tripped, purred and tripped, as the bike sped over the highway. The hair on Devon's white-knuckled hands whipped with the motion. His eyes, inside a black helmet, watched the road's lines. He'd been riding most of the day on the Midwestern interstates, passing shoddy hippie vans he knew were also headed for the next show. A gas station lay a few miles ahead. Devon looked at the cloudy gauge, it was only a quarter full, so he decided to stop.

He kicked his heels against the throttle and pulled the bike to a gas pump. Devon looked up at the bulbous shape of an orange sign, and letting his mind go blank pulled out his chained wallet and walked inside the shiny store.

"What'll it be sir?" the older attendant said, squinting at him. Devon noticed the man's stained button up shirt underneath a company smock. He saw dullness in his eyes that reminded him of a guard he once knew.

"Twenty on that bike out there," he said, shaking the thought of resemblance and ducking to look out the window over the man's shoulder, "number five, yeah, twenty on number five."

"Ok, anything else today, sir?"

"Oh," Devon said, his eyes wildly scanning bright food wrappers, till he settled on a long package of nuts. "And these," he said pulling the peanuts off a rack.

The man smiled and Devon walked out the door ripping open the package and pouring the salty snack in his mouth. While he waited for the gas to stream into his bike, he took a quick swig from his flask, mixing whisky with the salt. Devon wiped his red tank with a soiled rag and also the top of his helmet, smearing away black bug parts.

He hummed the highways for another good hour then cut to a smaller road that would bypass the bustle of Indianapolis and head east to Columbus. The sky began to streak with pink and clouds took on the bright lining from a fading sun. Devon rode through a forest, the tall trees waving their branches as he passed. He stretched his shoulders back under his stiff leather jacket and lifted his head to the forest. Crisp air filled his lungs and he closed his eyes for a second, reveling in the blackness and the movement of his bike. He wanted to see through his other eyes, the ones that gave sharp edges to everything around him. The ones that could see dark and light, simpler, and free from color. His human mind tried to track seeing that way. He knew one time he'd been able to, in New Mexico, when he'd finished the magpie buckle. He remembered looking at Emmajean's photo and walking out the back door. After that, he just remembered wanting.

Devon stopped his bike as the desolate road curved. He pulled up next to a cattle gate and turned the engine off. Slowly rolling a cigarette, he felt the weight of the deserted place. The way the land stretched out beyond a fence, prairie grass covering it, made him think of stretches of the California desert. He used to walk out those fields with his buddy, Andy, as far as they could go before seeing another building construction site. It was on those walks when he first felt the glimmer of his path, that might have started with PJ, but then became his own. Andy would be rattling away and Devon would disappear, then he would turn back, gentle, and walk home alone. Devon still had the memory of watching his friend from the top of a tree, from the sky above and there was such a deep knowing and acceptance in his friend's homeward gaze that Devon wanted to go back right away.

Devon struck a match on the small box and watched the smoke curl into him. His lungs sucked in the pleasure and he leaned against the fence, wiping away his mind and watching the pink streak to purple in the sky. He tried to track his actions from the night before: going to the Dead show, stumbling to a campground, crashing near an old tree. He remembered wanting to change there, too, and falling asleep before he could. Devon scanned the sky, and the isolated road. The stretch of land was soft and the sky clear and he just wanted to soar and dip his way around like a bird, even for just a minute. Devon dropped his cigarette and ground his boot heel over it. He climbed the cattle grate and walked in amongst some trees, running his calloused fingers along the bark. He let the sensations come into him and he tried to keep his mind blank and simple. He inhaled and exhaled, closing his eyes and trying for that other sight. He liked the calm feeling in his lungs. He could also feel the angle of his standing legs, the strength of his feet against the earth. These feelings were not close to flight but made him appreciate his human body. He kept breathing, feeling the sun on his face.

Behind Devon's closed eyes, a vision creeped in: the eyes of an old man, not unlike PJ The eyes were small and grey with little wrinkle lines all around. Those eyes looked into Devon's, real close, with kindness and pity. Devon didn't know what he was looking at. He just knew that he wanted his body to disappear, to fly and feel another way. It really felt connected to nature, and maybe his will. Heck, he didn't really know though. It wasn't like there was a handbook or anything.

The man's eyes came back soft again and Devon looked at them in his mind, quiet, amongst the trees on the side of a road. There was peace in them, and a glassiness. It made him just want to become the raven, fly and be free from thought. There was something else in that gaze, too, though. Devon whispered, "I just want to go, if I can't see Emma in this life, what's it for anyway?" The gaze kept steady but didn't offer anything but its mirror. Devon inhaled again, but felt the breath stick just below his ribcage. He felt a blooming in his upper chest of pain that fled to his head. The man's face disappeared and Emmajean, Cora, and his father and mother all came tumbling in. Their images confused him, and Devon dropped to his knees, knowing he couldn't be free with them near. He couldn't get away from the hurt he'd felt with each of them. The man in him pulled his body down closer to the earth and he sobbed, wishing to be free, wishing to soar, but knowing he was human and stuck.

Chapter 24
Rowen

Marked like a lost one, thrown into a show
Struggling with divine and you say, "no."

Rowen hunkered in his seat, legs barely tapping, hands tightly crossed. Next to him, Nick was up, moving wildly and hooting in between the chords. The boys were playing well, but Rowen wasn't paying much attention. He let himself hide in the dark below everyone's dancing knees, where he could avoid the lights streaming from the stage. Kentucky's small arena held the sound well, but there was a dark air about the place. The mix of concertgoers—Deadheads and folks in dirty jeans who liked to shoot guns didn't sit well with him. People screamed rough in between songs, and Rowen slid further in the seat. The band sang about outsiders and Bobby wailed about being different. Rowen felt it, even though he was in the place he thought he wanted to be most.

"Hey, man, what's got ya?" Rowen's friend, Nick, who'd lived in those parts for ten years, said. Rowen just shook his head, not saying anything. Nick sat down next to him, his whole body twitching, leg bouncing and sweat rolling from his temples and thick curly hair.

"They're sounding pretty good. Been way too long since I've been to a show," Nick continued, "You think they'll play 'Stella'?"

"Maybe," Rowen said. He knew Nick loved "Stella Blue". He used to tour in a big light blue van he called Stella.

"Probably some bluesy stuff first," Rowen said.

"That'd be alright." Nick stood up and started dancing to the next tune.

When the band rolled into an old Willie Dixon song, Rowen got up and bent his knees, too. He tried to let the music into him, but it didn't go very far. He decided to hit the head and made his way through the dancing row and out to the hallway. Some spinners occupied one cove, twirling near each other, dipping up and down. Two local-looking young boys with baseball caps slumped against a wall next to them. They were laughing hysterically and moving their hands like they were turning the dancers, as if they were spinning tops. Probably too high, but maybe on something good, Rowen thought. He went into the bathroom, avoiding eye contact with the non-deadheads there. Back out in the hallway, he walked around a bit, his hands sunk in his front pockets. Besides the rough folk, there seemed to be a whole bunch of clean-shirted, shifty-eyed, middle-aged men—most likely narcs. Rowen stood in line to buy a bottle of water. When he got it and turned around, he saw Picasso Joe.

"Oh, Row!" the old Deadhead said, lifting up his tinted sunglasses. The crazy guy always made Rowen smile. He leaned in, giving him a side shoulder hug.

"Just a minute, just a minute," he said and ordered a giant coke. Rowen stood by, waiting for him. Joe slurped his soda and motioned for Rowen to walk around with him.

"What do you think of this place, man?" Rowen asked.

"Groovy, groovy," he said, then pulled his glasses down glaring at Rowen, "and fucking weird!" Joe burst into laughter. Rowen laughed, too, mostly at the old man's craziness. "Come on," he said motioning for Rowen to follow him to the floor. All the roadies, hell, everyone on tour knew Picasso Joe, although some people called him PJ. He was a decent source of acid, but so hard to get a hold of, especially when Rowen wanted to sell some sheets. It was probably how he kept out of trouble. The two guys squeezed into a row of seats and Rowen let Joe's infectious vibe rub off on him. They danced easily to "Don't Ease Me In." Joe set his drink down, and while continuing to dance, handed Rowen a tiny piece of paper. Rowen saw the miniature face of a clown before discreetly putting the hit in his mouth. Yeah, he thought, a shift in mind, that's what I need.

The band's tunes slid a little deeper, and a big guy came into the row, glaring at Rowen who was standing in front of his seat. The guy just flicked his head up once. Rowen turned to Joe, "Hey, thanks man, I'll see you around," and clasped hands with him before sliding past the big guy and back out to the hallway. Already Rowen's head was tingling and the sound waves felt thicker. He tried to pay attention to the quality of the high, as he might want to swing some of those clowns later in the tour.

Chapter 25
Percy

Percy took a place at a bench and table set up with a long row of others inside the alleyway bar. The men near him weren't from America, their thick accents setting them apart. They were speaking English, but Percy could barely understand anything they said. Still, they were friendly enough, and didn't mind him. He sipped his mug of ale, trying to make it last. He didn't want to squander his wages. They were strictly for sending home.

After an hour, his mug was drained. He hadn't eaten and the alcohol had gone to his head, so when he stood up, he lost his balance and fell into the table behind him

"Watch it! You nearly spilled me ale," a broad shouldered young man shouted at him.

"Oh, oh, I'm sorry," Percy said. He was still wobbly, as two men on either side of the fellow stood up. They towered over Percy. He looked up and their faces were not kind.

"Really, really, I'm sorry he said," putting his hands up in the air. The men grumbled, grabbed his jacket front and shoved him.

"That'll show you. No one likes to be pushed,"

Percy hit the dirt ground pretty hard, side of his head first. He hated the roughness that pervaded in this place. He managed to prop himself up on his knees and scramble out of the hall, back down the dark alley and into the room he shared with six other men. He fell into his bunk, feeling awfully bad for himself. Missing Molly, missing home.

Chapter 26
Rowen

After the show, Rowen, Nick, Ollie and Changa drove to Jefferson Forrest Campground, following the line of Deadhead vehicles going the same way. Every so often a cop car, lights blaring, sped by them in the left lane. Rowen gripped the steering wheel and kept focused on the road and the cars in front of him. That hit did change his perspective a little, but it was weak and already wearing off. What remained were his own thoughts. He remembered his mom when he was younger, and they traveled to New Mexico where she grew up. He liked the dusty roads there and the dry heat. He remembered the way his mom and grandma fought about every little thing, but with a smile tucked behind their eyes. Rowen wondered about his grandmother, still out in that small cabin. He remembered that she called, and he really should call her back. She liked being alone, he thought, tucked up with her quilts and sewing. The line of cars slowed down and pulled into the park. The forest was thick with spindly trees and overgrown brush. Headlights were a stark contrast to the dark roadside. It seemed the camping spots were already taken, so cars just lined up and tuned their engines off. Ollie and Changa jumped out the side door to go scope the scene. Nick stuck around with Rowen.

"You gonna swing any beer here?" Nick asked.

"Nah, I'm tired. We only have two cases and no ice," Rowen said.

Nick nodded. Rowen climbed in the back and pulled two beers floating in the cooler's inch of cold water. He popped their tops and handed one to Nick.

"Thanks man," Nick said pulling on the Heineken whose green label was sliding off.

"Hey, Rowen, Ollie told me about your mom. I'm real sorry to hear that."

"Thanks," Rowen said, nodding and taking a long swig from his beer.

"You doing ok man?"

Rowen nodded quickly and then opened the van doors. He grabbed a jacket from the side bench and motioned for Nick to get out, too. They locked up and started walking down the park road. A crowd was forming around one campsite with some folks setting up shop to sell beer and food. No one was clear on what would be cool or not and didn't want to be the guinea pig for a bust, so they just kept things small.

"You hungry?" Nick asked.

"Yeah, think we can find anything?"

Nick walked around, looking for his local friends. He gravitated towards a VW van. A big bearded guy had set up a camping stove and placed a thick flat cast iron skillet on it.

"Sandy," Nick said, giving the burly man a hug, "What're you cooking."

"Nothing yet," he said looking around, "But I bet I could make some dough on a few sandwiches," he said. "We've got some cheese and bacon ones ready to grill up,"

"Sweet," Nick said, "hook us up man!"

"Sure thing," Sandy said, working quickly to lay buttered bread, already stacked with cheese and bacon, on the griddle. Rowen flicked his head up in greeting to the cook. They milled around close, waiting for the sandwiches. Others followed the scent towards the van, too, and a small line formed behind Nick and Rowen. Coolers were laid on the ground around them but not popped open yet.

As Rowen stood there, he looked into the forest surrounding them. The trees were close together and their darkened branches wove in and around each other. He squinted, looking at them, then noticed the branches moving and swaying. Rowen pulled his jacket on, thinking a wind had come up. He turned around to the group of people, and heard voices muffled and slurring. A guy's hand slapped his shoulder, and Rowen whipped around to see someone giving him a toothy grin.

"Line's up man," he said motioning for Rowen to move towards the cooking sandwiches. His heart lurched forward as he looked to the cooking griddle, now sizzling so loud Rowen had to put his hands to his ears. The acid had come on late, and it was way too speedy.

"Relax man," the guy said.

"What," Rowen tried to say, but his voice got stuck on his tongue. Nick came back from pissing in the woods and noticed the line, and Rowen turning around wildly. He walked up to Rowen.

"Yo, man, he's tripping something fierce," the guy behind said to Nick, flicking his head towards Rowen.

"Row, Row, it's me, Nick. Come on man, let's go."

Rowen let Nick lead him away from the line. Nick grabbed a sandwich from Sandy with his other hand.

"Dude, you ok?" Nick said, keeping his hand on Rowen's shoulder. Rowen still couldn't talk. His face was a little pale. Nick led them to a closed cooler.

"Got any water?" A guy sold Nick a bottle for a buck. He walked Rowen to a bunch of stumps and sat him down, plopping on the ground himself. He opened the bottle and handed it to Rowen who drank instinctively but dribbled a bunch of water down his chin, too.

Nick looked at him and started to laugh. "Rowen, what the heck you on bro?"

Rowen shook his head and started laughing, too. He laughed so much, he slid off the tree stump.

"Woah, woah, Row, must be turning good now," Nick said. Rowen looked over at Nick, and nodded, still laughing.

The two of them hung around that spot for a while longer then got up to explore. Rowen seemed to be fine and was able to use his mouth again. "That, shit… came on strong!" Rowen said slowly.

"Where'd you get it," Nick asked.

"Picasso Joe. Clowns."

Nick nodded, chuckling. A little bit of a Shakedown had formed along one of the campground's roads, with heads sitting on blankets and selling clothes, jewelry, and posters. Some had full set ups with tables and lamps, others carried boards. Seemed to be a free for all. Any chance to hawk wears was fully taken advantage of on tour. There were enough novice show and campground goers that a buck could still be made most places. The guys walked to a big circle opening, with a good-sized campfire going. Nick bounded forward towards a drum circle, and Rowen followed slowly. The drum patterns escalated, and they felt good to Rowen. He could feel the beats in his chest. A few uniformed park rangers stood near the fire, but they seemed to be having fun with all the Heads there, too. Rowen found a tall tree on the edge of the circle and slumped down in front of it. There he could feel the drums in his toes which stretched out in front of him. Nick joined a group of heads dancing to the drums, and Rowen watched his arms flail freely in the air. Rowen could feel the acid run up and down his legs, pulsing like a deep massage. He shook his legs out a little and watched as they swayed side to side on the dirt. The space around him was getting more and more crowded, but Rowen kept his legs stretched out straight. The dark behind the trees was complete, but tiny embers from the fire lit up the sky above the circle clearing.

Rowen's mind was fluid and he followed it to his grandmother's land, out there in the desert with that tall mountain in front of her cabin. He remembered loving that place in the daytime when he was young, but the night there was different. It was so vast and encompassing—it held lots of animal action. Rowen remembered his fear of the outhouse after dark and any place beyond five feet from the cabin's walls. He closed his eyes, thinking of night there: the scratch of a ground squirrel by the wood pile, a long moan of a coyote in the brush, a sharp call of a raven. Rowen felt himself recoil and want to go inside his grandmother's cabin. Then his mind violently skipped to the fear of his mom's pale skin, seeing her lying there, dead in her bed.

"Hey, watch it!" a girl shouted as a big man stumbled knocking her shoulder.

"I, ahh," the man mumbled falling forward.

Rowen jerked awake from the shout, back to the drums and fire heat and other voices, only to watch a man trip over his outstretched legs and land on the ground next to him with a hard thump. Rowen pulled back his legs and felt the tree bark press into his back. He looked at the man's face, half pressed to the earth, and saw his stringy hair. The man's eyes opened then closed and Rowen focused and unfocused as the skin turned black and feathered. A matte black beak where his nose was, oily feathers around a small eye socket. Rowen jumped to the side and back, scraping his arms on the tree. The man turned human again, and Rowen saw his sunken eyes, eyebrows, wide forehead. He heard a grunting sound coming from his nose and mouth. The big man came to and propped himself up on his arms, shaking his head side to side like a dog.

Rowen watched, horrified by his hallucination. Rowen's legs hurt and he found anger and he found his voice, "Hey, man, you fucked up my legs!"

The man sat back on his knees and looked at Rowen sleepily. "What, oh, sorry kid," he said running his hands through oily hair a few times.

"It fucking hurt!" Rowen shouted, startled by the volume of his own voice.

The man breathed like a rattled engine and stared into Rowen's face, squinting like he was trying to figure something out. Rowen watched the man's pupils swell and deepen into black. Rowen felt something hot and familiar.

"Cool it kid," the man said and pulled some tobacco from his pocket. Rowen felt he had and hadn't seen this guy around, like so many other Heads who came on and off tour. He was older than him by a good decade. Rowen scrambled on all fours, closer to the fire and the other people, shaken, but somehow remembering that he was on acid. Nick saw him and came around the circle.

"Rowen, Rowen, you alright man?" Nick asked. Rowen was sitting up now, shaking his head no, and trying to calm his breath.

"No. More. Clowns," he managed to say as Nick sat down next to him.

Nick chuckled, "Yeah, yeah, I always thought Picasso's blotter was no good. Come on man, let's get out of here."

Nick helped Rowen get up, and when they walked past the man, Rowen breathed. He convinced himself he was just another drunk deadhead. They got back to the van and Rowen laid on the quilt over the back bed, staring out the window for hours as the trip wore down.

Chapter 27
Devon

As Devon had watched the kid scamper towards the fire, he noticed the strands of black hair behind him. It was glassy black and appealing in the half-light from the flames. When he walked away from the campground, Devon knew he was familiar, and after a long while his mind settled back on the woman a few years older than him, who he kind of knew in New Mexico. She was broody and sullen is what he remembered, but with the same long black hair. Devon's mind was cloudy, as he sunk into the Earth, smoking. His eyes narrowed, and breath eked in, as he remembered a gravestone near his cabin. It was still there, small and rounded on top, with his sister's name and the short years of her life etched in. Growing up, he remembered seeing that long haired girl out the window, sitting next to it, and talking to herself. He'd stare out the window until his mother would scold him and make him practice school or something.

Devon came back to the present with the sound of shouting on the other side of the fire circle. He wanted to be alone. Devon trudged back to the spot where his motorcycle was parked, a few campground-rings over. A group of locals were standing around his bike, talking loudly—a flock of stupid crows, Devon thought. Glass beer bottles were strewn by their feet, near his tires.

He walked slowly, his head averting their gazes and reached his hands for his bike's handles.

"Well, looky here," one of the guys in tattered jeans and a frayed black Metallica t shirt said.

"This is my bike, 'scuse me," Devon said noticing the beer spills on his seat.

"Sc-use-me!" the guy mocked. Devon shook his head. He didn't want trouble. He just wanted to drink and sleep, carve a spot on the ground next to his bike. Devon tried again to move his bike, and one of the guys shoved him. Devon looked at the soft spot between the guy's chin and chest. He wanted to peck it with a sharp beak, send a shrill caw into the hoodlum's ear and fly away. He didn't move though, and the guy pushed him again while his friends laughed.

Devon felt defeat inside his chest. He knew the raven in him wouldn't come and he'd have to rely on his human traits. He conjured anger, anger that he didn't have his full power, anger that he had to deal with stupid humans. Devon kept his leg close to his bike, turned around and pushed his hand to that spot in the man's neck. The guy flew back, grabbing his throat.

"What the fuck man," another stupid one squawked, "He was just joking, Jesus!"

Devon shook his head and started to leave. A flashlight shone on all of them.

"Hey, what's going on here. Cool it, all a' you," a park ranger said coming towards them. The crows looked up, seemingly recognizing the ranger who shouted, "Billy, Hank, Jim, get on outta here. Stop causing trouble or I'll get your asses thrown back in jail!" The guys turned and stumbled away, helping their wounded friend.

Devon turned away from all of them, steering his bike over to another tree and avoiding eye contact with anyone. He pulled his blanket roll from the bike's back and laid it not too near a couple of other Heads sleeping on tarps and blankets on the ground. Devon pulled his flask from the bike pack and downed the inch of whiskey left in it. He dropped to the ground and lay still. Devon tried to relax on the earth, in his body, his bulbous body. He hated the shit and riff raff that hung around the Dead scene sometimes. Devon peered up at the pine trees, swaying tall above him. He surveyed the placement of branches, savored the stand out of the needles in the crescent moonlight, and rattled thick air into his lungs. He wanted to sleep high up there, with his feathers tucked in tight, his talons clamping bark. He blinked at the night, closing in on sleep when his mind flashed back to that tiny headstone near his cabin, grown-over with weeds and grasses to hide it.

Chapter 28
Percy

The other's prayerful harm when compulsion sounds alarm.
I struggle with the divine to carry or fall behind.

Percy woke before the others in the cramped room. He rolled out of the shared bed, adjusted his clothes and quietly pulled on his boots and jacket. He sneaked out amidst snores and grunts of the other working men still sleeping in the room. Outside the air was crisp, and even though black smoke trailed from the factory's chimney, the place wasn't bustling with workers yet. Percy walked down the small street to a strip of green grass that sloped up to the tracks and then a river. He heard the sound of water and let it flush out his mind like a bath. He squat down and tugged at the thin grasses.

He had gotten a job, in a sooty factory putting things together for people far away. Nothing his own children could have. The river shush softened his mind and heart. He wondered how the boys were getting on, if they were helping their aunt, if they were as sad as he was. Percy knew it had been wrong to leave, but he just couldn't stay there. He tugged grasses out and laid them in a little pile, thinking of the crops on his land far away. He had to make things right. He had to make this money and go back with it. Percy heard the breakfast bell clang-clang, and he peered down the bank to the river, where a black bird, hopped along the water's edge.

Chapter 29
Cass

"You're gonna be late," Joanne yelled from the kitchen. Cass rolled over in bed, dreading the start of a summer job. She flipped the stereo on and let the sound get her going—drum patterns and Jerry's cooing voice helped her tug on jeans and a white tee shirt. Joanne appeared in her doorway, tapping her watch.

"You start at 8:00," she said.

"I know, Mom, I'm almost ready."

"Turn that music down, get going!"

"I am! Ok, now leave me alone," Cass said closing the door in her mom's face.

She grabbed her purse and the little clear crystal, kissing it before shoving it in her pocket. Cass flew past her mom in the living room and slammed the front door before walking the two blocks of tree lined streets to the local Hen House grocery store. The wide streets and manicured lawns seemed so sterile to her. She wanted more dirt, more cars and buildings and more people—but not all the boring people in her Kansas town. She wanted to be where people were more friendly, and all working together or enjoying together. Someplace where colors and music and sweetness filled the air. She wanted to be at a Grateful Dead concert. On Tuesday, Hillary had called her from the road. She was in Kentucky and rambling on about how great the shows there were, and how Cass should come on tour.

"I mean, Chicago's so close to you. You could take a bus up there or something," Hillary said.

"I don't know, I mean, how would I get tickets? Where would I stay?"

"Don't you remember, you just put your pretty little finger up in the air and…presto," Hillary said cooingly.

Cass remembered her "miracle" ticket. It had worked.

"You can stay with me, wherever that may be," Hillary said.

Cass's mind rolled over and over after that conversation and she began keeping notes of what she'd have to do to get up to the show. She wanted a book like Hillary's, filled with stories and scraps and photos. She wanted something colorful and foreign like one of her father's postcards. The Chicago show was in two weeks. All she really wanted was to hear from Rowen.

The back room of the grocery store was piled high with cardboard boxes and plastic carts. The concrete floor was stained and littered with an occasional withered lettuce leaf or forlorn orange.

"You wear this apron the whole shift, and follow Ronda's direction," the store manager said, handing her a laundered green apron. Cass studied him, his clean button up shirt and tie, his tidy hair and sturdy shoes. She looked around at the storeroom and felt cold and empty inside. "Ok," she said, following him to the back corner where a woman was unpacking boxes and pulling produce onto a metal table. She looked up at Cass.

"Come here, dolly. You'll help me with these boxes.

Cass smiled and walked over to the table to join the woman.

"What's your name, Hon," she said.

"Cass. It's nice to meet you," Cass said taking a box from the woman's arms

"Good to meet you, too. Glad I'll have some company back here," she said. The woman must have been sixty, short with cropped red hair and a sagging bosom. Cass followed Rhonda's actions, pulling boxes open, cutting off rotten produce ends, sorting oranges and apples and prickly pineapples. They tagged and weighed and sorted and stacked for a good two hours.

"You're getting the hang of it, dolly," Rhonda said.

Cass relaxed, appreciating the rhythms of this woman. She seemed like someone Cass could trust.

"Hey, Rhonda?" Cass said as she rolled some limes out of a box and onto a table, the green of them against the silver table encouraging her. "Have you ever been to Chicago?"

"Sure Doll, many times. Why?" Ronda said raising an eyebrow at Cass.

"Just wondering," Cass said checking the limes before piling them into a basket. "It's not that far from here, right?" Cass asked.

"It's a little ways, honey, maybe about seven or eight hours," Rhonda said.

"Oh," Cass said feeling a little burn in her chest as she thought about how she could get up there. She stuck her hand in her pocket and turned the little crystal over so a different point of it pressed against her thigh.

"What's up there," Rhonda asked.

"Oh, nothing, just curious," Cass said, dropping the subject, pulling down her green smock and working with Rhonda in silence.

Cass managed to get through the shift at the store. On her walk home, she counted up in her mind the money she would get from the work. It was meaningless work, but maybe it would get her to Chicago, and to Rowen. Cass dropped her sweatshirt on the couch and went to her room, shutting the door. Her mom would be home soon, but Cass didn't want to talk to her. Cass locked her bedroom door, turned on the stereo and pulled out her notebook. She could take a bus or a plane, although the plane ticket was much more expensive. She pulled out a map of Chicago that she'd copied from the library. She found Soldier Field and circled it in pink pen. That's where she wanted to be, walking in the parking lot with all the Grateful Dead fans. Cass heard the front door open. She scrawled a few more notes then shoved the notebook and map back under her bed. Then the phone rang, interrupting Jerry's singing voice. Cass leaped up and grabbed it.

"Hello," Cass said.

"Hi Cassidy," a man's voice said, and Cass's stomach dropped, and then her heart raced. She knew who it was. A click was made on the phone, and her mom's voice blew through.

"Hello," Joanne said.

"I got it, Mom, it's for me. You can hang up, ok?" Cass said, trying to stay calm and in control.

"Uh, ok," Joanne said slowly and got off the line. Rowen had waited patiently

"Hello," Cass said again, "is that…"

"It's Rowen. How are you," he said.

"Fine thanks, and you," Cass could feel her whole body go towards his soft voice through the receiver. She closed her eyes.

Rowen became quick. "So, we're heading to Chicago next week, you coming to the show?" he asked.

"I— I'm thinking about it, yeah," she said.

"You should come. I have a ticket for you," Rowen said flatly. A smile spread up to Cass's face.

"Oh, cool, thank you," she said, trying to remember the outline of his face.

"You ever been to Chicago?" he asked. Cass sensed a tone in his voice, of annoyance or something.

"No, but I don't think it's too far."

"It's not. You could take a bus or plane if you can't get a ride. We won't be coming through Kansas."

Cass wondered who the "we" was.

"So, I can meet you in the lot. I really have to go now, but I'll try to call you again. Bye sweet Cass." He'd hung up the phone.

Cass cradled the receiver next to her neck, savoring where his voice had been. She slowly put the phone down and looked to make sure her door was locked. Cass rifled through her desk drawer, her sock drawer and the bottom of her purse looking for money. He had a ticket for her. This was gold in her mind. She remembered his hands tracing her body, and she remembered dancing freely at the concert. She would make it to Chicago, for sure. She pulled out a small flower print backpack she hadn't used in years, put the notebook and map in it and shoved it back under her bed. Her room was now a mess, and she noticed the edge of a postcard under a pile of clothes. She reached for it and turned it over, smiles of Himalayan people in their traditional dress gazed back at her. Their beauty was strong and so far removed from faces in Kansas. Cass turned it over to see her father's curly writing, minimal but there. She put the card under her bed, too. Her mother's knock on the closed door startled her.

Hettie's ancestor spirit was getting more and more comfortable arriving right after the candle was lit. But she still wasn't sure she understood why he was visiting, except to steal her cabin space, rocking chair movement or the small glasses of whiskey she offered him. Hettie also couldn't figure out if he had anything to do with the girl she'd been seeing now in her dreams. That girl was so carefree, and free flowing, popping up like one of the early summer flowers easily munched by deer. Hettie'd tried to get in touch with her grandson, wondering if the girl had something to do with him, but he was elusive, not returning her calls. Hettie's sack of bones felt like a windsock on a dull day. She didn't have anything to hide from the spirit but wondered what he was hiding from her. Did he do something to hurt someone? Why did he look so sad and beat up? Hettie did know that times were hard for folks in his day.

Hettie reached for the big candle, whose wick had burned a round hole the size of a shotgun shell right through the middle. She paused before lighting it and peered at the blue quilt. Again, she recalled that kerchief covered woman dropping it in her lap. Hettie looked at the material in between the blue points. It was a cream-colored pattern, tiny leaves and flowers inside of it. But when she squinted her eyes it looked messy like scattered dirt, pebbles and leaf scraps. That cream color was yellowed from years soaking up wood stove smoke inside her cabin. Hettie stared at the bird beak center. If she focused away from its trace, she saw the navy fabric puffed and punched through with quilt stitches. The bird's head looked cracked like this and stuck inside the star. Hettie blinked and let the water in her eyes slide down her cheeks as she lit the candle.

He was there, rocking away as soon as she turned around.

"Geez," Hettie said walking to the kitchen to get her tea cup and one for him. "Couldn't wait for me to take a breath, dang near sneeze," she said shuffling past him and sitting on the couch. He seemed different, perched up on the chair, not rocking, but bouncing his legs. Hettie could feel his racing inside her own body and took a deep breath. He shook his head, and clasped his hands together, ringing his thick knuckles and swishing the dead skin on his palms together. His clothes looked dirtier, and stained sort of a greasy black.

"It ain't so good," he said.

Hettie's mind flashed on an open-beaked, bristle-throated raven head. Hettie looked over at him, wondering what he might've seen. The vision was nothing of hers. The raven was a messenger, she knew, and a symbol of power.

"Need's medicine when he comes," he said, bolting up and leaving her place quick, the glass undisturbed.

Medicine, Hettie thought to herself. She knew about teas and twigs and spirit bits. She looked to the wall and the trace of the bird's head was solid in the folds of the quilt.

Later that night, after she'd crawled into her quiet bed, Hettie heard a creek on her porch. She perched up in bed and looked to the bureau where no candle burned. She was a little worried about the spirit, but he was dead. He could take care of himself. It was the "he" he mentioned, and the preoccupation with medicine. What did he mean by medicine anyway? There was actual medicine and there was spirit medicine, like the gauzy strings of a spider web or the pull through of a quilt thread. Hettie reached to her bedside table and a small stained bowl with sage leaves in it. She propped herself up more, before striking a match and singeing a few leaves. They flared, she shook them and dropped them back in the bowl. In the lamplight a plume of smoke rose by her bed and she breathed the strong scent, breathed it in like life and protection.

"Whoever comes here will have to contend with old me," she whispered to herself, banishing fear. She didn't hear anything for a long while and she slumped back in her bed, keeping her light on though.

Then she heard a strange sound, like a broom swishing against hard wood. *Swish-swish, swish-swish.* It stopped for a few minutes, then she heard it again. It didn't sound like the pattery feet of a mouse, or the heavier feet of an elk, or bear. It must be small, or made of dust. Hettie threw off her covers, annoyed by the illusiveness of spirits and ghosts in her life these days. She brushed more sage smoke to her and walked to the porch door. She pressed her ear to its wood and waited. She heard the swish again and then a low throaty croak. Hettie went to the window and peered out. There was no wind, no movement, nothing. "God dammit," Hettie cursed to her cabin air. She pulled her strength together and held the spirit's word in her mind before opening the door: medicine.

In half-moon light Hettie saw a black mass of feathers, laying half way under the porch bench. She nodded her head, "Aha," she said to the bird, "there ya are, I wondered about you." She said this remembering the bird who'd kept her up a few weeks back. Hettie searched the space around her porch. It was quiet with stars marking the sky. She came a little closer to the bird, noticing one wing spread like a fan. The other wing was tucked in and its body was pulsing, like a panting dog. Hettie surveyed its dull black eyes. As she approached, it tried to move, dragging its wing with a swish.

"Ok, ok, I ain't gonna hurt you, I just want to help." Hettie sat on a chair on the other side of the porch in her nightgown. "I don't know who ya are, or why you ended up on my porch, but I will help ya," she said. The sick raven tried to lift its body but wasn't able.

Hettie went to her kitchen and started making a tea on the stove. She watched the water boil, then turned off the stove and dropped in some crushed sage and eucalyptus leaves and a few budding chamomile flowers. Maybe, if she was lucky, it'd help him. As she waited for the herbs to soothe the water, Hettie looked to the living room and imagined the spirit rocking in her chair. She imagined him when he was calm and smoking a pipe. Feeling like she was doing some good, Hettie strained the tea into a bowl and dropped in a couple ice cubes. She found a dropper and headed back out to the porch. She sat down with the bowl cupped in her hands and sang, real soft, a song of healing. She imagined the prayers slipping into the tea, for this half-alive bird, knowing there was something larger at stake that she didn't really need to know. When the brew cooled, she set the bowl on the porch floor, squeezed a dropperful and slowly crouched by the bird. She could see it better from an inside light coming through the window.

"Ok, now, mister, just get this in ya," she whispered as she set the glass dropper in the slight opening of his hard beak. She gently released the medicine and watched as the bird's neck moved, swallowing. "That a boy," she said. Hettie noticed in its still outstretched wing, the missing section of feathers. It didn't look like it would keep him from flying but made him recognizable. Hettie hummed softly. She filled another dropper, and gave it to him, then sat back on her chair. Hettie felt pity for the creature. She thought of other animals who nursed their kin back to health. She thought about nursing her own daughter and her grandsons when they were little and around. This bird was clearly on his own. Hettie knew a little about how that felt, too. She looked over and saw his eye blink. The two of them out there in the New Mexico highlands in front of Crystal Mountain.

Chapter 31
Cass

Rows of yellow-green fields streamed by outside the bus window. Cass shifted in the straight seat, hugging her knees around the backpack nestled between them. An older woman was sleeping in the seat next to her, and Cass inched as close to the window as she could. Her mom's voice echoed in her head, "Don't think you are any older than you are, young lady." Her mom was far from pleased when Cass maturely informed her she was taking a bus to Chicago for the Grateful Dead show. Cass was out of school, she was almost 18, she could do what she wanted. But the way her mom's face set in a stern downturn, the way she turned and walked into her room calmly closing the door, bothered Cass. No amount of yelling would change Cass's mind, and her mom seemed to know that. Going off without her mom's support, though, was a whole new story. As the bus passed highway rest stops, and herds of cattle, Cass focused on her own details. Rowen had a ticket for her. She had $125 and a change of clothes. She had Hillary's voicemail, and a map of Chicago. Rowen said to find him in the lot of Soldier Field Stadium.

It was about 10 blocks from the bus station. She'd arrive in the early afternoon and the show started at 7pm. She could do it, Cass told herself. The woman next to her belched out a smoker's cough. The scent of old cigarette smoke fled from the woman's clothes, and Cass realized she was in the world now. She put headphones on and listened to the Grateful Dead tape for about the hundredth time. She knew all the words to those ten songs. Even if their story hadn't sunk in, the melody was something to hold on to, and the cheer of the crowd she imagined as each song ended.

She wanted to be in that crowd, watching everyone around her cheer and bow to the band.

When the bus neared the city, the highway expanded to four lanes in each direction. Cass could see the outline of buildings in the distance. She read the big green direction signs as the bus slid under them, and she could feel her heart swell. Rowen was somewhere in this city and she was going to see him again. About ten minutes on these new highways, and cars and trucks multiplied around the bus. The speed slowed down and Cass realized it was a major traffic jam. Shit. She looked at her watch. The bus was going to be late. Cass noticed other riders still snoozing. Cass took a deep breath and got out her map to study the streets she would walk to get to Soldier Field. It was near the water, so that should make it easy.

By the time the bus pulled into the station, it was an hour late. Cass held her backpack straps tightly. She knew her mom would be at work, so she found a pay phone in the station and left a message: "Mom, it's me, I'm fine. In Chicago. Bus was a little late. Talk to you later." She hung up the phone quickly. Outside, she stood up against a tall building, pulling her folded map from her pocket. She was on S. Clinton Street and she would have to get to Van Buren, one over. Business folk, bus riders, and a homeless man trudged by her. Cass looked around, trying to keep calm and tell herself she could do it. She could find Soldier Field. She noticed yellow cabs zipping by on the busy street. She could take a cab, but who knows how much it would cost, and Rowen would probably think she was stupid wasting money. In the direction of her destination, Cass spotted a tie dye shirt. The bright colors and swirly design on the young person wearing it was a good sign that brought a smile to her face. They must be going to the Grateful Dead show, too, Cass thought. So she took off in the same direction, checking her map along the way, and feeling the breeze blowing in from the lake waters. As Cass walked down Van Buren, passing Canal and Wells streets then Clark, the crowds increased and she felt like she was entering a parade. But she didn't know anyone. At every phone booth, she thought of stopping at to call Hill's voicemail, but a line of two of three people had formed. It was exciting though, going to the lot for a Grateful Dead concert, everyone there for the same thing. She had more to think about: Rowen. He was somewhere in the parking lot. He had a ticket for her and just the thought of hugging him was enough. The gray stadium towered to her left, like a Roman castle, with steps leading up to it and American flags lined up and waving. It was still some time before the place would open, but people were standing in line already. Cass looked to her right, and the sea of cars. Laughter and music blossomed in the parking lot, but Cass's heartbeat sped, as she realized she was supposed to just *find* Rowen. Cass didn't have a map to him. She breathed, and put some lip balm on, then started walking through the crowd, looking for his black van, looking for his long black hair.

"Ice cold soda, kind banana bread, cash for your extra!" she heard shouting around her as she wove through people. She wasn't making much progress down the middle of the crowd, so Cass cut over to walk between the parked cars. It was a great mix: sticker-laden VW buses, small run down cars, and sleek sedans with car alarms. She walked in between the cars, dodging side mirrors, and trying not to look inside when she noticed people inside. There were too many black cars, and each time she saw reflection on a sleek black paintjob, her stomach dropped. She was sweating, too, as it must have been over 80 degrees.

Cass stopped and looked back at the stadium. She'd walked so far she was coming to the end of the parking lot. It was one vertical row to the end. There were as many horizontal rows, too, and her mind swept back to her living room, and her mom shaking her head. "Fuck!" she said out loud, everyone was headed in the opposite direction she was walking. Everyone would be going into the show soon. What was she going to do! Cass could feel hot tears swelling in her eyes. She quickly walked to the last rows over. "Where are you?" she said to the empty cars, "How am I supposed to find you!" Cass beat her hands against her thighs and tears dropped to the pavement. She was stupid, this was stupid, what was she thinking. Cass walked past a guy tying up something on a motorcycle. He looked up and must have heard her talking to herself.

"You ok?" he said, making eye contact with her. Cass nodded, and quickly wiped her face and kept looking around, trying to conjure purpose. The man stood up. He was tall. He had long, dirty hair and a claw earring, but his eyes were kind.

"I can't find my friend," Cass told him.

"Sure, that happens," he said, "Want me to help?"

Cass looked at him again, then around her. She was in a giant parking lot, lots of people were around but she didn't know them, and this guy seemed nice enough. "Uh, thanks," she said. "He has a black van, and he has long hair."

The guy chuckled. "That narrows it. The show's that way, and if he got here early, he'd probably be by the stadium."

Cass nodded. Rowen probably did get there early. She remembered that it was ok to talk to all different kinds of people, and of different ages at a show. She remembered this from Bonner Springs. The thought was freeing.

"Do you come to shows a lot?" she asked him.

"Sure, and you?"

"Not so much," she said gripping the straps of her bag as she followed him through the rows, both of their heads turning side to side.

He stopped in an open row. "Is that it," he asked, pointing halfway down a row at a beat up van.

"No, it's bigger. Not a VW." He nodded and lit a cigarette. Cass kept walking, the stadium getting bigger. She looked back to see if the guy was till helping her. He nodded and pointed forward. "He sells things, I think," Cass said.

"Then head to that big row of people, Shakedown Street," he said smiling. Cass smiled at him, too, remembering Hillary telling her about the place hippies sold things at shows.

"Hey, what's your name?"

"Cass, Cassandra," she said.

"It's nice to meet you Cassandra. I'm Devon," and he stuck his hand out to shake hers. She placed her hand in his, and he squeezed. His handshake was warm and securing and Cass let her fear about not finding Rowen down for a second. She walked on the edge of Shakedown, carefully, still looking down the rows of cars. A couple more rows and she saw him! He was by his gleaming van, talking with a couple other guys. His leg was propped behind him as he leaned back, a bottle in his fingers, and his black hair straight and calling her. Cass lost her breath. Then she turned back to see Devon behind her. "That's him!" she said excitedly.

Devon followed her gaze and seemed to study the guys. "Ah," he said, "Good, have a good show, Cass."

Cass smiled, lifted her hand in a tiny wave and left him to weave back into the crowd. "Thanks," she said as she walked towards the reason she'd come there. Her heart beat in her head, and she smoothed her hair down.

She remembered his hands on her against the tree, and rolling in the back of that van with him. 100 yards away he saw her, coolly stood up, set his bottle down, and walked towards her.

"Cass, you made it," he said.

Cass nodded and Rowen enveloped her in a hug.

Rowen was surprised, but glad the girl showed up. He took her hand as they walked towards the stadium, losing the other guys.

When she'd first arrived, they all had snarky grins that bugged Rowen. He didn't want them to say anything. It was his ride, he was calling the shots, and whoever he wanted to bring along was how it would be.

"Your bus ride ok," he asked.

"Yeah," she said. Rowen knew she was so fresh to the scene. He tried not to get annoyed by that and focused on the weight of her hand, skin contact. They walked under massive columns and giant concrete beams. Rowen could feel her trepidation as she gripped his hand.

"It's huge," she said.

"Yeah, this is one of the bigger venues the Grateful Dead plays."

They moved through the hallway, past people Rowen knew and many others he didn't. The seats were first tier on Jerry's side—not bad mail order seats. The two of them slid down their row and settled in. Rowen slunk down and heard the metal clang of his clip key-chain hit the plastic seat.

Cass looked around the stadium wildly, like she thought the show would start any minute.

"It'll be a bit yet," Rowen said. His gaze was towards the stage, "See those guys moving around there, they still have to bring the band's guitars out, and then it'll be at least 30 minutes after that."

Cass nodded, studying the stage.

"Sometimes I like coming in here early, if I'm not selling things," Rowen said.

"Oh, are you not selling things today?"

"We'll do it after the show." Rowen looked over Cass's face, wondering if he could count on her, or if she was just another party girl not willing to pull her weight. They'd all see after the show. "Is there anything you want to hear tonight?"

Cass paused, "Um, scarlet something?"

"You mean 'Scarlet Begonias'?"

"Yeah, I guess. I think that's what it's called."

"It is," Rowen said, shifting up in his seat.

"That song's on a tape Hillary left me in Bonner Springs," she explained.

"I see," Rowen said, grinning, and reaching for her hand again, "Scarlet's possible."

"What about you, what do you want to hear?"

"Oh, 'Schoolgirl', 'Lovelight', or 'Good Loving' would be nice," Rowen said leaning in to smell Cass's hair, and watching her blush deeply. Rowen thought about his luck, and the responsibility of looking after this girl. It might be easy though, and she was damn cute.

The stadium filled out, and the sun crept lower. All the guitars were on the stage now. Rowen stood up, looking around and down at the stage. He didn't know where Nick or Ollie would be sitting, or if they even got into the show. He shared his tickets with them sometimes, but he'd only mail ordered two this tour. Cass was first in line. A few more minutes and the boys walked out on stage, welcomed by a loud roar of applause, shouting and whistling. Rowen clapped, too, and Cass followed his lead. Vince tinkled a few notes on the keyboard and Mickey and Bill patted a couple drums. Rowen leaned against Cass and whispered, "Bertha."

"Huh?" Cass said.

"They're gonna play 'Bertha'" Rowen said smiling, "That's my guess." Cass nodded. The music began like a steady train, and she started to dance. "Yep, I'm right."

"Cool," Cass said. Rowen swiveled his Van tennis shoes against the concrete, showing this girl that he did like to dance. Showing her himself in his scene. His hands slapped his thighs and his long straight hair flipped around. She was moving, too, and Rowen noticed her gaze locked on the stage. Rowen watched her hips slide side to side and her hands held out in front of her body. Her movements kept to the rhythm. Her dark gold hair shone in the stadium light. She's alright, Rowen thought, she's alright.

Chapter 33
Devon

Devon had scored a good seat on the floor, but after the first set, he didn't want to be that low and climbed many concrete steps to the top rows. There were lots of empty seats up there, and Devon liked being closer to the sky. He imagined his spot was on the top of a small mountain and with the stadium curving down into a valley. All the Deadheads were like ants moving around. Devon's mind went back to the parking lot before the show when he'd helped a girl find someone in the lot. She was naïve like a young deer or a cautious sparrow. Helping her made him feel useful. But as soon as she saw her slick, longhaired boyfriend, she was gone. Girls wove in and out of the scene all the time. She seemed a little different, though, trusting him so quickly. He sure hoped that guy took the right care of her.

Devon tapped his feet through Drums and twisted his fingers, watching the crowd through Space. Sometimes the guitar strings screeched like a bird call, and Devon wished he could caw back, for real. He would have soared right down into the stadium bowl, circling the rows. Devon closed his eyes, trying to feel extension through his shoulders, his back, his arms, but his human body was planted in a plastic seat. The music climbed with deep horn sounds and prickly high notes. The screech made him think of metal grates, sliding ones, prison gates. The softer notes flashed Emmajean's face—round flesh, thin pigtails. He would fly to see her. But that was a tortured thought, as he knew Cora would push him away. The band mercifully led into another song, and the energy of the place cooled down. It was a song he knew and loved well. Devon stood up, stretched his body and breathed in the high air. He tried to see all the way to the stage, tiny figures moving. His vision shifted to the left and right, his head bobbing. "The circle is moving and always goes around," the band played, "Wherever you go you'll always be bound." Devon shook his head at the truth and pain of the lyric. He wished for flight, as usual. The song shifted slower and Devon walked, clunking down the thick steps, one by one, in the glowing stage and stadium lights. Jerry's voice carried the sound of birds, of roads and slowing down. Devon longed for quiet space, the peace of earth and freedom.

That sick raven was on Hettie's porch for a day and a half, and then he was gone. Hettie was pleased she could nurse him back to health. She searched the porch and around the cabin to see if he'd only made it a few feet. No signs of him, though, so she got about her other business. The summer brought gnats and little ants that liked to parade along her inside window sills. It wouldn't do. She brushed them out the windows, This is my cabin. You all have the whole outdoors, now go, she told them. She just squashed the gnats with a rag and piled her counter food into the refrigerator.

Sometimes living out there in her isolated cabin, felt like the middle of the wilderness. She tired of the consistent battles with nature there, though she liked it better than battles with city sounds, and city dirt. Hettie opened the windows and doors, leaving the screens closed for protection. She flipped the ceiling fans on and ran a wet rag over surfaces. A slight breeze tinkled her wind chime on the porch, but thick heat and sunlight poured in, too. The memory of her dream returned to her, of the girl standing in the sun. She was young. Her face a little less carefree—a small line creasing her forehead. Hettie tried to remember more, but nothing came. She went back to dusting the photos on her mantle—Jessie, Rowen and his brothers, a stout photo of Wilson, and a photo of herself when she was 21. How sprightly she was, with long braids and a smile that didn't quit. Her path had been so clear then: married to a landowner, ready to produce babies, run a farm, live a good life. She'd done it, too, although Jessie was her only baby. She thought of

Jessie's path, moving to California in chase of a bad man. Having three boys, always looking for work, then being left to raise her sons alone. She did her best though, had steady work the last 20 years of her life, even if it was just in a breakfast shop.

Those boys had needed a father, but that just wasn't the way it turned out. In her mind, Tate and Lou were beyond repair—in and out of jail and scraping to get by when they were free. Rowen, though, Rowen she worried about. In the depths of him, he was a good boy. He stayed out of trouble, but his pain knotted inside him like a twisted thread. Hettie finished cleaning, and stacking some jars of garden vegetables her neighbor had delivered into the cabinets. She poured herself a glass of cold tea and lit the remaining wax of the candle. The flame was low, and she sat on the couch, staring up at the blue quilt. She was fonder of it these days and started wondering if it should ever come down from that North wall—maybe to be cleaned or something. The bird beak was somewhere inside the center star, and the other star points pierced out like the sharp angles of a wing against the sky. It was beautiful to imagine it like that, and she glanced to the window, hoping that raven was flying free somewhere.

She was just about to doze off, when the rocking chair creaked. The spirit was there, and calm this time, filling a little pipe to smoke.

"Glad to see you," Hettie said, waking up.

"Mm," he answered. It was too early for whisky, so she didn't offer him any, just hoped her cleaning made the space a little more welcoming.

"That bird get on?" he asked.

"Yep, I nursed him with some tea and song," Hettie said.

Her great-granddaddy nodded, looking at her before lighting his pipe.

"It helped," he said, "but he's still not free.

Hettie shrugged. How was she supposed to know what a raggedy raven needed to be free? She liked nature as much as the next person, but why was it her business? Her gaze drew up to the quilt. The bird stuck in there on her wall. She was the one who lived with that symbol, those star quilt points much of her life.

"Yep," he said, rocking slowly.

It bothered Hettie though, this obsession with a bird and a quilt. She wanted to help Rowen. She closed her eyes and pulled up the memory of him next to his black van, cleaning out coolers and ignoring the pain of his mother's death.

His relation, rocking in the chair next to her, nodded. He kept silent, though, and seemed to be thinking as he drew on his pipe.

"He's still young, needs something," Hettie said. "Please help him, he is your relation, too." Her great-grand daddy nodded. Hettie stood up to go to the kitchen. She watched more dust swirl in the stream of sun pouring through the kitchen window now. When she turned back toward the living room, he was gone. A trail of smoke lingered above the rocking chair.

Chapter 35
Cass

During the Drums and Space section of the show, Cass smoked a lot of pot with Rowen. He had a fat joint that he kept passing to her, in the dark of their seats. Others around them were smoking, too, so it was no big deal. She just followed Rowen's lead. He knew what was up, she convinced herself. The music slowed down as it came into her ears. She stood up with Rowen when the band played a pretty song, and Rowen said was called "Wheel" or something. She started dancing, but then found herself not moving, just staring at the stage, the pot coursing through her body more than anything. Then the song changed, and after a bunch of cheering, the big guy sang a slower tune about roads. Cass gazed at his fluffy head on the big screen and let Rowen grasp her hand. His grip was grounding and kind. She leaned into him, and they followed the other couples who swayed together around them.

"This is Jerry's new song," he'd told Cass.

The last part of the show was a frenzy. A song by Bob Dylan, Rowen had said, and then the harmonica player came back out for a tune that wound higher and higher. It was "Lovelight," and Rowen held on to her, bouncing his body against hers as they danced. Cass had regained rhythm by that time and moved along with him, realizing why this place and this band was so popular. She smiled, watching the stage lights and everybody moving. The skinnier band member in a tight blue t shirt screamed into the mic. The whole thing was so gloriously serious. The music was really tight. When the crowd roared and the band left the stage, a little movie played on the screens, first of a dancing skeleton and then stars spinning and flashing in circles. Cass tried to watch that, but it made her dizzy, so she turned to Rowen.

"Is there an encore,"

"Yeah, but we want to leave before the end," He said, studying the stage, "Let's just see what it is."

"Ok," Cass said.

A deep riff on one of the guitars started, and Rowen immediately said, "Yep, 'Gloria'."

"How do you know," Cass said, smiling at him.

"It's an easy one to tell," he said, winking at her. All the band's voices melded together singing that name. Rowen leaned down, pushed Cass's hair to one side, and kissed her neck. She was flooded with pleasure and turned into his chest. "Let's get out a here," he whispered in her ear. Cass nodded and let him take her hand to move past the others down the aisle. The rolling harmonica notes led their way. Once they got into the hallway, Rowen picked up his pace, almost dragging her hand as they walked. His legs were longer than hers, so he could gain ground easily. They wove through a growing crowd.

"Come on, we've got to make it out before the crowd," he said.

"Ok," Cass said.

Rowen let her hand drop in the darkened vast parking lot, and she hurried to follow him to the van. She wouldn't lose him in this lot, not after searching so hard when she'd arrive in Chicago, so she strained to keep her eyes on his flying black hair. Once they got to the van, he moved quickly, pulling coolers out and setting up a small table with a camping stove. Cass watched him lift the cooler top and shuffle ice and bottles around. Two coolers were packed with soft edged ice cubes and shining glass beer bottles and round tin cans of soda. Cass was impressed. She remembered how she met Rowen, hawking his soda at the campground. So this was how he made money. Seemed like a good idea. A jovial fella ran up to the van, panting and smiling.

"Hey there," he said when he saw Cass. "I'm Ollie, you must be?"

"That's Cass," Rowen said dragging a cooler in the aisle. "Here, take this one to Shakedown, man, I'll get the grill going and then we'll move the other one.

"Sure," Ollie said, "See ya later, Cass." He hoisted the cooler onto a small wooden board with wheels on it and took off for the crowded spot.

Cass just stood next to the van, hands in her pocket. She didn't know what to do.

"Wanna help?" Rowen asked, stopping for a second.

"Um, sure. What can I do?"

"Here, come in here," he climbed into the van where a large cutting board lay, stacked with slices of bread, and a huge chuck of orange cheese. "We'll make about a hundred grilled cheese sandwiches," Rowen said.

"Really?"

"Yeah, and it will happen quickly," Rowen looked out the van's windows, "and soon."

Cass sat on the bench, ready to work. The bread was buttered on one side and stacked butter sides together.

"Cut this cheese in slices, and stack them on the top of the two slices, then move to the next, until you have a whole stack ready to go," Rowen said, showing her how thin he wanted the cheese and how to place it. "Got it?"

"Sure," she said and took his place when he jumped out of the van, taking the first three sets of sandwiches. Cass gripped the plastic covered cheese block and began cutting. She could feel the weight of her wrist as it pressed down through the waxy substance that looked day-glow in the van's light. She carefully placed the bright slices on bread, moved the next buttered bread group on top and continued. She didn't know how much cheese Rowen wanted. Cass glanced out the window, and the growing crowd of concert-goers passing the van. The scent of grilling sandwiches crept into the van, making her hungry. The raw version smelled and looked pasty though. Rowen jumped in the van,

"Got more ready?"

"Yeah, but are these ok?"

Rowen lifted the pieces and began taking a few slices off each and filling an empty set. "A little lighter, so the cheese'll last," he said smiling quickly at her.

"Ok," Cass said. She handed him a stack and he jumped back out of the van to his grill spot. The hunk of cheddar was still so big, she could barely imagine all of it being used any time soon. She heard more and more voices just outside the van: "How much?" "Can you spare a sandwich, brother?" "Oh, I want one!" Cass leaned over and looked out the window at a flock of people gathered around Rowen. She looked back down at her task: more bread, more cheese, more cutting and stacking. She was getting tired of it but knew this was how Rowen's world worked. She piled another stack high, then jumped out of the van.

Rowen had a cutting board stacked with cooked sandwiches, "Here," he said, "Can you sell these?" And he handed her the steaming board.

"Um," Cass took the board, looked at the crowd.

Rowen turned back to the grill, adjusted the heat and slipped into the van, coming back with a fresh stack. Cass stood by the van still. "Go sell 'em," Rowen said, raising his voice.

His tone jolted her. He must have seen a hurt look on her face, so he came closer. "Just walk out into the crowd, hold the board up and say, 'Grilled Cheese!' loud," he said. "They're two bucks. Just take money and give them a sandwich." Rowen winked at her and went back to his own work. Cass walked down the row of cars, cautiously, keeping an eye on the sagging food. "Grilled cheese," she tried to yell, but she felt stupid. What the fuck, why did she have to do this. She watched all the people coming out of the show, happy. Maybe it was better than cutting cheese in the back of the van? "Grilled cheese," Cass said again. She passed people sitting on ratty blankets, milling around the back of cars drinking beer, people walking with floppy balloons, and lots of other people selling things. She watched them, shouting and holding up their goods. She tried to follow their lead, remembered when she stuck her finger in the air trying to find her first ticket.

A couple guys stopped her, "How much?"

"Two bucks," she said.

"I want one,"

"Me, too," the first guy's friend said.

Cass took four dollars from them and they each peeled a softened sandwich from the stack. Filled with some confidence, Cass walked on, shouting a little louder. "Grilled cheese! Two bucks!" A couple of girls stopped her. One had dreaded brown hair with beads and bits of other things in it. Her scent was really strong.

"I've got 50 cents," she said to Cass.

Cass looked at her board, the sandwiches were soggy now. "Um," she said.

"Please," the girl held two quarters out.

Her friend threw another quarter in the hand. "Here, we can share it," she said.

Cass looked at the two of them, "Ok," she said and took their money. They peeled one off, pulled it in half and walked away pleased and stuffing their mouths. Two other guys, obviously drunk, came up and bought her last three cold sandwiches. Cass turned around trying to orient herself to the parking lot. She walked cautiously, board down, searching the rows for the black van. She spotted it pretty quickly and the small crowd had moved in around Rowen's grill.

He smiled when he saw her. "Nice work, Cass!"

"Thanks," she said handing him the board. For a minute she feared he would pile it up again, but he had other ideas.

"Ok, now we'll have you sell out this cooler!"

Cass watched as he kicked a heavy cooler towards her, the sound of sloshing ice following its slide.

"As soon as Ollie gets back, you can go with him to sell these on Shakedown," Rowen announced.

Cass nodded. She wanted to be a team player and leaned down to inspect the contents of the cooler. It was mostly beer—green, brown and clear necks sticking out of watery ice. She then peered back in the van, where another two stacks of buttered bread lay on the bench. "Do you want more sandwiches?" She asked Rowen.

"Yeah! Just those on the board if you can do that,"

"Sure," Cass shouted and stepped in the van. It was hot in there and the dank, sticky scent of softening cheese and greasy butter filled the small space. Bread crumbs littered the matted down carpet and Cass eyed a thin metal knife coated with off white butter. She worked quickly, filling the stack with slices and brought them outside. "Can you watch these?" Rowen asked.

"Sure," and she took the spatula from Rowen.

"I want to put things away in there, so they'll keep."

Six sandwiches filled the grill and Cass lifted the edges, watching the bread brown. A non-hippy looking woman came up, holding the hand of a seven or eight year old girl. To Cass, the woman looked more like someone she would see in a Kansas grocery store instead of at a Grateful Dead concert.

The girl looked up at the woman and smiled. "Can we have one?' The woman seemed to inspect Cass and the grill and the van.

Cass smiled. "They'll be ready in a little bit," Cass said. She realized that she hadn't eaten one yet, and her stomach turned with hunger. "It's cheddar cheese," she said, "two bucks," Cass felt like she was getting the hang of this selling. She liked the idea of making something for someone who really wanted it. She flipped the sandwiches. Rowen came back out of the van, and Cass noticed the woman stiffen slightly and squeeze the girl's hand. Cass smiled at her again. "I think they're almost done, I flipped them," she said to Rowen. He took the spatula from her. "Do you want anything to drink?" She asked the woman.

"Do you have any soda or juice," she asked, "All we can find is beer." The girl squinted her face.

"I think there's some soda in the bottom, right side of the cooler," Rowen said, "Have a look, Cass, will ya?"

Cass knelt down, opened the cooler, and shoved her hand in the ice water. "Oh, cold," she said. She moved some bottles around and pulled up a Hanson's orange soda. "I found an orange soda, do you want that," she said looking at the woman.

"Sure," she said, taking the cold can from Cass.

Rowen finished grilling and they walked away happy. Cass watched them move down the row, wondering what the girl must think of this crazy scene.

Ollie slid up, bent over the rolling cooler. His head up searching the way through the crowd.

"All done," he said.

"Good! Thanks man. Now why don't you and Cass take this one back to Shakedown."

"Yeah," he said, "can I have one of those?" Ollie grabbed a hot grilled cheese from the end of Rowen's spatula and shifted it to his other hand before biting tenderly into it, stretching a string of cheese from his mouth.

"Me, too," Cass said. Rowen gave her one, switched off the grill and the three of them filled their mouths.

"So, 'Gloria', 'Lovelight'," Ollie said raising his eyebrows at Rowen.

"Yeah, man," Rowen said, making a silent flick with his head to let Ollie know what he was thinking and that he could stop there.

"That harmonica player was great," Cass said, glancing at Rowen and Ollie.

"Fuck yeah! James Cotton," Ollie said.

"Hey, can you wheel this cooler over, they might try to shut this shit down soon," Rowen said. "I've got to find D.B."

"Sure man," Ollie wiped his hands on his jeans, pushed his glasses up on his head and slid the cooler onto the wheels. "Come on, Cass, follow me!" Ollie took off sliding again through the crowd.

Rowen grabbed Cass's hand, pulled her in, their lips touching and slipping from butter. Cass could feel Rowen's tongue which sent a rush through her. "Thanks, Cass," he said before giving her a little push to follow Ollie.

After selling for a good twenty-five minutes, Cass and Ollie dragged the cooler back to the van. Rowen was there, packing everything up. They wouldn't have to leave the parking lot, and Cass started wondering what everyone was going to do, where she and Rowen would sleep and where she might be able to go to the bathroom. The parking lot had thinned out, but several cars, buses, and vans remained. The pavement was littered with cans, balloons and cigarette butts and pieces of food. A small crew of Deadheads trudged around with big garbage bags and orange vests, slowly picking up the debris. Rowen locked up the van, and took Cass's hand, pulling her across the big parking lot. Cass looked up at a clearing sky and the stark outline of Soldier Field Stadium, giant columns shadowed by lamplight and moon light. Grateful Dead music blared through the lot, and Cass went back to the show in her mind. The blazing speakers, the fractals and drum beats. Rowen led her to a long row of port-a-potties, and she was grateful, but the stench grabbed her and make her gag. She watched Rowen disappear into one and Cass held her breath and went into one, too, releasing her bladder and quickly retreating. When she came back out, Rowen was talking to another head. Cass walked up, took her hand, and continued talking. Other Deadheads and drunk people milled around, but there were no fires or circles.

"We can camp here," Rowen said to her as they walked back across the lot, "but we can't party too much."

"Oh," Cass said. "Where do most people sleep?"

"In their cars, or on the ground." Rowen said. Cass nodded and let him lead her back to the van. The other guys were gone. She wondered if Ollie would sleep in the van, too. Maybe Rowen told him not to. He pulled the slip chain from his pocket and opened the van door. Cass climbed in. It was dark with blankets up over the windows and the bed in the back made up with a patterned quilt. It seemed clean. Rowen lit a stick of incense and pulled a small pipe and bud from the side cabinet. He quickly filled the bowl and handed it to Cass with a lighter. She smiled, took it and pulled the smoke into her lungs. It was strong and burned.

"Careful now," Rowen said.

"Yeah," Cass blew the smoke out and handed the pipe back to Rowen. He pulled quickly and blew out, mixing the pot smoke with the incense. The small boxy van was filled with white and Cass didn't protest when Rowen cracked a front window. Cass pulled off her sweatshirt and tucked it on top of her backpack that was perched on the back bed. She realized how tired she was when the pot began coursing through her body. She let herself fall back on the bed, feeling her heart beat in her chest. She didn't want to think of anything. She couldn't believe she was in Rowen's van again, inches away from him.

"You good?" Rowen asked.

"Yeah, it's been a long day!"

Rowen turned the car stereo on and music poured towards her. Cass recognized Jerry's gravelly voice. Rowen placed the pipe and bud back in the cabinet and snuffed out the incense before climbing next to Cass on the bed. He propped himself up on his elbow and leaned close to her face. Cass studied his eyebrows and the way strands of his black hair hung over his shoulder. Her heart beat faster now, fueled by his closeness. His finger traced her nose and brushed her eyelashes. Her nerves climbed higher as he leaned over and pressed his lips against hers. Cass felt a racing in her mind, a surge down her limbs, as she gripped his lips back. Their breathing increased, and she felt Rowen's body against hers. His hands slid over her shirt and Cass felt a sharp stab of fear. Her mind shot her up, realizing she was in a van with a guy much older than her in a parking lot in Chicago. Something made her sit up. Her breathing increased, and her head expanded. She was too high.

"You ok," Rowen asked, gently putting his hand against her back. She looked at him and calmed, realizing it was ok, he was ok. This was what she wanted, she reminded herself.

"I think I'm a little high," she said.

Rowen chuckled, "Yeah, that stuff's strong, you probably don't need much." He got up and found a bottle of water in the ice box and handed it to her.

Cass focused her attention on the bottle top, twisting it and drinking deep. She was thirsty. She was hungry, too, but didn't want to eat anything. Cass set the bottle down and slowly climbed back next to him. She rested her head on one of the pillows there.

"This is our bed, ok," he said.

Cass nodded and tried to relax, even though her mind screamed at her. Was she going to have sex with this guy or what? Of course she wanted to, but.

"What are you thinking about?" Rowen asked, pushing her hair behind her ear.

"You," she said, letting out a nervous laugh.

"What about me?"

"I don't know. Anything. I don't think I know you."

"Well, you can get to know me."

Cass nodded, studying his face again, his dark eyes, the angled slope of his cheek bones.

"You know you're really beautiful," Rowen said.

Cass blushed, wondering how he could say that when it was clear in her mind that Rowen was more beautiful than she would ever be.

"You're soft," he said, slowly running his hand across her hair, her neck and her shoulder.

Cass felt her chest tighten and her nipples wake up, under her shirt.

"And sweet," Rowen continued, leaning over to kiss her again. His hair fell down around Cass's face. Cass focused on feeling Rowen, the weight of his chest, the heavy scent of his breath. She heard the music from the front. She could hear the drum pats, and keyboard notes. She could hear the voices, calming her.

Rowen lifted up, "Cassidy," he smiled at her.

She smiled at him, not feeling like herself at all. She wasn't sure she wanted to go that far with him. He clearly had other ideas. Maybe Rowen saw her face, studied fear in her eyes.

"We can just sleep," he said. "Would you like that?"

Cass didn't want to disappoint him, but she nodded and reached down to put her sweatshirt back on. He got up, got his pipe and took a few more hits. He went up to the front and turned the key, to stop the music. He leaned, looking out the window, then came back in and opened the side door.

"Hey, man, what's up?" he said to Ollie, who was hanging outside the van.

"Nothin'. Everything's cool."

"Yeah," Rowen said, defeated. "You should just sleep in here, man, it's no big deal."

Cass scrunched her legs up and moved to the back of the bed, when she realized Ollie was coming there, too.

"He's gonna sleep on the side couch, Cass," Rowen said, "You cool with that?"

Cass's face turned red, she nodded and smiled at Ollie quickly, who laid out a sleeping bag on the bench, climbed in—his head turned away from them—and lay still.

Rowen crawled on the bed next to her, sighing. He pulled a quilt over the two of them, moved his body next to Cass's and put his head on the pillow. He closed his eyes. Cass lay there, totally unsure how to be. There was no way she could sleep in there, next to a gorgeous man who, five minutes ago, was ready to make out with her. She could feel her heart still beating in her chest. She could see lights from the parking lot peeking through the window. She could hear Rowen's breathing, and Ollie's. Rowen blinked, giving her a sly smile before burying his face in her neck. She wanted to giggle, but suppressed it, and pulled the blanket over her shoulder. It was too quiet in there, but that was how it went. Space was shared. She was there. Again, she'd have to go along.

Shouting came from outside the van, and Cass woke up next to Rowen. She lifted up a bit to notice that Ollie wasn't in the van. Rowen's back was towards her. So she had slept, and nothing more happened with Rowen. She felt her stomach rumble and the summer heat creeping in the van. Rowen turned over, and with eyes still closed, wrapped his arm around her side, pulling her into him. Her nerves shot to every part of her body, racing her heartbeat up quickly. Rowen looked at her, his eyes sleepy and hair tangled.

"Morning," he said.

"Hi," Cass said, feeling embarrassed to see him in the morning.

"Let's get up," he said, releasing his grip around her, and moving off the bed.

They spent most of the day walking around the parking lot that took a few hours past noon to fill up again. Cass changed to a tank top and let the sun warm and start to tan her skin. People in the lot were so carefree, skipping, dancing, blowing bubbles, partying. She kept her eyes out for Hillary. In the late afternoon, Shakedown Street was grooving, and Heads lined this side of it, selling t shirts, jewelry, food and beer. Rowen had pulled five cases of beer from the back of the van, and Ollie showed up, getting a ride in a little car, carting four large bags of ice. Rowen and Ollie worked quickly icing up the beers and getting ready to sell them.

"Ok Cass, you ready to work Shakedown?" Rowen asked.

"Um, yeah, I guess so." As the guys hoisted a cooler on the wooden piece with wheels, Cass took a bottle opener from Rowen and shoved it in the back pocket of her jeans. This wasn't what she really had in mind, coming to meet Rowen at the Dead show. But the more she watched the people around her, the more she began to understand that this is just the way to make it work: taking dollar bills, selling beer, grilled cheese, and soda. It wasn't hard work, but she didn't like that Rowen just expected her to do it. He had given her a ticket to the show, she reminded herself. The alternate thought of sitting at the kitchen table with her mom seemed so far away. Her mom must be furious with her by now, and Cass thought she should probably call her—a dreaded call.

"You got this, Cass?" Ollie asked her as he slid the cooler off the wheeler.

"I think so," she said.

"Just watch what's going on around you. If it looks like others are closing their coolers, or covering stuff with a blanket, just close the cooler and sit down on it, looking the other way," Ollie said, "But most of all, have fun!" He pushed his glasses up and smiled, before walking away. Ollie was an ok guy; he was really laid back.

Cass stared at her open cooler, bottle tops sticking out the thick layer of ice.

"What have you got?" an older man in a clean tie-dye t-shirt asked her.

"Um, beer: Heineken, Bass, and some Sammy Smiths."

"How much," the guy asked, pulling out a wad of cash.

"Heineken and Bass, two bucks, but the Sammy's are four.

"I'll take two Bass."

Cass pulled out two and reached for the bottle opener. "Want me to open them," she said, smiling at the guy.

"Sure, babe," he said making Cass blush a tiny bit.

She took his money and stuffed it in her front pocket. As he walked away, Cass wondered what she looked like, standing in a parking lot, selling beer. She pushed her hair, that felt greasy, behind her ear, and adjusted the straps of her bra under her tank top. The top was a little tight but felt good in the hot parking lot. Three other guys bought beer from her, and the bills produced a nice little bulge in her front pocket.

"Hi sunshine!" a guy said reaching over the cooler and giving Cass a big hug. His little blond dreads hit her face. When he pulled back, Cass smiled.

"Remember me from Bonner Springs?" He asked.

"Yeah," she said, "Forrest?"

"Yes!" Forrest reached over and gave her another hug, his thick body odor almost made Cass sneeze, but it was really nice to know someone in the lot.

"So what are you selling," Forrest asked.

"Oh, beer, for my… friend. Want one?"

"Sure, thanks, Cass." Cass pulled out a green Heineken, opened the top and gave it to him. She didn't want to ask for any money, but they weren't hers. Would Rowen get mad? Cass decided it was ok.

"You going in the show tonight," Forrest asked her.

"Yeah, are you?"

"Maybe, I have to find a miracle. You seem like good luck!" Forrest's eyes sparkled.

"Well, I hope you find one," Cass said.

"We should dance again."

"Uh, sure," she said returning his cute smile. Forrest moved on through Shakedown, and Cass continued selling beer, fueled by the interaction. "Beer, two bucks," she shouted, "Sammy Smiths!" It had been about an hour, and she felt in the swing of things—just another vendor selling in the parking lot of a Grateful Dead concert. The cooler had more ice than beer in it, and Cass wondered what time it was, when Ollie or Rowen would be back, what they were doing while she gathered dollar bills. Cass looked at all the people walking around with their fingers high in the air looking for a ticket to the show.

"Do you have any more Sammy's," an older guy said.

"Yeah, I think so," she said, bending own to search in the ice. He bent down, too, and Cass looked in his face. "Oh, hi, didn't you…"

"Yeah, looks like you found your friend and your work."

"Yes. Hey, thanks again for that." Cass looked at the lines around the eyes of the man who had helped her find Rowen the day before. He gave her four dollars and took the open beer.

"Cass, right?"

"Yes, I can't remember your name though.

"It's Devon."

Cass stood up. The crowd was getting thicker. Devon came closer to her. Cass wondered about him. She wondered how strange it was that she ran into him again. The parking lot seemed so big. More people wanted beer, so Cass turned back to selling. "I gotta sell this," she said.

"Yeah, enjoy the show," Devon said.

She watched him weave through the crowd, his hunched shoulders hugging a denim jacket. He turned back and caught her eyes for a second. Then she was really busy, popping bottle tops, taking bills and emptying the cooler. Ok, she'd done her work. Where was Rowen!

"Cass, you almost out?" It was Ollie, and he hoisted the cooler on wheels. She followed him back to the van.

The outhouse at the bottom of her hill was wood, with cracks on all sides. A line of ants had taken up residence on one side of the door, and a few summer flies threatened to make the place uncomfortable. Hettie threw lime in the pot and let the heavy door slam behind her. Up the path, back to the cabin, she could feel her weight as she stepped up the rocks. She remembered having to crawl her way back to the cabin in the dark not too long ago. Her steps were not good, and she could feel the frailty of her ankle. It felt like she had a new kind of ankle or foot, everything stacked inside her skin a slightly different way. She wanted to brush it off, and just not walk down the hill much. When she had to go though, she had to go, even if it was every few days, which she seemed to have trained her body to tolerate. Before going inside, she looked out to the field. Tall yellowing grass brushed across, and in the strong sunlight, she thought it looked like a girl's waving hair. So different from her Jessie's black hair though, softer and a little more innocent. Inside, Hettie settled on the couch with an old shoebox filled with photos. She couldn't remember the color of Violet's hair. Violet and her girl were inseparable when they were young, bouncing all over the ranch and trails like they were invincible. She looked at pictures of Wilson on horseback near cattle, of Jessie grasping the neck of a dog, of herself holding up a prize quilt at the fair.

Jessie was only five or six years old when it happened. Hettie did come up with a photo of the two girls, arm in arm, making silly faces at the camera. Violet's hair was dusty blond, not quite like summer. She'd had a seriousness to her that Hettie always thought got into her own little girl too much. "Well, you're both in heaven together now," Hettie said to the photo. She wondered if the girl in her dream was Violet's spirit, but why would she come back instead of Jessie. Part of her knew that her daughter's ghost wouldn't come back to this land. It took everything she had to visit during her adult life, so much pain here for her. Hettie found a photo of The Maxwell's: Peggy and John and Devon, all standing with space in between them like they were strangers. Hettie thought about how many more years her own daughter had in this world. Yes, Jessie was gone, and the pain of that thought burned inside her every day, but she hadn't been young. She'd lived and had her offspring. Her life had something to show for it. Hettie found photos of the boys, all with thumbs hooked in their jeans pockets, looking like little cowboys at the ranch. Hettie remembered how rough those boys would play in the woods, while Jessie sat inside the cabin smoking cigarettes and frying her nerves to anger, worrying about them. Really she was just reliving the grief of losing her best friend to those woods.

Lou and Tate were used to the city and hopped in the car as soon as it was time to drive back to California. Rowen lingered, wanting to know everything he could about the animal tracks around the cabin, about how his granddaddy got the cattle to move, and anything physical having to do with real life—building a fire, setting a trap, catching bugs. Hettie should have insisted he stay in Cueva with her and Wilson. But, time passed on, the boys got older, and into things they couldn't let go of. Trouble really, and a lifestyle a single mother couldn't control. Hettie looked at the bird quilt, the blues and whites and black lines. She bet if Rowen was here, he'd have a whole explanation for the bird. He was imaginative like that. Hettie thought about the spirit. Rowen had some similarities to him— both quiet and knowing and headstrong. The times she could look at his weathered face, she could see their eyes were alike, too. Why wouldn't he want to help Rowen, Hettie wondered. He was more concerned with sick ravens and some pain from his own past. The fact remained that Hettie and Rowen were in the land of the living—where any real change or healing could actually take place.

Chapter 37
Cass

Two people stood in front of her to use the pay phones by the stadium entrance. *I'm just going to tell her the truth, that everything's fine, that I'm having fun, that I'm working here, too,* Cass thought. She knew her mom was pissed beyond anything. Cass walked out on her job at the grocery store, took a taxi to a bus downtown, made her way to Chicago alone. But in her mind, she wasn't alone. She had Rowen. He knew what was up. He gave her work, and tickets to the shows. Her memory of Rowen's hands on her shot energy throughout her limbs. She wasn't about to tell her mom about him. It was safer to say she was with Hillary. Even though she didn't like her, her mom had at least met Hillary. Cass decided to call Hillary's voicemail first. When she stepped up to the pay phone she dialed and turned towards the beautiful lot, excited to report where she was.

"This is Hillary, you know what to do!" the message played.

"Hi Hillary, it's Cass, you know, from Kansas City. Guess where I am! Chicago, in the parking lot. I went to two shows already and there's one more tonight. Are you here? Look for me!" Cass said in a cheery voice that didn't really sound like her own. She dropped more change in the pay phone and listened to the sound of it thud.

The phone rang, once, twice. "Hello," her mom answered.

"Hi, Mom, it's me."

"Cass! Where the hell are you?" Joanne screamed.

"In Chicago. I left you a message the other day." The other people waiting in line felt too close. She didn't want them to hear her mom's shriek. Cass turned towards the phone and tried to chuckle a little like there was a funny conversation she was having with someone, not her mom.

Her mom's voice broke and whined, "Cass! I'm worried about you! Jack and I were thinking of driving up there!"

"What?" Cass felt her muscles tense. "No! Everything's fine. Hillary has a nice hotel room near the concert. We are having fun and she has a boyfriend who walked us back to the hotel after the show. There's even an extra room for me." Cass tried to say things her mom would want to hear. Telling her she slept in the back of a van in a parking lot with two guys would not go over well. Telling her she sold coolers full of beer to strangers would also not be good. Cass mustered calm.

"Everything's ok. It's the summer. I'm just having a little fun. I'll be back tomorrow, I promise."

"Cass, everything is not ok," her mom countered with her own calm, "It's not usual for a girl your age to go traipsing off to a big city alone!"

"I'm not alone," Cass said, avoiding saying 'mom'. "There are tons of people here for the concert. They're all really nice. Dad would love this place."

Her mom got silent on the other end. "Your father has nothing to do with this. He's not even on this continent." Cass turned to look around the parking lot. She saw a news van, and giant camera on a man's shoulder pointed at the lot. How does she know, Cass thought. Her father could be anywhere.

"You've got to give me something, Cass. I have to know you're safe," her mom pleaded, "or Jack and I will be up there, contacting the Chicago Police Department."

"Mom!" Cass said a little too loud, noticing the person behind her raise their eyebrows. "I told you, I'll be home tomorrow! Don't be so crazy."

"Crazy? Crazy? Uh, I think we know that's not me, little missy," Joanne choked.

Cass wanted to laugh. It was odd to hear her mom so out of sorts. Their relationship was usually more like that of best friends. To hear her mom reprimand her, it didn't feel real.

"Ok, what do you want to know? The concert will be starting soon, and there are other people waiting for the phone."

"What's the name of the hotel?"

"Um," shit, Cass hadn't thought that far. "I think it's the Chicago Regency." she lied.

"Where is it?"

"Downtown."

"When does your bus get to KC?"

"In the afternoon, but it might be late," Cass added, knowing that could buy her some leeway. "How about I call you at the station before I get on the bus. Would you like that," Cass said, trying not to let her voice get sarcastic.

"Ok, but if I don't hear from you by noon tomorrow, I swear, Jack is going to call the Chicago PD, and then you'll have the whole city searching for you!"

This did scare Cass. Not because she was afraid of her mom's stupid cop boyfriend, but because she didn't want any cops in Chicago to know what she was really doing: selling beer, smoking pot, sleeping with an older guy, though she was old enough to do that. Cass tried to sound sweet and get off the phone.

"Ok, thanks for your care, Mom. I know you love me. I love you, too. I really gotta go. Talk to you tomorrow before noon." Cass hung up the phone before her mom could reply. She turned to the next person in line. "Sorry. It's all yours."

Chapter 38
Devon

Can something keep a wily one from harm, if he gets caught up in a storm.
Can he shoot his arrow cross the land, and wind up back where he stands?

The sun had been hot all day, and as it wore down and the show crowd increased, Devon could feel others coming too close to him. He stepped one row away from Shakedown and caught a shimmer of light. But then his senses dulled and a feverish thread of heat rose from inside him: up the black pavement through his motorcycle boots. Devon shook his head, took a deep breath. His heart was racing. He tried to reach in his pocket for tobacco, but his hand was shaking. He looked to the pavement, heard voices around him, sharp as bells. He felt his back muscles, and the beat of his heart against them. This was familiar. Devon's mind lifted, his eyes focused and refocused. He looked across the lot to glimpse something, anything. This was the sharpened sense he wanted to track and to help him lift above everything.

Devon took a step, and another step, feeling light in his body, moving through cars towards the stadium. If he had wings he'd make it across the lot in quick heartbeats. Yet as he thought this, his lumbering body came back to him, slowing him down. When he came to the end of the row, he shifted his head to the right, searching the vans and cars. His sharp sense caught people squatting in front of jewelry blankets. Others tripping over beer bottles. He watched a girl with long dreads bounce a toddler on her lap. He saw the edges of faces, curled into smiles.

Devon stopped, watching, letting people slide in front and behind him, moving towards Soldier Field stadium. He wanted to get closer, fly to the top of the concrete structure. His gaze was fixed on how people moved towards and away from Shakedown. One person caught his stance, squinting and seeming to recognize him for a second. But then he pushed his hair back, furrowed his brow. Devon felt exposed, unsure of his actions as a man, unaligned from his feeling as another.

Devon moved to the edge of the parking lot, the farthest point from the concrete columns of the stadium. He watched the ant bodies swarm to the entrance, pulled by the promise of song. His adult mind returned. He pushed the tracking of that elusive part of himself aside. He found his bike and unlocked the side compartment, pulling out a thin glass bottle of whisky. He sat against his bike, feeling the comfort of its red metal. The gas tank rounding underneath him. The motorcycle handles solid, like present friends. Devon unscrewed the cap slowly, feeling human and dull again. He swigged the amber liquid, letting the fire coat his throat—a feeling he knew well, and could trust. He would numb himself, willingly, again. Go into the show and listen like everybody else. He could do that, he told himself. No one would notice him, he could be anonymous, free like that.

Chapter 39
Rowen

"Deer Creek is up next," Rowen informed her. "It's only three hours away. We're thinking of leaving after the show." Rowen looked at her face to gauge whether she was really game for tour or not. He knew it was only a matter of time, or tour dates, before he could really sleep with her or she'd be gone. He liked having a chick around, and she was pulling her weight—selling two full coolers and helping with the grilled cheese. Her presence seemed to soften the tension between him and the other guys, too. She distracted from the truth people knew about him. He hated that everyone treated him like wet toast, as if he couldn't handle that his mom died and keep his shit together on tour.

"Right after the show?" she asked.

"Maybe after the lot clears a bit. We'll sleep on the way. That way we'll get a good spot in Indiana. The shows there are tricky, but if we can make a go, we'll pull in more dough," Rowen said watching her face contort a little. Rowen walked away to clean up the van, leaving her to decide some things on her own. He didn't want to be entirely responsible for her, but he knew he was being a bit of a dick, too. He thought of Penny—his girlfriend for a year and a half on tour. She was so independent and half the time drove her own car to the shows. He both liked and didn't like it. She took care of herself, and he never had to worry about her knowing what and what not to do on tour. On the other hand, she'd disappear for days and Rowen had to just hope he'd run into her in the show. Turned out, she'd disappear with some other guy too often and that was what ended it for him. Rowen peeked out of the van. Cass was just standing there.

"Hey, come here," Rowen said to her. She walked over to the side doors, and Rowen sat down, pulling her hips in to him. Her body was stiff. "You know," he said, carefully pushing her hair behind her back, "Deer Creek's a great place for shows, and it's not far from here. It's two days, and after you can get a bus back to Kansas, no problem." Rowen brushed her lips with his and felt her relax. He hugged her.

"Well," she said, "I'm supposed to go back to Kansas tomorrow."

"It's summer!" he winked at her.

"You're right."

"How about it. It'll be fun."

"Ok," she said. Rowen liked how easy it was to convince her. He stood up and took her hand, pulling her into the van. They still had a little time before the show. He closed up the side doors and locked the van. "Come here," Rowen laid down on the back bed with her and started kissing her deeply, like he wanted to. He could feel his desire climbing. She let him caress her breasts and crawl on top of her. They could hear people moving right outside the van, but he didn't care, the windows were all covered. After a few minutes, she broke their kiss, breathing heavily underneath him. She stared at him and had so much softness in her gaze. She wasn't like Penny, who would have teased and played with him, and then let him have his way. "You are so pretty

Cass," he said. Her skin blushed. He eased his weight off of her. "You ready for the show?" She nodded. He knew his desire would have to wane, again. He leaned in for more kisses though, and she grabbed his lips back, with hers. His feeling moved up from his sex to his chest and got stuck there. He pulled away and looked at her, before bending over and coughing.

"You ok?" she said placing her hand on his back. Rowen coughed again, a smoker's cough like he remembered his mom's. He nodded and got up from the bed and opened the ice box for a bottle of water.

"We should go in," he said,

"Ok," Cass said, wrapping a sweatshirt around her waist.

They walked with a crowd to the entrance, holding hands. She frequently bumped into him as others crowded close. Rowen focused on getting into the show. He stopped thinking about anything, just wanted to get in and get high, not feel anything close to his heart. He dropped Cass's hand for a minute and hit his chest so he wouldn't cough again.

When the looming columns towered above them, Rowen pulled out their tickets. They were second tier—not bad. Inside he took her hand again and they walked halfway around the stadium. "What do you want to hear tonight," she asked him playfully. "Oh, I don't know, 'Playing,' 'Scarlet/Fire,' 'Throwing Stones,'" he said.

Cass nodded, like she knew the names of those songs. They passed two guys with long dreads.

"Hey, man," one said to Rowen.

"Hey," Rowen returned and climbed the stairs, aware that he was holding Cass's hand. His mind jumped to wonder what they would think of him with the young clean chick. Rowen glanced back and the other guy nodded, not giving him any indication that he cared. It just wasn't his style, Rowen knew, to go for someone so young, so inexperienced on tour. It was a less-seasoned Deadhead's tactic. Really, Rowen didn't want to give a shit. He just wanted to feel alright and enjoy the tour, make some cash, and keep going. Getting laid wouldn't be bad either, just as long as it didn't require him to feel too much.

Chapter 40
Hettie

Hettie pulled her knees up onto the couch. The sun went down outside, and stillness filled her cabin. It wasn't cold, but she pulled the green afghan over her legs that felt brittle. She could feel her creaky hips in the sunken couch, she could feel the breath inside her lungs. She was alone, like she wanted to be most of the time. It had its silences, though, that sometimes felt so deafening. It was one of those days she couldn't get herself to do much, couldn't trick her mind into thinking that little tasks couldn't wait. The quilts hanging on the walls around her cabin seemed lifeless. She thought about how she'd surrounded herself with dead: dead ancestors, dead memories, her dead daughter. She might as well be dead herself.

Part of her knew such thoughts were useless, but why wasn't her life filled with screaming great-grandchildren or ranch hands to feed, or books to keep. Those thoughts exhausted her, but she knew she'd keep up if life presented her with more to do. Wilson hadn't gotten that far in their plan—imagining his heart would hold out way longer than it had. Hettie guessed she was lucky to keep the cabin, and bit of land. That had come from letting go of all the work, though, and the livestock. If Jessie was alive, maybe it would be no different. She would never have returned. Hettie knew that living in LA was a bigger death sentence to her own senses. She liked the quiet, and the rhythms of nature. Things moved slowly, though; sometimes so slowly, she only had her stupid breath to listen to. She hugged her knees tighter, felt the welling of pain bubble up like a stream. She gasped, letting it break loose, letting the sound of a sob spill tears over her weathered face. She let the feelings come, not knowing why or how deep they ran. She wasn't afraid. She knew it was just like rain, having its own plan to drench earth, and make things grow later. Her mind stopped on her daughter, beautiful Jessie, hardworking Jessie, in-pain Jessie. Hettie was proud her daughter had been so strong. Not everyone would have gotten so well through the death of a best friend, a failed marriage, unruly children in and out of jail, slinging never-ending plates of eggs and bacon. If only people stayed in one place and were forced to keep a family together. It wasn't like that anymore. Heck, she did it, too, walking out of her mother's Oklahoma home to move with a ranch hand to New Mexico. Hettie wondered what life had been like for her great-granddaddy. She imagined, in his day, families lived close, all under one roof. Hettie knew their history, and some of the movement from the East towards the middle of the country. Hettie thought about all she missed of her own daughter's life living near a thousand miles away. Tears continued to stream from Hettie's eyes. She let her head drop to her knees, let the blanket take the moisture. Rowen came to mind, settled like a cat near her feet. She missed him. He was still living. He had the long hair of his mother, her proud cheekbones, her strength and sensitivity. Hettie wanted to cuddle him, like when he was a boy, let him cry in her arms about his lost mother. Try and take the pain away as she'd done many nights with Jessie after Violet's death. Hettie looked to the bird quilt, squinting her eyes and wishing a raven would help bring him near, wishing his ancestor would look out for him in between the ethers where she couldn't fly.

Chapter 41
Cass

Cass sat in the front seat with the big atlas open across her lap. Her head was still buzzing from the show. Rowen was stationed behind the van, selling the last of the beer in the cooler. She could hear him flipping the bottle tops open, she could hear the ice swish in the cooler. Her head was buzzing. She looked down, tried to focus on the map. Missouri, Illinois, Indiana. She put her finger to the page and drew a line from Kansas City to Chicago. Then she drew a line from Kansas City to Indianapolis. The distance seemed the same. So, she thought, it shouldn't matter whether she came back home from here or there. She didn't want to think about telling her mom. She knew she'd fly off the handle. Once they got out of Chicago, there'd be no tracking them. Jack wouldn't waste his time on her. She pictured him, sitting in his cop car in the parking lot of her apartment building. Before, his presence seemed good, securing. But now, she didn't want him to track her. She wanted to be free, even though she knew the things she was doing were not exactly legal. Cass pulled down the visor mirror and looked at herself. Her pupils were huge. She smiled at herself, conjured confidence, shut the atlas. She'd call her mom in the morning. Cass came out to the parking lot, where the guys were shooting the shit.

"What'd you think of the show tonight Cass," Ollie said.

"Oh, very cool! I liked 'Shakedown' and 'One More Saturday Night'." Nick nodded, pulling a drag from his cigarette, and glancing at Rowen.

"She'll be a regular old Deadhead before you know it man," Nick said.

Cass blushed. Rowen lightly punched Nick's shoulder.

Ollie looked at Cass. "Hey, wanna go find some snacks for the road," he asked her.

"Sure," Cass said. Rowen flicked his head up at Cass and she walked away with Ollie. Ollie was kind to her and patient, she thought, as she followed him to Shakedown.

"Sometimes we can find good deals at the end of the show," he said, "What do you feel like Cass?"

"Oh, I don't know." Cass felt the inside of her mouth. It was dry and sticky. She put her hand on her stomach, wondering if she was hungry, or would be. They'd be driving soon, for three hours. She hadn't travelled with any of them, but she assumed everything would be fine.

"Maybe we could find some banana bread, or chips, or sandwiches."

"Sure. I'm thirsty, too. Maybe some juice?"

"Yeah, good call." Ollie wove through the crowd, searching.

Cass stayed right behind him. It seemed really funny to her, zig zagging back and forth across the aisle, as he peered at people's blankets and inside baskets and in coolers. Cass started laughing, and Ollie turned around. He smiled at her.

Ollie pushed his glasses up on his face, he reached out and grabbed Cass's hand. she let him tug her. "Come on silly, we've got to hurry. Rowen will want to load up soon."

Cass nodded seriously but then spaced out again, letting herself be led by Ollie. They found a cooler full of juice and he bought two apple juices and an orange juice.

"Here, hold these," he said.

Cass took the bottles and cradled them to her chest. As a girl walked by with a big woven basket, Cass stopped her, "Hey, what do you have in there?"

"Goodies, sister!" she said, "brownies, banana bread, chocolate chip cookies."

Cass now felt her empty stomach. "Ollie, how about this?"

Ollie looked at the girl, assessing her for cleanliness and reaching into her basket to touch one of the individually wrapped treats. "Looks good. They regular?"

"Yeah, man. Just for munchies."

"How much?"

"Two each, three for five."

"Cool we'll take six for ten."

Cass smiled as the girl unloaded the baked goods into Ollie's arms. The two of them turned around to head back to the van.

"Keep your eyes open for sandwiches," Ollie said. They wove through the dwindling crowd. Ollie veered to one side and a blanket with saran wrapped packages laid out. There was a dog stomping on the other end of the blanket, his leash wrapped around a girl's waist. Ollie glanced at Cass, and shook his head, before moving on. Other people were packing up their vehicles and starting engines. "We better get back, time to go," he said, lumbering through the aisles with his hands full. Cass loved it that they could just walk in the parking lot and find food for the road. When they got to the van, everything was packed up and it was started. They opened the side doors and hopped in to put the food on the bench next to Nick.

"Jackpot!"

"Come on man, where you guys been?" Rowen said from the driver's seat.

Ollie didn't say anything but hopped back out and searched around the tires to make sure there wasn't any glass, then came back in quickly.

"Cass in front," Rowen shouted. Cass grabbed a juice and a cookie from the bench and crawled up to the front seat. She looked at Rowen. His face was stern. She settled in to the passenger seat and snapped her buckle. Rowen threw the atlas back and it landed on the floor. Ollie picked it up and turned to the right page.

"90 South, to 94, then we pick up 65," he announced, before tucking the atlas behind the seat and settling in with his own snacks. Rowen popped a tape in and the car became quiet as they pulled out of the parking lot, and head down Lake Shore Drive to the highway.

Cass took small bites of her cookie, glancing at Rowen. He was paying attention to the road. His long hair was pulled back in a ponytail at his neck. Cass looked at his jawline, sharp and angled. She saw his cheeks, rough with some stubble. He didn't look as attractive with his hair pulled back, but the seriousness she could see in him did impress her. She needed to feel confident in him, in what she was doing. He turned the music up and tapped his hands on the steering wheel. Cass looked out to the traffic just outside the stadium, small and big cars, many with stickers— of dancing bears and skeleton heads and peace signs. She was traveling with all the others. From one show to the next. Cass liked the feeling, the idea of the road. Before getting on the highway, they passed two cop cars with circling red lights going. They were in front and back of a big yellow school bus, loaded with people. Several deadheads were on the street next to the bus talking to police officers who stood with hands on hips.

"Bummer," Nick said from the back. Rowen kept his eyes straight, focused on getting the van gently onto the highway. Cass sat up straighter. She sipped her apple juice, thought about Jack. She would be so embarrassed if he saw her in the van with Rowen and the other guys. His world seemed so far away from the world of the Deadheads. Those black uniformed cops by the side of the road seemed so different from the folk in colorful, flowing hippy dresses and corduroy.

The van streamed along the highway, the Dead's music flowed from the stereo, the guys in back stayed quiet. Cass liked that everyone was calm. She would have liked to be talking to Ollie in the back. Rowen's mood confused her a little. Cass focused on the yellow lines of the road. They moved out of Chicago and onto 94 South. A quieter song came on, and Cass could feel her eyelids getting heavy. They drove for a solid hour. Cass thought she had dozed a few times but perked up when they slid into the parking lot of a truck stop. Big yellow and red signs lit up the building and gas pumps. They pulled up to pump three and Rowen jumped out. Ollie was out right after him. Rowen handed him forty bucks and cleaned off the windshield, while he waited. Ollie came back out, and Rowen filled the tank. Cass came around the side of the van.

"Hey, girl," Rowen said.

"Hi. I'm going to have to pee."

"Sure, I'm gonna pull over there and park. We'll go in and get some food. You hungry?"

"Kind a," Cass said. She realized that she hadn't had any hot food, except for grilled cheese, in the past two days. She pulled on her dirty sweatshirt, retied her tennis shoes and went into the truck stop with the guys.

"Gary, Indiana, Gary Indiana, Gary Indiana," Changa mumbled as they walked. Cass looked at him and smiled. As they walked back to the restaurant, Cass felt like everyone in the place was staring at them: big burly truckers, a red-haired waitress, and some guys wearing black leather jackets. It was about 1:00am. They moved to a round booth near the window, Cass next to Rowen, then Nick and Ollie and Changa on one end. A waitress came and dropped off thick plastic menus.

"Howdy, what can I get y'all to drink?"

Ollie glanced at Rowen, "I'll have an iced tea."

"Just water," Rowen said.

"A cup of coffee please," Nick said, smiling at the woman.

"Water, too, please," Cass said.

"Me, too," Changa said, "Water."

Cass looked at the menu that was a little blurry. The bright lettering sort of hurt her head. She had no idea what to order. Rowen leaned over. "Eggs are good," he said. Cass nodded. When the woman came back, she ordered two scrambled eggs and toast. Rowen ordered an omelet, Ollie one, too, Nick a cheeseburger, and Changa nothing. Cass ate everything on her plate, surprised at how hungry she was. Ollie left a quarter of his omelet and Nick put a half-eaten burger onto Ollie's plate before they slid it over to Changa who'd been sipping his water quietly and sorting some ticket stubs on the table in front of him. Cass watched Changa perk up, nod at the guys and begin eating their leftovers.

"How long till Indianapolis?" Rowen asked Ollie who was slurping down the rest of his tall iced tea.

"Maybe bout two and a half hours. We cut over before Indianapolis."

"You good to drive?" Ollie nodded vigorously. "Good." Rowen leaned over and whispered in Cass's ear, "We can get some sleep."

Cass could feel her bladder screaming at her now. They all slid out of the booth, as Changa stuffed the last bite of cheeseburger in his mouth. "I want to use the bathroom," Cass said.

"Sure," Rowen said, "It's over there. See you back outside." Cass nodded and walked away, as Rowen went to the front to pay and the other guys dispersed in the place. Cass passed some pay phones and thought about calling her mom. If she knew she'd traveled with strangers, she'd hate it. She didn't want Rowen to overhear her, and besides it was in the middle of the night. In the bathroom, Cass looked at herself in the mirror. Her hair was greasy, her eyes bloodshot. She looked like shit. She tried to untangle her hair, pat some water on her face, wipe eyeliner from under her eyes. She wished she could take a shower, look pretty for Rowen. She remembered him with his greasy hair pulled back. He was dirty, too. Maybe it was ok. She smiled at herself and decided it was just part of the scene. As she walked towards the door, a middle-aged man passed in front of her. He had long stringy hair, too, and a jeans jacket. Cass watched him go towards the restaurant. The roundedness of the man's shoulders reminded her of that guy she'd run into in the lot twice. What was his name? He had been nice, but something about him also seemed sad.

Back in the van, the guys were joking and talking. Rowen was in back, lounging on the bed. Cass climbed in, and Rowen moved over. She crawled to the back with him. Ollie was in the driver's seat. Nick was sitting on the floor, with the atlas on his lap, rolling a joint. "Ok, let's go man," Rowen said. Ollie pulled out slowly, and Nick put the atlas away and hopped in front. Changa sat on the bench close to the front to chat with the guys.

"You tired Cass?" Rowen said, pulling her to lie back on the bed.

"Yeah,' she said stiffening as she lay down. She sighed, not knowing what they were going to do there, with all the other guys just a few feet away. Rowen moved over so she could lie next to the back van doors. He positioned a pillow under her and smiled. He loosened his hair tie, and his black hair dropped heavily to one side. His body odor was so strong that Cass wrinkled her nose, but she also liked his smell. They lay on the back bed, not touching much, as the van moved down the highway to the next show in Deer Creek.

Chapter 42
Devon

Devon bumped his bike onto the grassy part of the lot, following other cars to a stand of bikes much fancier than his. All those shiny chromed Harleys decked out with silver Steal-Your-Faces on the back. Yeah, he liked the shine, but the dull red of his Indian motorcycle was home. The show wouldn't be for a good few hours, so Devon left his bike and started walking.

The day was warm, but cloudy. There'd been rain there the night before, and Devon could feel the matted grass and mud give way to his heavy boots as he walked. The thought of raven was in him, but way to the back of his mind. He was feeling defeated in his desire to change. It just wouldn't happen. Still, there was some power in him below the surface. The crowd wasn't just deadheads. Corn-fed, big-bodied cops lined the stadium's entrance, and identical overweight men dressed ridiculously in Hawaiian shirts and jeans, paraded the parking lot—the most obvious narcs he'd ever seen. Deadheads were walking around them in a wide berth and Devon chuckled. What a joke. Part of him wanted to trick every one of them, just for fun. Devon moved towards the far end of the lot, where people were and were not trying to start a Shakedown. No one wanted to be the test case to get busted, so deals were taking place quietly up against and inside cars. What a shame that the Midwest couldn't just let things be. Yeah, the Head ways were different from the Bible Belters, but it wasn't the 50s anymore.

Plenty of young chicks milled around, looking cute, holding fingers in the air for a ticket. Devon figured he'd find a face value ticket closer to show time, but really he didn't care so much about the show. He looked for coolers. Only tailgated ones were visible. Then he saw that black van. The one without any stickers, a California license plate, shaded windows. Real cool. He felt annoyance at that slick and familiar young Head. He knew the kid was that young gal, Cass's, boyfriend. Didn't seem like Cass knew anything about the Dead scene, and a guy like that could take advantage of her. He'd put her to work already, slinging his beer. But really it was none of his business. He just didn't like people being treated bad. Devon stopped at the end of the row and rolled a cigarette, keeping cool, keeping his sights all around the lot. He pulled the ease of tobacco into him and thought about Emmajean. These days Devon couldn't protect her to save his life, if she ever needed it. As Cora wished, he was mostly dead to Emma.

Two girls passed behind that black van, one in an expensive looking pink skirt. The fancy girl had her arm wrapped around Cass and Devon thought the two looked like a popstar and a teenager. Cass didn't match her at all and it just reinforced Devon's thought that the girl didn't know anything about the Grateful Dead scene. He wanted to tell her about the music, about the history, about the way things were and what ideals they were supposed to manifest there. Devon dropped his cigarette and noticed his hand was shaking. He coughed and felt the bottom of his lungs. Devon suppressed the shaking in his chest, he stood up, shoved his hands in his pockets as the girls walked towards him. The fancy girl kept her arm wrapped around Cass. As they neared, she wrinkled her nose and looked him up and down before passing. Cass recognized him though. "Oh, hi," she said as they walked past him, but nothing more. He lifted his hand halfheartedly at her. The fancy girl looked back at Devon with disdain, reminding him of Cora's judging eye. Devon stamped his boots, turned around in a circle, watched the two walk across the parking lot. He looked towards the black van. A group of guys there, like stupid crows.

Chapter 43
Hettie

Hettie lit the candle every day at dusk now. The wick was lower and set near the candle were two little shot glasses of whisky that he never came for. She wanted to appeal to him again, to help Rowen, and also maybe to understand why that sick raven had been so important. Hettie walked out onto the back porch clutching a broom. She let the door slam behind her, maybe he could hear her. She began to sweep the wood slats, sending black roly-poly bugs and dust off the edge of the porch. She angled the broom under a bench and pulled more dirt from there. In the messy pile, a black feather stood out. Hettie looked at it, remembering the swishing sound of that bird's wing. Part of her wanted to pull it out and put it next to the candle, just in case it might bring her ancestor's spirit sooner. But it looked half mite eaten, so she gently swept it off the edge, too. She watched it tumble and settle on the ground, covered with dirt. "Go back to the earth. Hope your other feathers are stronger now," she said, thinking of the blinking black eyes of that poor bird. Hettie sat on her porch bench and looked up at Crystal Mountain, the pattern of pines zig zagging up its left side, the rocky slants at the top, and the softer looking green down the right slope. It seemed so simple viewed as a whole, but Hettie knew that many of the forests and patches of brush up there were deep and varied and held their own hundred-year secrets. She liked living opposite the mountain, in its own wholeness, as she tried to maintain hers. Shadows slid slowly across, as the sun began to retire. Hettie went back inside, letting the door close slowly against her back.

She set up her dinner plate and ate standing up in the kitchen. Then she poured a small glass of whisky for herself, and another half shot for him. She lit the candle again, and settled on her couch, thumbing through a magazine that was months old. She heard early evening birds and the crick of trees, changing their temperature for the night. Some squirrels scampered over the roof, and she smiled at the natural sounds, trying to listen closer for clues of a nearing dead man. She wondered what he might be doing in his world: working, sleeping, playing his fiddle. Hettie wanted to know more about his history. It was her history, too, even if she didn't experience it right off.

Hettie stared at the quilt again, studying the edges and squinting her eyes to see exposed thread lines. Its patterns were intricate, and she knew it must have taken someone, or many people, a long time to make. She wondered if it had been made with something or someone in mind in the first place. Being crafted only for Wilson didn't seem right. It landed in her lap at the memorial; that old woman had probably pulled it from a cupboard, maybe a cupboard that would get emptied one day by someone other than a family member. It must have been valued enough to be right for a give-away. Hettie hadn't really thought about it those years ago. It was just beautiful, so it had gone up on the wall. It really was more beautiful than any she'd made—tighter stitches, finer shapes. Whoever made it knew more about quilting than she ever did or would. Hettie got up and walked over to the quilt. She flipped an edge up, rubbing the old material of it in her fingers. It was thinning, but still solid. She pulled the quilt slightly out and sent a wave up through it. Shadows from the moving candle flame danced over the blue and white. Hettie smiled. When she turned back to the couch, her granddaddy was there, settled into the rocker. He was dressed in dark pants and a cotton shirt. He looked respectable, like a rancher, with his hair greased back. Hettie sat carefully on the couch, not turning completely towards him. She didn't want him to leave so quickly like he had the last time. She watched him smoke his pipe, and rock in her chair. He seemed happy and calm just to do that. Hettie sat quietly, folding her hands and watching the shadow of his movements.

"You wake in the morning, you turn your bedclothes back up. You wash and set out dishes, you light a candle, you talk to the Earth," he said.

Hettie looked at him, his focus and words, spoken with head down. She nodded but wasn't sure where he was going.

"You mark time, pull threads through on a quilt."

Hettie nodded again, looking up at the quilt, then at her hands. The wrinkled skin stretched over was enough to know that time marked her more than anything these days. He shifted and creaked the chair against the wooden floor.

"You love this land?" he asked her.

I do," Hettie answered, glancing out the window to the darkening sky.

He nodded, "good, stay as long as you can."

"I intend to." Hettie was a little confused. She settled into the couch and closed her eyes. She saw a wood cabin. A porch with a chair, a door left open. The place looked empty. Hettie opened her eyes to glimpse his pipe smoke trailing to the ceiling, he was still there. She closed her eyes again and saw a garden plot, grown over with weeds, a gate fallen inward. It looked like just another abandoned plot, the likes of which she knew were all around her neighborhood in Cueva even. Although, the cabins near her were mostly made from adobe bricks. Hettie closed her eyes one more time and saw the side of a mountain blown open with rock crumbling down the side.

The dirt was clean and loose. It looked like it wasn't supposed to be like that, like something strange had happened. In a nearby tree, strips of faded, colored cloth fluttered in a breeze, like the half of a clothesline.

When Hettie saw this, she shivered and opened her eyes. He was rocking, his shoulders hunched over. Hettie felt an emptiness, looking at him. He's dead, she reminded herself. Maybe he lived there once, before what she saw. Maybe he misses it.

"Like I said, stay as long as you can," he mumbled, "don't go leaving."

Hettie studied the lines on his face. They were deep, drawing down his face like tears, or blood, or paint. Part of her wanted to worry about him, but that was probably no use—what was done was done.

"It's all we had," he said, leaning over and touching some black ash from his pipe. Hettie stared. Hettie heard the whinny of a horse, and saw his gaze turn, saw him stand and walk away. Back in her cabin, he'd gone, too, right through the solid walls where he'd come from. Hettie looked to the dresser, and the thin trail of smoke from the candle. What he'd shown her was interesting, dreary, but it wasn't anything having to do with Rowen. Wherever that place was, she didn't know, but he seemed awfully sad about it, like he didn't get to finish something there.

Chapter 44
Rowen

Rowen watched her walk back towards the van, close to that chick, Hillary. What a fucking joke, he thought. He hated girls like that, so cool and calculated. He didn't want Cass to pick up her ways. He noticed Cass had a different shirt on, a blousy one, didn't look like her. She was smiling though and laughing.

This girl's getting to be a regular tourer!" Hillary said when the two walked up.

"Yeah," Rowen said flatly. Cass saw him and dropped the girl's arm, looking down and walking towards him.

"So, Rowen is it?" Hillary said, swaying her body side to side as she spoke. "Where are you guys sitting at the show? Are you on the floor?"

"Don't know, maybe."

"Mail order?"

Rowen nodded, and shot a glance at Cass, wishing Hillary would just fuck off. Cass turned away from him, staring at Hillary with wide doe eyes, like she was a princess or something. It turned something in Rowen's chest, made him want to spit or slam something. That girl had an aloofness that he remembered in Penny—the parts of her he could have done without. He didn't want Cass to become like her, or, he was just going to say fuck it. She was riding with him though.

"Well, maybe we could meet up in the show?" Hillary said to the two of them, but really more to Cass, sounding like she was trying to be innocent, "I'm on the floor, but can come up."

"Whatever," Rowen said. Cass turned towards him and gave him a half-smile. Rowen wanted to pull her into him, but felt it wasn't cool. He didn't like being judged by Hillary.

Nick came around to the back of the van. "Hey, sister," he said to Hillary, breaking her barrier and enveloping her in a wide hug.

"Hey, brother," she said returning his hug. "You riding here, too?"

"Yeah," Nick said, "far away from New York."

Hillary perked up when he said this. "Oh, really, what part?"

"Brooklyn," Nick said. Hillary nodded, and went over to straighten Cass's blouse, that had pulled to one side.

"Listen, Cass," she said to only her, "I'm going to find Ron. I'll look for you in the show, okay? Let's dance!"

"Sure, thanks for the blouse, Hillary," Cass said politely. Rowen watched Cass watch Hillary as she skipped off back to Shakedown, lighting a cigarette on her way.

"She from Kansas, too?" Nick asked.

"No, Texas," Cass said, "but I met her in Kansas. She's the reason I came to my first show." Cass said this enthusiastically.

"Cool," Nick said, then gave Rowen a look, before disappearing in the van to get some things before the show. Rowen could tell Nick wanted him to chill the fuck out. Nick was one guy who could see right through him. He was older, and sometimes Rowen thought he looked after him, but Nick was much more free-wheeling than Rowen would ever be.

Rowen didn't take Cass's hand as they walked to the venue's entrance. He was moving pretty quickly, and Cass hurried to follow. When they got up to the line, Rowen did steer her in front of him. She straightened her blouse again and ran her fingers through her hair. Rowen could smell her body odor, and it turned him on. He put his hands on Cass's shoulder. She turned around and smiled at him, making the feeling stronger. Maybe they could just have a good show, stay in their seats, get close, he thought. Once inside, he took Cass's hand, and they walked through the halls to the Friends of the Earth table set up. Jane was there, arranging pamphlets.

"Rowen!" she said, coming around the table to envelop him in a hug.

"Hi Jane, how's it going here?"

"Oh, fine, fine," she said smiling and glancing towards Cass. "Hi honey, I'm Jane," she said leaning in to hug Cass.

"Hi, I'm Cass."

"Nice to meet you sweetie."

Cass blushed, smiling big, and leaning in to look at the material on the table.

"How's the Midwest treating you Row?"

"Oh, well as can be. Way too many narcs out there, couldn't really sell anything before the show."

"Yeah, I've seen a bunch in here. They just come to our table and pretend to be interested. When I try to start up a conversation they just seem confused and walk away!" Jane said chuckling.

"Yeah, and they're the ones you really need to get through to."

"Everyone really."

Rowen nodded. "Scout here?"

"Yeah, somewhere. He's gonna get the first set, and I'll get the second," she said.

"Oh, good!"

"Well, enjoy the show, you two."

"Thanks," Rowen said, reading Jane's face as she admired Cass's beauty. Some part of Rowen didn't mind Jane witnessing him with Cass. She wouldn't judge. He knew she just wanted him to be happy, but having Jane see Cass, made him feel more responsible for her. They settled in their seats, right side, Jerry and Vince's side, one tier up from the floor. Good seats.

"Does Jane go to all the shows?" Cass asked.

"A lot of them. It's a good place to teach people and get folks involved. They're a lot of people who care about the environment here," Rowen said. Cass nodded. She sunk down in her seat and leaned a little towards Rowen. He liked this and leaned over and kissed her. "You glad to be here?" he asked.

"Yes," she said quickly.

"Is everything ok? I mean, does your family know where you are?"

"Yeah," Cass said, but Rowen thought she sounded a little guilty. He didn't want to press anything. He figured she was old enough to take care of her side of things.

"Good," he said. "Not sure what's after these shows, but we can drop you at the bus station in a couple days if you want." Rowen could feel Cass stiffen, but he didn't budge while she just nodded again.

"What do you want to hear?" She said, obviously trying to change the subject.

"Oh, maybe 'Fire,' or 'Terrapin,' we could get a 'Stella,'" he said. Rowen reached into his shoe and pulled out a small sack of weed and began rolling a thin joint. They smoked it between them, sinking down in their seats, as the lights went out and the crowd roared. Cass sucked in more than she had before and Rowen was pleased she was getting the hang of smoking. The boys came out and began picking their guitars. Rowen listened for clues of the first set.

Chapter 45
Cass

During drums and space, Cass felt confined in her seat next to Rowen. She viewed the rows below them on the floor looking for Hillary. Cass liked the idea of dancing freely with her like they had in Bonner Springs. She liked being near Rowen, but he could watch half the show from the comfort of his seat, just getting higher and higher smoking weed. Cass wanted to explore, be up and move her body crazily.

"You wanna toke," Rowen said holding another joint out to her.

"No thanks."

Rowen took her hand and entwined his fingers with hers. His hand was clammy and a bit cold. Cass wanted to let go, but she also wanted to stay close to him. There was a current running inside her veins that seemed to buzz as the band members thrashed odd chords on their guitars. She knew already that she could do without Space. Still, she was mesmerized by the Heads standing in the aisles, who seemed to move every little whirl and buzz coming from the stage through their bodies—even if it sometimes looked like the movements were making them sick.

"I think I'll go to the bathroom," Cass said.

"Yeah, you know where it is?"

"Sure, just up there."

"Cool," Rowen said, he sounded sleepy. "Here's your ticket stub," he handed her the half of a thin ticket with glittered writing on it.

"Thanks," she said, looking up the rows to the top where the bathrooms were.

"Come back," Rowen said, as she stood up.

Cass smiled at him, then took off, climbing the concrete steps. She was out of breath, halfway up, but liked feeling her chest move with her breath and her heartbeat. At the top, the entrance to the hallway was crowded with dancers, some flailing their arms, others spinning in circles. Cass watched skirts billow out to perfect circles as men and women twirled close to one another. Also, standing within good distance of them, with hands shoved in pockets, were bigger men in Hawaiian shirts. Cass found the bathroom and had to wait in a short line. The toilets seemed overused, with bits of toilet paper scattered on the floor. She was grateful that it was a flush toilet though. She hated the Port-a-Potties. Cass looked at herself in the mirror while washing her hands with soap. She was still dirty, but Hillary had helped her comb her hair and tuck it back. The blouse made her look more like a Head, and she liked this. It was freeing. As she walked back to her section entrance, Cass saw Forrest. When he spotted her, he ran up and hugged her, picking her up off the floor and twirling her.

"Hey! Cass,' he said as he let her back down. The whoosh excited Cass, and she blushed.

"Hi! Forrest!"

He took her hand and she couldn't help following him as they moved to another hallway entrance nearby. A bunch of Heads, with dreaded hair and huge smiles, made way for them to enter into their dancing group. One guy enveloped Forrest in a bear hug.

"Hey! brother, so good to see ya!" Forrest beamed, and started shaking his body unreservedly, but matched to the music that was now coming from the stage. The band opened the second set with, "I Need a Miracle." At the chorus, the whole group lifted their fingers in the air. Cass followed along with Forrest. She liked being in the center of these folks, who seemed so carefree and loving of one another. It was nothing like Cass had ever seen anywhere else, except inside a Grateful Dead show. Apart from his dreads, Forrest seemed like someone she could have known in high school. Maybe he was closer to her age. It felt easier to be with him. She wasn't so self-conscious. Cass swung her hips with the rock and roll beats, listening to Bobby sing. She knew she should go back to the seat with Rowen, but she was having so much fun in the hallway. She didn't want to sit down or be confined by the narrow space between the seats. The whole group around her was jumping up and down, twisting and twirling, hollering and whistling by the end of the song. Several of

Forrest's friends spontaneously came up to give Cass a big hug, spreading body odor and sweat on her. But she didn't care, there was so much love she felt from everyone.

The music changed, slowing way down. Cass thought she really should go back, and sink into Rowen's shoulder, but she found herself in the middle of a gentle sway. It was "Standing on the Moon," and Cass recognized the melody. The Heads around her were moving like one—a breathing, peaceful animal, or an angel of some sorts. The high notes of the song lifted her, made her want to reach her hands above her head, and sway. She felt free. Forrest, with his hands clasped at his heart, beamed at her. He looked so innocent. He could be at church, praying. Cass stayed inside this peaceful circle, closed her eyes and listened to the music. She thought of the freedom and community her dad must encounter in his travels around the world. This experience, too, was so far removed from Kansas life.

Jerry's voice eased her and Cass's mind went to the postcards from her Dad, the ones from Katmandu, and Kerala, and China. His scrolling handwriting—the only thing she'd held of him in years. The presence she felt and didn't feel from those bits were mixed up in her, but somehow in the center of this circle of strangers, in a hallway in the middle of America, listening to the high music, she felt closer to him. Cass let her eyes swell with tears, and she kept them closed, letting herself feel the pain around her heart. Towards the end of the song, Forrest must have known she was feeling it, and wrapped her in a hug, swaying with her. Cass let her head drop to his shoulder. He was a friend, a good friend, he understood, and let her be just who she was, let her feel what she needed to feel in that moment. It was all ok. Then he took her hands in his and moved her around in a circle, till her smile came back. She felt fresh, revived. She'd liked thinking about her dad with that song, even if it was sad. But the time for excitement came back with the next song.

Cass moved towards the steps and looked out trying to find Rowen's aisle. There were so many people standing now and dancing that she couldn't see him. She looked to the stage and the hot lights coming from there. She squinted to see the guitarists' hands strumming and moving up the guitars, the drummers pounding away, the keyboardist flying his fingers across the keys. Cass looked down the stairs one more row over and saw a girl skipping up the steps. She wore pink and seemed so happy.

It was Hillary! Cass rushed back up through the hallway, shouting at Forrest, "be right back!" He smiled and extended his prayered hands out to her. Cass went left to the next entrance and met Hillary at the top of the stairs. "Hill!" she said, surprising her with a big hug.

"Wow, sugar, you must be having some fun!"

"Definitely! Come on, there's a good place to dance."

"Alright then!" Hillary followed Cass back to Forrest's group. She smiled, and said to Cass, "I see you've found the spinners, and your little dreaddie friend," Hillary said, winking.

"Yeah," Cass said. Hillary started dancing on the edge of the circle. The music was climbing higher, as folks kept steady on their dancing groove. Cass reached out and took Hillary's hands moving around in a circle.

Hillary smiled, "Careful, I'm no spinner girl. Hey, where's Rowen?"

Cass's face dropped a little. He's down there, sitting," Cass shouted over the music.

"I see," Hill said. The music drew up into "Sunshine Daydream" and the two girls lifted their arms in the air, so carefree, so beautiful. Cass looked at Forrest who was shaking his head back and forth and stamping his feet into the concrete. He looked funny and lovely and Cass laughed, her heart lifted. She also knew that she'd been "going to the bathroom" for almost four songs, and Rowen told her to come back. She was close by, just up the aisle, and she went to the side again to try to find his row. At the end of the song, Hillary gave her gentle hug.

"You know the show is almost over, right? You and Rowen going to sell things in the lot?" Hillary asked with a bit of sarcasm in her voice.

"I don't know, probably."

"Alright then. So, I'll catch you later, doll. So glad you're having so much fun!"

"Me, too!" Cass beamed. She watched Hillary sway into the hallway, then glanced at Forrest who remained reverent amidst all the shouting, whistling and clapping. She joined him, holding her hands at her chest and looking to the stage, hoping for another song. She could feel the anticipation, the wish, the buzz of this little waiting. She looked down the aisles again and noticed some people climbing the stairs to leave. The encore started, and it was cool and mellow like a walk down a dusty path. She wanted to be back with Rowen then. "Forrest, I gotta go, thanks so much! See you later."

Forrest hugged her again and even placed a scratchy kiss on her cheek. "See you later, sweet Cassidy!"

As Cass rushed back out to the hallway, she saw, leaning against the wall quietly watching the group of hallway dancers, that man, Devon. He stared towards her, but Cass dropped her head, not before feeling an odd rush around her heart. Why did she keep seeing him? In the lot, in the show, at the next show? Cass looked back, and saw he wasn't leaning against the wall anymore. Cass brushed it off though and kept moving to the right aisle, heading down the steps. Halfway down though, Rowen came up towards her. "Rowen!" She said.

"Oh," he said, "Come on, let's go." He didn't take her hand, just kept climbing up, and expecting Cass to follow him, which she did. She wanted to talk to him, reconnect, say she was sorry she didn't come back sooner. It seemed he didn't care though, and Cass raced after him, out the doors and into the parking lot. She practically ran to keep up with him. "Are we gonna sell something to the crowd?" she asked.

"Not sure." He wouldn't even look at her.

"Well, I can help." she said.

"Good."

They made it back to the van and Ollie and Nick were already there.

"Good show!" Ollie said.

Rowen flicked his head up, agreeing. Nick dropped a cigarette on the ground.

"Cassidy, how'd you like the show?" he asked.

Cass glanced at Rowen before answering, "It was great!"

Nick came up and put his hands on her shoulder. He was looking towards Rowen though, who'd disappeared in the van. "I danced in the hallway some," she said.

"Oh yeah, cool!" Nick said.

"Are we going to sell stuff now?" she asked Nick.

"Not sure, I think. We've got beer and could do grilled cheese."

They could hear the crowd cheering inside the venue, they could also hear Rowen raising his voice as him and Ollie moved coolers out and shuffled ice.

"Oh, geez," Nick said.

Cass just stood by the back of the van, waiting to see what she was going to do. She wished she could talk to Rowen. His mood seemed really foul, and she didn't like it. But she was there with all of them, she needed to make it work.

"Why don't Cass and I take this cooler to Shakedown," she heard Ollie say.

"Whatever," Rowen said, dropping his side of the cooler on the pavement by the back of the van. Cass moved out of the way.

"Row, let's stay here and work the other one, man," Nick said. Come on, and he got Rowen to go back in the van to ready the other one.

"Here Cass can you take the other side of this?" Ollie said.

"Sure" and she lifted the heavy cooler with Ollie and walked with him away from the van. She tried to look back but couldn't, so she let herself focus on all the happy, wasted people flooding into the parking lot looking for a cold beer.

Chapter 46
Rowen

Rowen ripped the beer boxes open and pulled the glass bottles out, swinging around to the inside of the van, and slamming them into the cooler, making a lot of noise. He was pissed. Where the fuck had she been the whole second set? He didn't like the idea of financing some chick's tour, just for her to go traipsing off and dancing or whatever else she was doing with other Heads. It made him feel like a fucking loser. If he was walking around with her, if she was riding with him, sharing his bed, paying for her tickets, people would take notice. He didn't want to be the last one noticing what everyone else did, like with Penny. He knew Cass was different. Much younger, for one thing, and so new to the scene.

"Hey, man, take it easy," Nick said crawling into the van and arranging the cooler ice so the bottles sunk down. Rowen slowed, took the last two bottles from the carton and handed them to Nick.

"It's just…" Rowen started, then stopped.

"Just what, Row," Nick said giving him a look that said he knew Rowen was pissed about the girl.

"Never mind, man."

"She's cool, you know. Just new to the scene. I wouldn't worry about it."

Rowen shook his head. The two of them hoisted the cooler out of the van and set it on the pavement. They lifted the lid and Rowen plunged his hand in to pull out two cold Bass beers. He flipped the top with a lighter and handed it to Nick, then opened one for himself. "I don't know," Rowen said. "She's too much of a freshie."

"Oh, who cares? She seems sweet, a little young," Nick said raising his eyebrows at Rowen, "but seems cool to me."

"Yeah, I guess so. But that other chick, that Hillary, fuck that shit," Rowen said.

"Yeah, she seems like a handful, for sure. Still, man, I wouldn't worry about it. That other girl can't have a pretty one like Cass trailing her, it would cramp her scene—going after a rich boy at every stop."

"Fucking A, you're right!" The guys laughed and downed the rest of their beers. After-show crowds moved in and they got busy taking dollar bills and popping bottle tops.

Chapter 47
Devon

Devon walked endlessly—circling the edges of the lot. It was a wide path for his legs. He wanted to be higher, soaring, seeing everything in a matter of minutes. The lot was full of campers and tarps and tie dyes hung up for cover. Folks slept on the ground in sleeping bags, people sold things quietly. Everyone was under the radar of the Midwest cops' gaze. But drums beat somewhere in between the cars and shouts and loud, drunk voices carried. Devon walked around the east edge of the lot to a grove of bikes parked close together. A round barbeque flamed with a fire. Devon saw Charlie sitting in a circle of plastic chairs with other bikers. He walked up to the few folks he actually knew there, standing on the other side of the fire. The sting of lighter fluid filled his nose. Devon dug the orange flames, over the dull black of the barbeque metal. He looked at the men there, letting his eye move to their middles and the glint of light that hit their belt buckles. He recognized two or three. Silver, dull, placed between great bellies and limbs. The etchings he'd made, lost among denim and leather. The guys around him nodded their heads up, raised small liquor bottles to acknowledge him. When Charlie noticed Devon, he raised his arm, snubbed his cigarette out, and lumbered out of his chair. Last night's show played nearby. It was the end of the first set—good bass, Jerry's rough scratching voice.

"Hey, man," Charlie said, holding out his hand and clasping Devon's. He gave him a plastic cup and poured in a couple inches of whisky.

"Thanks," Devon said, kicking it and burning the back of his throat. He sucked in air and felt the good fire spread in him.

"Good show," Charlie said, sniffing, rubbing his hands on black jeans and putting his lips against the bottle.

Devon just nodded. He set the cup on the ground and rolled a cigarette, tucking the brown twills in the paper with his longer thumb nails. This group was fairly chill, but Devon could tell, as the night moved past midnight, booze would get them rolling.

"You moving further East next, Devon?" Charlie asked.

"Not sure. Might just head back West. How about you?"

"We'll all roll into DC for a bit. Business is rich there."

Devon nodded. He picked up his plastic cup. Charlie waddled over to a cabbed silver pick up and came back with another bottle out of a box of whisky. He unscrewed the cap and poured the amber liquid in the white plastic, filling it halfway. Devon raised it, "Thanks man." On Charlie's hand Devon saw the silver cuff he'd made years ago, with a proud Steal-Your-Face and skeletons on either side. It made him smile. It still had a shine, even in the dull evening light. Voices raised around them, a Harley started up, grumbling along with the music. The whiskey fire moved down through his body and Devon wanted to walk more, to align with the trees, or Earth. Charlie tucked his chubby fingers in a front pocket and pulled out a small plastic baggie. Devon saw a few clean white pills inside. Charlie picked out one small capsule and held it out to Devon.

"This is some real clean shit Devon. It'll make you fly high," he said, winking and chuckling. Devon popped the pill in his mouth and washed it back with whiskey. He knew anything Charlie carried was really good and would trip him in just the right way.

"Thanks man." Devon gazed across the circle and looked a couple biker chicks up and down. The leather hugging thin legs made nice shadows behind them. The orange end of their lit cigarettes trailing smoke around their round chests. These were the kind of women he knew, hard-edge, like Cora. He looked away, he didn't want it anymore. The only power he wanted was in the folds of feather and wing. Devon held out his hand and Charlie grabbed it, shaking and then rearranging his fingers in another hold, before letting go. Devon tipped his head to the women as he walked on.

He sought the edge of the lot and the grassy fields that lay beyond the pavement. He looked to the left and the cop car that was at the entrance, lights circling, as if the Heads needed that kind of marker. It was a humid night, and summer bugs buzzed louder in his ears. Whatever that white powder in the capsule was, it was starting to ease its way into Devon's blood stream. Most likely high-grade MDMA; It felt good. He could feel every little stick under his foot as he walked into a nearby field. The waving grasses were hidden by dark. His frame was hidden, too. Devon's eyes adjusted, looked to some trees ahead. He walked to the sound of scratch under foot, to the distancing hollers of partying Heads behind him. He came to the clump of trees in the middle of the field and brushed his hand against the rough bark. The wood snagged his skin slightly and he moved slower, noticing the feeling of his human skin, the softness of it compared to leathery talons. Devon gazed up into the branches, noticing the crossing pattern of branches thrust to the sky. The view was beautiful, a labyrinth or a web. He closed his eyes, saw the limit of perching amongst that web, grasping onto one branch, hopping to a second, but not seeing the whole. Devon turned his back and slid down the tree's trunk, bending his knees and feeling his feet root into the ground, then press and push his back against the tree. It was a solid feeling, and he played with arching and relaxing his feet. The subtle movement stirred his blood and connected him to the tree, to the Earth, to a gentle breeze. To himself.

Devon closed his eyes, breathing his humanness, finding space and weight. His mind returned and he nodded, knowing that the MDMA was working just fine. He squinted, looking back to distant lights among those camping. He saw yellowed plants in the field waving, he saw the circling red and blue of cop lights. Then he heard a shuffle and crunch. Devon turned his head to the right, feeling a lag, and inability to move quickly. His eyelids languished down, and up again. He heard the sound again. He wanted to stand, but his legs seemed planted comfortably against the earth, against the tree's trunk. The sound continued until a man stood in front of him.

The man was dressed in old work clothes and a tan leather hat. Tucked under his arm, was a black lump. Something alive, but not well. Or was it dead? The gloss of black startled Devon. He felt his breath increase, fear move under his skin. The man's face was streaked with sooty lines from his forehead to his eyes, down his cheeks, to his chin. The man stood still, unthreatening. Devon opened his mouth, panting a bit. The man nodded his head down, gently, and sat, five feet away, waiting while Devon's human body relaxed. Devon studied him. It was probably a hallucination, but the scent of this man came through Devon's nostrils, a sweet smoky, earthy dung. It calmed him. Devon saw trees behind his closed eyes, and the up-close green needles of pine, the sticky sap of pine bark. He saw the sky stretch out before him, the release and freedom of expanse.

Devon could feel his throat open and the sounds he wanted to make, close to the surface. He could feel the blink of a small eye, and an itch under feathers. The man sitting near him, grumbled under his breath. He wasn't speaking a language Devon could understand. His sounds were clicks and shushes, like some type of song. Devon looked at him, his eyes were at the same height as Devon's gaze, but the man was looking well past him, into another field. Devon let his head lean back against the tree again. He closed his eyes, felt the MDMA coursing through him.

Behind his eyes, Devon saw Cora standing in her bedroom, stacking his clothes and things, shoving them in black plastic. He felt his lumbering body in the doorway, watching her, the pain of endings; her quickness, and the sharp words she spewed as she pushed past him. There was no more comfort in that room for him, no light brushes, no laughter with Emma. Devon breathed, remembering this scene he had played over and over while lying on his hard prison cot. He'd gone there in his mind to try to recreate something, that had been dead for a long time. The thought of prison and trying to escape it through his memory was an old pattern he didn't need anymore. He was free, sitting in a field at a Grateful Dead show. Devon opened his eyes and stared at the ground. The man was rocking back and forth, with his legs crossed, mumbling. Devon stretched his arms up and back, brushing the rough edges of the tree. He was grateful to be outside, to have the ground underneath him. Devon looked at the man, "Brother?' he heard himself say. The man didn't move. "Brother, why are you here?" The man kept rocking and grumbling. Slowly the vision of him clutching a bird faded for Devon, until it was just the field grass around him. Devon bent his knees, stretched his back, and felt pain shoot through his tailbone. He'd sat too long. He pulled himself up and could feel sweat soaking his shirt, and his ankles swollen inside his boots.

Chapter 48
Percy

Percy didn't last too long in the factory. People were not kind there, and the work was endless, numbing. The same hammer slammed into a piece of wood, over and over again, to where his arm ached with the one motion. He'd hopped the trains again, moved further West, crawled into the Earth every morning, and chipped away at black mountains. It seemed so futile, the whole prospect of chipping black coals out of the mountains. It was odd and messy work.

Still, he did it. Percy felt closer to the others who had soot on their faces, too. He'd been able to send back two letters, padded with twenty one-dollar bills each. He hoped to God that they'd made it. It was nearing four months that he'd been away and every day, he wanted to get on a train back.

Percy entered the cabin that'd become a place for folks to gather and drink after hours. This time, he brought his fiddle with him. He knew others played some music, too, and he could keep up with them. Percy held his fiddle down, stood up next to the others, and nodded, listening. At the second round, he started playing and the sounds felt so good. The joining with other musicians, the tap of heavy boots on floorboards in front of him. People were liking it; people were clapping their hands. Birds soared in his chest and Percy thought, if he had to be out on the road like he was, it couldn't get much better.

Chapter 49
Cass

Cass liked the gentle weight of Hillary's small hand in hers as they walked towards the arena and the phones there. Hillary had come back by the van, in the morning. She was staying in the lot, too, which seemed unusual for her. Cass was glad her only female friend on tour was close. She needed Hilary's confidence to call her mom. Cass's heart beat fast as they trudged down the rows of Heads sleeping in their cars, and in tents on the matted grass.

"So what're you going to say," Hill asked.

"I don't know. She's going to be so pissed. I was supposed to call her, like, yesterday."

"Oh, come on. It's only been a day. She'll get over it," Hillary said, swinging Cass's arm playfully.

Cass didn't think so. She knew her mom, and she'd really never been this pissed before. Cass's chest burned, and she could feel some juice she'd had, ready to make her barf. She dropped Hillary's hand and zipped up her sweatshirt against the light breeze and the various ripe scents lingering through the lot. There were only a few people in line for the phones.

"So, is Rowen going to take you back to Kansas?"

"Uh, I don't think so. He didn't really offer," Cass said.

"Oh, that's kinda shitty. But he's probably planning to go East for the next shows," Hillary said matter-of-factly. "Heads tour, that's what they do," she gave Cass a wide grin, "You should, too!"

"Yeah, I really want to, but…"

"But what? You can make some cash on tour. Rowen does have a pretty sweet ride, if you like being in the lot."

"He does, but I don't know. I probably should be working back home."

"Hey, didn't you just graduate?" Hillary said, stamping her hands on her hips.

"Yes, but…"

"But nothing! This is the summer of your life! What better place to be than on Dead tour, I mean, come on!"

Cass smiled, catching her enthusiasm. She was getting used to the scene. She did love the music. She loved dancing. She could make cash on tour, selling beer and grilled cheese. The line moved up. Cass pulled a calling card from her back pocket. As she punched the numbers, she imagined her mom sitting at the kitchen table, her hands gripping a mug. The space opposite her empty, where Cass would have been. The ring was loud and piercing, in her ear, like a siren.

"Hello," Joanne answered.

"Mom?"

"Cass!" her mom whimpered, "oh, Jesus! Honey! Where are you?"

"Mom, calm down, I'm fine," Cass said feeling the burning spread in her chest. She felt angry, too. Her mom was overreacting. Hillary stood close by and when Cass looked at her she raised her eyebrows sarcastically. This calmed Cass and even made her smile a little.

"Cassandra! I've been worried sick over you! Don't you dare tell me to calm down."

Cass held the phone silently. She did feel sorry.

"Cass, honey, are you there?"

"Yes, Mom."

"Are you still in Chicago?"

"No."

"I didn't think so. Jack contacted the Chicago PD and they said the Grateful Dead shows were over there. Anything could have happened to you."

"Mom, I'm totally fine. I'm in Indiana, where the next show is. I'm with Hillary." She turned to her friend who straightened up and mouthed 'want me to talk to her?' Cass shook her head slowly. "I'm sorry you were worried about me. I really am fine. I'm just trying to enjoy my summer."

"Well, lying and running all over the country is not the only way to enjoy your summer. Besides, I thought we had an agreement that you would work this summer, save some money for college." The thought of more school felt like such a drag to Cass. She could work on tour. Somehow, she didn't think her mom would equate a job at the back of a grocery store with making and selling grilled cheese sandwiches out of a van. "I know, Mom. I can still do that. I'm sorry. I really am fine. I'm with Hillary. She's right here," Cass looked at Hill, who held out her hand and mouthed, 'let me talk to her.' Cass let the receiver slide from her hand into Hillary's.

"Joanne? It's Hillary. Cass and I are doing just fine."

"Just fine! Listen here Miss, Miss…" Hillary held the phone away from her ear and made a shrieking face at Cass.

"Constantine," Hill said.

"Miss Constantine, Cass is my daughter and I worry about her. I don't know what kind of life you have, but this is not one for her."

Cass, hearing her mom's shouts through the phone, made her fearful of both hurting her mom, and embarrassing herself in front of Hill.

"Yes, ma'am," Hillary said.

"Where are you exactly?"

"Noblesville, IN, by Deer Creek. The second show will start in a few hours. I am looking after Cass. She really is fine," Hillary said, working her Southern manners well.

"Do your parents know where you are, Hillary," Joanne said softer.

"Yes ma'am. They trust me. I leave them a voice mail every few days," Hillary looked at Cass, nodding and smirking.

"Well," Joanne said, "this is not usual for my daughter. Please put her back on." Hillary dangled the receiver from her hand till Cass took it. She stepped back from the phone booths then and lit a cigarette.

"Mom?" Cass said.

"What?"

"Please just trust me a little. You know I will be safe."

"It's not you I worry about, Cass, it's other people."

Cass was silent. She took a deep breath. "So, Mom, I'm going to stay here for the show tonight, and then I'll get a bus back. Hillary can drive me to the bus station," she lied. "Really, I'm just at this concert hall in the middle of a corn field. There are lots of cops around, keeping everybody safe. I'm being really careful, I promise," Cass said, knowing her mom was already questioning the words, 'I promise."

"Ok Cass. I know you're almost an adult, but I still worry about you and I love you so much."

"I know, Mom, I love you, too."

"Please call me again, ok?"

"I will. I've got to go. There's another person who wants to use the phone."

"I love you, Cass" Joanne said.

Again, Cass could hear the break in her mom's voice. "Me, too," Cass said and hung up the phone.

Chapter 50
Hettie

Shoe marks Hettie's granddaddy left on her wood floor were still there, faintly. Every time she walked past the smudge lines, she imagined him working someplace dirty in the American West. In the days since his last visit, Hettie had climbed up to the tiny attic space near her front door, pulling out old shoeboxes. Most were dusty on top and scattered with mouse droppings. She brushed them off with a rag and opened the tops of these cardboard vaults that had been ignored for three, five, maybe seven years. Most were filled with spools of thread, some had disorganized papers, or birthday cards, a couple kids' drawings. She looked for clues of her family. She remembered when she'd traveled back to Oklahoma, right before her mother died. She was so distracted with the weight of her duties. Wilson shoved her and Jessie onto a bus but didn't come with them. He'd found someone to take care of things while she was gone, but she only stayed a few days there, plus a few days travel. In that old cabin where she'd grown up, Jessie found the quietest spots to hide: in the corner of the living room; next to the kitchen stove; around back by the tool shed. The scent of her grandmother dying was too much for the girl.

Hettie remembered sitting and holding her mother's hand, watching breath go in and out, checking the rise and fall of her chest almost imperceptibly. In between sitting with her, Hettie had rooted around the old house, looking for anything she'd like to take back to New Mexico. There was a lot of junk in that house, and it all overwhelmed her. She knew she wouldn't have much room for things and trying to haul stuff on the bus seemed crazy. She'd filled two boxes, wrapped one in an old buckskin bag, and the other in a wool blanket. She figured she and Jessie would be able to hold them on the ride back.

Many years later, the scraps that remained in the dusty boxes seemed useless and tired. There were tools of Wilson's, a compass, metal files, a draft card. Hettie spread a stack of papers on her couch. Most were letters, from Jessie and Rowen, ones even from Lou and Tate. There were older letters in her mama's uneven handwriting. There was a stiff photo of her mama and daddy standing in the yard, him dressed in work pants and a shirt, her in a long, high collared dress. They looked like old ranchers. Hettie pushed the papers around and found a black and white photo of a group of people in front of a log cabin. The men in hats sitting on chairs that had been pulled out onto the grass. Hettie turned the photo over and read 1910. She squinted her eyes to see two girls standing in front of a tree, wearing long dresses. One must have been her mother. It was probably in Oklahoma, where they'd moved. The cabin didn't look so bad to Hettie though. It was similar to the one she'd grown up in.

When she'd fallen for Wilson, there was no keeping her on that land. Hettie shoved most of the things back in the box but left that photo on the table. In the days that followed, she looked at it a lot, even with a magnifying glass, to see if one of the men looked anything like her ancestor's spirit. He must have been in that photo, or nearby, anyway, but maybe not.

Hettie went out on her porch, with the sun high overhead. She liked the warmth of the early summer. Flies buzzed around the dark wood, and she heard the quick zing of hummingbirds playing. Hettie closed her eyes and imagined the pretty girl with light colored hair. The thought of her softened Hettie's mind and heart. She liked thinking about her more than black ravens or all the dead people she'd been thinking about lately. Of course, that girl could be another spirit, too, for all she knew. Hettie thought about Rowen, perched in his van, driving highways. She knew he must be feeling the loss of his mother. She knew he was probably doing everything he could to not feel it. The grief, though, was real. If he didn't let himself feel it,

Hettie worried he'd burry it way inside of himself and it would be like a rock, pulling him down into water. Hettie wished he could soften enough to just feel things instead of continuing to run away.

Chapter 51
Rowen

They spent most of the day just lounging in the back of the van with the windows and doors cracked; it was pretty hot out. Rowen laid on the back bed with Cass. Her body odor had increased after two days without a shower. Her bare, sticky arms pressed against his. It was too hot to close the doors and find privacy, so he just relaxed, feeling good next to her.

"So, what do you think of the band, Cassidy?" Rowen asked.

She turned towards him and smiled. "They seem to do a lot in one song, like all the improvisation"

"That's kind of their thing. And a lot of songs segue into each other."

"I think I like the big guy's voice the best," she said.

"Yeah, Jerry. We're so lucky to have him. You know, he's had a lot of rough patches. Most of them have, really."

"Like what?"

"You know, drugs and rock and roll! Yeah, but Jer dabbled in heroin. That shit sucks."

"You ever try that?" she said looking at him with innocent eyes.

"Nope." Rowen sat up and checked the time. He thought about his older brother Tate. He was probably still wallowing around the apartment, messing with tin foil in the bathroom. The last time Rowen had seen him, his eyes were so sunken, he looked like he could fall over. Worrying about his downfall into smack was the last thing he could do now. He knew his mom would have given him a talk if she could. It was beyond anything anyone could do though. Tate would go down and probably follow his mother to the grave. Rowen ran his hand through his hair and stopped that thought in its tracks. He climbed to the front of the van and grabbed the keys from the ignition. "Come on, lets walk around, it's too hot in here," Rowen said.

The show was in a few hours. They'd sold everything they had the day before, so it was just chill, as far as Rowen was concerned, unless he could score an ounce or something. Indiana was still the Midwest. He'd heard, in the lot, that busts were pretty low, but it wasn't really worth risking it. He knew he'd be back in Cali and pick up his regular route soon enough. Cass peeled herself off the bed and slipped her tennis shoes on. They walked towards Shakedown, Cass a few steps in front of him. She seemed eager to see what was going on. Rowen remembered her disappearance in the last show, he'd let it go, but decided he wanted her to stay closer to him. He stepped forward and reached for her hand. She let their fingers slip into his and slowed her gait.

As they moved closer to the crowds, Rowen could feel Cass's excitement. Even after four shows, she seemed less reserved, more open to party and be there. She was naïve though, and this kind of worried Rowen. There were so many groups in the scene, the true dreaddie Heads, the religious spinners, the bikers, the rat pack, the environmentalists, the groundscorers, the beggars and the rich kids. It kind of depended on who you hung out with, and who you aligned with. Rowen liked folks who respected others, the scene, and worked hard, helping each other. He hated folks who broke shit, started fights, tried to sneak in to the shows, or got so fucking drunk and high on nitrous that they fell on the pavement and cracked their heads open. Or the speeders who banked on tanks, selling balloons for $10 bucks each, and never even going into the shows. Cass only knew what she could see in front of her, and people were deceptive.

"You hungry?" Rowen asked.

"A little bit. Are you?"

"Sure. Let's see what we can find." As they slipped into the crowd and stayed close to one side, voices and colors and scents of cooking food every few feet caught their senses. Rowen held on to Cass's hand and inspected things. One guy had a grill going with sandwiches, but a stack of Velveeta and a pile of plastic wrappers floating around on the ground under his table. Another Shakedown vendor had a table laid with pre-maid burritos. The food and the folks selling them looked clean, but the wraps not so tasty. Rowen pulled Cass forward. Then he spotted Rex, a tall spindly guy with a giant wok full of steaming vegetables. Rex had a bandana over his head, and even a white chef's apron on. He smiled when he saw Rowen coming.

"Hey, man," Rowen said, "good on you, cooking in this heat!"

"Everyone's gotta eat," he said, scooping a spatula into the wok with his long arm. "You guys hungry?" He winked at Cass and she smiled.

"Yeah, looks great!"

Rex scooped a huge pile of steaming veggies onto a thick cardboard plate and handed it to Cass. He then picked up a plastic fork, twirled it around and handed it to her like a cool magician. She smiled and took a bite of carrot, pepper and onion.

"Yum!" she said.

Rowen handed Rex $3 and the two guys clasped hands.

"Hey, what did you think of that "Stella" last night?"

"Oh, so sweet brother. You know I'll take that any day."

Rowen nodded and took another fork from the table, and the plate from Cass. Rex kept tossing the vegetables, and Rowen and Cass moved to the side, to make way for another customer.

"Hey, thanks, man," Rowen said. "Enjoy the show!"

"You, too, brother, and you as well, pretty gal."

Cass blushed, her mouth full of vegetables. They finished eating, found an overflowing trash bag to leave the plate. Shakedown was getting more and more crowded and Rowen looked over the crowd: heads, party-goers, freshies. Lots of people had fingers in the air for miracle tickets. Rowen was surprised at how many times he heard, "buds! doses!" as Heads walked by. Even if he was selling, he'd never just advertise like that. Rowen would just visit folks he knew. Open selling was pretty much asking for it, in his mind, unless they were in Oakland or someplace West. Rowen took Cass's hand again and they moved through the crowd. Cass was learning how to weave through people, and Rowen followed, watching her back and her hips. She sped up and pulled him towards a young dreaddie who was selling beer. Cass dropped Rowen's hand and dove into the guy, letting him wrap his arm around her waist and pull her in for a hug.

"Hey, Cass! How's it going, girl?" the guy said, beaming.

"Great, thanks! Hey, Forrest, this is Rowen," she said.

Rowen pursed his lips, feeling heat spread through his face and chest. He flicked his head up but kept his hands in his pockets. "Hey, man."

"You guys want something to drink?" he said, winking at Cass.

She nodded and he handed her a Heineken after popping the top with a lighter.

"Thanks Forrest," she said.

"You want something Rowen?"

Rowen shook his head and felt pissed that the dreaddie even used his name. "Come on, we should go in," Rowen said to Cass.

"Sure," she said, raising her beer at the guy and following Rowen down Shakedown.

When they were a few yards away, Rowen said, "who's that?"

"I told you, Forrest," Cass said, looking at him sarcastically, like he was crazy.

"How do you know him?" Rowen said trying to suppress the annoyance in his voice, but aware he wasn't doing a very good job. Cass didn't seem to notice, she was in a good mood.

"Oh, I met him in Bonner Springs, at my first show."

"I see," Rowen said, tugging her towards the show's entrance, and trying to walk off the anger that was bubbling in him. What the fuck? Did she meet him before she met me? That stupid Hillary. Forrest's face came in to Rowen's mind, and a big part of him knew a guy like that was no competition. He probably didn't even have a car to ride in. Rowen looked at Cass while they stood in line and tried to smile at her. She brightened back at him, oblivious to the inside of his mind.

The show opened a mellow vibe: "Good Times," "Hell in a Bucket," "Lazy River," "Stuck Inside a Mobile." It was fine for Rowen. He relaxed on the right side of the lawn not too far from the covered canopy section so they could see the stage. He leaned his leg against Cass'. They got high and the pot seemed to subdue them. Rowen thought about going East after the shows. He didn't think Cass would go to RFK. It was a bit of a crap shoot for one show. He could just head back West. Going to California, he could find lots of places to hang before the Shoreline shows. Really, he needed to go back to his mom's neighborhood. That's where all of his pot customers were. The last thing he wanted to do, though, was walk back into his mom's apartment. He could almost smell her dead body, even from a thousand miles away. Rowen stiffened. He couldn't fucking save Tate and hanging around his other brother Lou was worthless. Lou was so fucking stupid with his petty coke deals, and drama queen girlfriends. No, there'd be no room there for him. Rowen's mind wandered South to his grandmother's property. The wind that blew through those tall pines, the wood of her cabin, the winding deserted roads it took to get there. It felt like peace. He hadn't been there in a good five years. His grandma's face came to mind.

Cass was still next to Rowen. He liked her being chill with him. She wasn't up dancing around, running with dirtier hippies. Rowen clasped his hands, refocused and studied the stage. The boys calmed him. Their steady playing let his mind relax. Phil stepped up to the mic, and the guitars slowed down.

"This is Phil's new one, it's a Robbie Robertson song."

"It's sweet," Cass said. She reached her hand towards Rowen's. Then she leaned her body towards him and let her head rest down on his shoulder. This made Rowen's chest hurt. He breathed in, training his mind on Phil's voice.

Chapter 52
Cass

Cass couldn't really believe she was sitting in another Grateful Dead show, two states away from her home now, and with a guy she never imagined she'd ever talk to, let alone be dating, if she could call it that. The rules of interaction seemed so different on tour. She was basically living with him, albeit in his van. She let her body sink into the matted grass of the lawn. As the music entered, her mind pushed away all the things she knew she should think about, but didn't want to. While she held Rowen's rough fingers in hers, she looked to Phil, the tall bass player on the left side of the stage. His voice belted, *"Changing, shifting my life upside down."* His words were true to her experience. Rowen was changing her whole life. She loved it, snuggled into him. He stayed still, reclining. Cass let her mind go to their time in the van. Let the memory heat her up. He likes me, she thought. It was easy to convince herself that was the truth. What she'd experienced there was far more than anything with anyone before.

At the set break, Cass followed Rowen up around the giant lawn space. She had to rush a bit behind him. The entire lawn was crowded and she was glad he slowed down and reached for her hand. They walked close to the Friends of the Earth table. It was swarmed with people, but Jane caught their eyes and waved. Cass smiled and waved back at her, hoping she had been looking at them.

"They're busy!" Rowen said, "That's good."

"Yeah," Cass said, bumping gently into Rowen as they walked. She liked being with him, where everyone could see them. He knew the scene well, made her feel cool. Far removed from her boring Kansas town. Hanging out in Deer Creek, Indiana, she felt a million miles from there. She squeezed Rowen's hand.

Three-quarters of the way around the lawn, something in Rowen changed. He quickly dropped her hand, as they came towards a tall woman with pretty straight brown hair and a small hoop nose ring. She looked older than Cass and definitely a seasoned Deadhead by attitude and her gorgeous, flowing tie-dyed skirt. She stopped three feet in front of them.

"Hey, Ro-wen," she said, leaning in and kissing his cheek. Cass watched, wondering who the hell the woman was. She didn't really like the way her stomach felt as she watched the girl's lips touch Rowen's skin.

"Hi Jasmine, how you been?"

"Oh, fine. Nice tour, good shows, can't complain," she said winking at him.

"Yeah, it's been alright, better than Spring Tour," Rowen said, focusing his attention on the woman to the point that Cass felt like she was invisible. Jasmine glanced at Cass but didn't smile at her or anything. "Oh, this is Cass," Rowen said offhandedly. Jasmine looked at Cass, giving her a smile that really said fuck you.

Then she said to Rowen, "You know, Penny's on this tour. She didn't make it to the East shows, but she's back."

"Nope, didn't know," Rowen said.

"Mmm-hmm," Jasmine sighed, "I'll tell her I saw you and…"

"I'm Cass," Cass said, feeling bold and angry. She gave the girl a fake smile.

"Oh, ok," Jasmin said, smirking.

"That's ok," Rowen said, reaching down for Cass's hand, "Enjoy the rest of the show." Then he pulled Cass away quickly and they headed back to find seats in the same area where they were before. The pressure in Cass's chest made her feel like she could puke. What the fuck was that, she thought. She'd felt so small next to that woman and realized that there was a lot about Rowen that she didn't know. They settled on the dirty grass, and smoked pot again, which Cass tugged into her lungs in an effort to push away the tears she was on the edge of dropping. The musicians came back to the stage and started beating the drums, Cass let the reverberation come into her body. The drum beats were like signposts.

Cass knew she could just listen to them and the screech of guitars and everything would be alright. The middle guy stepped up to the mic and sang about old characters in "Sampson and Delilah." Some of the drums sounded like they had water in them. She smiled, watching one of the drummers belt out a good beat. The next song shifted to the keyboardist, whose long wavy hair shaped his face. The tune made her feel sleepy and she leaned into Rowen. He leaned in, too, and brought his lips to hers, kissing her slowly and deeply. His kiss slid all the way to her toes, as the band made strange sounds. She smiled at Rowen and closed her eyes again. It was amazing to her how a simple, well, maybe not so simple, kiss could push away everything else.

The keyboardist wailed about home. While she clutched Rowen's arm, the thought of Kansas crept in. She heard her mom's voice, through the guitar chords. Part of her felt bad, like something between them had broken. She wondered if they'd ever be friends again. Now that she'd graduated high school, her mom wanted to discipline her. It seemed stupid to Cass. She was done with school, she finally wanted to get into the real world, like her dad. Cass could imagine him taking pictures of this band, walking around the stage with his big camera, snapping priceless moments. It made her smile, and she looked around the stage for cameramen. Of course, he wouldn't be there though, in Indiana. It was too tame for him, but she was there, capturing the pictures of her own experience. It was her time.

Chapter 53
Devon

And then the bard gives up his words amidst the burning wood.
The lock is fully opened now, and he can be returned.

Devon had slept all day in a field, under a big oak. When he woke, he was covered with sticky sweat and his body hurt. The sound of a crowd muffled in the distance and it took him a while to realize where he was, that he'd slept and the sun was slowly making its way down the other side of the sky. He rolled to the side, pushed himself up and ran his swollen, heated hand through damp hair. Flies buzzed near his head, and when he closed his eyes, he saw flashes of dark, circles and trails. He winced as pain entered his head, too. The remnants of a drug his body hadn't finished with yet. He rubbed his eyes and closed them again. The face of the weathered man, clutching a dark bird under his arm came back to Devon. He didn't really know what to make of it, but somehow, it gave him a feeling in his chest like sour honey. Sweet to see the shiny black feathers, held tight and safe under an arm, but also unmoving like a dead chicken going towards supper.

When Devon re-entered the lot, the show was soon to start. He had a ticket, scored from the other day, and stumbled into the entrance line. Another show, and another chance to feel the music. He got a beer, slugged it down, and went in. His ticket was for the lawn, but he walked on both sides of the fanned section under a canopy. He moved slowly his body still coursing drugs. During the set break, Devon circled the lawn twice, feeling restless. The MDMA was almost out of his blood but left a feeling like he was trying to get somewhere but couldn't. As the second set began, he went back to the top of the lawn. He liked being outside. Still his eyes darted to all sides of the grass, to people with their lawn chairs and plastic containers, to bits of trash and ratty blankets. It seemed just an extension from the parking lot. People dragged their stuff inside and made camp again. As music settled in, people did, too, some just lounging, others getting into dance grooves. After two new songs, the first easy cool licks of "Terrapin" locked in. A deep sigh and hum spread through the crowd. Devon loved the song, too. It was like stepping off the ground for a few minutes, akin to flying through the air, past the tops of trees and close to clouds. Devon got up again and walked slowly down the right side of the lawn. The music reminded him of the whole other part of himself. The part he wished for more than anything else, but Devon realized why he was there, at the concert. The music, when it was good like this, wiped things away. The lawn was coming to an end, and Devon turned and looked back up the sloping grass. As his eyes came back down, he saw a girl, knees pulled up, chin resting on them. Her arms hugged her body and she was rocking slightly to the music. She lifted her head, and Devon saw it was Cass. There was an empty space next to her. She looked sad, kind of like the day he'd met her searching for that guy. Devin glanced to the stage, then back at her. There were lots of people on the grass. Maybe it would be no big deal if he just sat down next to her. As the last licks of "Terrapin" crooned from the stage and easy swaying dancers slowed, he stepped through and sat down. She straightened up quickly, startled. He looked the other way, then back at her.

"Um," she said, "someone's sitting there… oh, hi!"

"Hi there, oh, sorry, it just looked like an empty spot," Devon said casually. She looked towards the aisle and back at him. But then she smiled, and relaxed. "How are you?" she said.

"Good, good," he said, "how are you liking the shows?' I see you've made it to the next venue!"

She looked to the aisle again and crossed her legs. "Oh, it's fun. I like the music. How about you?"

"Same old shows," Devon said, conjuring his coolest smile, "That 'Terrapin' was pretty good though."

"Is that the name of that song?"

"'Terrapin Station.' It's a real storyteller's story," he said.

Cass smiled at him. Devon leaned back on the grass.

"Um, my, uh," she paused, excluding the word that could define what that slick guy was to her, "is coming back here soon."

"Oh, sure, I'll get up. Don't worry."

"Thanks." She looked to the aisle again. She seemed uncomfortable that her boyfriend, or whatever he was, could walk back and find his seat taken. Find him there. Find that she'd let someone sit there. Devon just played it cool, staring down at the stage, stretching his legs out in the small space there was to do so. He leaned back on his elbows. Cass pulled her knees up again, glanced at his stretched body, then back to the aisle. The drums section subsided and Jerry toyed with some notes. Devon leaned over and whispered to Cass, "We could get a 'Dark Star'."

"Oh?"

"Never know," he said. As the song formed on stage, her guy came back, standing on the edge of the lawn, staring at them. Cass pulled her body in and flicked her head towards the aisle.

Chapter 54
Rowen

Rowen had ducked out during "Terrapin" to go to the bathroom. He wanted to push that song away. He loved its melody and the entry it made into another world, but that journey was too much for him now. He felt it took all he had to stay connected to the ground, or to not break down crying like a little girl. He remembered sitting in Nick's Brooklyn apartment a few years back, blasting the "Terrapin" from that show where Penny's friend, Angie, peaked too hard after the show and jumped off the side of a building. She thought she could fly. Rowen didn't want to think about it. Penny moped around for months and turned her grief into anger. He remembered trying to soothe her and imagine that Angie was in another world, being free and doing ghostly things, like trying to whisper into Bobby's ear what he should play next or controlling the soundboard when she didn't like the length of Space during a show. He tried to make her laugh. It had shaken him though. "Terrapin" was always mixed for him after that.

He couldn't fucking believe that he'd run into Jasmin. What a bitch. He'd hated the way she looked him up and down and judged Cass. So, Penny was on tour. Who the fuck cared. Rowen hadn't seen her in half a year. It was easy to avoid someone on tour, as long as you didn't go looking for them. But as Rowen had come out of the bathroom, he imagined what she'd look like, standing there waiting for him like she had many times. She'd give him a big smile, skip over and take his hand. She was bold, and gorgeous. But she was no good. He knew that. When Rowen walked back to the lawn, his hands were shoved into his pockets as "Terrapin" played out. Nah, he didn't need her cunning shit. He was better off on his own, or with a more innocent girl like Cass. He could teach Cass things about tour and she would soak it up, if she could keep up and not have to slink back to Kansas. Cass wouldn't act like she knew everything. She knew practically nothing. This made Rowen grin to himself.

He walked down the concrete slope, scanning the grass for Cass's back. When he spotted her, he noticed someone sitting next to her. Eh, people moved in to empty spots all the time. He'd just go in and make some space. As he got closer though, he saw it was a big, older dude and he was leaning into Cass and she was smiling a little. Hmm. When he came to the row, Cass turned her head and smiled, but with a short look of panic on her face. She turned back and told the guy he had to move. He nodded and got himself up. Rowen waited.

"Bye Devon," Cass said.

"See ya gal," he answered her.

Those words unnerved Rowen. Ok, so she knows this guy, too. As the dude walked towards the aisle, Rowen could swear he knew him. His eyes were caged with wrinkles and his scraggly hair, oily. Rowen pursed his lips and when the guy got closer, he turned his back to pass him. Rowen smelled a strong scent, like fire and dirt but also something sweet and dead. "Hey, man," the man's deep voice shot into Rowen's chest. He contorted his face, trying to remember who the fuck the guy was. Rowen didn't say anything but stepped onto the grass and sat down next to Cass. Who the fuck?

"Thanks for holding my spot," he said sarcastically.

"I'm sorry, I," she shrieked.

"Hey, it's ok, I'm kidding," he said smiling. Rowen caught Devon's frame out of the corner of his eye, noticing he was still around. Rowen then leaned in to place his lips on Cass's. He put his hand on her hair, too. She just melted into him. Yeah. Show that fucker, he thought.

Tour could be so brutal, just like life. Everyone, when they were out to party, often let their morals fall down and hide under the gaze of partying. But, when tour was life, it wasn't so fun to do that. He'd been burned. He would mark his things and his territory now, like a fucking coyote if he had to. Rowen settled in and lit up a pipe to smoke with Cass. That guy was still hanging around, leaning up against the railing, right where he could still see them. Cass wasn't going anywhere; she had moved even closer to Rowen. She was naïve about people. She liked them too easily. The bud soothed him. The boys began a new song, and the crowd swayed. *"The circle is moving"* Rowen took Cass's hand and could feel her nerves alight. It didn't make his chest hurt so much but made him feel powerful. He looked to the aisle and saw the guy looking straight at him, his nose pointing. Rowen saw the guy's one sharp, curved earring and he fucking remembered. The guy had run into him in Kentucky, at that campground. What an asshole, Rowen thought. But he also remembered the fear of that bad trip and the way the acid gave him visuals. Rowen looked over and saw it again, the guy's face, not as a face. Not as something normal.

"And it's coming back around," he heard and gripped Cass's hand.

She shouted a little, "Ow! That hurts!" she pulled her hand away.

The guy turned his bird-like head to the side, and Rowen's flash subsided. But as he watched the man's rounded body walk away, he felt something even more familiar, like he'd seen him off tour somewhere.

"Oh, sorry," he said lifting Cass's fingers to his lips. Everyone around them had stood up as the band moved into the last song of the set. Rowen stood and helped Cass up, too. He looked to the aisle, trying to glimpse that guy again. The one Cass knew as Devon. Bobby was crooning into the mic. Rowen wrapped his arms around Cass, standing behind her, and tried to bend his knees to the music. He stayed close to her, and he could tell she was cool with that. But his mind was somewhere else, trying to track something familiar and strange, in him, in the air.

Chapter 55
Percy

Percy trudged his mud caked boots down the rain-ravined streets with ramshackle houses built on both sides. The other miners wanted those houses, wanted to make a life right there for themselves. All Percy wanted to do was save money and leave. It wasn't easy though, the pay was slim, and the mining company had everything set up to make them spend every last bit of it, right there. Percy carefully kept track though and ate only what he absolutely had to, and didn't drink his wages away, like many men did.

He swung open the screen door of the little post house. Five men were cooling out in there, their faces drawn low as Percy felt his was most of the time. They just shook their heads.

"No mail this week," one man with soot smudges across his forehead said. The weight in Percy's chest just built upon itself, and the damp from the consistent rain ached in his bones. He nodded his head and left the place. At least there was green surrounding the hole he crawled into every day. It was after hours. He knew he should conserve his energy for the next day's work. Yet, he climbed the hill, keeping his head on the dewy green shoots. He was one of the few that sought foods from the earth around there. For one, he had to walk a ways to find hills untrampled by others. And when he did, the miner's lettuce was few and far between. Still, when he did get a spicy mouthful, it brought him back home, just for an instant. He knew it was full of vitamins for him, too.

Conserving, keeping strong, working hard, was the most important thing. The sound of the train drew close by and Percy let the screech of tracks soothe him. Soon, he'd be back on the train again, soon he'd get back home. Soon he'd be able to resume his life in the Southeast, even if Molly wasn't there no more.

Chapter 56
Hettie

"Where you at, black cat?" Hettie screeched into the receiver, "It's your grandmother. Give me a call, I'm wondering about you." She hung up, not knowing if the message would reach Rowen or not. It'd probably take a few days anyhow. He could be far across the country for all she knew. Lately, Hettie found herself sitting on her couch, under a ceiling fan, praying that somehow, Rowen would stop all the traveling and get into some real work, real life. What he kept up doing just seemed scattered to her. She didn't think anyone could be grounded or sane without being connected to a piece of ground, the rhythms of land or habit. For so many years, her own life was ruled by the sun going up and the sun coming down, by cows and mealtimes and times when calves were born. She didn't ever have time for wanderings. Occasionally, she'd join the ranch hands on horseback to go look for a stray cow, but most of the time she spent in a cramped kitchen churning out meals for hungry workers or solving numerous numbers problems having to do with the ranching business. When she had time to stop, she always hung laundry, tucked her girl into bed, pulled thread through cloth for a new quilt.

It seemed, these days, that the hot sun took so long to find the horizon, and Hettie just waited inside for its heat to dissipate. She'd pulled photo albums out and had been looking through them. Everyone was so young, so full of life. She saw her Jessie, in a photo taken from the cabin's window: hair flying behind her, long and ravenesque. She saw her with the three boys crouching close. Then a loose photo tucked in between the dull plastic pages, of her and Violet, maybe when they were five tumbles out. Those two. They'd always grasped each other like sisters. They looked nothing alike, Jessie with her dark hair and pointed features, and Violet with gold-brown hair and big eyes.

Almost as soon as the sun slipped away, and she was fiddling in her kitchen for some dinner, she heard the creak of her rocker. Her granddaddy was back, rocking and bouncing his leg. He looked dirty this time and broken. It made her wonder, and she poured a little whisky and walked back towards the living room, making a wide arc around him and taking time to sit on the couch. There was no candle. It seemed too hot for that. Hettie breathed in the strong scent of him. It was like a days-old campfire, and leather and sweat. It reminded her of the ranch hands who used to tromp in and out of the big cabin.

She looked over at him. His head was down, and it looked like he was staring at that dirt, but his leg kept bouncing. "What is it?" she ventured to ask. He lifted his head but didn't look straight at her.

"What're you doing with all this land you got," he asked, looking over his shoulder out towards the window. Hettie's gaze moved out the window. She thought for a few minutes. The land was just the land nowadays. Before, it'd been for grazing and growing alfalfa. She liked that it'd been able to return to its more natural state, like her days. She knew she could rent it out, maybe, but the thought of noisy tractors going in her front yard, as she now thought it, didn't seem so nice.

"Nothin', I guess," she said. Her granddaddy looked out the window again, real sad, and she wondered what he would do with it if he could. Guess, she didn't realize how good it really was. Maybe through his old eyes he could. She turned her thoughts to Rowen again and wondered what his life would've been like if he'd grown up with her and Wilson. Hettie watched her granddaddy's gaze move up the wall to the quilt. He was squinting at it, maybe studying the pattern.

He looked back down. "You don't know how good you got it here," he said and shook his head, let his leg tap up and down again.

"Mm," Hettie said, closing her eyes and nodding. In her mind's eye, she flashed on all the work that'd been done over the years there. She knew the land was getting hard. It was not being used. She didn't want anything happening there anymore. It was too much for her to think about.

Chapter 57
Cass

Cass watched the black van drive away, down a street, one she didn't know. Rowen had bought her a $67.00 ticket in the bus station, back to Kansas City. They shopped in the little convenience store and he bought her food for the nine-hour bus ride. Then he hugged her limply and left. He left. Stuck inside Cass's chest was a hole the size of a baseball. She looked around at the somewhat grimy bus station. She noticed people sitting, people reading, people sipping coffee, shuffling newspapers, going in and out of the bathroom. She checked the big red-lettered board. The bus left in an hour. Rowen left to head East. Cass wanted to go with him. She wanted to be near him all the time. What the heck did she have to go back to Kansas for.

"Oh," Rowen had said, when she told him her mom was kind of mad. "You should go back to Kansas." Did he want her to leave? Cass's mind skipped back to standing in the hallway at the Deer Creek show, and the way that girl looked her up and down. The memory singed the skin around the hole in her heart. Then she remembered the way Rowen did grab her hand and pull her down the hall. She remembered the way his body felt next to hers on the back bed, not three hours before. Now she found herself standing alone in a bus station.

Cass tried to calm down and sink into the plastic seat. Her foot tapped unconsciously, and she took a deep breath, pulled her backpack into her chest, on her lap. It was summer, she was away from Kansas, she'd just seen a slew of Grateful Dead concerts, she had a boyfriend, maybe. Across the station, Cass spotted a young couple, definitely Deadheads. They were weighted down with big backpacks and sleeping bag rolls. Cass smiled, feeling slightly less alone and let her gaze hook to their colored tie dye shirts and dreaded hair. They seemed very different from Rowen. Even though he lived his life on the road, he kept clean, cleaner than many of the hippies she'd seen. But being on the road was being on the road, and Cass could smell her own BO, seeping through her t shirt, making her smell like her high school locker room at the end of gym class. Her mom was not going to love the way she smelled. Cass went into the bathroom. Looking at herself in the scratched mirror, she seemed different. Her hair was messy and greasy, her lips red and puffed out, her eyes full of tiny reddened lines. She was exhausted. She hadn't really slept and had consumed more pot than she ever had, hadn't eaten much and danced her ass off. She smiled at herself and liked the way her teeth stood out. She was dirty and tired and sad and lonely and moved, but she knew she'd done something more interesting than anything else in her life before. She was not in Kansas anymore, and she liked it.

Cass walked in the front door at 6:30pm. Thank God, her mom wasn't home yet. Cass beelined for her bedroom, tore off her clothes and got into the shower quickly. She was beyond tired, and every part of her body hurt. She scrubbed her skin and hair and got out and used the hair dryer. She wanted to look clean; she wanted to *be* clean. It seemed necessary to fit in there. She pulled on clean jeans and a plain t shirt and pulled her hair into a ponytail. Her mom still wasn't home at 6:50pm. Cass opened the fridge, felt her feet on the kitchen tile. She started to relax as she pulled a tin foil covered pan out of the fridge, cut a wedge of some lasagna that was in there and put it in the microwave. The shush of the microwave and little pops and hisses from inside it caught her ear. She thought she was listening differently. She'd heard so much music, so many sounds other than the ones she knew so well in this kitchen. The beep went off three times, and then the front door creaked open. Cass took a breath in, pulled her hot plate out and took it to the kitchen table. She sat down casually and started to eat. She heard her mom's keys clang on the coffee table, she heard her bag thud to the floor, she heard silence and space in between those movements. Then she heard her mom slowly close the door and lock it.

Cass looked up. Her mom came into the kitchen, leaned against the wall and stared at her. She looked just about as tired as Cass felt. Her mom stood there with her arms crossed and shook her head slowly. Cass looked down and kept eating. She could feel heat rising in the back of her neck. She hated her mom's judging. "What?" she said a little too loud, with lasagna still in her mouth. Cass's mom stopped shaking her head, turned and walked out of the kitchen without saying anything. Cass finished and put her dish in the dishwasher, like an adult. She got a glass of water and sat back down. She put her head down on the kitchen table over her arms. Damn, she could fall asleep right there. Cass was actually happy to be home. The comfort and smell of that kitchen let her relax for the first time in over five days. Life on tour was a blast, but it was fricking hard, too, and she didn't know anything. She knew this place though. Knew it like the back of her hand. Her eyes got droopy, and she was nearly falling asleep when her mom came back into the kitchen.

"How could you do this to me,"

Cass sucked in some air. Her mom was staring, tears streaming down her face. Cass rubbed her eyes and looked again. "What?" was all she could say.

"What the hell do you mean, what!?" Cass's mom sneered, "Cass, I was worried sick. Sick, like puking, shaking sick."

Cass straightened up, tried to find someplace inside her head for this. It was the last thing she wanted. She just wanted to rest.

"I'm sorry," Cass managed to say. Her head started to hurt. She didn't like seeing her mom like this. She knew she was in trouble, but she hadn't wanted her mom to be sick about it.

"You have no idea how upset I've been."

Cass crossed her arms and felt the chair slats against her back. Her folded arms were keeping her upright. She shook her head.

"Well, you should think about it. What in the world has gotten into you? It was that girl, wasn't it?"

Cass shook her head again, not really having the energy to do more to defend Hillary.

"And you look like hell. Have you been doing a bunch of drugs or something?"

Cass let her head drop into her hands. This was stupid. Her mom was stupid. She wasn't a little girl anymore. Lots of people her age partied. Just because she hadn't before, didn't mean she'd never wanted to. Jeez. Cass slugged some of her water. Through her exhaustion, she felt annoyance, she felt resentment. She just wanted to do what she wanted to do. Her mom was overreacting. Cass stood up.

"Answer me!" her mom shouted.

Cass turned around and glared at her. "I'm not twelve, Mom. Jesus, I just graduated high school!"

"Hmm!" her mom said. "Well, you're a long way from being an adult!"

Cass had had enough. She filled her water again and left the kitchen. She went into her room, shut and locked the door and fell asleep on top of her bed with her clothes on.

Chapter 58
Devon

Devon decided it was time to go back West. He longed for the quiet and solitude of his cabin. As his bike buzzed down the highway, his mind whipped to the last show, when he'd sat down by that girl Cass, and her slick ass boyfriend. He'd tracked him, in his mind, to Mrs. Jones' daughter, the one he sort of grew up around. The one he knew had moved to California and had a few kids. He vaguely remembered her return, seeing her on his road, and carting her three boys.

That Rowen was one of them. He'd just been a kid. Now he was on Dead tour and acting all cool and apparently not treating young women well. Devon's mind switched to Emmajean. Someday, she would grow up to be a young woman, too. The thought of her ever being treated unkindly irked him. His hands trembled on the bike handles. His ass ached from riding so long. He wouldn't be there to protect her; he wouldn't be there to school a young man if she was ever treated like Cass. Anger welled in Devon's chest and he sped his bike up and passed a Sudan. He just wanted to get home. He thought of the dusty road, and the steep curve of Crystal Mountain. He thought of the quiet sway of trees behind his cabin and the other birds that darted around there constantly. He wondered if he would ever see Emmajean, if she'd ever get to walk around the land and cabin he'd always wanted to share with her. She was in some stupid suburban neighborhood in California. He knew he could teach her so much more about life and nature than Cora ever could. Devon wondered if Emma ever thought of him. If she could form her own opinion of a father who had been unallowed to see her. Devon was sure Cora painted him a devil or a no good. Devon could hear Cora's meanness as she told his daughter that her father was in jail, was never coming back. Someday, maybe he would. She might get to an age when she could think for herself, and he imagined being there for that.

Chapter 59
Rowen

Rowen steadied his gaze on the lines at the edge of the highway: white, white, white, black pavement, white. He tried to clear his head with the monotony of driving on 70. Just driving. It was another long stretch from Indianapolis to D.C. Part of him was tired, but the road was what he had to focus on, what kept him occupied.

When he'd driven those nine hours, and traffic started backing up near the city, he toked up, listened to music, followed the route he knew. He had a mail order ticket for RFK. It was a big stadium, impersonal, but he wanted to be there. Now with the jumble of cars trying to thread through a jammed city, he wondered. Why the fuck *was* he here? It was about as far as he could get from California. As far from the memory of his mom. It felt good to be thousands of miles from there, even if for a few days. He knew he'd go back, he'd see shows in Oakland and San Francisco and at some point he'd be right back in her apartment parking lot in the San Fernando Valley. She just wouldn't be there anymore, that's all that would be changed. Rowen tried to get his head around that as he pulled into the Dead parking lot that somehow had opened to Heads the night before the show. It was pretty quiet and he jumped out, locked up and started walking. There were johns on the far side of the lot.

A little while later Rowen was curled in the back of the van, pulling the quilt around him. It was quiet, there was no one else in there with him, Ollie had said he couldn't afford it and needed to check in with his family in Indiana. Nick was riding with some gal he'd met and Changa never showed to ask for a ride. Rowen could feel a swell in his chest, burning like he'd eaten a bad cheeseburger, like he had a bruise there. He thought about how his mom must have died, alone, scared, shaking and writhing by herself on her bed. The burn swelled to Rowen's throat, and he pulled the quilt tighter around him. Fuck, fuck, fuck. He didn't want to feel it. He wanted it to leave him. But now nothing could keep the hard set he always held. Rowen gasped, then coughed, as tears streamed down his face. His limbs trembled, he pulled the quilt tight, he could feel the strength in his gripping fingers. Fuck this, fuck this. Rowen heard himself sob. It was so fucking pitiful; he was acting like a baby. Stop it, he told himself. But he couldn't stop his body from shaking, his skin felt cold, his nose was clogged. He pulled an old shirt from under the bed, and held it to his face, blowing hard. He sat up, leaning into his knees and trying to steady his shaking. All he could think about was the way his mom looked, so disheveled when he found her, so still. It was a fight, she'd fought death. Rowen smiled a little thinking how strong his mom had always been. Shit, he shook his head. Why'd she have to go. Rowen realized that he'd actually needed her strength. It kept him solid when he traveled everywhere, doing his thing. The fact that she wouldn't be there, back in Cali, was terrible, empty, tragic.

Rowen stumbled to the front of the van, reaching to the visor and pulling it down. Nothing was there. A panic flared in his chest, and Rowen heard himself gasp again. Then he looked out the front window, aware that he was packed in a tight parking lot, but no one was looking at him. Then he remembered, and his trembling hand opened the glove compartment where the folded photo was laying on top. He took it back to the bed, curling up again under the quilt and holding it out, staring with his head sideways. He had the photo; it was his mom. She was happy then, outside at Gran's place in New Mexico. She was much younger, and free. It seemed like she loved the place, loved being away from L.A. She always told them to run around in the forest on the flat side across the road from the cabin. Things were safe there, she said, and Rowen knew she meant compared to L.A., where for years she tried to keep him and his brothers close. Once he started skateboarding and drinking and meeting girls, Rowen thought, she just hoped we'd come home at night. Rowen's heart ached as he thought about how hard it must've been for her keeping tabs. He knew he was the least wild. Lou was always bad, and made his mom take off work to go to principal's offices, and later, police stations. Tate just broke her heart with the drug use. He hung around her apartment, but she was always keen-eyed with him, studying the sag of his posture or the droop of his eyes. Rowen had decided it was best to stay away, give her one less to think about. But, thinking back now, imagining her hand on his back when he'd come in from tromping the forest near Gran's house, he realized maybe it would've been better if he'd stuck around—instead of being always on Dead tour.

Rowen heard a small crowd shouting outside his van. They were obviously drunk and starting the party a day early. Rowen wiped his face again, gently set the photo on the ice box and turned into his pillow to sleep. There was no point in getting off tour now, she was gone.

The show fucking sucked for him. That's all Rowen could focus on as he buckled his seat belt and steamed out of the parking spot. It was far enough after the show, so the lines out were moving. He didn't even want to listen to The Dead. He searched the middle console for other music, Bob Marley, CSN, Phish, Van Morrison were lined up there. None of it sounded good. Rowen opened the window, pulled the side mirror in a little, and hopped on the highway, in silence. His head hurt, his heart hurt. He sped up, dodging some slow-moving trucks and hippie vans. Now, he just wanted to cover ground, get away from the big fucking city. He had close to 3000 miles to cover till he reached California, and he was driving alone again.

When he cleared the city limits, he calmed down a little and popped in Bob Marley, "Trenchtown Rock," it was 11:55pm. He held the wheel with his knee and pulled the Velcro cover off the steering wheel. His little pipe was there and he filled it quickly, glancing up at the road. He found a lighter, and sucked hard, then blowing out and filling the van with white smoke.

He'd decided to go South, through Virginia and pick up 64 to Louisville. He was getting tired of the fucking Midwest, Ohio, Indiana, Illinois—all those corn-fed assholes. The pot soothed him, and he cracked the windows and relaxed back in his seat, for the long haul. He thought of Jerry mixing up the words to "Warf Rat," then "Stella" in the second set. It made him sad. Why had he gone to RFK, anyway. Somehow, the movement was all he'd wanted, now he had a whole bunch more of it stretched out in front of him. The hum of the van steadied him. He saw signs showing he'd passed into West Virginia. Bob Marley went around again, and he let it. Rowen tried breathing, in and out, in and out. The road was dark and empty. Fine, he thought, just fine. He sped up a little, wanting to catch ground, make good time.

A few minutes later, he looked in the side mirror and saw rolling red lights coming up fast behind him. "Shit, God Dammit," he said aloud, pressing his foot into the break, turning the stereo down. Then he heard the sirens. He scanned the console, looking for anything incriminating. pot was tucked back, and he pressed the steering wheel to make sure the cover was secure. "Here we go," he said, pulling over to the side, listening to the gravel come under his tires. He straightened up, kept his hands on the wheel. The cop car pulled up right behind him, the lights still twirling and piercing Rowen's eyes in the side mirror. He waited. The man that emerged was tall and big, and wearing a fucking Smokey The Bear hat. Great, fucking highway patrol bastard, he thought. Rowen watched the man saunter up next to his van, hand on gun. Rowen waited. It would be better if he'd had Cass with him, he thought for a minute, she was so innocent looking. He glanced out the closed window, hands still on the wheel, so the fucker could see them. Knuckles rapped hard, and he motioned the window to be rolled down. Rowen watched his eyes, then slowly rolled the window down, placing his hands back on the wheel.

"Well, well," he said in a thick Southern drawl. "What you doing out here, with your California tags?"

"I am driving back from D.C. sir." The guy smelled like cigarettes and shit.

"Long way from home."

"Yes, sir."

"License and papers," the man nearly shouted.

Rowen looked at him. "They're in the glove box. Can I get them?"

"You better hurry," he said, placing his hand firmly on his gun.

Rowen slowly reached over and opened the glove box. His license was on top, but the insurance papers were buried. Fuck. He started shuffling through.

"What the hell you got in there, boy?"

Rowen's mind wanted to explode. Maybe the Midwest would have been better, these Southern fuckers just wanted to prove their worth to anyone out of state. "my insurance is in here, I just…"

"Hurry it up!" Rowen looked over to see the man step back and reach

for his gun. Papers started dropping out of the glove box and the picture,
of his mom he'd put back there, fell to the floor. He glanced down, her
face darkened and smiling. It burned his chest. He searched some more
and found the paper. He slowly leaned back up and stuck it and his license
out the window. The cop looked at him, narrowing his eyes. He shined
his small flashlight on the papers.

"Van Nuys, where the hell is that?"

"California, sir. Near Los Angeles."

The cop snickered. Rowen's stomach turned.

"Get out of the van, Mr. Slater."

Rowen looked at him, started getting angry. This fucker. He was
determined to keep his cool though. He knew that was the only quick
way out of this.

"Yes sir." Rowen opened the door, and stepped out, he let his bare feet
hit the black pavement. The cop immediately looked down.

"What? You drive this fancy van and can't afford shoes?" Shit, Rowen
forgot that could be a problem.

"I have shoes officer, it's just more comfortable to drive barefoot."

The cop slowly shook his head, slicing the air with the rim of his broad
hat. He tucked Rowen's license and paper in his pocket and put his hand
on his gun again.

"Up against the van, spread your hands and feet!"

What the fuck. Rowen did what he was told. Now his bladder was full
and he wanted to just piss all over the stupid man. He placed his hand,
spread out on the van's side, and opened his legs. The cop came up right
behind him and started patting his body roughly. The hands hitting the
back of his greasy hair.

"You smell like a sty."

Rowen bit his tongue, until the cop reached in his pocket. Rowen
flinched.

"Don't you move."

Rowen started sweating. He looked around at the ground lit by his
headlights. It was fucking dark beyond them and it was a desolate road.
He started getting scared and telling his body what to do if the cop went
too far. He whipped a small piece of paper from his pocket. A ticket.

"Well, looky here, a concert ticket. The Grateful Dead. RFK Stadium,"
the cop read.

"Yes, sir. It's not illegal to attend a concert."

"Don't you tell me what is and isn't legal!"

"Yes sir." This was getting old. Rowen felt sleepy and defeated.

"Don't move. I'm gonna run your numbers."

Rowen was silent, keeping his hands and feet planted. He could feel the gravel pressing into his calloused feet. He turned his head to watch the cop walk slowly back to his car. Once inside, he turned a spotlight on Rowen. It was so bright, it stung and Rowen just kept his face forward, closing his eyes, trying to breathe again, in and out, in and out.

Chapter 60
Hettie

"Get out of my field, you no good son of a bitch," Hettie shouted. The man in the dirty jeans and work shirt didn't hear nothing. He was gazing up at Crystal Mountain, so Hettie barked again. She leaned over the edge of her porch and raised her walking stick in the air.

"Did you hear me?"

The man didn't move. Her feet creaked on porch wood. Hettie watched the man's uneven swagger as he walked on, his brown boot heels sinking into the mud. No good fool. She'd seen it before, the mountain's call, pulling the unsatisfied to its slope. She'd seen the young or the stupid scaling its edges that were steeper than they looked. She had her own relationship with Crystal Mountain. Leave and let be. Watch the sun climb over its head only.

Next day, round noon, Hettie saw the man again. Same spot, same look. She yelled at him and he didn't budge. She waved her stick, making a nuisance of herself. And when he turned around, Hettie saw a weathered face, thick lines creasing his skin. But again, he walked off. Maybe he's a ghost, Hettie thought, feeling the weight of too many of them walking around her parts.

Another day and a knock at her door kicked Hettie's stomach. "What do you want" she said, moving to the door. She surveyed the man standing in the doorway: greasy long hair and thick motorcycle boots. "Who are you? Why you bothering me?" Hettie said. Then after studying this face, she realized he was probably Peggy's son, the one who'd been in and out of jail in the past few years.

"I live up there, Devon Maxwell," he said, his movements were slow as he pointed up the road. "I'm not bothering your land, just want to climb," and he let his hand sway lazily towards the mountain.

"Why?"

"Just want to."

"It's a dumb idea," she said, wondering again how Percy Maxwell's kid could grow up so bad. As far as she knew, all he did was run a loud motorcycle past her place.

"Why's that?" he said in a low raspy voice. Hettie saw dullness in his eyes. He was glazed in a way she knew. A way grief can grip the nerves and twist things up to couch the dead. She turned her back and moved inside. She left the door open, left it up to him.

"I know you're Peggy's son," Hettie said from her living room.

"Yes."

"Sit down," she said. He sat. She plunked in her rocking chair with a sigh that seemed to deflate her anger. Hettie both wanted to keep this delinquent son of her husband's dead farm hand in check and also some part of her wanted to keep him from doing something foolish, or dangerous.

"You know those trails ain't marked up there," she said, measuring two scant pours of whisky into two cloudy glass cups.

"Ma'am—what do you know about that mountain?" Devon asked.

She just looked at him and poured another swig for herself. He said a few more words about height and climbing, but as he spoke, Hettie could feel her own grief swirling and cutting off her sensible mind. Hettie looked at the blue quilt and the bird's head trace that had become crystal clear. She swallowed her whisky and slid the other cup towards this man. "I've lived by it for forty years, that's all," she said. Hettie watched his calloused hands lift the cup and down the whisky. "It's too steep from the middle up and there ain't no damn crystals up there."

Devon smiled a little. "I just want to get up there, up above everything, you know?"

"Do what you're gonna do," she said and got up, moving towards the kitchen. She didn't say anything else, just glanced once back at the door. He was old enough to make his own bed, this one, she decided. Devon stared at the empty cup on her table, got up, nodded at her once, and walked out the open door.

Chapter 61
Devon

Devon had been home for nearly a week, and at first the solitude nurtured him, but then he just felt sad. He couldn't clear all the things in his mind: Emmajean, Cora, wanting so badly to be something other than human that it hurt. He started drinking during the day. He walked out into the fields in front of Mrs. Jones' cabin. The clouds gaining clout above her cabin. She'd cursed him, filling the air with obscenity. All he'd ever heard from his Pop was that Mrs. Jones was not to be crossed. Devon was thinking he should climb the mountain. He used to think that as a kid, in the summer, but everyone kept him home or working on the ranch. He wanted to be closer to the sky. The pines jutting, the black rock peaking at the top, promised height. Devon wanted lift.

Finally, he just went up to her house. She seemed so bitter, as she left her door open for him to come inside. The cabin was dusty, but the walls were hung with bright quilts that made it feel friendly. She thought climbing the mountain was a stupid idea. Who cares, Devon didn't feel like he had much to lose. He wanted out of his skin. Maybe being in his skin and exercising or something could help him.

The next day Devon laced his boots tight. He brought a jacket and a bottle. Nights of whisky and burned out mind, alone in that low-ceiling shack had cramped his blood. He went to the field in front of Mrs. Jones' cabin, but cut down the side way, so he didn't have to pass too close to her place. Three hundred yards up the mountain and Devon was winded more than he thought he'd be. Smoke-scented breath heaved in and out of his chest. Even this slight elevation thinned the air and made it enter the lungs like mint. It was late morning, and the birds darted from pine to pine, gathering twigs and bugs. He couldn't see a buck's big antler poked though pines, or a beetle stopping its crawl near his black boot heel, or two squirrels leaning over branches and studying the oily surface of his head.

As he marched on, Devon shifted his mind from Emmajean's face to the rock face. He stepped up, leaving flat land behind. He walked for nearly two hours, not noticing much at all. Then, somewhere up through a tall stand of trees, Devon thought he saw a person. He thought he heard the low whine of a harmonica. He slowed his pace, cautious not to scare the man. Closer now, Devon saw a beard so mangy and tangled it looked like a bear's face. The man had a leather cap and a large, hunched body.

"Well, looky here," the man said as Devon approached. He stood up and moved, severely bow-legged.

Something in Devon turned over and he almost retched, sensing the man's odor. He drew his elbow close to his face and sneezed.

"*Gazunderheighten!*"

"Uh, thanks," Devon said. He watched the man sit back down on a boulder and smile.

"What are you doing up here?" the man said.

"Just walking," Devon answered. But when he said it, he felt as though he'd needed somebody's permission, not just his own feet deciding to climb.

"I see that," the man said. "But what are you doing here?" he repeated. The man didn't wait for his answer and went back to his harmonica, playing a cowboy tune.

Devon waited a minute, then lifted his hand and walked on, feeling the slope of earth incline. That was fucking weird, Devon thought as he listened for the lingering harmonica, or the jovial and reprimanding voice, but both had faded. Instead he noticed the sun and the pop of its rays on tree trunks, hot sap releasing. Maybe the elevation was causing him to hallucinate.

Three hundred yards more and Devon entered another grove of trees. These seemed to be set in ringed patterns, one two three four five, then another set of five—all with five feet circling in between. Devon's boots pressed the ground layered with pine needles. It was spongy. Standing in the center of one ring, Devon stretched his arms to the side and touched the bark of two. His breastbone lifted. He sought a deep breath that wouldn't come. When a bird, nothing stopped his breath, no shudders. He closed his eyes, freeing his mind, trying to conjure.

Little girl's laughter broke the reverie, and Devon dropped his arms. He looked out the ring and watched as a girl in a yellow and pink dress skipped through the trees. She was being chased by another girl in three-quarter pants. Their giggles sounded through the forest. Devon ducked, not wanting to be seen, trying to get his heart rate to slow. What the fuck. Why are little girls up here? They didn't seem to be with an adult. He would never let Emma go running around on the side of a mountain forest alone. Are these ghosts or something? He wasn't afraid, just startled, and a little concerned. The two kids wove in an out of the tree patterns, oblivious to anything but their game. The air around Devon felt thick, viscous. He lifted his bottle from the ground, took a good swig and left that part of the forest, fast. He started thinking there was a reason folks didn't climb up here when he was young.

Just keep going, just keep climbing. The day was clearly half gone now, and still a thousand feet of mountain sloped above him. Devon renewed his conviction, the one alternative to moping in his shack for days. Just go up there and find it. Find that part that flies. Yeah, Crystal Mountain was not an ordinary place. Yeah, probably ghosts, but they were no different from thoughts that'd sucked his mind in prison.

Devon, ravaged without water, without shade, found a boulder and collapsed on its flat top. He watched the clouds streaming overhead, squinted his eyes to see tiny particles swimming everywhere in the air. Then he rolled a smoke, lit a match and drew in comfort. As he pulled tobacco into him, Devon wondered what his life would have been like if Cora had let him stay.

A loud caw cut through his thoughts and Devon saw the black body of a raven looking down on him from a treetop. He blew out smoke and let it cloud his sight; let it stand between him and the bird. It cawed again and lifted, flying to another nearby tree. Devon watched it, wished for it. Didn't want to say anything to it. It was a solo one, just like he wanted. The bird leapt again, and Devon saw a jagged wing, missing some feathers. It flew towards the top of the mountain.

You're fine, Keep going, keep walking. Devon heaved his legs. He was close to the angled rock slope, black slate that led to the top. He could see down the mountain now, too. The old woman's house was small like a building block. He could see the snake-wind of the stream on her field. He was a long way above.

Devon crouched as he climbed the rocks. They were hot and slick and sharp. He felt his blood race and lungs constrict. His hands shook but he kept going up, the swatch of land like this was wide and unburdened by trees. I could slide down and die right here, he thought, but Devon kept going, and once, when he had to stretch his leg up to reach the next rock, the bottle in his back pocket slipped out and tumbled down. Glass crashed and whisky sizzled to the ground. Shit. Devon leaned against the mountain, felt his chest heaving. He pressed his face against the slate, closed his eyes and heard, inside his mind, the glass crashing again—this time on hard pavement, too close to Cora's feet.

The top of Crystal Mountain was flat and scattered with pines, bent by the wind. After throwing up sour liquid, Devon laid on the ground for a long time, sometimes watching the clouds, sometimes following the fast part of sky behind closed lids. He did feel clearer up here, more himself.

The sun was now making its descent. Devon walked, upright, to the edge of the mountain, overlooking rocky cliff, overlooking grove after grove of sloping forest. He saw the slice of shadow over fields way below. Again, he opened his arms, steadying his feet, closing his eyes. He was on the edge. He breathed one long, deep human breath. And a loud CUH CAW broke behind him.

Chapter 62
Cass

Cass had been home for two days, and there was no word from Rowen. She wished she had a photo of him. All she had were so many details of him in her mind: his black hair, the way he swiveled his feet when he danced, how he held the steering wheel while driving, the length and tone of his arms when he picked up a cooler. She also had the memories running through her nerves, that even now, made her face go hot and her stomach drop. He was so different from the boys she knew from school. Well, being five years older than her helped that. He was a man. But a man who didn't really have a job, who traveled and lived in his van, and who, she suspected, sold drugs to keep afloat. Not exactly someone to bring home to her mother, but Cass didn't care. She thought Rowen was exciting and beautiful and he liked her, she thought. Cass remembered his call before Chicago. So, he did have her number. Cass went to the little pile of ticket stubs and pieces of paper on her desk. She smoothed the mail order and general admission tickets.

They were the remnants that went along with the songs in her head. The far-away sound of the Grateful Dead's music was with her all the time now. She liked "Birdsong," and "Jack Straw," and now "Terrapin." She thought she was becoming a Jerry fan, but Bobby was kinda cute. She knew Shakedown was the place to get anything on tour, and you just had to be patient driving in and out of the lot. She also knew that there were narcs around the scene, and also stupid people who got drunk and made the real Deadheads look bad. Cass's eyes were now opened beyond her small Kansas world, and she'd met people like Changa who got along without much and found everything he needed on the ground. He also had a giant heart and always a smile for her. Being on the tour made Cass question everything. It made her want to be out there, to explore, to discover people, places, songs, love. Cass took the ticket stubs to the shoebox under her bed and lay them on top of the postcards from her father. The wishes she'd always had of seeing the places in his photos seemed to be fading. She didn't need to go to Mongolia or Costa Rica for adventure. Fun times were right in America, beckoning her to Dead tour.

Chapter 63
Hettie

In her mind's eye, Hettie saw the black etch of a raven's wing, she saw the hunched shoulders of John Maxwell's son and the glimmer of spider strands in the air. It was nighttime and the hot slide of whisky had coated both her throat and her thoughts. As she moved back and forth, with the rocking chair's easy glide, she pictured Crystal Mountain—its steep slope, its sordid history, its ghosts. One thing for certain, that Devon didn't know what he could encounter up there.

Back in 1954 when the world followed straight lines and pretty dreams, when nearby cities were pictures of polish, Cueva, New Mexico was still in the dark. They all had outhouses back then and when someone's horse gave birth, everyone knew it. Stories had lingered for sixty years—native rustles with pioneers, gold diggers and wanna-get-rich men with hard land and weather—the place had been rough at the edges before and in '54 it pretty much still was. As far as Hettie was concerned, it made no difference whether tussles and outbreaks had happened six decades previous, because the spirits flying around the land made it seem like only yesterday.

It had been a busy year: Wilson planting hay in three fields, six calves born, Hettie's little girl almost five. It was well after late summer's end because the leaves were golden and orange, pumpkin and cocoa-brown by then. Peggy Maxwell was eight months pregnant then with her second, who came out in a wake of grieving. The two girls liked playing in all the wrong places—by Wilson's tool shack, the splintery wood piles, dusty rooms of neighbors' attics. Every which way Hettie turned around, seemed like those girls had a problem needed solving by someone else.

It wasn't an easy time for her neither, with the growing ranch, and all the details of paying ranch hands and getting the proper shots for every animal. All that was up to her, all the bills and such, plus cooking for nearly twenty two times a day.

Hettie's Jessie and Violet Maxwell had been gone way too long, and as the cows moaned in the lower field, Hettie started worrying. Finally, she sent the ranch boys out on horseback. When they came back an hour later with no trace of either girl, Hettie laced up her own boots. She sent one of those boys on over to sit with Peggy, who, if she didn't want that baby in her belly to come out too soon, just needed to stay calm. Hettie remembered her own long and horsing call: "V-i-i-l-e-t! Jessy-girl, get on home now!" Then she tried every which way of whistling and screaming, till her horse had just about had it. When the girls didn't come out from some hiding place or answer back with high pitched "Coming Mom!" Hettie looked up the mountain. None of them went up there, and the girls knew it. But they were short enough that brush had not fully covered the old trails to their eyes.

Hettie and Wilson, John and three other hands started up there, one horse's careful foot after another, the light leaving the sky. The shrill cries and low "Hiyah" of the men's voices seemed to slide through the air, become too thin to matter, and leave them all with heavy answering silence. Hettie remembered the black birds dipping over trees up there, eyeing their presence with unwelcomed glares. Even though the stories of the mountain spirits were on everyone's mind, their desperate search party overruled.

John saw 'em first, crumpled at the base of a rocky slope, not a quarter up the mountain. His daughter's left leg twisted and still bleeding. Her hair damp and sticky, framing small motionless eyes. They must've fallen from way up and gotten knocked clear out, Violet wracked by the rush of ground against body. Hettie remembered hearing John gasp as he sucked in the thin air of shock. Then she remembered her own little girl coming to. When she saw them, she started crying in long wails against her mamma's shaking chest. She rocked that girl, crying herself, and knowing that nothing would be the same around there again.

Wilson was the one that laid Violet's body over the front of his horse, John slumping, falling off his horse on the way back down, and finally needing to ride along with the smallest ranch hand.

At home Hettie laid her little girl with Wilson and went on up to Peggy. John crying like a lone cow, had sent that woman right into labor six weeks early, and eighteen hours later, Hettie's own hands caught the boy. Nobody talked about what happened after that, just trying to get Peggy to focus on the new baby in her arms.

Most people stayed away, for fear of what that God Forsaken mountain could do. Don't even think that boy got a blessing blanket, and Hettie and Wilson did all they could with money and land deeds, over the years, for the Maxwell's. John declined quickly though, day by day, drink by drink, and both that boy and Hettie's girl got out of town as soon as each could drive. It was ten years before Devon came back.

Chapter 64
Devon

Devon listened to the crisp rustle of tree leaves, to the coyote's moaning howl and the sharp breaks in his own thoughts. It was no picnic being up there in the half-light that trailed from a crescent moon. He wavered back and forth from fear of wicked, angry ghosts to not caring if he was torn to bits. Mostly he wanted to be part of the night, and the comfort a black raven found in shadowless spaces.

Crouching near two boulders that sheltered from the wind, Devon felt the cold earth near his ass. He trembled, drew tobacco from his pocket, rolled it and lit it with a match. Fire flared, illuminating the dark close around him and cutting out starlight. Shapes in the near distance rose and fell as the match ignited his white stick then burned out fast. Devon sucked in smoke, hoping the tobacco would keep away spirits. He didn't really know where he was on the mountain, just that it had gotten too dark to see a trail and was better to just stay where he was.

It gave him time to think, time to feel the raw power of nature—in her bold element. Somehow if I slow my blood down, he thought, that bird part might swoop and take me. Devon both wanted the shape-shift and wanted to let go of its promise. That search for unhuman feeling was like walking on a glass rope, easy to slip and fall to hard earth. On that slope, he'd felt it, and wishing on the edge of the cliff, he'd needed it. Devon was a junkie to his own dark longing. A longing that left him utterly alone— far away from any good memory.

"What're you doing up here?" a rough sound slid through Devon's ears. He leapt back, hitting his body against the rock and pounding with the sound of his heart in his throat.

"Who are you? What do you want?" Devon said, trying to stake his ground, trying to gauge in near-space the speaking shape. He quickly lit another match, as if light could banish a creature. It was a gaunt man, in an old jacket, and a worn hat. It looked like the same man who'd had a bird under his arm when he'd taken MDMA. Devon coughed and spat up phlegm.

"I said, what're you doing up here?"

In an instant, Devon heard his father's voice, mixed with a prison guard's tone and the sound made him sick. He retched on the ground, over burned out matches. He wiped his mouth, thought that somehow this man or this spirit knew him. He didn't want to be afraid and he let anger lead him. He'd wanted raven, not an intermediary. "I was walking. Trying to find something."

"Well, it's not up here, son. All your gonna find up here is death."

Devon didn't like the tone, but it reminded him of the old man who'd picked him up when his bike had crashed. That man just wanted to be kind, Devon remembered. But in his own thoughts, he wanted to rage, to spit and demand that the raven let him fly. He was sick of being a stupid man. But then quicker than his anger, a scene passed through Devon's mind. A little girl lay still on the ground. Then he viewed his father's face—crumpled and sick. Devon couldn't yell, he began coughing and coughing and feeling his insides heave. He turned towards the ground, felt the chill earth. The cold, an ally. "All you're gonna find up here is death." Devon wanted cold, he also wanted death to rip through and leave him unhuman. He felt a breaking in his chest, in his stomach, in the sharp ends of all his hair. This man watched him, unmoving and not quite kind.

Devon's body shook, and he heard his own wails like a train in the distance. He sobbed dry like a baby for a long time, flashing on his dead father's face, on his dead mother's face, on his dead sister's gravestone and finally on Emmajean's face, till sleep took hold and numbed him to the night.

When daylight spread swift, with its own open wings, Devon felt light on his face. He wasn't cold, but stiff and smooth like a train's empty track. A blue jay landed on the boulder and screeched, actually making him grin. His memory of the night was fuzzy. He just knew he wasn't at home and needed to get back to warmth and food. His legs barely bent, and for a long while, sloping downhill, he limped. Then the trail cleared and, over an edge, he saw the wide field, Mrs. Jones' cabin, and the other distant hills. He head for his shack, trying, but not able to remember why he'd come up there.

Chapter 65
Rowen

Rowen drove hard across the southern states, only slicing the top of Texas. He'd stopped at rest areas to sleep and kept to the speed limits. He didn't want any more brushes with the law. By now, he just wanted to be back in California. When he finally came to his home state just below the tip of Nevada, he felt like he could breathe better: the moist air, the proximity to the ocean, the fact that the Dead played most comfortably here. He drove on Highway 40, also taking comfort in the dry bush and low hills that continued the desert landscape he'd been watching through Arizona. He knew he'd need to dip down to the 10 and make his way into the Valley. He needed to get a pound, portion it and bring it 'round to his regulars. It'd been almost three weeks and folks would be running out about now. The dough Rowen would make fueled him, but he knew everyone would know about his mom, and he really didn't want to face their pity.

He dreaded condolences, pats on the back and, "let me know if there's anything I can do, man." That road would lead to an end, which he couldn't face yet. Eventually, he'd have to go back to his mom's place, where Lou would no doubt be blubbering, high and making stupid deals at the apartment, and Tate would be heating bits of tin foil in the bathroom and passing out on the couch. Not comforting. His tires buzzed through Barstow, and he instinctively took the turn for the 15 that would get him back to LA. He needed money. Before getting into the tangle of traffic, Rowen got off the highway for gas. He filled up, then pulled around to a pay phone. He heard the change of sounds, the first long ring, and then another.

"Hey, man, it's Row. What's going?"

"Hey, man. Ok."

"Alright."

"The same?"

"Yeah, two hours?"

"Sure. See ya."

Rowen clicked the phone, securing he'd meet his pick up for a pound of Mexican swag at a strip mall parking lot just south of Van Nuys in two hours. The guy would front the pound to Rowen and in a day or two Rowen would bring him back the money for it, like usual. It was a good connect. The guys were staples of the San Fernando Valley, deeply well connected and knew how to not get caught, despite their shiny ass, pumped up trucks. Rowen had been working with them for three or four years. He never socialized with them. They were probably into guns, and shit, but they worked with him well and he could trust them. Rowen dialed another number, read from the tiny scrap of paper where she'd written it. It would be about 9:00am in Kansas. The phone rang three times, and he was about to hang up, when he heard her voice.

"Hello."

"Cassidy?"

"Rowen? Is that you?"

He could feel a lighter feeling in his chest, when she said his name. He then knew he wanted her around. She could soften all the blows. Everyone would be so distracted that he had a new girl with him, that they'd barely mention his mom.

"Yeah. How's it going?"

"It's ok, but, you know, it's Kansas…"

"Ha! Yeah. Hey, wanna come out here?"

"Where are you?"

"Back in California. I could send you a ticket in a day or two if you want. There are shows in Oakland on the weekend."

"Oh my gosh, yes, that would be great! Thank you!"

"No problem. Hey, I'd like to chat, but I have to go. I'll call you back and let you know when."

"Wow, ok, that sounds good." She made some more sounds like she was about to ask him a load of questions, but he didn't want that.

"So, I'll call you back." Rowen hung up the phone. That was that. He'd get her there. They could just bum around The Valley till the shows on the weekend.

Hettie walked out on her back porch and gazed up Crystal Mountain. The sun was high and keeping things hazy. She scanned here and there, focusing on individual trees and straining her eyes to try to see him. She figured he'd gone up there, despite whatever she might have said about the mountain. Maybe he needed to face something, in himself. Still, Hettie worried about that giant man, who she'd once pulled out of his mother. She'd never had a maternal instinct towards him, but she knew about him, and she could feel his sadness. Besides, the fact that that bird in the quilt became crystal clearer to her when he'd been in her cabin, made her wonder. Hettie creaked on the wood slats of the porch and could feel tinges of pain from her ankle. It wasn't fully healed, maybe never would be. She'd probably have a little limp for the rest of her life. Who cared though, as long as she could get around ok. Hettie gazed down the hill to her outhouse. Indoor plumbing would be nice, damn, wish she'd insisted on that when she'd moved from the larger cabin ten years ago. But she'd got used to it and it had made her feel tough. Now, she mostly dreaded walking down there, worrying she'd twist her ankle again and have to ask for help from someone. Maybe she could have someone level the path out or build some stairs and a handrail. Shit, she was getting old. The ways of living she'd taken for granted, her body's ability, seemed less reliable these days. But she was only 75, she was 75. The knowledge that she was out there, on a large stretch of land, with a looming mountain, all alone, was becoming more apparent. Instead of the solace her solitude had made her feel for so many years, she was starting to feel its burden. Hettie didn't want to have to rely on anyone. No one relied on her anymore, and having to just look after herself had been an afterthought. She surveyed the mountain again, catching a darting bird, watching the wind blow a tree limb. Maybe she could help Devon. The thought of helping someone other than herself was more comforting. It was easier to just ignore herself and carry on like she always had before. Too much time to think of oneself never did anyone any good. Devon might be up there, he might have gotten lost, but he was a grown man, had been to prison even; he could take care of himself.

Hettie went back inside, noticing the dust swirling around the cabin. She really should clean the place. Light came through the windows and hit upon the blue quilt. Hettie looked there, like she'd looked at the mountain, squinting her eyes, till she saw the bird's head in the center. Then the black diamond-shaped patches shooting out from the center caught her attention as a whole. They looked like black feathers and it made her smile. Hettie went to straighten up her kitchen and the phone rang.

"Nan?" a voice barked through.

"Black cat? Is that you? Where you been?' A smile broke all over Hettie's face.

"Yeah, it's me, Rowen. I just got back to California. How are you? How're things?

"It's the same around here." Hettie looked around her dusty cabin. She remembered Rowen from the bus window, "You still following that rock and roll band?"

"Yeah, I am."

Hettie was quiet for a few seconds. "Are you doing alright?

"I'm fine. How are you?"

Hettie shifted her weight onto her good ankle. She wouldn't tell Rowen anything that'd trouble him. It was enough that he'd never been around for his mom. With his sensitivity, he probably had guilt swirling around him most of the time.

"I'm just fine." She sure would like him to come visit and build some kind of railing for him. But California was far away and she hated being a bother. They really didn't have anything to talk about and the weight of Jessie's absence was thick as hard honey. She could hear him breathing and sounds of a street in the background.

"Well, I gotta go," he said.

"Sure you do," Hettie said, and at the last minute, "maybe come down here sometime." He clicked off the phone, so Hettie didn't know if he'd heard her. She walked to the light stream from her window, and saw that big man, moving across her field. He wasn't going fast and seemed to limp, like she did now.

Chapter 67
Cass

Every few minutes, Cass looked at the telephone. She was driving herself crazy staring at the one on the kitchen wall, then on the living room table, and again on the desk in her room. He said he'd call back less than 24 hours ago. He was going to fly her to California. Shit. How in the world was she going to be able to do that. Her mom was already dead pissed. But, somewhere in Cass, as she remembered traveling to Chicago alone, then to back from Indiana alone, it all didn't seem like such a big deal. She'd gotten an idea of what tour was like, and what traveling in Rowen's van was like, but he was from California, so he must have some kind of place there.

Cass had never been to California. She knew she totally didn't really know Rowen. She didn't care though. The thought of his kisses and the way her heartbeat picked up near him was enough to make her travel to the ends of the Earth. Meeting him and traveling to Dead shows was the most exciting thing that had ever happened to her. She felt done with Kansas anyway. But how to tell her mom, or rather how not to tell her mom, was a big problem. There was absolutely no way her mom would allow her to go. Cass could hear her mom's sarcastic tone: "Are you out of your mind?" So, Cass thought, she'd just go. She'd write a note, but somehow, leave it somewhere so she wouldn't see it till Cass had already arrived in California. If, Rowen ever called her back. Cass picked up the receiver from its cordless cradle and pushed it on. The dial tone was like a blank stare and she listened to its dull, monotonous pulse that resonated over her thumping heartbeat and the knowledge that he might not even call her back. She pushed the off button and returned the hard plastic to its cradle. She put on a Grateful Dead tape to cool her nerves. Cass smiled as she was able to remember the words to "Jack Straw." She thought of Ollie, and Changa and Nick, of Jane she'd met inside the show at the Friends of the Earth table, and she thought of that guy, Devon. She liked sitting next to him on the lawn in Indiana. He must be like her dad's age. That was the neat thing about the Dead scene, you could talk to anyone, and it didn't matter how old they were or where they were from. Everyone was there for the same thing, and it all had to do with good music, fun and good vibes. Except for that bitch who'd looked her up and down in the hallway. Cass could feel a hot streak through her chest when she remembered and then she wondered how Rowen knew her, if she was from California, too, if she had been his girlfriend once. Shit. Fuck. Cass's mind collapsed into doubt. He probably won't call. And what if her mom is home and answers the phone or something. It was 4:45. She would be home soon. Dammit, there was no way she could go to California. She barely had money for a ride to the airport. She could take a bus, she thought. Cass reached for the shoebox under her bed and lifted her father's postcards and the three Grateful Dead ticket stubs. She had a 20, two 10s and three fives. She thought about how she'd sold beer and helped make grilled cheese. It was easy to make money before or after the show on tour. Rowen seemed to trust her, she worked, and then it didn't seem so weird that he paid for everything. It was like they were just working together, like a family or community. Their times together were kind of like dates. Guys pay on dates, she thought, although she hadn't been on many dates. Really, Cass didn't know anyone who had been on Dead tour, or even traveled much, except for her dad, but that was a professional job. Hillary seemed so confidently living on a parallel universe. Maybe she came from a lot of money. Cass thought about how she'd looked around, kind of judging-like, when she'd first brought her into the apartment. Her mom hated Hillary, but, she was not a twenty-three-year-old guy, so her mom would probably feel better thinking she went to California with Hillary, when it came to her having to tell her mom more.

Cass was cleaning the kitchen counters to get on her mom's good side, when the green wall phone rang. It was a little after 5:00. On the second ring, she lifted the receiver. "Hello?"

"Is Cass there?"

"It's me. Who's this," she said, recognizing Rowen's voice, but wanting to make sure.

"Rowen here."

He sounded a little funny, like he had an accent or he was somewhere with a lot of other people. Cass could feel her heart beat. She didn't really know what to say.

"Hey, I got you a plane ticket, for the day after tomorrow. Is that cool?"

A smile spread wide across her face, and her chest bounced with beats. "Yeah, that's great! Thank you. Um, where will I fly into? What do I need to do? Will the ticket be at the airport?" Cass could hear a cough on the other end of the phone and she felt very juvenile. She wanted to ask him so many more questions, like what she should wear and where they would be sleeping. Part of her knew that she had to just go with it.

"Yeah, yeah," Rowen said, adjusting his voice to be slower and quieter, which felt kind. "Just go up to the ticket counter at American Airlines and tell them your name. Bring an ID. Here's the confirmation number. Can you write it down?

"Ah, yes," Cass said opening a drawer and pulling out a pad and pen.

"Ok, so LAX is pretty busy. Here's my voicemail number." Cass wrote another set of numbers down.

"When you arrive, walk outside and stay close to the signs for American Airlines. I'll circle around and you can just look out for the van."

"Ok. That sounds good," Cass said. She had so much more she wanted to ask him, but she didn't.

"Hey, I've gotta go. So, I'll see you the day after tomorrow, sweet Cassidy."

Cass could feel her cheeks blush and even when he'd hung up, she listened to the dial tone as if it was an extension of his voice, the receiver snug to her ear.

Devon's heavy boots sounded like bricks dropping on his cabin's wood floor. He turned the kitchen faucet on, bent over and drank sideways from the streaming water. His throat slowly softened as he gulped and the dry edges of his mouth filled with moisture. Three or four flies buzzed near some half-clean plates and the place smelled sour. Devon realized he'd have to do more if Emma was ever going to be there. That was a little too much to think of just yet, though. His body ached, and he felt like lead. Devon switched on his old stereo and let "Workingman's Dead" pound into him. He turned open a couple tins of beans and slopped them into a pan. He'd have to do better in the kitchen. His desk was strewn with silver dust from filing, and papers were scattered all over it. He'd have to clean up his messes. Devon opened the side drawer and pulled out her picture. His empty belly contracted, and his chest burned. He sat down, placing her photo on the edge of the desk carefully. She was so good. He could see himself in her cheeks and the squint of her brown eyes. Devon's leg started bouncing, his nerves leaving him unsteady. He rolled a cigarette, watching her, and listening to the gas hissing its heat from the stove. There was no goddamn reason why he couldn't be a part of her life. She was his daughter. Devon licked the rolling paper, and stood up, walking to the kitchen to stir his beans. The statute of his probation was over, or nearly over. He could see her. She was only a couple days ride away. His mind flashed to the top of Crystal Mountain and some of the stuff he'd seen up there. Those kooky visions, and the bird, and the…Devon sloughed it off. That was up there, he was down here, on the ground, as a man, and he felt conviction for his life, for his Emma. That was it. Emma would be part of his life. Devon poured the hot beans in a big bowl, and his stomach leapt. He tucked the smoke behind his greasy hair and sat with her photo. The beans dropped into his stomach as Pigpen screamed through the stereo. When he was finished eating, Devon stumbled to his bed, taking Emma's picture with him and propping it up gently on the night table. His exhausted body sank into sleep, like a weight falling to the bottom of the ocean.

Chapter 69
Rowen

Rowen gently guided his van into the apartment parking lot, Hardees wrappers and broken CDs were scattered in the empty spot next to his van. He felt sick as he opened the door and jumped out, dreading even the walk up to the apartment where he last saw his mom's dead body. His mind flashed to the swirling cop cars and an ambulance with the lights turned off. He creaked open the building's front door and trudged up the dirt-stained stairs. Sounds of loud TVs, children crying, wafts of onions frying, and cigarette smoke seeped from the other apartment doors. Number 2B, was closed and a thick black streak fled across the bottom of the door, probably Lou's stupid boot kicking it.

Inside, the TV blared a news program—lines of text streaming across the bottom of the screen. The coffee table was strewn with bills and candy wrappers and filled ash trays. The place smelled sick and old, of sour ketchup and pot. Rowen dropped his small duffle near the door and shouted.

"Hello! Anyone here?"

Lou bounced out of the back bedroom, his eyes bloodshot and sinking, his hair a greasy mess, and sweatpants sagging from his tall frame.

"Hey, man!" he said coming to awkwardly hug Rowen. He stepped back after their brotherly bodies touched for a second. "What are you doing, Row?"

"Just got back to Cali. How's it going here?"

"Oh, man, things are ok, mostly shit, though. How long you around for?" Lou said, glancing furtively back to the bedroom.

"Don't know. Just got here." Rowen could hear rustling in the back and a small dog waddled out. Lou picked him up.

"This is Alfie," he said, smiling big and exposing the small crack in his front tooth.

"Hi there" Rowen said, reaching to pet the dog, whose fur was greasy like Lou. The other bedroom door was closed. "Is Tate around?"

"Uh, yeah, been sleeping most of the day though," Lou said, laughing in a strangely pitched tone and coughing with a phlegmy rattle. Rowen walked into the kitchen, surveying the dishes piled in the sink.

"Place is kind of a mess. Sorry," Lou said, reaching to stack more dishes from the counter into the sink. The whole scene made Rowen want to vomit. His mom had kept the place neat as a tack. He hated all of this. But, if he was going to stay there, which was really uncertain at this point, he'd want it to be halfway decent, even just for his mom's memory. And, if Cass came there, well, she wasn't a slouch. She was probably used to real nice places. Rowen blocked his senses and started cleaning. Lou was propped in the other room in front of the TV, smoke trailing into the air. Rowen pulled a new trash bag out from under the sink and started filling it with newspaper ads, paper plates, fast food bags and half full plastic sauce containers. Then he opened the fridge and the stench almost broke him. He remembered how his mom had kept it. What she'd had in there: cottage cheese, hard boiled eggs, tomato juice, and usually a candy bar or two. He just reached for open bags of molding vegetables, stale pizza, a half-eaten cheeseburger and fries and bottles of dark slimy protein shakes, stuffing it all in the black plastic bag. When the shelves were mostly empty, he closed the door again. He opened the small dishwasher and started stacking plates and cereal bowls and glasses. He popped in some liquid and started the thing. Lou came to the kitchen's entrance, dangling a cigarette from his mouth and holding the dog to his chest.

"Well, aren't you the regular old maid," he said, crackling with yucky laughter again.

Rowen just looked at him, suppressing his anger and wish to just strangle his brother, knock him back to the ground and scream obscenities at him.

"Well, doesn't look like you are."

"Nope. Got a gal," he said glancing back into the living room, "but she's no good for much other than, well."

"Spare me," Rowen said, not wanting to get into it with his brother who used to tackle him on that kitchen floor. He was, or had always been, much stronger and tougher than him. Rowen found a bottle of industrial cleaner and went to work on the counters, the sink and then onto the floor. It was all a far reach from the natural body odors, the cool attitude of the Heads on tour and the way he kept his van clean, when he could, but the ammonia smell reminded him of his mom. Rowen stepped back from the cleaned kitchen and went to peer out the window. He scanned the parking lot for unmarked cars, for thugs and gang members who, he knew, populated the place.

"What kind of shit are you into now?" he asked Lou.

"What do you mean. I'm clean. I'm here, no problems, really."

Rowen rolled his eyes. He looked to the hallway and remembered the slow walk back to his mom's bedroom. A room that was now occupied by Lou and whatever fucking floosy he had in there. He didn't trust his brother any more than he wished he could knock sense into him. It would take a sledgehammer.

"Right," Rowen said.

"You got any bud," he asked Rowen.

"Nope," Rowen looked at the edge of the coffee table and a small smudge of white that he knew had been a line of coke. His brother was so fucking stupid he could barely stand it. There were three bedrooms in the place: the one now occupied by Stupid and the one his brother must be sleeping off a heroin dose in, and his own. Rowen walked back and opened his door. The room was stacked with boxes, and all of his mother's old clothes piled on his bed. Her restaurant uniform on top. He could feel the bile rising into his chest. Rowen promptly went back to the kitchen for another trash bag.

"What're ya doing now," Lou said.

"Cleaning."

"Oh, whatever. Knock yourself out."

Fuck you, Rowen wanted to say. But he steeled himself again, hung her uniform in the closet and shoved all of his mother's other clothes into a bag. He hauled it out and set it next to the door. He opened the closet, pushed all of the shit, including his own shit, to one side, and stacked the boxes of his mom's old photo albums in there. He could see the carpet again. The sagging, dirty carpet. He couldn't believe all the shit. How come no one had done anything? It was a useless question, he could answer himself, knowing his no good brothers. Wish Nan was here, he thought, or his mom. Rowen didn't stop to feel, he pulled the vacuum from the hall closet, and sucked up dust and dirt from the carpet, all while trying hard to ignore a burn in the middle of his chest. After half an hour, he closed his door, wrapped the cord around the vacuum and shoved it back into the closet.

"See ya later," he shouted to Lou.

"Ok, bro. Hey, can you pick up some tacos for me?"

"No," Rowen said and shut the door, hauling the bags of clothes and trash outside. He threw the trash into the large bin and set the bag of clothes next to the garbage. Fuck, he should take them somewhere. He didn't have the energy for that. He knew someone would find them and probably put them to use. That was better. He started up the van and drove in circles around the blocks, smoking and getting as high as he could to push away the reality of being back in L.A.

Chapter 70
Devon

The roaring of his bike flew into his ears, ten times louder than it had on the highway the past two days. He was in her quiet neighborhood, with the bland, same-shaped houses pressed together and creating a barrier for the sound to echo. He hated this suburban humdrum. He wanted Emma to grown up with nature, like he had. Devon's heart thumped under his leather jacket, as he passed, one, two, three houses on her street. It was number 2111 and he slowed his bike, approaching. The lawn was immaculate with a small tree near the end of the driveway on the left, by the curb and a few green bushes hugging the side of the house. Devon tried to stay calm. He knew Cora was flighty and would flare up like wood in lit fuel if he moved too quickly or seemed to be any kind of threat. He just wanted to see Emmajean, nothing more, nothing less. She was his daughter. There really should be no problem with this, he thought. Devon pulled his bike in front of the house, under the tree. He looked at his watch. It was half-past six. The sun was still high enough in the sky. They should be home for the night though, maybe making dinner. Devon's empty stomach gnawed. He remembered Cora's cooking. She wasn't a half-bad cook. He remembered her cooking for him. He remembered Emma's high chair pulled up to the table. Devon took a deep breath, climbed off his bike, and set his helmet on the seat, carefully, quietly. He would just go up and ring the bell. No big deal. Devon walked towards the front door and could feel his feet prod the ground. He remembered what it felt like the first time he walked on the free Earth after being in prison for three years. It was amazing. He remembered that. His heart pounded. He breathed again. He thought he heard a child's shriek from inside the house. It made him smile. His little girl. A few cars passed on the street. Devon rang the bell and waited.

The door creaked open slowly and a little pig-tailed girl peered around its edge. Her head cocked to one side as she looked at him. Then she blinked and smiled big,

"Daddy!"

"Hi Baby, yeah it's me, your Daddy." Devon's chest cracked open like wings ready to fly. His whole nervous system exploding awake.

"Daddy! Daddy! Daddy!" she squealed. She tried to push the screened door, but it was locked. Devon could hear Cora from the other room.

"Who is it Emma?"

"Mommy, Mommy, it's Daddy!"

"What?" Cora said as she walked towards the door, and crumped the dishtowel in her hand, throwing it with force on the floor, and yanking Emma's arm away from the door. "Go to your room Emma! Now!" She screamed.

"But Mommy," Emma whined.

"Now, I said!" Emma ran away.

Devon breathed.

"Hi Cora, I'm sorry for just showing up but," he started.

"But nothing! What the fuck are you doing here? You know the rules. You have to call my lawyer. And that's after your probation ends."

"I know, I'm sorry, I just," Devon could feel his blood racing through his veins.

"No. No!" she screamed.

Dammit. There it was, that hard-ass head of hers, flying at him like a knife.

"Cora, come on, please. I just want to see her," Devon kept his voice low.

"No! It doesn't work like that. Now get the hell off my property, before I call the cops." She started to close the door, but opened it again, to shake her finger at him through the screen, "and if you ever try this 'stopping by' again, I'll have you arrested. Is that clear?"

"Fucking A. ok, ok," Devon said, holding his hands up in the air in front of him, "I'm sorry, ok."

The door slammed, hard. Devon walked back towards his bike, his legs feeling like jelly. Well, that didn't go so well. Devon clipped on his helmet and steered his bike away. He looked back to the house and saw Emmajean's face pressed against glass. She looked so sad and so small. Fire entered Devon as the roar of his bike reverberated like hot coal inside glass pipes. He sped out of there.

Chapter 71
Cass

Back at home, Cass didn't feel all that right. Her mom was still incredibly mad since she'd gotten back from Indiana, so she barely wanted to even be in the apartment. Tuesday night, knowing her mom would be home, Cass went over to her friend Cecilia's. Supposedly, she was having a party, and Cass could do with a little company, even if it wasn't Rowen, yet.

Cecelia lived in a giant house off Ward Parkway and walking up by the three-car garage to go in the back door, Cass shook her head. Yeah, she'd been there a dozen times before, and half her friends from high school were from wealthy families, but she thought about Rowen. She really didn't know where he'd grown up, but she'd bet it wasn't with a lot of money. She wondered what he might think walking up to that house with her. He'd probably think it was excessive. Hell, he could get by sleeping in the back of his van most of the time. Cass noticed the way her eyes looked at the trees, the manicured landscaping. It was beautiful, but a bit too pristine. A bit too perfect.

Cass turned the knob and walked inside. Cecelia's parents were out of town, and the kitchen counter was littered with bottles of liquor and Solo cups. She could hear sounds in the back room, screeching and laughing and some punk music playing. Cass felt a little wobbly, and she remembered walking into the last show. She opened the fridge and found a Heineken, not as good as a Sammy Smiths, she knew now, but it would do. Another friend, Tommy, walked in the kitchen.

"Hey there, Cass! Long time no see," he said, well slurred because he was drunk. "I heard you joined the circus?"

"Ha, ha," she countered looking around for a bottle opener, "I've just been traveling, seeing shows, ya know."

"Turning all hippy, I hear."

"Am not. Shut up, Tommy. What would you know anyway." Ugh, Cass thought, high school boys. She felt so different dating Rowen. He was a man, doing his own thing. Not living at his parents' house, like she and most of her high school friends still were. Cass settled on the couch and listened to the conversation. They were talking about parties, other parties, and colleges and summer jobs as lifeguards at the fancy country clubs. Cass felt pretty out of place. She knew she was tired though, her brain still foggy from partying and then not sleeping and traveling back to Kansas.

"Hey, Cass," Melanie, a girl a year younger said, "I heard you went on Grateful Dead Tour! Is that right?" She seemed really interested.

"Yeah, I went to a few shows in the Midwest."

"Oh my gosh, that is so cool! I saw the Bonner Springs show, but that's it."

"That was a good show," Cass said, smiling. She remembered how she felt at that first show, and compared to now, after five shows. She knew so much more about the scene. She'd heard songs played multiple times and knew which ones she liked best.

"Maybe I'll get to go to another one, like you."

"Yeah, it's fun. You should." Cass was so glad she was out of school. If she was still in high school, she'd never be able to do what she was doing, and a man like Rowen probably wouldn't take her seriously either. Melanie was sweet. From a good family. From lots of money, too. She might end up like Hillary, though, if she went on tour. Cass was kind of proud of herself that she could get along on tour with those guys the way she did. She liked working in the lot with Rowen, although trying to sell anything while you're really high is no picnic. Tommy walked into the living room.

"Hey, did you all see Cass? She's back from Dead tour," he said, mocking her.

"Whatever. Don't listen to him," Melanie said.

"Yeah, I know," said Cass, "Dead tour sure beats Kansas summer!" Cass swigged back her beer. They had no idea what life was like outside of their little world. L.A. was worlds away.

"Where's the next show, Cass?" Melanie asked eagerly.

"Oakland, California. That's in the Bay Area, like near San Francisco."

"Oh, that's a bit far away."

Cass nodded. She wanted to tell Melanie about her older Deadhead boyfriend who was going to fly her there, but then she thought better. Kansas City was small, and she didn't want things getting back to her mom. Her mom still had no idea about Rowen, and Cass thought it best to keep things that way.

When she got home, Cass's mom was sitting on the couch watching TV.

"Hi, Mom."

"Hi Cass. Where have you been?"

"At Cecelia's house."

"Oh." Her mom had muted the TV and was looking at Cass with a scowl on her face.

"Someone called here twice and hung up," she said.

"Oh," Cass said, nonchalantly, heading into the kitchen. "Do you know who it was?"

"No idea."

Cass didn't look at her mom, tried to remain calm. It was probably Rowen. Damn, and she missed it. Cass hoped he would call back. She could leave him a message, maybe. There was a spark inside her that worried their plan had changed. Kansas was feeling way too stifling. The TV sound had started again and Cass went into her room and shut the door. She lifted her telephone receiver, heard the empty dial tone. Checked that the ringer was on. Please call back Rowen, please. Cass reached under her bed for the shoebox of things. She rifled through the papers, the Dead tickets, the map of Chicago. She was looking for someplace she might have written Rowen's number. She pulled out the postcards from her Dad and dropped them aside. Then she found the little note from Hillary. She could call her, see if she was going to California.

Cass remembered the last conversation with Hillary in the parking lot. Rowen really didn't like her. The two of them were like the sun and moon, like NY and LA, worlds apart for both being Deadheads. Cass put on "American Beauty" and felt the comfort of the guitar, the easy melodies.

Damn, she wanted to be on the tour. She dialed Hillary's voicemail and kept her voice low, "Hey, Hillary, it's Cass. You going to the Oakland shows? I'm back in Kansas, yuck! Maybe I'll see you there!" and she put the phone back in its cradle and pulled it over next to her bed. She crawled in bed as "Attics" came on the tape player. The song lulled her, into dreams of something she wanted, something out in the world, far, far away. Her clean, cozy bed allowed her to dream and imagine sleeping next to Rowen, imagine hands in prayer swaying at a show, imagine the kind of life she wanted, exploring the planet and being good to it.

Cass had been dreaming, when the phone rang. The ring stunned her for a second, like a squirrel caught in traffic. Then her mind jumped and she leaned over the bed and snatched the receiver. "Hello?"

"Cassidy?"

"Oh! Hi! Hold on a second. Cass knew her mom would pick up the phone, too. The clock radio read 7:35am. She would be getting ready for work. Shit, she really didn't want her to hear Rowen's voice. There was no other click on the phone though. "Hey, just one sec, I'll be right back, just stay on the line," she directed Rowen, her heart pounding. She didn't want Rowen to think she was a fucking baby, but the wrath of her mom if she knew about him would be ten times worse. Cass leaped out of bed and opened her door and walked out. "Mom?" She didn't hear anything, "Mom?" Maybe her mom already left for work, fuck. Cass went back in the bedroom and picked up the phone. "Hi there, sorry, I just woke up."

"Oh, yeah, I know it early, it's even earlier here. So, you'll leave two hours later than I thought, ok?

"Um, yes, definitely."

"Ok, so you leave tomorrow early afternoon. I'll pick you up, there'll be a good run in Cali and then we can drive North to the Oregon show. Sound good?"

Cass heard a click on the phone, "Oh, you're on the phone."

"Hey, yeah, Cecelia, that sounds perfect. Thanks so much, bye."

"Ok, bye," Rowen said in his deeper voice than her high school friend would use and clicked off. Fuck. Her mom heard him. She slammed the phone down and opened her door.

"I'm off the phone; you can use it now." Her mom hadn't left. Dammit. Cass wondered if she'd heard Rowen's voice. Cass quickly thought she could make something up about Tommy being on the phone, too. She would go to the pool with them later. Really, she would be getting her shit together to go to California and Oregon! Yes! Cass went in the bathroom and locked the door to avoid her mom. A few minutes later, she heard pounding and her mom trying to open the door. "I'm going to the bathroom, Mom, what?"

Her mom shouted through the door, "Who was that on the phone?"

"Cecelia, she invited me to the pool today."

"It didn't sound like Cecelia. And how about looking for a job instead of lounging by the pool like some princess."

"Tommy was on the phone, too. Ok!" There was silence.

"I'm going to work. Clean up the kitchen and your shit before you go, and start looking for another job!" she shouted.

"Ok, Mom, have a good day, love you." More pause.

"You, too."

After a few minutes, she heard the front door open and close. When she got out of the shower, Cass cranked up Grateful Dead on her stereo.

"Flight 224 to Los Angeles, boarding now," Cass heard over the speakers. She had slouched in an airport seat, as close to the corner as possible, just trying to blend in and carry out her plan. That morning, as soon as her mom left for work, Cass sprang into action, pulling her small, already packed duffel from under her bed, putting her ID and money in her back pocket, and the little clear crystal from Rowen in her front pocket. She laced up her Converse tennis shoes and walked six blocks to the bus stop. She would have to change buses three times, but it was the cheapest way to get to the airport. The whole time she listened to "American Beauty" on her Walkman. She'd left a card in an envelope on her mom's bedside table. Cass tried to be as nice as possible and as mature as possible. *I know you don't like this, mom, but I'm going to be fine. I promise I'll call,* she'd written. It was one thing to have her mom mad at her for doing something she didn't like, but she really didn't want her to worry. Cass could still see her mom's face in the kitchen when she'd come home from the other shows. She looked really bad, worried.

It was super easy to get the plane ticket. Wow, Rowen must really like her to do that, she thought. Her seat was against the window, and as Cass peered out at the air traffic controllers waving their orange wands, she couldn't believe she was flying to California to see him. No one else, of her friends from school, would be doing that. It was so cool. Dead Tour in California.

Damn, she thought, smiling to herself. She fast forward her tape to "Box of Rain." It was one of her favorites. Cass stared at the logo on the cover of the tape she'd bought the weekend before. It seemed a good studio tape to start her collection. Classic songs, Rowen would think. The circle on a wood background with a rose in the center, inspired her. This is what America is about, the beauty of freedom, music, travel. Her back leaned against the plane seat as they moved into the air, and Cass loved it.

The woman next to her patted Cass's arm a little and she woke up. People were standing up in the aisle already. She was in Los Angeles. Cass pulled off her headphones and shoved them in her duffle, unbuckled her belt and got ready. She peeked out the window, it was sunny California! Oh, wow. She would see Rowen so soon! Cass followed the herd of people off the plane and into a busy airport. She remembered all the crowds at the shows. This was nothing. And these people, she thought, scanning the business suits or women tugging children's arms or sporting designer dresses and heels, probably have no idea how cool a Dead show is. Cass followed the signs for Drop off/ Pick up and Baggage Claim. She griped her backpack on her shoulder with one hand and swung the small duffle in the other as she walked.

Outside, the California air was warm and thick, but Cass felt like she could smell the sea somewhere, mixed with the car exhaust. The place was a zoo. Cars inched and then bolted forward, horns honked, people lugged baggage and whistled for cabs that swiveled to the curb. Cass started searching, black van, black van, black van. That was all she needed to find. Her mind leapt back to the parking lot in Chicago when she had to search for the van and Rowen. That totally sucked. She didn't think she would find him, ever. But she did, and that guy Devon had helped. She liked that about the scene. She almost felt that here, too, in LAX, looking for her pick up like the adults around her. It was a new world, one she was finally getting to be a part of. She watched the people around her, knowing everyone had a purpose here and place to go.

It was taking a while, so Cass sat outside the airport on a bench, waiting for Rowen. She knew he might be late because it was rush hour, and it was a big city. She couldn't believe that she'd made it there, after all the fighting, and tension with her mom. Shit, she knew she was going off the rails, like her mom said, but who the heck wanted to stay on the rails if it meant a boring existence like her mom led in the middle of Kansas? Nope, she wanted to be like her father, at least live the kind of life he was living, off somewhere exotic. Cass reached into her backpack and pulled out the two postcards she'd brought from him. One was from Katmandu, and the other from San Francisco. The one from California was really old, with frayed edges and a photo of a streetcar that must have been from the seventies. She didn't care, it just made her feel good, like close to him in a way, because she was now near there.

Rowen's cool van pulled up in front of her, and Cass could feel her cheeks blushing. She tucked the postcards away and grabbed her two carry-on bags and hopped in the van.

"Hey!" Rowen said, "You made it."

"Sure did!"

He leaned over the seat and gave her an awkward kiss. Then she heard a jangling and noticed the little dog in the back seat.

"Thought he could get out for a ride," Rowen said smiling.

Cass reached down and pet the little scruffy dog.

"Everything alright in Kansas?" Rowen asked.

"Oh. Yeah, I guess so. It's just boring, and my mom—" Cass stopped herself.

Rowen nodded as he drove them out of the airport traffic. "So, you know, shows in Cali are pretty much the best. It's the home scene. You'll see."

"Sounds great!" Cass said, trying to maintain her wide-eyed excitement for getting out of Kansas, back to the Dead scene and back with Rowen. She looked at his long hair, that did seem a little bit cleaner than she'd remembered. She studied the outline of his jaw, the bronze of his skin and the deep green of his loose army pants. She could smell him from where she sat: a mix of incense and body odor that excited her.

"You hungry?" he asked.

"Oh, not so much, I will be later though," she said, "Thanks."

"So, we'll do some selling in the lot. I got fourteen cases. And they'll go over the next few days. but we won't have to worry so much," Rowen informed her.

Cass nodded. Oh yeah, she'd forgotten all that selling. It was a little intense, and illegal, but she did like it when things moved quickly and she could make someone happy just by selling them a beer.

He pulled the van up to the bland Valley neighborhood—small ranch houses lined up like pinball markers. Rowen hopped out, grabbing his small backpack. Cass didn't move, probably because he'd had her stay in the car for the last few runs, but Jackson liked him to smoke and chill out a while. He'd just be getting in after his plumbing job, and his shiny ass orange truck sat like a trophy in the driveway. Walking around the front of the car, Rowen nodded his head, and Cass, like a little puppy, opened the door and got out. She shoved her hands in her pockets, shoulders hunched up. Just be fucking cool, will ya, Rowen wanted to say. But he just walked to the front door, and expected she'd follow.

The front door hinged open, and the tall man in jeans and a clean shirt clapped Rowen's hand, then pulled him into a side hug that lasted a few seconds too long and Rowen knew he knew and could feel a little stab in his chest. Rowen pulled away and nodded his head, like just don't say anything man, please. Jackson seemed to get it and ushered him inside. "This is Cass," Rowen said nodding to her.

"Hi there!"

Rowen could see Jackson blushing a little and getting awkward. This guy, in his mid-thirties, working man, had some kind of strange fear when it came to women. Rowen rarely saw a chick around nor did they talk much about any in the ten years or so he'd known him and been selling him weed.

They walked through the tidy kitchen, past a brown wall phone with a long tangled cord brushing the floor, and a shop calendar with a half-naked chick on a truck like the one in Jackson's driveway tacked up next to it.

"How ya been man?" Rowen asked him.

"Oh, just fine, just fine. Same old shit in the pipes and clogs in the drains, but yeah. My brother and I are going up to Santa Rosa tomorrow for a car thing."

"Cool, cool," Rowen said, as the three of them settled on a cushy sectional couch. The carpet was tan and stained, but clean from a vacuum cleaner. Rowen's knee tapped as he loaded a pipe and passed it to Jackson.

"Thanks man." He pulled the smoke in like an expert and blew out a big cloud of white slowly, and a few goofy smoke rings. Rowen smiled. He liked his customers happy.

"Mmmm," Jackson cooed, then started hacking a little but promptly stopped when he peered over at Cass. He passed the bowl over to Rowen who handed it sideways to Cass. Rowen watched out of his peripheral vision, as Cass lit and pulled in on the pipe. She was fine, and blew out her smoke pretty quickly then passed the pipe back to him. Rowen was a little annoyed, and worried that there'd be another incident of Cass revealing just how little she knew about smoking pot. It didn't matter really, but somehow Rowen didn't like feeling he was tagging along a teenager with no experience. It didn't make him look all that good. But, she was cute, and that stood for something, and mainly her presence was just enough distraction that everyone might avoid mentioning his mom. Rowen laid a quarter of green bud on the table. It was mid-range, but the right strain for Jackson. And Rowen was glad that it wasn't the ditch weed. He didn't really like smoking that with folks too much. It was too much like tobacco to him. Jackson unrolled the little sandwich bag and nestled his nose in.

"Oh, yeah, this is good bro, thank you!"

"Sure thing."

Jackson leaned over the side of his couch and brought out a one and a half foot bong. He pulled off a small nug and loaded it up. He leaned over the coffee table and handed it to Cass, like some kind of gentleman.

"Oh! Thanks," Cass said, blushing a little.

Jesus Christ, Rowen thought. She probably never even used a bong. Rowen sniffed, pulling his composure together and slyly leaned over to her. He took the lighter from the table and twirled it in his fingers.

He nodded as Cass put her mouth in the bong top, as he lit it gently, he whispered, "just suck it up," he smiled at her and her mouth curled in a smile inside the bong, so she looked cool and practiced, at something. When she'd filled the chamber, just enough, Rowen lifted the stem. Of course it was too much, and the smoke trailed out the top as she exhaled quickly. Rowen glanced over at Jackson who was rubbing his hands on his jean legs. Rowen thought he must be like, what the fuck, man, that shit's expensive, so Rowen sucked up the rest of the smoke, and held it in reverently while he set the bong in front of Jackson.

Rowen and Jackson each took two bong hits, filling the chamber with thick smoke and pulling like they knew what they were doing, because they did, from years of smoking. They joked about cars, and tours, and the riff raff that was moving in all around the Valley. Every so often Rowen glanced at Cass, who was sunk back into the couch, like she was stoned to it. She looked like she could fall asleep. Whatever, Rowen thought. Now sufficiently high, Jackson leaned in over the coffee table and looked up at Rowen like a helpless rabbit. Oh, fuck, Rowen thought, looking down.

"Hey, Rowen, I heard about your mom. I'm so, so sorry, man."

Chapter 73
Cass

Cass gripped the side of the car door, noticing the smoothness of the metal. She knew she was way too high and started worrying that something unpleasant could happen. She glanced over at Rowen, cool and comfortable in his driver's seat. She barely knew him, and she was riding in his van, all over the Valley, as he called it, what, selling pot? I guess that's cool, Cass thought. But it also tightened her stomach, when she thought about Jack, her mom's stupid cop boyfriend. She knew he was thousands of miles away. Cass wondered if her mom had read the note she left for her yet. It was right on her bedside, so she should find it. It wasn't all that cool on her part, she knew, but what the fuck. Sometimes you just have to get out there, take a chance. Now she was doing that. Cass listened to the Dead music from the stereo and tried to relax, tried to breath and slow down. It was summer.

"So, we've got one more stop and then we can chill. Show's not 'til tomorrow night. You good?" Rowen asked her.

"Oh," Cass heard her voice, and felt heat enter her face. "I mean, cool." Rowen must think she was such a dork. Cass had done her best to be cool, in all the houses they visited and the enormous amount of pot she just kept smoking and smoking, like Rowen did. It was too much for her though. Separating her reality and his reality was getting a little complicated. She had never even been to Southern California, and he grew up here. The van pulled up in front of another small house in a suburb. There were four cars lined up in the little driveway, two side by side. Across the street, a couple guys were milling around a souped-up truck, and they revved the engine higher and higher, rumbling the air, even inside the van. Cass could feel it. The guys there looked a little rough.

"I'll just be a minute," Rowen said.

"Ok," Cass relaxed a little, easing into the front seat, thankful that she wouldn't have to meet more random pot buyers or get any higher. Rowen hopped out and locked the door from the outside, which he hadn't done when he left her in the car before. Ok, whatever, she thought, and gazed across the street again. She rolled the window down a tiny bit so she didn't feel like a trapped dog.

Later in the early evening, they pulled into a parking lot of an apartment building that was a little beat up. Cass didn't want to wait for Rowen to do another drug deal. She was getting tired and had to pee.

"Let's go," Rowen said, "Bring your bag." Cass climbed in the back and stepped out the side door with her full backpack. Is this where he lived? Rowen didn't say anything, so she followed him, again. It seemed like he was pissed or something. He did hold the glass door open for her and Cass's senses were bombarded by stale cigarette smoke, fast food, and farts or something worse. It was really gross, but she followed Rowen up a set of stairs. He opened the door with a key, and they walked in.

"I have to go to the bathroom," Cass said

"First door on the right."

Cass set her bag down on the thin carpet and shut herself inside the small bathroom. Cleaner entered her nostrils and something else, more pungent, like burning plastic. Cass held her breath as she put the toilet seat down. No, she didn't want to sit down. It felt dirty in there. After laying paper on the seat, she relived herself and could hear loud voices from the living room. It wasn't Rowen's voice, but another one. His family? His roommate?

When Cass came out, a tall guy in basketball shorts and a t-shirt stood in the living room. He had long hair like Rowen, but when he smiled, Cass saw a chipped tooth.

"Well, hello there!" he said, looking her up and down, which instantly made Cass uncomfortable.

"Cass, this is my brother, Lou," Rowen said and walked towards her grabbing her backpack. Cass gave the guy a little wave. "Come on," Rowen said and entered a back room. She followed and he shut the door. Rowen collapsed on the bed and closed his eyes under a dangling plant above the pillow. Cass walked carefully to the bed, too.

"You have one brother?'

"Two," Rowen said without opening his eyes. Cass came to the side of the bed and sat down on the floor. Ok, the guy was 23, lived in this shitty apartment with his brothers, that is, when he wasn't in his van. He sold pot to regular people. It was a long way from Kansas, and Cass started to feel an emptiness in her belly. Is this what being out in the world looks like? She peered at the hanging plant and Rowen's lengthy frame. I can do this, she said to herself. I mean, it beats summer at a grocery store in Kansas.

One side of the room was piled with boxes and picture albums and books and some cloth was spilling out of them. Cass could see a picture of a child's crayon artwork in a little frame and a photo, also framed, of three boys and a woman. Cass went over and picked up the picture, "Is this you and your brothers?"

"Yeah, and my mom," Rowen said turning on his side and resting his head in his hand.

"Your mom is pretty," she said, studying the photo.

"Was," Rowen said.

"Oh?" Cass said, looking at him.

"She died."

"Oh, I'm sorry," Cass said, gently putting the photo back and coming over to the bed. Rowen turned away from her. Oh, shit, Cass thought, she had no idea. She wondered if Rowen was crying and didn't want her to see his face. She sat on the bed and gently placed her hand on his side. Just sitting there.

It look him a bit, but then he turned back around, "It's ok, I just miss her sometimes," he said. Cass nodded and then smiled a bit. Rowen pulled her down to lay next to him. She could see he was trying to overcome his sadness with desire instead. Cass felt for him and hugged him tightly.

Cass rolled over on the little bed, yawning and stretching. She was in the room alone. The door was closed. She had no idea how long she'd slept. She had been so high. Cass reached down and felt her backpack next to the bed. She needed to brush her teeth, but even more pressing, she needed to call her mom. Cass groaned and got up. She needed to find a phone. The idea of calling from Rowen's house just seemed bad. Who knows how her mom would react, most likely angry as hell, and Cass didn't want Rowen to hear that. She went out into the living room and the tv was blaring a game show. Rowen's brother was slumped on the couch with a bunch of food wrappers on the table in front of him.

"Oh, *hi-i-i-i-i*," he said sitting up straight, "heard you passed out!" and he laughed loudly with phlegm caught in his throat.

"Hi," Cass said, "Is Rowen here?"

"Nope, went to run an errand."

"Oh."

"But you can hang with me," Rowen's bigger brother said, patting the couch next to him.

Yuck, Cass thought. Her chest tightened. "Hey, is there like a mini mart or something close by?"

"Uh, yeah, what kinds of things you need?"

"Oh, just girl stuff," Cass said, knowing that should shut him up.

"Okay," he said, still poking curiosity at her, "There's one two blocks up, before the stoplight on the right."

Cass popped back into the bedroom. She didn't want to leave her stuff there, with Rowen's brother. He didn't seem exactly trustworthy. So she pulled out some of her clothes and set them in the corner, next to a box that was filled with knick-knacks, like little cheap statues of animals. Seemed a strange thing for Rowen to have in his room. They looked like something that belonged to an old person. Cass zipped her lighter backpack and head down the gross hallway and stairs. The neighborhood wasn't all that nice, either. Trash collected by some of the sidewalks, notices stapled into posts advertised cheap tacos and an Indian buffet. Cass found the mini mart and walked up to the pay phone outside.

Cass readied the calling card she'd bought and braced herself for her mom's tirade. She didn't really even have to call her, but Cass didn't want her mom getting sick over her. Cass gripped the greasy phone and stood close to the plastic hood over the phone.

"Hello?" Her mom's voice sounded angry and terse.

"Hi, Mom," Cass said.

There was silence, then, "Yes?"

"It's me, I'm just checking in," Cass said, doing what she thought her mom wanted.

"What do you want, Cass?"

Cass paused, thinking. Then decided showing care was best.

"I don't want you to get sick."

"I'm not sick."

"Ok, good." Cass felt a little panic. What was going on? "Did you get my letter?"

"Yes," her mom said, coolly.

"Ok. So, are you ok?"

"Cass!! What the hell do you want me to say?"

There it was. The anger she was expecting. "I don't know. I just thought you'd want me to check in."

"Check in? Check in! Ha! Cass, you are so far off the mark, I don't know what to say."

"Mom! It's not a big deal."

"Well," her mom said calmly, "If you want to start living as an adult, then you can start taking responsibility for yourself." She paused, before saying, "and that will start with you finding another place to live. Your things will be on the lawn, or better yet, in the apartment trash bin, in one week."

Cass could hear the weight of her mom's breath through the phone.

"What?" Cass said softly.

"You heard me. If you are not going to contribute to this, to my household, you can find your own way, get your shit and deal with it yourself!"

"Mom!?" But the line was dead. Her mom had clicked off! What the fuck. Cass quickly thought about calling back, apologizing, starting the conversation over. People came in and out of the mini mart, looking her over before walking on. Shit. Now what? Fuck. Cass pulled herself together and walked back down the street, trying not to freak out, trying not to cry. When she came back into the apartment, Rowen was sitting on the couch with his brother.

Devon pulled his bike into the Oakland Coliseum parking lot in front of the grey building that looked like a stone fort. Unfortunately, the place reminded him of a prison. Devon shook that off, and reminded himself he was in one of the freest places in Cali that he could think of. Not behind bars, not in a bar, not on his isolated road, not watching his little girl through glass. He took in the scene, hippies milling around holding up fingers for "miracles." Tables being set up to sell food, sticker boards leaning against cars. He was way early, but it didn't matter. Devon parked next to some other bikes but then walked away. He didn't have a ticket yet, but that shouldn't be a problem. He heard the tweet of small birds and found a sidewalk to sit on and roll a smoke. The place was so familiar, and relaxed—not like the Midwest or East Coast, everything was chill here, at least around him. He replayed Emma's voice inside his head, "Daddy, Daddy, Daddy!" It was the best sound he could ever wish for, high and pure and unreserved. Just love.

But then he thought of Cora and the way she yanked his daughter's arm from the door, from him. The thought lined up in his head, next to a cement wall. One that wasn't about to let things happen. The kind of wall in his mind made him want to rise far, far above it, and everything. Devon watched the vans and buses and dilapidated cars roll in and line up in the parking lot. In a few hours the whole lot would be full, and the start of a five day show stint would commence. Shakedown started, where it always did, in the center aisles. He recognized so many faces, but everything looked the same. It was both comforting and pushing. Devon shifted his shoulders under his heavy jacket, feeling weight. He tracked his senses, going for shiny metal reflecting the California sun, hot dog buns on the pavement, kind bud wafting through the air. Towards the end of the forming Shakedown, Devon got a glimpse of a man in striped black and white pants, a floppy hat and a low-slung bag hanging off his lanky frame.

Devon squinted, and traced the shape of the man, the weathered look of his skin as he moved forward. Fucking A is that PJ, Devon thought. As he moved closer, Devon watched the man moving his arms, animated, talking loudly, fingering a long spliff. A smile cracked across his face and Devon walked up slower, till the man turned around and recognized him. He started shaking his head, like he couldn't believe it.

"Oh, brother! Oh, lord! Where in the world have you been?" PJ said, slapping his thigh. Devon smiled and stuck out his hand, but PJ wrapped his arms around him. The man's body was bony, and Devon noticed the feeling of his elbow in his back.

"Hi brother, good to see you."

"I'll say!" PJ's face wrinkled into a happy, toothy smile. He passed the spliff to Devon, who toked long and handed it back.

They got to talking about Emma and how much Devon missed his little girl. Devon worried he'd miss out on being a father. It would slip past his life like birds avoiding him in flight.

"I know man, but I'm sure she remembers you," PJ said as he bent down to tie his tie dye Converse high tops.

"I don't know. She's so young, so impressionable, so sweet," Devon said, "I wish there was some way to let her know I'm thinking of her, to let her know I still care every day." PJ tapped around the space in front of the VW van he was riding in. He shook his head wildly and scratched his chin. He was probably on some speedy acid. Devon shook his own head and smiled at his friend's antics.

"I've got it, I've got it," he shouted. "What if we, well I, get something to her, like a rock or a piece of candy or a shell or something. Is there anything that reminds her of you? Anything that you two used to look for in nature of something?

"Feathers," Devon said, "and white shells and white rocks." He flashed on a day before his prison time when they'd gone to Long Beach and walked together on sand. She was younger then, but her little eye always searched and found white shells. "I used to bring feathers home and stick them in a vase we had in the living room. She liked looking at them and always pointed in the direction they stood up in the vase." Devon remembered she used to say, "yer, yer," her little stubby arm thrust up in the air.

"Perfect," PJ said. "I can deliver them to her, and she'll remember. When you see her again, and I do believe you will brother, give her another one. The connection will be made on its own man. Easy-peasy."

"Hmm," Devon said, "I like that." He watched PJ rifle through the opened van and throw things around before finding a pen and a scrap of paper.

"Ok, ok, what's her address, what's her address?"

"You have to promise me you won't just walk up to her door or some shit. Cora would not be so favorable to you either. She knows the colors of the Dead scene, remember?"

"I do, I do. Poor girl, never could let her freak flag fly," PJ said shaking his head like it was something tragic.

"That's for sure."

"No, no, I know that. I know. I have something else in mind," he said, grinning wide,

"Does she have a windowsill?"

"Sure, but she'd have to know to look there."

"Maybe that could be encouraged."

"Come walk with me," PJ said, and Devon followed him as he walked quickly several aisles over, weaving through cars. The feeling of following him, was freeing. Devon kept his sights on him and had to move fast. He could feel his breath increasing and his eyes sharpening. It was like flying after another bird. For a few minutes, it took him away. Away from the fucked place in his head to something else. He hadn't even spotted PJ most of the summer, and his presence was welcomed. He finally stopped by a yellow VW and opened the side door.

"This your new digs?" Devon asked.

PJ looked at him, and grinned, "Wouldn't that be my luck. No, just got a ride from across the Bay."

"Hmm. Where you been this tour, man?"

"Here, there and everywhere, brother. How about you?"

"I went back East and then South to New Mexico."

"Ah, the Land of Enchantment."

Devon nodded and waited for PJ to stuff his bag with a few sheets of what looked like colorful blotter acid. Devon looked around. Damn, still doing that shit. PJ was crazy, even if they were on the West Coast.

"Come on, man," I want to show you something."

"Oh?" And he was off again, and Devon followed again, like flying through to the other side of the lot. This guy was so crazy, but Devon remembered the magic he had. He remembered the weight of his grip as he helped him shape shift years ago. Such freedom, what he'd been longing for. And it showed up here, in this dirty parking lot that became more and more crowded by the minute. Devon wondered how it could be possible to find it here, instead of in the forests by his place in New Mexico. Somehow, PJ's enthusiasm was infectious. Devon kept his eye on him, wondering if he would disappear before they got to the end of the parking lot. He felt like a boy, chasing his loved dog or something. The sun blasting down on him. Free, free.

PJ stopped suddenly between some cars, and without looking, reached his hand back. Devon rushed forward and clasped it, and it was like a claw, pressing into his skin. He could feel his chest lift and his legs retract. He could feel the sky coming towards him. He could feel everything melting off him. But, as soon as he was in the air, not man, Devon's sense of anything earthbound disappeared. He wasn't thinking about flying or how to do it. He wasn't thinking about seeing his daughter or hating his ex-wife. He wasn't thinking, period.

And the next thing he knew, he was in line ready to go in the show, gripping a mail order ticket and feeling his legs a bit wobbly, his head twitching from side to side with the closeness of other bodies moving in front and behind him. It was showtime. He'd flown. Somewhere, somehow.

Chapter 75
Cass

Cass and Rowen sold a few cases of beer in the afternoon. Things were pretty easy in Oakland, and Cass liked the scene even more than in the Midwest. It was like everyone just knew what to do there and weren't so afraid of getting busted. The show wasn't for another hour or two.

"I just wanna rest before the show," Rowen said.

"Ok, yeah. Me, too," Cass said, although she'd really rather walk around the lot. She wanted to learn more about the scene every time she got the chance. Just as they were hauling the empty coolers back into the van, Hillary waltzed up.

"Hey, girlfriend!" she screeched. "How are you?" Cass smiled that someone other than Rowen knew her there.

"Hey, Hillary! I made it out here! How's it going," Cass said, stepping to the side of the van, while Rowen stayed in and continued cleaning up.

"You guys going in the show tonight?" Hillary asked, leaning into the van a little to look at Rowen. He didn't even get out to talk to her, kept his back to her, "Uh, yeah," he mumbled. Cass looked at Hillary and smiled sheepishly. Cass knew that Rowen didn't like Hillary, but he didn't have to be a dick about it. She wouldn't even be there if it weren't for her. Hillary grabbed Cass's arm, starting to tug her away, "Come walk with me sister," she said tilting her head to the side. Cass looked into the van and caught a sour face on Rowen. His eyebrows bounced up. "I'm just going to walk around for a bit. I'll be back soon," she said.

"Suit yourself," Rowen said, flopping on the back bed.

Hillary smiled and dragged Cass towards Shakedown. Cass felt a small stab in her chest. She didn't want Rowen to be pissed, but she also wanted to explore. This was her time. It was summer! Hillary hooked her elbow on Cass's as they walked down the center of an aisle. She was wearing flowing clothes and Cass could feel the slight swing of her body as they walked together. Cass felt like they were parading down the street, and she noticed others looking at them as they passed.

"Oh my God," Hillary said, "So I was at this party the other night and met this guy, Jason. I think he's involved in booking the band in California. Anyway, he's invited me to his flat for the weekend. It's in San Francisco, right across the bay." Hillary turned and winked at Cass. She was clearly excited and surprised at her own luck.

"Wow, that's cool," Cass said, though her mind was reeling with questions, like how did she meet the guy, is it safe?

"Totally! Wanna come with me? I bet he has a friend," Hillary smiled, "Who knows, maybe there'll be a party with some of the band members we could go to!"

Hillary's excitement started blending into Cass and she liked the thought of meeting more people. A party in a fancy flat? San Francisco, where it all started? Seemed too good to be true.

"What about Rowen?" Cass asked.

"Uh, I'm not sure," Hillary said, unhooking Cass's elbow to light a cigarette. "Maybe not. It'd have to be just us girls, ya know," she said winking at Cass again.

"Oh. Yeah, I don't know, Hillary," Cass said, shoving her hands in her front pockets. Hillary rolled her eyes at Cass and dragged her cigarette.

"What do you see in that guy anyway? He's kind of lot trash, ya know."

This burned Cass even more than disappointing Rowen earlier. Why did Hillary have to be a bitch! Cass took a deep breath and sighed.

"He's not trash!" She shrieked, while keeping a smile in the corner of her mouth, to keep things playful with her only other friend there. But she thought about the apartment bathroom and the kitchen that was even worse because of his messy brother.

"Oh, come on girl, a sweet thing like you, you can do way better," Hill goaded. Then Cass thought of the way Rowen was when they were alone and the patient way he taught her about the scene, and he fricking paid for her plane ticket out there.

"Yeah, it sounds fun, but I can't go off to a party without him. I mean, he flew me out here!"

"So," Hill said, walking quicker, and blowing smoke from her mouth. Cass slowed her walking; she wanted to take her time along Shakedown.

"Do you have a ticket for tonight?"

"No, not yet," Hill said.

"Oh." That was one good thing, Rowen had tickets for them when she was with him, and they were pretty good seats, even if she didn't want to be in them the whole show.

"Ok," Hill said, shooting her hand in the air as they neared the greater crowd, "Don't say I didn't invite you if it turns out to be the party of a lifetime!"

"Alright. Hey, have fun, and go get a miracle!" Cass smiled, Hill winked, and she was off. Cass turned around and took her time walking back to the van. There was so much to look at, the space behind cars set up with blankets and things spread out: jewelry, posters, multicolored teddy bears and tie dye shirts. Cass felt like she understood the folks selling. That was what she and Rowen did, too. Yeah, Hillary might have more exciting plans, but they seemed to change all the time, like she was always doing something different, with different people. The scene felt more like a community to Cass and the thought of seeing and being with and partying with and travelling with the same people is what made it comfortable.

As Cass neared the van, she worried that Rowen would be pissed at her. It seemed like he wanted her with him, when he did, and anytime she felt like doing something else, he seemed to get pissy. Something to keep in mind, she said to herself. Cass carefully opened the side van door. Rowen was crashed out on the bed, his back to her. Maybe he's sleeping, she thought. Carefully Cass lay down on the bed next to him, and Rowen leaned a bit, farther away from her. She decided to just be quiet and pretend like she was napping, too.

Cass woke up about 20 minutes later with Rowen draped across her body, snuggling into her. It was hot inside the van, but his weight felt good. Cass could feel her heartbeat pulse in her neck. Even though they were the only ones in the van, there was no real privacy—people streamed by right outside the cracked windows. At least at the apartment there was a door they could close. Cass wasn't used to being with a guy, let alone in the middle of a crowded parking lot. But, when Rowen began kissing her tenderly, she let everything melt away and kissed him back. He might be an asshole sometimes, but he made her feel mature and sexy. His body and desire kind of kicked everything else aside, everything she probably should have been thinking about.

Devon's mail order ticket for August 12, 1991, shimmered in his hand and he followed the seat numbers, down, down to a spot in the second row back from the stage. Woah, Devon looked around, wondering if he'd picked up someone else's ticket. He remembered being with PJ, and he could swear that he'd flown, but he didn't remember seeing the ground from above, or searching for shiny objects, or chasing after his friend by flying over the lot. No, maybe it was just a dream in his mind, maybe one of the hits PJ was selling, pressed into his hand. Devon could feel all the muscles in his body just a little more taught. He sat in his prime seat and stretched his legs back and forth under the plastic in front of it. He felt calm, for a minute and let the sun warm his face.

People moved in around him and the band opened with "Iko Iko" which was upbeat and welcomed. Then they slid into "New Minglewood," "Big River," "Birdsong." Devon closed his eyes, thinking about the roots of the songs, the roots in his mind and heart. All these songs he'd spent so many years with. They were like friends, like the comfort of his shack's living room, like the comfort of being in nature. That's all he wanted, to be in nature, and to share it with Emma. She should be in New Mexico with him, learning the rise and set of the sun, the crunch of leaves under feet through forest, the beauty that he'd grown up with. Devon thought about her cardboard neighborhood, about Cora's gruff style. Devon's mind flashed back to the little gravestone by his cabin and early death of his sister up Crystal Mountain, just because she'd been curious. Devon took a deep breath. He knew everything was way more complicated. He didn't even need to have Emma full time, maybe he wouldn't know how to take care of her. She needed so much. But, trusting Cora to really raise her right, with heart, was like trusting honey to just form in a swarming beehive. If he could, Devon would carefully reach his bare hand into a bee box and pull the honey out. He knew one had to do it that way. Otherwise, they'd be stung.

The music sunk into him, and Devon peered at the blue sky overhead. Even though he couldn't track the flight with PJ, Devon knew it had happened. Just that thought was comforting. It was like getting all the nutrients he needed, like drinking fresh orange juice or something. And the music of the Dead shows was like cake, easy to eat and sweet. If he still had his little family, he would take Emma to the shows. Devon knew she'd love it, so many colors and sights and sounds. He knew he'd be one of the parents who'd have their kids wear earphones, like you're supposed to. He could be good. The band settled into the first chords of "Birdsong." He heard Emma's sound, high pitched, like the notes the keyboard hit. Devon didn't know how he was able to turn into a bird, how PJ knew, too… but what if it was an inherited thing and Emma had it, too? What a gene gift to give his daughter, the freedom of flight, maybe. Devon let the top of his mind wander like this with the sweet melodies of the music. Maybe he was thinking crazy, but life was obviously crazy, so what did it really matter. Devon imagined flying with his little girl. Her wings spanned, his wings spanned, dipping and soaring. It was like a dream… it was a dream.

Devon came back as the song slowed, and he thought about Cora's house. It wasn't all that secure. He could get his daughter, just take her to New Mexico for a while. Teach her about the trees, about bugs and how to do small work on a farm. Not that he had a farm, but it was the way he was raised. It wasn't so bad, and Devon knew he could be ten times the father that his own father was. Devon thought he could be patient, kind, loving, all the parts of being human that he liked. Somehow, he felt more invisible, having flown in the parking lot without even knowing, like maybe he could escape or fly, shift after all. Maybe he could go into Cora's neighborhood without being seen. Maybe he could push up the bedroom window quietly and gently touch Emma's back. Wake her up and play a game of it, going out the window with Daddy. Spending time together, like he knew she wanted to. "Daddy!" he heard again and smiled.

He had a good show, and later walking in the lot, he saw that girl, Cass. She was standing on Shakedown like she kinda knew what she was doing, although it really looked like that boyfriend of hers had just put her to work again. Another fucking kingpin, carving his small power on tour. Devon ambled up, his hands slunk in his pockets.

"Hey there."

"Hey," she said.

"Remember me?"

"Sure, hi Devon, how's it going?"

"Oh, pretty good, pretty good. Whatcha got in there?"

"Oh, mostly beer, Heineken, Bass, a few Sammys."

"Looks like you're becoming a regular tour Head, selling full coolers a beer by yourself?"

"Oh, yeah, well it's nice to help out. We all kinda do, I guess."

"Sure, give me a Bass. You go in the show tonight?"

"Yeah, you?"

"It was a good one for me." As Devon talked to her, he could see Cass's attention directed around her, like she was kind of looking for someone. Again, like she had in Indiana.

"Is everything alright, doll?"

"Um, yeah, I guess so. Rowen—that's the guy, uh, you helped me find, in the black van, in Chicago, said he'd be back a while ago, and I don't know where he is."

"I remember him and his black van. Hm, I'm sure he's just toking up somewhere," Devon hesitated, but then continued, "you probably don't know this about him, but he has two older brothers."

"Oh? How d'you know Rowen's brothers?" Devon could see concern or anger in her eyes, like she didn't like someone knowing things about her 'boyfriend' she'd just learned herself.

"I know of them all, his mother, too."

"Oh, wow, really? How?" Cass said.

"A long time ago, his mom and I lived in the same town." Devon decided to leave out the part where the town was under 500 people and they lived down the street, and his family worked for Rowen's family and his mother was best friend's with Devon's older sister, who died.

"Oh, that's kinda strange. Does he remember you?"

"I'm not sure, I wasn't around there much."

"Where's there?"

"Little town in New Mexico. I believe his grandmother still lives there."

Cass had bent down and was readjusting the glass bottles and ice, letting things knock together and make sound. She looked up and down Shakedown. She opened Devon's beer and took his two bucks and stuffed them in her jeans picket with others that were just stuffed in and starting to make her pocket bulge. Tour's gotta be tough for the ones who are used to it, he thought, but young one's like her, seems like they could be taken advantage of too quickly.

"I think Rowen's mom died recently," Cass said, kind of quietly. "He doesn't seem to want to talk about it with anyone though," she said, looking around to make sure no one heard her.

"Oh, man, really?"

"I think so."

Devon's mind went to watching a girl with flying black hair out his kitchen window as a boy, sitting next to a small tombstone. That girl, Jessie. Fuck. Something swelled up in his chest and he had to cough to keep it down. He found the curb behind him, set his glass beer bottle down and slowly rolled a cigarette. Shakedown was starting to swarm and Cass continued selling her beer. Rowen's mom, Mrs. Jones' daughter, dead.

He shook his head and smoked.

"You alright?" Cass asked, looking behind her.

"Oh, yeah. Looks like yer selling now!" he said, mustering a different energy for her, before going back to his thoughts. His stretch of land in New Mexico. The devastation he'd heard washed over his family right before he was born. The devastation that spared the Jones'. And then Jessie went off to California and had three boys, one of whom was a deadhead now and acting like a little prick. But it made sense, Rowen was probably grieving—or not grieving. Still, no reason to be an asshole to an innocent girl like Cass. Devon got up and stood next to Cass again. She smiled at him and he could tell that underneath, she really was good. Maybe he'd keep an eye out for her.

"You always go into the shows with Rowen?"

Devon noticed she made a face. "Yes! why?"

"Just asking. You've got some other friends about here though, right?"

"I guess so," she said, clearly annoyed. Devon tried to soften.

"What'd you think about the show tonight? It was a pretty good one, especially all Bobby's cowboy songs.

"They were fun. I liked the second set better though."

Good, Devon thought, she was paying attention to the music. "You doing the rest of these shows" he asked her.

"I guess so," her brow scrunched up again. Then she looked in his eyes, clearly stressed. "Really, I shouldn't be here at all. I don't know what I'm doing and my mom is going to kill me!"

Ok, now the truth comes out. "Uh oh," Devon said, laughing gently, "Seems like you're doing swell. I mean, all ya gotta do right now is sell this beer, right," Devon moved to the side of the cooler to talk to her easier, and let other people come up to buy from her. "Then you go in the show, enjoy yourself, dance, have a good time, right?" She softened a bit, "Yeah, I guess so, thanks Devon."

"Supposed to be a good time here, right?"

She nodded and stopped looking around all frantically.

"Mind me asking how old you are Cass," Devon said, giving her a sly smile then sipping his beer.

"Eighteen," she said, "Old enough to make my own decisions."

"Right, right," he said. "And what does your mom think you should be doing?"

"Not this! That's for sure!" Cass laughed with him, becoming more comfortable, it seemed. Devon wondered what it must be like, having an older child, one who could make her way out in the world. That'd be a good many more years for Emma.

"Well," he said, trying to be cool, trying not to upset her, trying to offer some good advice.

"She thinks I should be working and going to school," Cass said flatly.

"Well, ya are working, although looks like you still got a lot more beers to sell" he said.

Cass smiled and shouted right into Shakedown, "ICE COLD BEER!" Devon laughed, but heads turned and she sold three more quickly.

"Not bad, not bad. So, it seems you got one thing covered, you ARE doing some work."

"This isn't exactly what my mom had in mind, I don't think."

"Well, it's still summer, you can still go to school, sometime. Just don't make your mom worry too much," Devon said and thought about how crazy Cora might get if she didn't know where Emma was. Probably a whole different thing for a teenager. Oof, he didn't want to even imagine what that'd be like.

"Ok," Cass said frowning. "I just…" she trailed off when she spotted Rowen walking towards them. He looked stern.

"Hey, man," Devon said, shrugging up his shoulders. He wouldn't say anything to him, even as he watched Rowen look him up and down.

"Oh, hey," he said, then turned to Cass, "You almost out?"

"Sort of," She said. Rowen bent down and made the bottle and ice clank, getting them in the icy water and pulling a few up so the labels could be seen.

"Hey, Rowen," Cass said, "Do you know Devon?"

"Uh," he said not so friendly, "I guess."

"Hey, man," he said again, "Yeah, seen you around."

Fucking little punk, Devon thought. Not decent enough to be a good brother on tour. Ok, ok, he reminded himself, his mom died. Must have been not too long ago. Cass looked at Devon, like, what's going on? Rowen stood up and looked at him. Devon stuck out his hand. Rowen paused, then stepped towards him and slapped his hand in. Devon held on and could feel a touch of fear in him. Really, he just wanted Rowen to know he knew him, he knew the truth and that it was ok, without having to fucking say anything. He held the younger man's hand, "Yeah, I've been on tour off and on. You, too, I see you around." Rowen nodded, until Devon let his hand go, and he watched him shoot a glance at Cass. She turned pink and bent down to stare into the cooler.

"Anyways," Devon said, "You all have a good night." He walked away, weaving into Shakedown and peered back to see Cass following him with her gaze. Clearly it was too much for Rowen, he seemed so tense, a quarter could bounce off him. Not time to confront him or offer condolences. Devon felt a shitty knot sitting in his own chest, hearing about Jessie. He could only imagine how Rowen felt.

Hettie wondered if Devon was even in the neighborhood. Was he still limping as she'd seen him moving across her front field after he, apparently, climbed Crystal Mountain. It didn't matter. She was just glad he was down off that crazy hill. Hettie didn't want any more fatalities up there, or anywhere. Hettie continued her task of cleaning the cabin. Every time she took a damp rag to some edge of wood, or windowsill, and came away with streaks of dark dust, she imagined someone else doing this task. Like if she wasn't there anymore. Hettie couldn't think of spending her days anywhere else, and there wasn't much room for another person in the cabin. It wasn't like her great-granddaddy's ghost stayed there or anything. He just popped in now and then. It had been a few weeks since she'd seen him, and Hettie remembered how sad he'd was last time.

Towards the afternoon, when she'd made some progress on the cabin's dirt, she heard a low thud. Thud, thud, like something dropping on the Earth, like heavy boots or a wrecking ball. Hettie moved towards her porch and heard it louder. She went outside and looked down. To the left and about 300 feet beyond her outhouse, she saw an old man lifting a giant, tarnished pick axe up behind his head and then letting it thud to the earth. He did it again and again with slow movements. The sound of that tool and the small tremor she could almost feel up there on the porch, widened her eyes. What in the Devil, she mouthed to herself. The man's clothes were baggy and worn, and as Hettie squinted to study the side of his face, she realized it was her granddaddy. He was working the land, he was breaking the earth, he was baking in the afternoon sun. Once the axe thud again, Hettie leaned over the rail. "Yoo-hoo," she yelled, "Oh, you! What're ya doing?" Before lifting the axe again, he slowly moved his head to the side and up, peering at her on the porch. But he didn't say anything, just kept swinging metal behind him, up and down into the Earth. Hettie looked to the spot on the ground down there, but there wasn't much of a hole or groundbreaking, if that's what he was trying for. He didn't seem like he was going to stop though. The sun beamed down on the scrubby Earth. She could feel the heat through her clothes. It was not the time of day to be outside, if one could help it. Hettie went back inside, letting the screen door slam behind her, hoping to make near as much noise as his work or whatever it was. She emptied her ice cube trays into a big glass pitcher and filled it with the jar of iced tea she had in the fridge and then more water. The liquid popped and cracked over the ice. Hettie grabbed two glasses from the cupboard and walked back to the porch with the jingling pitcher. She let the screen door slam again and shook the pitcher to let the sound of ice and water on glass, run off her porch. Hettie leaned over the rail and shouted as casual as she could, like she'd do to anyone working outside in the New Mexico heat. "Come and get something cold to drink." Hettie heard two more slow thuds and then silence. She poured ice and water into both glasses and sat down on the bench.

In a few minutes, her granddaddy's ghost was up on the porch, sitting down, too, and reaching for the other one of those glasses. He downed the liquid in one slow, very long swallow. Placing the ice filled glass on the wood table, Hettie thought how strange and unsettling his movements were. "That's real nice, thank you," he said.

Hettie just nodded and diverted her eyes from him. She leaned to the table and filled his glass again from the pitcher, letting the little clinks and ice pops fill the space between them. She sat back down. "What were you doing down there?" she ventured to ask.

"Well," he said slowly, pushing his hat up onto the back of his head. "You got all this land that's being neglected. It needs someone to make it fertile, to work it and plant something.

Hettie nodded and moved her mouth into a tight smile. "Used to be real fertile here," she said. "We'd alfalfa and hay and a big ole garden."

What happened?"

"Wilson died," she said thudding her drink glass onto the table with finality.

Hettie watched her granddaddy take his hat off and reach for a handkerchief from his pocket. He slowly rubbed the top of his head and thinning hair.

"I's sorry for ya," he said, "I knows how it feels."

Hettie could feel his sorrow seeping from the stained shirt he wore, from the sweat he mopped. She knew life had been ten times harder in his day and she knew, from story, that his wife had died before him. Hettie nodded her head gently and for a long time. They ended up sitting on the porch, silent, till the sun slid behind the front of the cabin, and the heat stopped its oppression.

She'd studied the deep lines carving his face. The spaces around his mouth that could go up in a smile or down in a frown, and Hettie felt a little sad remembering him swinging that pick axe. He said the place needed to be planted, cared for. Hettie remembered the time when she had a big full garden, and hay planted in the front field, alfalfa on the side. Crops that were real, that grew and were harvested. But that was back when it was a working farm. It was just her now, and the thought of planting and growing or overseeing a crop just felt like too much, so did walking down a rocky path just to use the bathroom.

"You don't know how lucky you are to even have this ground," he'd said while shoving hands in his overall pockets and stepping down the stairs of her porch. Hettie felt really fortunate that she didn't spend much time in Appalachia, where folks were bought off their land for very little and the whole community and structure of the people who lived there was forced to change. Everything in her life might not have changed so abruptly as in his, but her place was nothing like it used to be. Her land, as a working spot, really needed other people, and now there weren't any. This usually didn't bother Hettie. She most often wanted to be alone anyway, but the young and the strong, like someone Rowen's age, could bring the place together, also maybe build her a bathroom. Though, she doubted Rowen had the skill for that even, maybe a better path to her outhouse was the most she could hope for.

Chapter 78
Rowen

It was the third of five days in the Oakland run. He still had eight cases of beer left and needed ice. Rowen wished Ollie was there, he was always so good with ice runs. He knew Cass couldn't do it herself and the likelihood of them both hitching a ride to and from a shop was unlikely. Rowen pulled the wheeled board out from the back and brought it around to the side. Cass was just lying on the side bed in the van, doing nothing.

"Hey!" he said a little too abruptly, and she jerked up, "think you could help with something?"

"Uh, sure," she said, sitting up and tugging her tennis shoes on.

He had to lay everything out for her, which was tedious. "So, we need ice. Gotta go outta the lot to get it," he said, pulling the two empty coolers out the door. "We can't both go. I've got to get a ride there and back and load up someone else's car. People are used to these runs, but they cost about $20, which is a rip-off." Cass peered at him, now outside of the van, too, waiting for further instruction. "So, I need you to wait by the edge of the parking lot with these coolers. When I come back, we'll load the ice in here and bring it back. Understand?" He said, dropping the wheelie and placing the coolers one on top of the other on it. Cass nodded and put her hands on the wobbly empty coolers. "I don't know how long I'll be, but you can head to the entrance in say 30 minutes."

"Ok, Rowen, I can do that." Her voice kinda creaked, but Rowen didn't question.

Work needed to be done on tour and if she wanted to ride, he'd need her help. "Ok," he said and walked away. Rowen booked it to the edge of the East parking lot entry. A ratty dude was idling in his small hatchback, looking like he did runs.

"Hey, brother, you running? For ice?"

"Sure am," the guy said, dropping his cigarette and stepping out of his car.

"How much?"

"$40."

"What? That's robbery, man?"

The guy put his hands up in the air, "You need ice? I need cash," and he turned around to get back in his rusted car. Rowen looked around, it was the only car, apparently, he had a monopoly, in that no one else was doing runs, and pretty soon new folks would be coming in the lot and the lineup would make it harder to get close to the entrance. Fuck.

"I'll give ya $30," Rowen shouted.

"Nope."

Rowen looked back in the lot. He could try to go find someone else, but if they had a good parking spot, they probably wouldn't want to lose it. A few other beer sellers he knew, started walking to the entrance, too, probably also needing ice. The stupid little car was hatchback, two seats. Really only enough room for one rider and 5 big bags of ice in the trunk. Shit. Cass would be over in 30 minutes. This was Ollie's gig. Rowen wished he didn't have to sell in the lot, even in Oakland. He never did that with Penny. She always had money. And touring with the other guys, well they did most of the grunt work.

"Fine," Rowen said. He got in the passenger side, and creaked the door closed. The car smelled like shit, BO and meth. Rat Head, Rowen thought. "You know the closest spot for ice."

"Ya brother and cool it. Give me $20 first."

Rowen shook his head, such shit, this lot life. He pulled a $20 from his pocket and handed it to the guy. They had to go to two stores because the first only had an empty ice cooler. By the time they headed back, it had been about 55 minutes. Rowen didn't see Cass. He didn't see his coolers. Fuck.

"Ok brother, there you go. Now give me the other $20."

"Here," Rowen said, "and thanks a lot," he peeled another twenty off a stack of bills and tossed it to the guy. Other heads were milling near the entrance. Where the fuck was Cass, Rowen raged. He got out and creaked open the hatchback. The giant bags of ice were starting to condense in the plastic. He needed to transfer them to the coolers.

"Ok, who's next?" the swindler said. A dreaded Head Rowen recognized flipped up his head. He walked towards the car, leaving a friend who was standing next to two coolers. Rowen shouted at him, "hey, man, my gal's not here with my coolers. Think I can borrow yours for a minute?" The guy looked around then lifted the cooler's lid. It was three-quarters full of glass beer bottles. Maybe enough room for one or two bags. Rowen shook his head, pissed that he couldn't execute this easy task without stupidity. He started to sweat. The other head closed the lid and flicked his head towards the hatchback. His ice was ready to unload.

"Hey, man, I feel ya. How bout I help you and you give me one of those bags to start cooling my glass?" It was a fair deal, but meant he'd probably sell less himself. Unless everything could move really quick. Rowen searched around for Cass. Where the fuck was she? His chest was tight and the meth head started beeping his stupid car horn.

"Hey, get yer ice, bro! I've got work to do!"

Rowen just shook his head, flicked it up at the guy, and said, "ok, brother. Help me out." The two guys lifted the ice bags, broke one in the cooler and stacked the others on top. They both bent down on either side of the stack and breathed out as they lifted. The weight felt like lead in his arms, the sharp ice edges poking through the plastic against his face. When they made it to the van, Cass wasn't there either. Rowen made quick work with the ice and one remaining cooler, and the van's small ice box. One bag was still left to sit on top of the open cooler.

"Hey, thanks, brother. Want me to help you carry your cooler back?"

"No that's ok, man." Rowen clasped hands with the guy and watched him easily hoist the cooler up and walk back towards the entrance. The East Entrance. That head was clearly stronger than Rowen; he probably did manual labor off tour. Rowen cracked the van's back doors, four cases still unpacked. Whatever. If he didn't sell them, it wasn't the end of the world, but what the fuck, where the hell was Cass? Rowen locked everything up and went searching for her.

Chapter 79
Hettie

Hettie looked at the colorful diamonds under her sewing needle. The quilt spread out over a rectangular table. She continued her stitch with the needle and length of string, then her eyes moved to look at the whole quilt. It was so familiar, and the colors of it were as vibrant as Fall leaves: red, brown, purples and orange and blues. The table seemed iridescent, shimmering in the little farmhouse room. Then Hettie heard voices, slowly getting louder and around the table were three other women. She listened.

"That's no good, man," one said.

"That's right! Going off with his fiddle like some explorer chasing gold."

"All Percy's gonna find is a lump of coal, and it'll bring him right back here." Hettie noticed the women around the table. They were familiar, too.

"Betty Ann, pass me that stretch of string, will you?" a woman with shoulders hunching towards the table said.

"Here you go, Dear," The other old woman said, stretching her hand across the table. Hettie watched them but didn't think they could see her. She looked down at the quilt bit in front of her, and it'd shifted to a star point. The colors weren't burnt, but now bluer. She knew this quilt better.

"That poor sister of his, just dropped with his children!"

"Oh, Melinda's a smart woman. She'll put those kids to work before they know their daddy's gone away. Gone away, gone away like the blowing wind," She hummed and the other women shook their heads slowly and continued pulling string through cloth.

"What do you think, Henrietta?" her great-grandmother, Betty Ann, said. Hettie's eyes got wide, and she felt flushed. Hettie felt like she was in trouble, like she'd been colluding with the devil or something. In her mind, Percy was a fine man, just a little lost maybe. Betty Ann shook her head slowly and Hettie felt the weight of her judgment. She looked down at her quilt again and the spot was the bird tracing, the needle in her hand about to pierce its eye.

"Now, don't you go confusing the girl," another of the women said, "She's just trying to help.

"The way for that man to help, would be staying on his own land, plowing it every day. Just because his wife died, doesn't mean he should up and leave!" Betty Ann said.

"Yes, it does," Hettie found herself saying.

"No, it doesn't!" Betty Ann piped, "Who do you think you are, saying such things?"

"She's your great-granddaughter," one of the other women in the quilting bee said.

"Oh, no she ain't, not if she's housing that no good bum, Percy."

"I, um," Hettie tried to say. She looked down and the black bird from her porch was sitting on the quilt, squawking like a chicken, his black beak opening and closing like it was going to bite her.

Hettie shot up in bed, her hands out in front of her, but no black bird, and no quilt. The dream fading as she realized she was still in bed.

Hettie peered anxiously out her window, gripping Wilson's stick, the one she'd have to use to get down the driveway into Marni's car, or to snap anyone who told her something she didn't want to hear. Hettie closed her eyes and heard fiddle music belting out and saw her granddaddy in her mind tapping his foot. She looked down. She couldn't tap her foot like him if she wanted to. It was still swollen, and any number of herb wraps she tried on it just wasn't working. It wasn't until Marni had come in the other day and yelled at her for not calling sooner.

"What in God's great name happened to you, Henrietta?"

"Oh, shush you, I'm fine. Just a little sprain."

But when Marni started wafting her hand in front of her face from the slightly musty scent of urine, perhaps a little drop still left in the jar she used, Hettie got embarrassed, and finally let her younger neighbor set up an appointment in the clinic in town to get it looked at.

"Tweep! Tweep!" The stupid little car sounded, and Hettie made for the door. She tried her very best to stand straight and ignore the pain in her ankle as she walked towards the car.

"Alright, Henri, you can get that scowl off your face and just thank me for coming," Marni said with a grin as she pulled out of the driveway. Hettie just looked out the window most of the way to town, letting Marni jabber about all the things she always jabbered on about: Jim, Jim, and her dogs and cats, and books and stews, and pies and the mail that'd come from her kids. Her voice wasn't steady and pleasing like her grandad's and Hettie wondered about the fact that she liked the company of her dead Granddaddy more than someone alive.

The clinic was in one building, a newer one that'd popped up long after she'd needed it with her Jessie for stitches, or Lou when he dang near lopped off his hand with a hacksaw. No, they'd had to drive 45 long minutes, kids wailing to get the help they'd needed.

Hettie wouldn't let Marni help her inside, even though she'd left her stick in the car. She didn't want the doctor to think she needed it.

"Well, hello Mrs. Jones," the young buck in a white coat said when she'd gotten up on the examining table. "What happened to your foot here?"

"It's my ankle and I think I just stepped on it funny, that's all. It's just a little swollen, should be fine," Hettie said and watched as Marni, who'd insisted on coming into the room, too, shifted and re-crossed her arms.

Without even being asked, she piped in "Mrs. Jones' outhouse is on down a little hill and the path is not so straight," Marni explained. Hettie shot her a glance, like, mind your own business!

The doctor helped Hettie lay down on the table and rest her feet up on it. The overhead light was really strong in her eyes, and she opened and closed her lids a few times to acclimate.

She couldn't see what the doctor was doing now. She couldn't see his face or Marni's when her sock was removed and they saw the purple, and that little place where her ankle bone was ugly and now more misshapen.

"Ah, I see," the doctor said using his doctor's voice that unnerved Hettie. "Mrs. Jones it looks like you might have broken your ankle." He was using a loud voice, as if she was hard of hearing and this made Hettie clench her body. This was the last place in the whole world she wanted to be, but she willed herself to take a deep breath and let it out really slowly, like she'd done in the years of her marriage when Wilson trampled on her nerves one too many times.

"Well, what, what has to be done about it," she said, relinquishing control over her own health, she felt.

"We'll take an x-ray and then maybe put you in a cast for a little while," the doctor said.

Hettie could feel herself starting to sweat. More constriction. Great.

"How long do you think it'll take to heal?"

"Oh, maybe six weeks?

"Six weeks of hobbling around with a big cast on my foot?"

"Yes, ma'am, maybe longer if you don't rest as much as you should."

Hettie let the young doctor and his nurses x ray and then wrap and plaster her ankle. She felt like a kid's craft experiment. And then they gave her some crutches, sticks, she thought, that dug into her armpits. They made her practice up and down the small hallway of their office and Hettie was really sweating by then.

Three hours later, after letting Marni grocery shop for her while she sat in the car, Hettie closed the door to her cabin, one crutch crashing to the ground like she felt, broken, needing to be picked up, needing other people. She just wanted to cry or spit. Hettie hobbled into the kitchen and poured herself a half a cup of whisky instead. Then she hobbled back to her couch, downed half the strong drink and sighed, her ankle looked like a giant snowball. It was so ludicrous that she had to laugh. Hettie let laughter pour out of her, loud and snorting, till it nearly turned to sobs.

Devon parked his bike down the street from the house. It was late afternoon on a Sunday. From what he remembered of Cora, she'd be napping about this time. Devon walked their street quietly, hands in his pockets. He didn't have a solid plan, he just wanted to spend time with Emma again. He thought, if he could just get her away from Cora—even for a little while, they could be free to be father and daughter. The street was pretty quiet. A kid on a bike sped down the other side, a dog barked behind a chain link fence, the early summer fronds of a palm shook above. Devon could feel his heartbeat in his throat. He tried to calm himself, get up and over the reality of what he was doing.

Cora did say she'd call the police, but clearly trying to see his daughter the normal way, by ringing the front bell, was not a choice. Nearing the house, he could feel himself sweating a little. He paused before quickly and very quietly stepping his leg over the fence, placing his motorcycle boot down on the grass of the backyard. He walked to the side window, where Emma's room had always been. The window was cracked, the screen in place. Devon crouched down and looked inside. Emma was sleeping on the bed. Hallelujah, he thought. Devon conjured the stealthy quiet he remembered from his flights, the swift movements of the raven. Devon lifted the window, and then the screen, using his fingernails to pry it up and open. She turned in her bed but did not wake. The bedroom door was mostly closed. There on the windowsill, were two tiny white shells and a little feather small enough to be from a hummingbird. Courage opened in his heart and he felt PJ's good work. Stepping across the room, Devon remembered that when Emma was younger it was easy to pick her up from the bed and carry her someplace else without her waking up. Still holding his stealth, Devon scooped up his daughter, turned, and carefully got her out the window. She was heavier than he remembered.

His flesh and blood, cradled in his arms, as he stepped over the fence. He wanted to be invisible, to fly with her all the way back to New Mexico. Devon shifted Emma's body so her head was resting against his chest. She breathed, and sighed, almost shuddered. Devon stopped, half way down the street with her in his arms, feeling elation, but also tremendous amounts of fear. Fear that anyone would see them, fear that she'd wake and not know him, fear that Cora would call the police. Devon had made it down two streets, back towards his bike. He needed her to wake up now. He shifted her dangly body to his other shoulder.

"Baby? Baby? Time to wake up," he said softly She stirred and lifted her hand to rub her eyes. They were near a shady tree, so Devon knelt down and held his daughter a little away from him. When she focused, she flinched, and seemed stunned, but then a huge smile spread across her face and she giggled,

"Daddy!" and she wrapped her arms around his neck, then whispered, "Mommy's gonna be really mad. Like she was the last time you came over."

"Oh, it's going to be ok, Emma. This is just time for you and me."

"Really?" she said, rubbing her eyes again, "Can we celebrate? Can we get ice cream, please, please, please Daddy!" Her squealing was kind of loud and Devon looked around.

"Ok, come on," he said, lifting her back up to sit on his hip as they walked.

"Tasty Freeze is just a couple blocks over, you know where it is?" she said, acting very adult.

"Ok, we can get some quick ice cream." Devon thanked God that she wasn't afraid of him or anything. Her focus on ice cream seemed like a good distraction from her realizing just how mad Mommy was going to be. When they got across the street, from the ice cream shop, Devon set her down on the sidewalk and took her hand. Her fingers were so thin and her skin satiny. She looked up at him,

"It's real good to see you Daddy!"

"Oh, baby, it's real good to see you, too," Devon could feel the corners of his smile reach all the way around his head. He hadn't felt this happy since… since… he remembered flying.

"Let's go in Daddy," Emma said tugging him. They got inside, and Devon looked for the least visible place. It was a booth near the back, and Devon sat on the side facing the door, facing his daughter. The part of the place they were sitting in was a restaurant, but you could order ice cream from there, too. A young kid came to take their order, and Devon was thankful it wasn't someone older, or a woman, someone who would be more likely to think something wasn't right.

"What can I get you?" he said.

"What do you want, Baby?"

"Ice cream sundae," she said confidently.

"Vanilla, or chocolate ice cream?"

"Both," she said smiling.

Wow, Devon thought, here was his little girl, all grown up and knowing what she wanted. Devon could barely believe it. He ordered a cup of coffee and an extra spoon. He wasn't sure how a little girl like Emma could eat a whole sundae.

"So, what's the occasion?" Emma asked, "Mommy says sundaes are for celebrations. But it's ok with me, if it's a regular day sundae." Her smile, her cheeks, her small kid teeth. Devon felt so lucky to be sitting across from her. He wanted time to stop, like it did when he remembered flying. He didn't want anything to take this away from him.

Bells jangled on the shop door, and Devon's heart lurched as he looked up to see two teenagers walk inside. Sunday afternoon, the place could get busy. Cora could walk into Emma's bedroom at any minute and fly off the handle, call the police, scour the neighborhood. The giant sundae arrived, and Emma was so excited she did a little clap over the bowl.

"Let's celebrate you Daddy, just you," she said looking at him.

"Thank you, Baby. How about you celebrate me, and I'll celebrate you!"

"Oh, that's a good idea." The way her voice curled up, pronouncing "idea" was just like Cora's voice. Devon watched his little girl shovel ice cream in her mouth and chew big slices of bananas. He snuck a few bites and washed them with the bitterness of coffee. He just wanted to stare and take in everything about her: the way a few strands of her hair circled down the side of her forehead, the way her small fingers gripped the spoon, how her head and shoulders came in line with the bowl.

"Did you drive your moto-cycle here, Daddy?"

"Yes, baby, but it's parked closer to the house."

"You mean Mommy and my house?"

"Yes," Devon said patiently, "It's nice to walk though, isn't it?"

"Mmm-hmm. I wanna go on your moto-cyle sometime," she said wiping her ice cream–smattered face with the back of her sleeve.

The ice cream in her bowl slowly disappeared, and Devon knew the time was disappearing, too. He couldn't take her away. Devon wasn't sure he'd even know how to care for her. Devon thought that someday he could have a home and provide for her. Someday, they could live like family again, but for now, he needed to be content with this small time. Devon's chest hurt with the weight of the reality, and under the table his leg bounced nervously. Now, he had to figure out how to get her back home. He had to convince her to keep a secret. Devon remembered the little white shell in his pocket. He pulled it out and set it on the table in front of her ice cream bowl. Her little hand shot out and grabbed it.

"Oh, Daddy! This looks like the other two I found," and she looked up at him with curiosity and a sly knowing, then smiled really big. "Were those from you, too, Daddy? They were on my windowsill."

Devon nodded and watched delight reign over his daughter's face, as she gripped the shell in her little palm. Devon took one long deep breath of light with her, before he realized time was slipping. "How long do you usually nap, Baby?"

"I don't know, Daddy. Til I wake up?" She gave him a big smile, as she shoveled in the last of her sundae.

"Ok, yes, that's usually how it works," Devon said winking at his little girl. He'd have to take her back. He paid the bill and slowed his breathing as they left the shop. He took her hand and they walked down the street. It had been about 30 or 40 minutes. When they neared the house, Devon swooped Emma up in his arms. She was so small, so sweet, and so much a part of him. He noticed a little chocolate smudge on her cheek and rubbed it with his finger until it was gone. When they got close, Devon could see the front door was open. His stomach dropped. He held on to Emma.

"Daddy you're squeezing me," she said and giggled.

"Oh, I'm sorry baby. I love you so much," he said, looking at her, "you know that, right?" She nodded her little head. He wouldn't be able to get her safely back into her bedroom, to make it look like she was still sleeping. Shit. Devon started to shake and he scanned the side of the house wildly.

"I can go back to sleep, right Daddy?"

"Yes, sweetheart," he said. Cora was bound to be waking up soon and would probably be walking into Emma's room any minute, calling the police. Shit. He set Emma down on the sidewalk in front of the house. "We're gonna go back through your window and you can crawl right into bed, and sleep off your ice cream?"

"Good idea, Daddy"

"Now this little time was our special secret, right?"

"Uh huh," she said as she nuzzled into his shoulder.

Devon stepped one leg then the other over the fence, slowly, carefully, quietly pushed the screen window up with one hand, and lifted her curled body back inside her house. She leaned out the window for a second and kissed his cheek.

"I'll be quiet and I won't tell anyone about the ice cream," she said and winked both her eyes at him. He watched as she crawled back in her bed, pulled the covers over and lay still. He stealthily closed both the window and the screen and leapt one leg then the other over the fence. Jesus, he'd made it. Then his sense of flight picked up. Devon took off. Running down the street towards his bike. Devon glanced back and saw the house and the sidewalk were still. His boots stabbed the pavement. Almost to his bike, he heard the sound of his boots, louder than anything else, and he stopped, looked back, nothing. He made it to his bike, climbed on and let the loud roar of his engine take over. He sped down the suburb streets, onto the main drag, pumping gas into the bike. Devon looked at his hands on the handles, and they were visibly bouncing. He let out a sigh through his teeth, sped up onto the highway and into the fast lane back up to Oakland and the Grateful Dead show parking lot.

The Oakland scene seemed way more open and free than in the Midwest to Cass, if that was possible in the Dead lot. Rowen was more relaxed, but he'd been a fucking asshole when she'd messed up the cooler meeting. Her mind switched to his tone when she'd rolled the coolers back to the side of the van.

"Where in the hell have you been?" he shouted, yanking the coolers inside and ripping open beer boxes.

"I was waiting by the entrance, like you told me!" Cass shouted back. She remembered wanting to cry. It wasn't her fault she didn't know the Oakland venue like the back of her hand. It wasn't her fault she didn't know the intricacies of selling beer in a parking lot. Jesus.

"Well, you weren't there," Rowen said coming up next to her and pointing to the East Entrance." She remembered smelling his body odor and wondering what she was doing with this dirty hippie. Maybe Hill was right.

"I was over there!" Cass said pointing in the other direction. Rowen dropped his hand, turned to the van, and shoved the coolers in further.

"Oh," was all he said.

Well, fuck you, too, Cass wanted to say to him, but she didn't. She just walked away, hot tears streaming down her face. People who'd heard them stared as she walked by. She hated having this confrontation so publicly. She hated everything being so public on tour. It was like suddenly living with a thousand siblings. Cass hadn't known what that was like. It had just been her and her mom. Everywhere she could see people hanging out of buses: yellow, orange, stickered and painted. Heads moved through the parking lot like they owned the place. Cass spent hours walking all over the lot. She let her mind flow to cartoons, and characters in books she'd read when she was younger, *Charlie and the Chocolate Factory*, Bugs Bunny, Peter Rabbit. She talked to random, people and even laughed with them. It wasn't until nearly showtime that she waded through the thickening crowd back to the van.

Cass watched as Rowen kicked the cooler closed and handed over three beers to a customer. Two other empty coolers lingered nearby. He'd sold most of the beer, by himself. He gently reached out and took Cass's hand and led her to the open side of the van. He sat down and pulled Cass close to him. She let him.

"Look, I'm sorry," he said, "I know this place is new to you."

Cass nodded and let him kiss her. Ok, she thought, at least he's not still being a dick. They rolled around on the back bed, with everything going on outside for nearly an hour. Then it was time to go in the show, and Cass had forgiven Rowen.

Cass stayed close to Rowen during the whole first set. He kept his fingers twined in hers. During the set break the two of them climbed the stairs together. Even though the experience was different from letting loose and dancing in the hallways, she liked being close to Rowen and she was happy he wasn't being a jerk. Rowen stopped in the middle of the hall, as a middle-aged man clasped his hand.

"Hey, Rowen, how you been, man?" the guy said.

"Good, good, happy to be back in Cali," Rowen winked at him.

The guy looked Cass up and down. "Hey there, pretty mama, who are you?"

"Hi, I'm Cass," she said and let me man lean in to hug her. He didn't smell. He seemed like a business man. Rowen chatted with the guy a little more, and then before they headed out, he handed Rowen a half a ticket stub, which Cass thought was strange. He already had his ticket. Back at their seats, Rowen tore a small corner off the other guy's ticket and popped it in his mouth.

"This is some real good stuff. You ever take acid, Cass?" She shook her head.

"You wanna trip?"

Cass had no idea what it'd be like, but she figured if it wasn't safe, he probably wouldn't give it to her. She trusted Rowen that much. "Ok, sure," she said. Rowen tore a piece about half the size of his and Cass put it on her tongue. She could taste a little tinge of something sharp, but mostly it just felt like a bit of paper in her mouth.

An hour and a half later, in the middle of space, Cass's head and body felt like water. The sounds coming from the stage sounded like bubbles and she almost thought she saw fish swimming through the air in front of her. The cheering and whistles of people around her were a giant wave, crashing on the shore and Cass closed her eyes so she didn't get swept away. Rowen was standing, watching the band members come back on stage. Everyone was standing, except Cass. The darkness of legs and closeness she felt to the concrete floor made her feel like she was at the bottom of the ocean. Cass gasped, wondering if she'd be able to breathe under there. She reached for Rowen's dangling arm and saw her hand through water. She wondered if she had feet or fins. She didn't think she could stand up. Rowen looked back and down at her, and leaned over, grabbing on to her arm. Cass tried to focus all her energy on reaching him, but everything melted under her. "Rowen," she eked out, "I feel really weird."

Cass didn't remember what happened after that, only that she woke up in the back of the van and everything smelled like sour cheese. She knew water would be good, but she still felt like she couldn't move. Her eyes felt thick in her head. She wondered if she had peed in her pants. No one was in the van, but the light was on and staring at her. She rolled over and peeled back the quilt over the window. Streetlight pavement shone on the ground, and she knew they were still in the lot, but where Rowen was, or how long after the show it was, she didn't. It felt hot in the van. There was a small duffle on the side bed, and her socks, shoes and hat were bunched on the floor next to the back, probably mixed with orange cheese bits.

Chapter 83
Hettie

Hettie woke with the afternoon sun warming her face. She heard a tune, and the slow whine of Percy's fiddle. Hettie rubbed her eyes, and focused on his slim frame, sitting in her rocker and playing for her. He was a sight for her sore eyes, and she shifted her body gently, and pushed her elevated snowball foot a little closer to him.

"I don't worry 'cause," Percy sang, but then broke into a smile, "it's sitting on top of your foot." He laughed hard then, making Hettie a little sore. "What in God's name is on your foot?"

"It's a cast!" she said, "I hurt myself, apparently," Hettie let the rock thud gently on the floor and positioned herself up.

"Well, whatever white rock that is sitting on top of your foot, it looks awfully silly," He covered his smudged face and snickered again.

"Well, thank you very much!" Hettie hated the cast more than anyone. It itched and was heavy to tote around the cabin. Her mind skipped back to her dream, the one where her grandmothers bad mouthed her granddaddy. She'd known that he'd left Appalachia, but she hadn't known that he upped and left his kids. That wasn't so good, but, Hettie thought, there must've been some reason for his doings. Now, acting like a school kid, she wasn't so sure he had a good reason.

Percy started playing again, and real concentrated like, with notes that seemed more complex and clearer. He was really good. Maybe he thought he had a shot at recording back then. Hettie didn't think it productive to hold a grudge against a dead man, and she kinda liked his music playing in her cabin. She brought him a small cup of whisky, and a glass of water which took a lot of hobbling to get to the table for him. She set back down and continued listening to him. Hettie studied his concentration as he played: the furrow on his brow, the steady angle of his elbow. He did produce beautiful music, but Hettie wondered what made him leave his family like he did. He strolled through another tune, and even started a high-pitched signing, which made her smile. Then he rested his fiddle on his knee and knocked back the whisky. He seemed relaxed enough, so Hettie asked, "How come you left your home?"

Percy looked at her and raised his eyebrows. Hettie kept calm. She was laying back down on the couch with her snowball perched up. She was just curious and kept her gaze soft. Percy rubbed his forehead and head and started rocking the rocking chair. "I don't know," he said, "guess I was looking for something. It seemed I was losing everything. There was just too much..."

Hettie stayed quiet. She wasn't about to call him out on leaving his kids behind. Percy put the fiddle under his chin, sat up to play something, then pulled it away. He did it again, like he wanted to play or say something, and again pulled it away.

"It's just... It's just..."

Hettie watched his knee bounce the fiddle resting on it up and down, up and down.

He wiped his face. "She was gone," he said, "My Molly was gone." His gaze seemed to fix on a point on the wall. Hettie did remember the name, Molly. She was his wife. She'd died and Hettie had overheard this from her parents. They did have three kids.

Percy put the fiddle under his chin, and pushed the bow forward real slow, making a low, long whining sound. He paused in the middle of a stroke, "She was real sick," he said and continued, pulling the bow back. He changed the position of his fingers and pushed again, slowly like breath going out. "She couldn't near breath," he said, pulling the breath and the tune back in. He was mesmerized in his thoughts and the making of a deep, sorrow song, and Hettie could see his sunken cheeks more clearly, his lowered head and thin legs. His pain was like tall, dry grass yellowed by wind and sun and ready to fold back to earth. Hettie closed her eyes, listening to the steady in and out, the screechy sound of a death fiddle. She felt really sad for him. The lines of sound became thinner and thinner, and when Hettie opened her eyes again, Percy's ghost was gone.

Chapter 84
Rowen

Rowen gripped the steering wheel, watching the center line, trying to keep himself calm as they sped through the edge of Arizona, almost into New Mexico. His mind was all over the place, his heart even worse. It was just him and Cass now. She'd freaked in Oakland. She was just tripping hard. He knew that to take her to the medic's tent would just mean a shot of Xanax or valium and trouble for him. Rowen's impulse after the show and getting her back into the van, was to flee, hit the road and not really stop. Now she sat next to him, arms crossed, eyes straight forward, clearly still uncomfortable, but not talking much. Even though Rowen was getting used to having her around, he could just as easily send her back to Kansas. She insisted she couldn't go back there—some shit with her mom.

"The Wheel" came on the deck, an old version with Brent. Rowen eased back in his seat. It was up to him to keep the cool head, to act like everything was going to be ok. But, shit, he didn't want to be responsible for her, and now with Hettie needing his help, the reality was feeling a little too real.

"Who's this?" Cass asked, when Brent's high gravel voice punched in.

"The singer is Brent Mydland, The Dead's keyboardist from '79 to '90."

Cass nodded. It was about all she'd said in the past 100 miles. Progress, Rowen thought. She took her tennis shoes off and propped her sweet, small feet up on the dash. Rowen smiled. Let things chill for a minute or two. The road sign said: Welcome to New Mexico, the Land of Enchantment. Rowen wondered about his grandmother. He hadn't seen her in near half a year, and he could still feel the tar weight of circumstances the last time. He wasn't sure what it would be like to see her. It'd probably remind him of his mom. Dammit. Rowen knew she was the closest thing to her, in essence, and it might just be too hard. He could feel his lips tightening, trying to hold his feelings inside.

Chapter 85
Devon

The weight of his head in his hands felt like a hallow bowling ball, hard shell, heavy, reeling. His clothes smelled like the road, and fear. He'd sped back up to Northern Cali in almost a straight shot. No cops appeared, but they could have. They could have. His leg bounced on its own, tapping his boot tip against the warped wood floor. He listened to the silence, for a moment, and then it filled up again with all his racing thoughts. Coming down from the road was one thing, trying to gauge what Cora would do next just made him angry. Made him want to hit something with metal, something as hard and round and confining as her actions made him feel. He'd hated being behind bars, it was like lost time, while his little girl had walked through her days, maybe wondering where he was. Emma's face came into his mind, and his throat closed. He'd captured a moment, the real kind, that he could replay over and over, and let bloom in his heart when he needed it. Like he'd savored in prison, at night, in the dark, in his bunk, when no one was giving shit or acting tough, when he didn't have to look over his shoulder, and could settle down and just think. Emma would be there, waving at him, running to him in the park, smiling her big smile, and even earlier when she'd taken her first steps. No one or nothing could take those memories from him.

Devon knew it was stupid, stealing Emma out of her window like a burglar. Real fucking stupid, man. What were you thinking, he asked himself. Devon felt the soft give of the motel bed, took a deep breath and blew it out. He'd needed something more current. Kids grow up so fast.

He didn't want to miss everything. He needed to see how her thoughts were forming, that she didn't forget him. He could still feel the gentle weight of her in his arms, on the sidewalk in front of Cora's house. The shock and then delight he'd experienced when she woke in his arms. The picture in his mind, made Devon smile, he could feel the memory moving into his chest, etching there, calming him. It was enough. It was enough. Devon stood up from the bed, feeling all the aches in his arms and legs from riding the highway.

Chapter 86
Rowen

owen popped the old tape in the dash, Legion of Mary. "Let it
Rock" came on sweet and slow. Rowen bobbed his head a bit then
climbed to the back of the van, side doors opened wide. He could
feel the cooler New Mexico air on his bare feet. Fucking Cass, she should
have just stayed in Kansas. What the fuck have I got myself into, he
thought, rubbing his forehead and brushing his hand down his oily hair.
He knew his grandmother was pissed, and she didn't know the half of it:
a twenty-three-year-old dosing up a barely out-of-high school girl and
riding with her across the country. Shit. He was stupid. The cops could
track him just for that.

Oh, and that casual mention that her mom's boyfriend works for the
KC Police Dept. What the fuck. Rowen sucked in air through his teeth
and let Jerry's guitar soothe him. Cass was gonna be fine. She just had
too much too fast, he told himself. She was presently sleeping it off on his
grandma's couch. He'd pack her up on a bus tomorrow and be done with
it. He was pissed enough that he'd had to leave the Oakland shows early
and give up his mail orders. He pulled the envelope from the cabinet and
looked inside. There were two tickets for the end of the tour shows in
Arizona, for the next day. Rowen studied the colored stripes on the end
and the capital letters: F-L-O-O-R. These were special. The thought of
missing this, when the band clearly honored him with floor seats for the
last show of the tour, was close to criminal. Rowen tapped the tickets on
the bench. Cass needed an off-tour break. He knew that. He'd seen that.

Rowen's heartburn came back and he wanted a toke. He packed the bowl, lit up and sucked in. He could feel the pot reaching his lungs and the burning space in the middle of his chest. His mom would hate him, think he was stupid. She never used to think anyone was good enough for him, even Penny. Everyone could see Cass was a good girl though, and he had no business with her. The sax lit up and blew out his thoughts. It's fine, he told himself. Rowen turned to the open doors, and there standing in front of him was an old man.

"Hey, son," the man said. Rowen jumped back. He hadn't seen anyone there a few seconds ago.

"Shit! You scared me, man," he said, slowly setting the pipe down.

"Real sorry," the man said, grinning big.

Rowen rubbed his eyes. What the fuck. The man was wearing threadbare clothes, not like a hippie, but a genuine hobo.

"Who are you? My grandma's neighbor?"

The man grinned again and showed some cracked teeth. "Ha, ha, guess you could say that."

Rowen pulled himself together and stretched out his hand.

"Rowen," he said. The man clasped Rowen's hand and gripped in a way that gave Rowen some goosebumps.

"Percy." The man held Rowen's hand and when he wanted to let go, fear leapt into him. Who the hell is this guy.

"I said, name's Percy."

Rowen's mind did a flip. He'd heard that name before.

"Where do you live?" Rowen asked, thinking it must be up the hill, around the bend, where he remembered a number of old families had always lived.

"Here and there," Percy said, nodding to the music, "like your sounds. Who is that?"

"Oh, thanks. That's Legion of Mary."

"Legion of what? Religious music?"

"Nah, just some slow blues rock."

Percy nodded. "Henrietta's gonna need your help, son," he said, sounding much older than he looked.

Rowen nodded. "Yeah,' he said, "I know."

"You treat her good, alright?"

Rowen looked at the man and felt a very strange feeling, like his insides were made of twine and bone, scratching in upon himself. The guy did seem pretty harmless, though. Rowen turned to the van's console and when he turned back around the guy was gone. All he could see was the wind brushing the tall grass in the front field.

Chapter 87
Cass

"**I** can't go back home!" Cass shouted at Rowen as he inched towards the van.

"Why not?" he said.

"I told you, my mom has practically disowned me, and the last thing I want to do is show up all burned out from acid." Cass watched Rowen shake his head and snicker.

"You're gonna be fine. You just need a break, that's all."

"I just need to be with you," she said, stepping towards him. But Rowen stepped away again. Cass's heart dropped. Her head throbbed, too. How could he go to the next show without her. How can he be so cool and composed. Cass hated him in that moment, but she still liked him. Ugh, it was all infuriating and tears started streaming down her face.

"Look, you'll be fine. I'll be back in a day or two. Or I can take you to the bus station right now."

"No!" Cass shouted. She was surprised by her own anger, by the force of her shout. Then, she watched Rowen shake his head again, get in the van, and leave.

"I hate you!" she shouted, but he was too far down the drive to hear her.

Cass sat on the grassy gravel driveway, knees up, forehead down and caught her sobs as they pushed themselves out. She stayed there for about an hour like that, and no one bothered her. Then she got up, wiped her nose on her sleeve and walked down the hill to the outhouse. She had to fucking pee. As she moved down the rocky and uneven path she noticed the wide field was glowing. A yellow that calmed her and called her past the outhouse to stand in the middle of the field, like a beacon. It was a peace after her storm and the sun warmed her face and dried her tears. For a minute she stopped thinking and just breathed. Then a big black bird soared overhead and she looked up, listening to the swishing sound of its wings over her. She remembered the bird she'd seen at her apartment complex at the beginning of the summer. Before she even knew who the Grateful Dead were, before she'd met Rowen. Before she'd ended up in the middle of New Mexico in a field by herself on her boyfriend's grandma's land.

Chapter 88
Hettie

Hettie watched the girl out of the corner of her eye, keeping her own hands busy untangling strings. She was curled up like a wounded badger, staring out the spider-webbed windowsill. It wasn't worth trying to figure out what possessed her grandson to take off like he did. If he was any younger, she'd school him something fierce. Really, Hettie knew. Grief could wrap itself around the throat like a tightening snake and only be released by bold action, hungry movement away from everything. She didn't know Rowen's life, his friends, what made him tick, but she had a sense that getting in some type of relationship was the least of his capabilities now. It was ok, the girl seemed fine, just a little young and unexperienced. She was safe, and maybe she did hold some clues to help Hettie. Maybe she was there to help her untangle the rat mess of strings around that bird. The girl turned over, fluttering her eyes like she was pretending to sleep. Hettie knew she was restless; knew she'd had too much of something. But time would take care of her. Hettie just had to be patient and now share her cabin.

When Jessie was a teenager, Hettie remembered her sullen attitude most of the time. the way she dressed in all black for a whole year until Wilson told her he'd had enough of living with a zombie. He threw jeans and a work shirt at her one evening and said, "new uniform, starting now." Hettie remembered how Jessie's hands griped those clothes and actually pulled them close to her, like they were a gift releasing her daughter from the strain of a morbid existence she'd taken on too early. The scar of Violet's death would always be with her, and she'd taken that on when she was old enough to understand what had happened. But she didn't have to wear it on her body every day.

"How about some lunch," Hettie barked across the room, loud enough to get through her headphones. Cass's head moved and she slowly peeled the music headphones from her ears. Her legs swung out and she stretched, fake-like, as if she'd actually been sleeping. "Are you hungry or not," Hettie said.

Rowen watched the stage, slid down in his seat. He'd left Cass at his grandmothers, that was fact. He didn't want to be responsible for her. Heck, he didn't want to have to be responsible for anything. The band moved into "Cassidy" and Rowen let the music filter into him. Dusk light pierced him and he tried to focus. Rowen remembered the look on Cass's face and the way she turned away from him, sobbing. Fuck. It was too much, she was too good for him.

He didn't want any of it. His mind jumped to his mom, when she was younger, corralling him and his brothers to their grandma's in what he always thought was the middle of nowhere, New Mexico. It was a time when he just wanted to be back in California, just wanted to be back with his friends, and his weed and his closet full of Grateful Dead tapes. It was a time when he didn't want to do anything, and his mom's sighs lashed him like tiny paper cuts. He knew the song was about Neal Cassidy but all he could think of was the sweet girl who'd given him a chance, and he'd royally fucked it up. He shouldn't have given a freshie so much killer clean acid. He shouldn't be in this show without her. He shouldn't have been all over the country when his mom needed him.

Rowen put his head down in his hands, thinking of all the shit his brothers put his mom through. She just tried to work and sleep and scratch off her lottery tickets. Rowen could feel the burn in his heart, the sickness he had in him. It wasn't fair, why did she have to just go like that. Why couldn't he have gotten his shit together. Why couldn't he now. Rowen crossed his legs, tucked his foot around his ankle, pulled himself in, in.

He wanted to be alone, curled up in his van to let the pain just eat him in silence if it had to. He shouldn't be there, he knew it, but his body was stuck there, in the middle of the show, surrounded by thousands of people. He'd backtracked the highways to Arizona, in time for the show, after only looking at his grandma's outhouse path once. She wanted him to dig and add posts and a railing. He barely knew how to do shit like that. As the band moved into "Brokedown Palace," he closed his eyes. The slow tune wracked him, twisted him, and came bubbling up, into his throat, into his head. He hid inside himself, let it just well up, let it spill out the corners of his eyes.

Later after Hettie and Cass had eaten some supper, and the girl had gone out for a quick walk in the forest across the street, they both settled. Hettie in her bedroom, with the door just cracked, and Cass in the living room, curled on the couch. Hettie turned off her bedside light, so she wouldn't be bothered. It was strange having someone else sleeping in her cabin. She wondered if her great-grandfather's spirit would stay away, or if he would be curious and show up in the middle of the night. Hettie wondered if Cass would be able to see him too, though she suspected not. Darting bats swung by outside her window, marking shadows through the thin drape. The moon was high and strong and Hettie could see its light coming through, too. From the other room, she heard rustlings, the girl turning over and over again, trying to get comfortable. It's all I got to offer, Hettie thought to herself. This girl looks like she comes from princess pads really. Well, too bad, she's here now, and she'll have to figure it out. Hettie sighed, but not too audibly. Everything in that small cabin could be heard one end to the other. Someone could pass wind and it would travel. The space was really meant for one and occasional daytime visitors. When she'd moved into it 20 years ago, all she wanted was the alone space. The thought of sharing with others seemed impossible. But here she was, with an overnight visitor.

The rustling had stopped and now Hettie heard a loud sniffle, trying to be suppressed. She also heard little gasps. Instead of getting annoyed or angry at the sound, something in Hettie turned. She wanted to go out to the girl, hold her and rock her and tell her everything would be ok, as if she were her own girl. Her girl, who was six feet below the surface of this great Earth now. Her girl, who went through so much pain, right here on this very land. The thought that she'd never get to console her daughter again made everything rise in Hettie like a bubbly stream, too, and soon her own cheeks were wet with tears. She smeared them with her bed sheet and readjusted her old body on the lumpy mattress. It was a shame. So much of it was a shame. Jessie gone, Rowen lost out of his wits, this new girl abandoned. Hettie made a silent prayer for Spirit to give her a good dream, one that would wash over all this and leave her new like a soft summer rain.

Chapter 91
Devon

Devon pulled his bike into the Oakland used car lot, letting the engine idle. It was a sound he kept close to him, like his solid boots or the buckles he made. It was pure and reliable. He felt the seat he straddled and remembered how many roads he'd coasted on it. That bike had given him power and a presence to feed the rumble in his own head. He'd had it for near fifteen years and the thought of parting with it made him feel sick.

Devon lifted his eyes to the black-rimmed, neon yellow sign: Rob's Used Cars, Trucks, RV. He'd chosen the spot because it looked like they might have cheaper trucks and he'd spotted a couple bikes on the lot, too. Devon breathed in smog and asphalt and dug his fingers into the handlebar rubber. He clenched his arms, too, and reminded himself that there was a greater purpose to his life, and it required sacrifices. He could do this. He had to do this. There was no way he could get Emma back to New Mexico on a motorcycle. The negotiations were swift. His bike was sweet and he'd only had to pay $300 to get the title to a 1983 sand color Chevy truck. It felt weird to be in a ride like that with no wind or sun touching him, but it did take him back to the truck he shared with Cora when Emma was first born. Devon looked over to the passenger side of the cab and imagined the baby carrier strapped in and Emma's little face all scrunched up sleeping. Devon could feel a bloom in his rib cage and he knew he was doing the right thing. The truck bumped out of the lot and Devon drove back to the motel.

It was the only way. He knew fighting Cora for real custody would be terrible. She'd fight him like a nail gun, shooting down everything he tried for. No, he'd have to do it his way. Devon was half amazed that he'd been able to hold his little girl two days before. There was no harm that came from it. Devon was perched on the edge of the motel bed. He spread the atlas out over the ragged brown bed cover, he inhaled stale cleaner. His eyes traced the smaller lines like capillaries going from LA to New Mexico. It would be their own little adventure. He had a ride now. He'd checked the seatbelts. Shit, he even bought a little seat to prop her up in front so they could ride nicely together.

By this time, Devon had trained his mind to stay focused on the goal. Show her the land where he grew up, take her on a walk through the forest, tuck her in at night and make her breakfast in the morning with all kinds of birds signing just outside the cabin. The joy spread in his chest and lay like a soft blanket covering something harder underneath. He was tough enough to keep other thoughts at bay. He trained himself to think of his baby.

Devon stood up and paced the cramped room. He'd have to do everything perfectly. He'd have to be smart and stealth and careful and keen. Devon picked up a small pad and pen from the bedside table. He'd need water and food for Emma, he'd need some clothes for her and a blanket and pillow so she could sleep most of the drive. It would have to be at night, and he prayed hard that it'd be a night when Cora took a sleeping pill and Emma stayed in her own room. He had no way of telling and the risk stank like fire smoke.

Devon sat back down, put his head in his hands and breathed really slow. He made his mind blink to New Mexico and smell pine sap, hear the wind through trees, hear Emma's giggle, feel the change of seasons. This was the change. It's the way it would now be. He'd return home and Emma would, too.

Chapter 92
Cass

Cass let the porch screen door slam as she walked out of Rowen's grandmother's cabin. She circled back to the side of the place and onto the gravel road. She turned right, heading deeper up the hill that was flanked by thicker forest. Cass heard buzzing, saw crickets hopping, shielded her eyes from the sun. Her body still felt slightly liquid, even though it'd been three days since she'd set that piece of ticket on her tongue.

She couldn't believe that Rowen had really left her there. His grandma was ok, and didn't seem bothered too much, but, what the fuck? Was she supposed to help his grandmother or just hang out or keep out of her way? Probably it was a combination of all that and Cass kept walking, scuffling her tennis shoes on the small grey rocks and sending little puffs of dust up. She had to admit to herself that walking near nature, not in the lot, was appealing. Also being away from Rowen for a minute and his sharpness, and sour moods, wasn't all bad.

As she veered off the road and tucked under a barbed wire fence, she took stock of her life. She was finally finished with high school. She hadn't gotten into college like most of her classmates. She'd blotched her grocery store job, probably missed registration at the community college, and her mom was about done with her. That was the hard part, Cass hated being so estranged from her mom.

Cass's shoes crunched on the trail and she smelled vanilla radiating from the warming trees. Her mind skipped back to the shows, Jerry cooing into the mic, twirling in the hallways with Forest, Jane and Hill, and the fact that she was probably falling in love with Rowen. Living at her mom's was safe and comfortable, but she wouldn't give back all she'd experienced in the past couple weeks. Not in a million years, not for a thousand postcards from her dad. If she couldn't ever be with him, maybe she could be more like him. Traveling, listening, really experiencing life and something that seemed to make more sense than the doldrum of a regular, safe Kansas life.

The forest path Cass had followed started to narrow, then widen and curve and open up to another field. In that field was a small cabin, more rundown than Rowen's grandma's. It looked like no one was there. Cass squinted and caught the red and blue on a large Steal Your Face. It was a circle with the skull in it and up on the side of the dark wood cabin. "Ha!" she said, "The Dead are Everywhere!" It made her smile and shake her head. It was some kind of confirmation, she thought. Cass turned around and started walking back down to the road. Maybe she would try to help Rowen's grandma. She thought of the way she saw Heads helping each other in the lot, in the shows. Maybe it was no different.

Chapter 93
Percy

The train depot was packed with people: mothers and babies, old men, teenagers, scrappy dogs sniffing around the suitcases and bags stuffed with clothes. Percy found a spot to lean up against the wall. He had his fiddle wrapped and tucked under the crook of his arm. Sometimes he thought it was too valuable for him to let others see it, especially others who looked so desperate and poor.

Percy had just enough dollar bills to pay for a ticket back to his land, back to his children. He sure hoped his sister and kids got the money he'd sent. It wasn't a whole lot, and it only happened three times over the whole summer, but it was something.

"Get back there. Go help yer brother. Pick that up!" Percy listened to the woman trying to corral her kids on the dirty floor of the station. Only two of the kids had shoes on and the woman also held a baby in her arms. Percy wondered how hard it'd been for his sister, taking care of his kids. Did they mind her? Did they help out? Watching the woman from his stalwart place against the wall, hat sloping down his face, he wondered what it would be like to show back up. He'd had no contact from them in the past four months. He didn't really make it easy for anyone to know where he'd gone. Heck, if they remembered him at all when he showed up, he'd be happy.

The constant image of his wife dying right there on her little bed, tattered breath just leaving her, wasn't going away. Percy had come to expect it, right in his mind and memory whether he was working in a factory, mining in a hole in the earth, or riding some rails. Even getting miles and miles away from where it happened, didn't stop anything. Percy realized the running was no good. Sure, he'd worked and sent money back, but had that been the right thing? The fear grip of Molly dying, the image of her white skin, had become a death presence and he couldn't, wouldn't be able to get away from it. He'd found no comfort working bleakly with men across the country. The only solace he had was in playing music. But Percy knew he could do that anywhere. What he really realized was that having a parcel of land, even if it was scrubby and dry, was something. Percy wondered how his sons were coping. Did they miss their momma as much as he did? Were they staying busy, growing into men, too? Lord knows there's always something to do when your living on land in the hills. He reckoned his sister wouldn't put up with anything, just like she'd whooped him when he was a boy, two years younger than her.

The land Percy's sister and him had in those Appalachian mountains wasn't much, but they could at least grow something to eat there. If they worked together, it just might be ok. He'd tried to make some money other ways. What he'd found was a lot of heartache, a lot of desperation and many men who just wanted to buy a piece of land for their families.

The sound of a rooster wafted into the station and Percy longed to hear the one around his barn. It'd squawk and talk, the whole time Molly shouting back and addressing it like one of her children.

Devon sat in the back row of the bus, watching the strip malls and parking lots glide by. This was Emma's neighborhood, void of nature, packed with commodities, all day and all night, buzzing as an extension of LA county. He was going towards her house. It was about 9:30pm. Devon wouldn't get her this night, but he needed more insight, about the neighborhood, about any land mines he'd have to hop with her. People got on and off the bus. They were working folk, mostly Hispanic, carrying plastic grocery sacks and there were a couple kids with skateboards. Devon was wearing a baseball cap. Very odd for him, but it was about the only thing he could find to conceal himself a little. With tufts of graying hair sticking out the sides of the cap, he looked like a tradesman. All kinds of men were fathers, he reminded himself. The thought made him straighten and feel his back against the bus seat.

The sand-colored truck was parked in the back lot of the motel. He figured the less he drove it around there before picking Emma up, the better. He'd filled it with gas, checked all the tires, and the oil, even fucking put more windshield wiper fluid in. That truck was just stationed now, like a good horse, waiting to go.

Devon got off the bus three streets from Cora's house. He walked as casually as he could, surveying the street widths, the street lights, the telephone and electricity wires and looking for any cameras. His plan might be ballsy as fuck, but he wasn't entirely stupid. He walked with purpose, like he knew exactly where he was going, so nobody would even notice him. It was a pretty quiet neighborhood, and Devon made mental notes which streets to turn on and which not, too. He noted the end of one street where he could park his truck out of the way and only have to walk around the corner with Emma. He was careful not to get too close to the house. He didn't want to be seen. From several hundred yards away, he squinted at the house.

The side gate was the same, the edge of Emma's window was the same, the tree flanking their front lawn the same. Ok, he thought, I just did this the other day, and that was in the afternoon. The evening should be a piece of cake. Devon turned around and walked back to the busy exit street, the one that led two miles down to the freeway entrance. The one that would lead him East and South.

Devon unwrapped the small headphones from the Walkman he used to listen to on his bike. He needed to chill and turned the bootleg over so it could play side two. It was an '89 show, one of his favorite years for the Dead. But the knocking rhythm of "Victim or the Crime" flooded into Devon's brain in a way that pulled him down. He stretched out on the motel bed and crossed his boots, just listening and breathing. When he closed his eyes, Devon could feel the whip around in the air, facing North, pumping away and within. He had a peripheral vision that surveyed black feathers, that watched wings pump.

Devon blinked his eyes open, staring at peeling wallpaper and paint. He grooved on the dark tones of Bobby's guitar and reminded himself what he was doing. It was the thing that made the most sense, being with Emma, his daughter, his flesh and blood. He wanted the time with her so much because she was the closest thing to a mirror back presence of God or something greater. For whatever it was worth, she was the closest he felt he could get to himself. The purest version of himself.

Devon closed his eyes again and soared in between Bobby's notes, up and over Jerry's guitar to the lot and PJ and all those little trinkets he'd left for Emma. Devon breathed in and out, in and out, like the raven part of him. Just like letting go of his bike was an end of an era, so was the release of bird feel, the release of slipping in to some other realm. He wouldn't be able to do that now. In his mind, the high up raven began to drop straight down, and Devon watched it, gasping a little and wondering where that part of him would go when he had Emma. He wouldn't be able to just disappear again. He'd need to be there for Emma, every moment of every day. The dark and free strand of his life would have to be just that, dark and free, but not part of his life much longer. Devon turned and curled into the bed, pulling his knees up to the side, feeling himself as man, conjuring himself as father.

Chapter 95
Hettie

The girl seemed to be getting comfortable in her place, and that made Hettie feel both calm and cautious. Rowen hadn't even called, and if Hettie had a quarter for every time Cass looked at the phone on her kitchen counter, she'd be able to put in a toilet. Rowen would come back, she knew it. It'd been less than 48 hours.

"Did you make all these quilts?" Cass asked.

Hettie stopped rocking in her rocking chair and pointed to the ones on each far wall. "I made those two, but not the one in the center there."

Cass nodded, "They're all really pretty."

The ones Hettie had made were box and ring designs, but the blue one was a star quilt. "Do you know how to sew?" Hettie asked her.

"Nun uh," Cass said, staring more intently at the blue one in front of her. "Who made that one," she asked pointing.

"I don't know," Hettie said looking from Cass to the quilt and back again, "it's just been there a really long time."

"I like that there's a bird in the center," Cass said matter-of-factly. She was curled up on the couch, gazing at it.

Hettie smiled. Aha, she thought, so she can see it, too. "Where exactly do you see that," Hettie said.

Cass jumped up from the couch and went to trace her finger along the center of the quilt, easy-like, as if it was clear as day. Hettie nodded.

Cass stood there a little longer. "I also like this fabric with the little yellow and white flowers here, she pointed. Cass slowly walked over to Hettie's desk. "Is this where you do your sewing?" she asked. The desk top was covered in threads. A tangled mess, all clawed at like a squirrel had sat and swished back and forth, turning things with its tail.

"Used to," said Hettie, "As you can see, it's a bit of a mess right now."

Cass smiled at her, shoved her hands in her back pocket and peered over the mess. "I could help you if you want," she said, clearly bored and wanting to get her mind off Rowen.

"That'd be swell, if you can." Hettie watched Cass take a gentle seat at her desk and survey things. She moved the tangle back and forth, easing it and creating more space in between the threads. She was patient and attentive and Hettie winced when the sunlight shone through the window onto her light gold hair. When Hettie stopped talking to her, Cass put her headphones on and continued unraveling. Her head bobbed as she pulled threads. She stacked bits of fabric, wound up spools, brushed dust off.

Well, look at that, Hettie thought, her grandson had found a young woman worth something. She took initiative and helped out. She was jovial in her work. An hour and a half later, Hettie surveyed her transformed desk. It was an organized platter that beckoned creativity, that beckoned newness.

Chapter 96
Rowen

The road swung around to the right for a mile, then back to the left. Rowen liked the slide, but also felt how his own emotions had swung in the past two days. It was frivolous to take off to Arizona and leave Cass at his grandma's, but it was also perfect. He needed that time alone to just be, to go in the show, to not be babysitting or worrying about being cool.

Now, he was headed back to New Mexico, and the landscape guiding him was warm and radiant. Rowen thought back to traveling with his mom and brothers from California. The last time they took that drive he was 19, and he remembered how much his mom liked to ride in the passenger seat, on vacation, smoking her cigarettes, ashing out the window, letting her hair get blown in the wind and propping flip flop feet up on the dash. She was like a teenager, while Rowen was the grown up—in his new van. She really had wanted to go to Mexico, to the beach somewhere and drink pina coladas.

Rowen suspected his mom didn't get to party like she'd wanted to in her life. He couldn't imagine having one kid at 23, then two more, two years later. She was locked in. And after his Dad left, she just went to work: carted fried eggs, cleaned up ketchup bottles, and poured coffee. That diner was her home though. Everyone knew her, and Rowen could remember countless pats on the back from the customers, until he was about 12, and started smoking pot, and stopped going in there. Too many local cops liked to dine there, too. Rowen didn't want to have anything to do with them, but he was happy his mom kept them looking the other way, at least he thought that was the case with Lou and Tate, who were much worse hooligans then Rowen ever could be.

Rowen knew his mom loved him, he knew she forgave him, and he knew she was watching over him. In songs like "Black Muddy River" and "Jack Straw" he felt her gentleness and the years she took to live her simple life.

His grandma was a different story, all holed up in a cabin and living the vestiges of a country life. She was spiritual for sure, but Rowen worried she wouldn't be able to take care of herself, someday. The thought exhausted him, but he also felt responsible—like if he didn't get the chance to be there for his mom, maybe he needed to be for his granny. Rowen wondered what was happening at her house now, with Cass. Cass was easy, his grandma was smart, there shouldn't be any problem. Maybe they can learn something from each other, Rowen thought. Mostly though, it was a load off him, and he needed that time. What was gonna happen with Cass, no one could say. Rowen liked her enough, but if she came out to California, he'd have to figure everything out. He wasn't ready for that. Soon it'd be time for Fall Tour, then winter. Maybe she wasn't one to give up her Kansas life and go on tour. Maybe she was smart enough to go to college. Maybe she should go to college.

Chapter 97
Devon

Wake up, darling girl. Let me see you smile.
Take up, fate's up. Keep moving through the night.

L a Cueva was in the Northern part of New Mexico. Devon would have been much more comfortable driving far south, close to the border even, but that was not where they were going. He gripped the steering wheel as early morning began and the gold-pink sun rose from the horizon in front of him. Mesa, Arizona, they were near half way. Brent's voice soothed him, one side of the headphones propped over his ear. "I Will Take You Home," cooing. I will take you, Emma, Devon thought, I'm here now with you. He could feel the speed under the metal of the truck as they moved along, closer and closer to his small cabin in the woods. He glanced at her, leaning to the side of her car seat, tiny hand up to her cheek. She was his now, to take care of, to protect and love.

Devon turned the truck onto 191 and began winding North through the Apache Forest when Emma stirred. She let out a muffled whine and Devon placed his hand on her front. She wrapped her arm over his hand and held it, as she squirmed a little in the seat. "Hey, baby, good morning," he said, pressing his hand to let her know she was alright.

"Where… where am I?" she said, blinking her eyes open and turning to look out the window.

Devon could feel the hummingbird flutter in her chest as fear and the motion startled her awake.

"Where are we?"

Devon realized he would need to hold her and soothe her. He carefully pulled the truck over to the side, near enough to a pretty stand of trees, and far enough off the road that other cars could speed by. When the car was in park, he slid over on the front seat and unhooked her belt. She crawled out towards him. "Come here, baby, it's ok. We are taking a trip, to New Mexico, to home." Emma rubbed her eyes and laid her head down on his shoulder. The tenderness of her little frame and the way she breathed in and relaxed into him more, made him feel right and good. He was doing this for him and for her. As he held her, Devon looked out to the forest, and the shafts of sun lighting the tree bark and dust. Small birds flew from branches and over rocky ground. He could stay there forever, his little girl snuggling into him. A truck sped by them and he held her closer.

"Daddy, I have to potty," she said.

"Ok honey, I'll help you out the door." Devon set her back in her seat, got out and carried her to the edge of the trees. "You can just go on the ground, like when you go camping, ok." She nodded and squatted down. Devon stared through the stands of trees and for a flash, felt a pull to fly through them at a high height. His daughter was at his mid-calf, his eyes met mid-tree, but with wings he'd be tree-top level, soaring.

"Daddy, I don't have paper."

"It's ok baby, just drip dry for a few seconds."

"Ok," she said and stayed still. Devon was proud of himself for having answers. They needed to keep driving, keep going to get home. Devon helped her back in the truck and secured her seat belt. It would be another few hours until they got to a larger road, and Devon put a scratchy radio station on. Another 10 minutes and Emma was sleeping again—it was still only 6:10 a.m.

Chapter 98
Cass

Now Hettie wanted her to start working on the path down to the outhouse. Cass put on the floppy wide-brim hat she gave her and took the shovel. They stood out by the beginning of the path down. It was pretty sloped and rocky and Cass wondered what the old woman had in mind to make it better. She was no construction worker, but she thought she'd be able to dig a little dirt to help her.

"See how it's got all those rocks juttin' out? It makes it real hard to get this crazy thing down, without all kinds of banging."

Cass looked down to the plastic bag tied around her casted ankle and foot. She nodded, knelt down and used her hands to scrape the dirt from larger rocks. Then she placed a couple to the side and patted the dirt back. She knew this was going to make the path even more sloped. It could almost be a slide.

"Maybe I need steps," Hettie said.

"That might be a good idea," Cass said, "maybe Rowen"

"Aw yeah, whenever he comes back."

Cass's chest tightened when she heard this. Here she was, stuck at this old woman's house, and her boyfriend, if she really could call him that, was taking his sweet time at a show.

"Well, least you can help me get down there," Hettie said reaching out to take Cass's arm. Cass helped her down, brushing up against the scraggly bushes and letting her own feet slide as she tried to steady Hettie. At the bottom, the outhouse door slammed and Cass walked out in the field to give her some time. It was beautiful there and serene and Cass smiled at the chirping of the crickets. She could hear water, too, in front of her, and feel the sun getting higher and warmer. Cass gazed up the mountain, which Hettie had called Crystal Mountain, and wondered how long it took to get to the top. She wasn't that ambitious though. She'd rather lay around and listen to the Grateful Dead and wait for Rowen to get back. He'd left the day before yesterday, so it was getting time, in her mind at least. She really should call her mom. Was her shit really going to be by the dumpster? Fuck. Cass heard the door creak and started walking back to help Hettie up the path.

"Don't worry too much," Hettie said, as if reading her mind, "Rowen will come back. He's just going through a lot right now."

Cass nodded and let his grandma lean on her as they climbed up. It was all a little weird. She smelled like lavender and baby powder. She'd known Rowen all his life. Cass had pretty much just met him. When they got inside the door, Cass said, "Sorry about your path. I'm sure Rowen has a better idea and I can help him."

"That's right honey. I'm gonna take a nap."

Cass asked, "Do you have a telephone I could use?"

"Sure," Hettie said, "It's right there," Hettie pointed to the kitchen counter, "You'll have to dial 1 and the area code, too. Try not to stay on long, it costs money."

"Ok, thank you," Cass said politely. Hettie hobbled into her bedroom to lay down, but left the door cracked. Cass sat on the kitchen stool and held the plastic receiver close to her, leaning in and sloping her shoulders. The phone rang twice, and Cass prepared to leave a message. She took a half breath. The machine came on, and Cass waited, then spoke: "Hi, Mom, it's me. I'm fine. Just wanted to check in. I hope you're well. Please don't leave my stuff in the dumpster. Thanks," and she hung up.

Cass actually missed her mom. She missed going into the kitchen and having coffee with her. She missed watching TV on the couch with her. She missed asking her homework questions and laughing at silly things with her. While Rowen's grandmother snored in the other room, Cass curled up in the window nook and turned on the Grateful Dead. "Operator" came on and Cass bobbed her head. It was 2:00 in the afternoon. Was Rowen coming back today? Would she go back to Kansas? Would she and Rowen build stairs for his grandma's outhouse path? Really, it was all pretty simple, but the unknown was creeping in to Cass, and she worried things would get much worse or no better. She closed her eyes and remembered the shows. She did love the music and being in the scene was just about the best there was, but how to make it work was another story.

Chapter 99
Devon

Devon watched his little girl curled up on his bed, light streaming through the high window above the bed, and showing the lingering cabin dust. The patter in his chest was a cool river, moving, moving over a glassy calm surface. They'd arrived late in the night and the length of Emma's acceptance of what was going on broke down. She was just really tired, he knew it, but the way she screamed and cried and called out, "Where's Mommy, where's Mommy," slit him. Devon worried she wouldn't forgive him, would be screaming her head off for days. He let her kick her small legs against the floor board, squirming on the wood slats, until she was exhausted. Then he picked her up and carried her to the bed where he rocked her in his arms for a good hour. Tears streamed down his face, too, feeling the weight of having had to change her life so abruptly. He knew the whole thing was not ideal. It was crap, in fact, but he'd had no choice, he'd convinced himself.

Before Emma woke up, Devon put on "Bear's Choice" and let the simple acoustic guitars and Jerry's soothing voice fill the cabin. He made coffee, like he would any day, and straightened her things up. He'd cleared space on his desk and placed a new coloring book and bright pens there for her to discover. He placed little white stones and rocks and a few feathers he'd pulled from the mantle and wiped the dust off next to her book.

From the other room, Devon heard a little whimper and small cough, like a lost puppy caught out in the rain overnight. As Devon walked to be there when she got up, he realized that getting Emma to the cabin might only be half the battle. She would have to like it there, would have to trust him, too, would have to let go of being a mama's girl. It was delicate, she was delicate and brave and so beautiful. Devon suppressed his own smoker's cough, and heard his heavy boots plod the floor as he walked to the bedroom. He sat gently on the edge of the bed and smiled at Emma. She rubbed her eyes and her sleepy self climbed into his arms. Devon could feel his heart beats bump against her body and they slowed down and love washed over him. "Good morning sunshine," he whispered.

"Morning Daddy." She squirmed a little, and Devon held her away from him for a moment, looking into her deep brown eyes.

"Are you hungry, Baby? I can make you some oatmeal. Would you like that?" She nodded, and Devon thought maybe, just maybe, it was going to be alright. "I got you something special and a little place to do some coloring while I make your breakfast." Devon set her on her feet, pulled down and brushed her cotton dress. He took her hand, "Come, I'll show you."

Emma was delighted when she saw the desk and slipped into the chair and opened the book and took caps off three marker colors right away. Yes, Devon thought and went to make her breakfast. Bobby started signing "I've Been All Around this World," and Devon's heart grew as he remembered all the times he'd spent at that desk thinking of her, making silver buckles with memories of her as his guide. And now she was there, blessing his workspace, blessing him.

She ate all the thick oatmeal in her bowl, chewing up the raisins and pecans he'd put in it. She even walked her bowl to the kitchen sink and stood on her tippy toes to place it in the porcelain. "Good girl, finishing all your breakfast, and thanks for helping clean up, too," Devon said.

"Mmm-hmm," she said, and was about to go right back to her desk, when Devon beckoned her to the couch. He'd pulled a thick photo album down from the shelf and it opened with a sticky cracking, unearthing the pages from one another. The photos had rounded edges and fading colors. They were from the late sixties and seventies and pressed under sheets of thick plastic with edges wanting to curl. Emma ran her fingers over the pictures.

"Who's that Daddy," she said pointing to his mother, standing in the yard with hands on hips and a stern look on her face like she didn't like having her picture taken.

"That was your grandma, Baby," Devon said.

"Oh, and what's that," she said pointing to a piece of farm equipment they used to use to clear the fields.

"That was for farming. Did you know your grandpa helped farm right around here?"

"Really, Daddy," she said. Devon's little girl seemed genuinely interested. It was her history, and Devon mused if he'd ever told her this before. There were years when he didn't come back to this land, when their life was occupied in Southern California and on tour. It wasn't until he'd gotten out of prison that he'd come back.

"Can we see the farm, Daddy?" Emma asked smiling up at him.

"We can see where it used to be, and the forest and mountains. It's really beautiful around here." Devon turned one more page of the album and Pig Pen blew out the harmonica notes on "Smokestack Lightening." Emma peered over the next page and the faces there, which Devon pointed out, as his father, his aunts, and himself, a tall and gangly teenager, with hands stuffed into faded jeans and eyes squinting at the camera. On the far right, was a picture of the headstone in the front yard. Devon had learned, when he was old enough, that his momma insisted on his dead sister being buried near enough to the cabin to keep her close. He often thought it was strange, especially when he'd seen Mrs. Jones' daughter, Jessie, camped out by it talking to herself. Emma leaped off the couch and went to use the bathroom. She could do that by herself, and Devon was proud. When she came out, Devon helped her on with her tennis shoes.

"Should we go exploring, Baby?" He suggested.

"Yes, let's!' she said. The boys' guitars were jangling away and Devon went to turn the stereo off before they left. "Who's that music, Daddy?"

"That's the Grateful Dead," he said and Emma nodded her head, dancing a little like she liked it. This made Devon smile.

Hettie squinted out the window in late morning haze, sun peeking from behind Crystal Mountain. Her eyes caught two figures moving through her field. She set her cup down, placed the quilt squares beside the couch where Cass's were, and moved to the porch. It was two people and one a good yard taller than the other. She creaked on the porch and heard the wood sap pop. A finch soared by and streaky clouds continued their flee from the sky. Hettie saw the little arm reaching up and that other was Maxwell's son.

"If he Gawd dang climbs up that mountain one more time," Hettie said under her breath. They were walking side length to the mountain, probably near to the creek, but she didn't like that whimsical urge to climb. And who is that child he's walking with? Hettie limped to the side of the porch railing and hollered over.

"Hey there. Hey." The two lazily looked back and Hettie waved her arm in the air. It was her land. If other than wild animals going for a drink come by, she wanted to remind them it was private property. "Where you two going," Hettie shouted. Inside she could hear the kitchen tap go on, then off and Cass walking towards the porch.

Devon waved his arm in the air with a little hello, but he didn't look up to the porch. Instead he bent down and picked up the girl, lifting her above the taller grass, as they moved closer to the stream.

It didn't seem Hettie could do anything about those two, not with a silly snowball still plastered round her ankle. She hobbled back inside and let the screen door slam like a heavy book closing. Cass was straightening the rags in the kitchen and making herself useful. Hettie was beginning to teach her about quilting, using some square bits to run string through. Cass seemed happy to have something to focus on. Hettie was sure she was preoccupied inside with thoughts of Rowen and what would happen when he returned.

"Did you get enough breakfast," Hettie asked Cass.

"I did, thank you," Cass said. Hettie had taught her how to whip up eggs and flour and make a light, thick and fluffy cake to be browned on the griddle. "Do you think Rowen will be back today," she asked Hettie, just a twinge of pain in her voice.

"I don't know, Miss Cass, but I imagine soon." Hettie leaned against the kitchen counter and arranged some things that had been there far too long. Then the phone rang, the sound like a cockatoo learning to shout. Hettie picked it up on the second ring and said hello. Then she waited for a minute.

"This is Mrs. Jones," she said. "oh, yes, yes she is. Would you like to talk with her?" Hettie held the receiver against her chest and raised her eyebrows at Cass who was settled on the couch. "Um, I believe this is your mother on the phone."

Cass leaped up and looked like she was going to dive for the phone, her face a hot beet pink. Hettie held the phone out to Cass and moved past the coiled cord slowly to the other side of the room. Cass waited then, put the phone to her ear and tentatively said, "Mom?"

Hettie watched Cass, hand tucked under her arm, shoulders hunched over, head down. Clearly she was in the wrong, Hettie thought, and seemed very embarrassed about her mom calling, which she deduced was not an expected call.

"I know, Mom." "I did, Mom." "I will, Mom." That was mainly what she heard Cass say.

Then, "I'm sorry, Mom." Cass repeated all these phrases two more times, and was on the phone for about ten minutes, her body curling in, then straightening in defiance, then recoiling again. Hettie could only imagine that this girl's mother was less than pleased with her traipse around the country. She didn't know exactly how old Cass was, but she suspected barely old enough to set out on her own with a twenty-three year old who practically lived in his van.

Still, Hettie wasn't worried about Cass, with Rowen having left her there. He might not be college material, or all that responsible, but Hettie knew he had a good heart and would feel sorry for any wrong doing he did to Cass. Hettie knew he was grieving, too. And the matter of her arriving hungover, or whatever it was, well that was just kids being kids. She'd had too much but was safe and now off it. Finally, when Cass got off the phone, she grabbed a jacket and beelined for the door.

"Sorry," she said to Hettie, "I'm gonna take a walk."

Hettie tried not to snicker much and just nodded as Cass opened and closed the door quietly behind her.

Well, at least they'd talked. At least there wasn't some mystery of where she was, at least what state she was in. Her mom probably had Jack show her how to trace the call from when she'd left a message. A different area code. She could hear her mom's voice inside her head: angry, sad, disappointed, hurt, all fucking rolled into one.

Cass walked down the road towards that path she'd taken before. So she might not know what she was doing with her life, like her mom had shouted, but who fucking cared. She didn't want to be like everyone else, a funnel into college, job, marriage, house, babies, carpool and death. Fuck no. She wanted a vibrant life. She wanted a life more free and in the world, like her Dad. Cass wondered if he'd ever show up and show her something interesting. She probably wouldn't like him though. Her mom sure didn't. But the thought of sharing a home with her mom, and stupid Jack, who was probably moved in by now, was less appealing that dumpster diving at a Dead show.

Cass knew money didn't grow on trees, but she'd learned a little bit about hustling and selling and she thought she was actually pretty fine at it. She liked selling coolers full of beer and making a hundred bucks in ones and meeting people, making them happy. It was a stark contrast from the back of a grocery store, chasing away misshapen fruit.

Cass ducked under the fence again and walked with purpose up the forest path. Rowen was going to come back, he was going to love her, they were going to tour together and make money and live life. Why the fuck not? Cass wanted to go everywhere in the world, and she wanted to start now. She had no interest in office buildings, or babies or big houses. She had no interest in Kansas anymore. Unless the Dead is playing there, she chuckled to herself.

Cass realized she was coming to the field again and the place where she'd seen the Steal Your Face. It was comforting, and as she walked into the clearing, she saw two people walking up to that cabin. The man was tall and familiar, and he held the hand of a little girl. Cass stopped and breathed and squinted, until the man looked up and saw her. He stopped, too, and looked down to the little girl. Cass watched him scoop her up. Then she realized it was that guy, Devon, from tour! Cass walked across the field like it was a natural, welcomed thing to do. She noticed Devon wrapping his arms tighter around the little girl as she approached.

"Devon? Is that you, brother?" Cass said. She liked using the word "brother" and thought it might relax him and help him remember her from tour.

"Oh! Cass? Hey, what're you doing here?"

"I'm staying with Rowen's grandmother." The little girl looked at Cass and back at Devon and back at Cass.

"Hi," Cass said to her.

"This is my daughter, Emma."

"Oh, wow, I didn't know you had a daughter. It's nice to meet you Emma. And how old are you?"

The little girl looked at her Dad like she was scared.

"You can tell her, Baby, this is my friend, Cass."

"I'm seven," she said.

"That's a great age!" Cass said.

She squirmed in her Daddy's arms, and Cass took a step back. "Is this your place? I noticed the Steal Your Face when I took a walk around here the other day. It's a beautiful spot."

"Aw, thanks," Devon said, "this is where I grew up."

"Wow, that's so cool. Hey, did you see the shows in Arizona?" Cass asked, as he shifted a bit and seemed like he was ready to go inside.

"Oh, no, I didn't" he said, "we're gonna go inside and get some lunch. It was nice to see you Cass. Welcome to the neighborhood." And Devon turned to walk back to his cabin. Cass waited for a second, then gave Emma a little wave and turned back towards the path.

Wow, what a small world. This is what I'm talking about, Cass thought, just getting out in the world, there's always something good and people to see. She glanced back as Devon closed his cabin door. He was a little abrupt saying goodbye, but maybe his little girl was tired, or hungry or both. Wow, he's a Dad, Cass thought. She wouldn't have thought. It made her like him more though. It made him soften in her mind. Rowen must've known him a long time, if he grew up down the street from his grandmother. So he wasn't just a Deadhead, he was a father.

Chapter 102
Devon

Devon closed the door and felt a tiny bit better, as he watched Emma go straight back to the desk and her coloring. He arranged things by the front door, hanging a fallen coat on the wood peg, lining his boots and Emma's new tennis shoes under the bench. He could feel sweat sliding down his back, he could feel a subtle tremble in his movements. It was so strange to see Cass. He knew the connection through Rowen, but he didn't think he'd be back around, especially with tour going on. He thought about it for a minute as he looked over at Emma perched on the chair, occupying herself quietly. Seeing Cass was a slight collision. Now someone else knew where he was, had seen him with Emma. It wasn't a secret, but reality washed over him like lava and Devon wondered if there was time to make things right.

"Daddy, come see," Emma squealed, "I've colored the bird." Devon walked over and knelt down next to her. She seemed truly proud of the pale blue back and forth lines and the circular navy blue lines that lay mostly inside the black borders of a bird in tree branches.

"That's beautiful, Baby! Good job," he said, and at the same time Devon wanted to break down crying. He both knew that these were the moments that he wanted and missed so much, and he might not have them again past these walls. He just wished time could stop right there, as her brown butter eyes gazed at him, and the sides of her smile curled. Devon put his arm around and hugged her. "You know I love you so much Emma. You know that, right, Baby?"

She nodded and laid her head against his shoulder. "I know, Daddy.

I love you, too," and she leaned away to kiss his cheek lightly.

Devon had to be strong. He had to believe. He couldn't break down. Emma needed him now.

Rowen turned onto the dirt road and bumped along, slowing down, feeling the weight of his actions, feeling the weight of having to face Cass and his grandma. It only took a few rotations of his tires though and he sloughed it off. The only way to make something right, was to believe it was right, to believe that he knew exactly what he was doing and not show otherwise. He saw the big cloud of mocha dirt billowing behind the van and smiled. He did love this land. As soon as he angled the van up the small driveway, the cabin door opened and Cass flew out.

"Thank fucking God," Cass said under her breath. It was about time, and instead of running to the driver's seat and wrapping her arms around Rowen, like part of her wanted to, she stood there, arms crossed, staring him down. She watched him take his time, turning off the ignition and crawling in the back before popping the side doors open and sheepishly getting out. He walked up to her, let his bag drop to the ground, and wrapped his arms around her rigid body. Cass sighed and eventually hugged him back. They stood there for a long time, until Hettie creaked the front door open.

"Well there ya are," she said, grinning and waiting for them to let go of each other.

"Hey, Gran," Rowen said. He wasn't going to apologize for anything. It all was what it was. Inside, he sat on the couch next to Cass, holding her hand, and peering at the quilt squares on the table in front of her. Good, she was keeping busy. She probably could do a lot more crafts, Rowen thought. She could sell them on tour. With her body close to him, he started to think he'd like to keep her on tour. They could make it work. She just needed a bit more schooling, life schooling that is, and she'd be a decent Head.

"How were the shows?" Cass asked.

"They were alright. The mail orders were good."

"Did you take anyone in with you?

"What? No," Rowen said and got up to get something to drink in the kitchen. He seemed pissed by her question, and Cass could feel her cheeks turning red.

"Ugh," she thought. How did she know? He could've taken that fucking Jasmin girl into the show, he could've met someone new. Cass took a deep breath and closed her eyes, trying to reign in her mind. She felt a little like a roman candle that probably shouldn't be pointed at Rowen. She'd spent the past half week wondering if she'd be left at this guy's grandmother's in the middle of fucking nowhere, forever. She remembered how many times she wondered if he was ever going to come back. It wasn't all that cool, and she tightened her body again, crossing her arms and sealing herself into the couch. Did he even like her anymore?

Clearly, he'd have to deflect some poison from Cass, Rowen thought. Ok, so he had just upped and left, but she didn't know him. He'd done it for both their own good. Nothing was going to change this perspective. He sat on the other side of the couch, talking to Hettie about her outhouse, and crossing his arms, too. Rowen spent a lot of the dwindling day helping his grandma hobble around by her path down the hill and around her outhouse, listening to everything she wanted him to do. He'd popped back into the van two or three times to toke up and help his mind process the good intention of wanting to be there for his grandma like he wasn't for his mom. He'd decided to deflect Cass's little arrows and barely answered the questions she fired at him about his time in Arizona. It was tedious. He didn't have time for that shit and tried to make that obvious by focusing on the project at hand, but by afternoon, he found her sulking in the back of the van.

"What's up?" Rowen said, leaning in and staring at Cass who was laying on the back bench. She had her bag on the floor.

She was not going to be left again, so Cass was ready when he was. She liked being in the van. She even liked the faint smell of grilled cheese and sour beer. "Are we going to another show?" Cass said leaning on her side, trying to be casual.

"There isn't one for a few weeks," Rowen said, "I thought we'd stick around here for a few days, help my Gan."

"Oh," Cass said, flopping back on the bed. What the fuck, she thought, she'd been hanging around in this wilderness for what seemed like forever. She wanted to be with Rowen, and she was grateful he was back in the same vicinity with her, but she wanted to be close with him.

"Unless you want to get a bus back to Kansas or something," Rowen said.

He watched her turn over and bury her head in the pillow. Oh, man, he thought, but Rowen climbed in the van and pulled the door half shut. He sat on the bed next to Cass and laid his palm on her back. "Hey, I don't want you to go back to Kansas. Not yet. Unless that's what you want?"

"It's not what I want," she almost screamed and turned to look at him, her eyes filling up. Rowen thought her tears were cute. They made her even prettier, and he leaned down gently to kiss her forehead and her cheeks and then her lips.

"Ok, what do you want?" He asked softly.

"To be with you. To go to more shows. To stay away from Kansas."

"Shouldn't you be going to college or something," Rowen asked. In his mind he imagined that was the natural path for a girl like her, or a girl he imagined was like her. Someone from a good home, someone who finished high school, and probably came from money, unlike him.

"Until I met you, the only place I'd ever been was Kansas and Missouri. I just want to live a little and get out there. Plus, being at a Grateful Dead concert is the most interesting and joyful thing I've experienced in my life. Why would I want to do anything else?" Cass looked at Rowen, his long hair oily from not washing it, his eyes and his broad smile. She just wanted to stay with him, as long as she could.

"I hear that, but I don't want to keep you from a life you should start living," Rowen said, looking away.

"But, I am starting to live it," she pleaded with him.

Rowen coughed and felt a burning in his chest again. He just didn't want to be responsible. Part of him wanted to hide. He rested his head in his hand, pushing back onto the side bench. She probably wouldn't understand. She couldn't understand. His mom had just fucking died. What was he supposed to do with that.

"Rowen?"

"What?" he snapped, not looking at her.

Cass leaned towards him, and Rowen leaned away. She went to hug him and his body became stiff as a rusted fence. He didn't want to have to tell her everything, for fuck's sake. He tried to move away.

"What's wrong with you?" Cass said.

Rowen shook his head slowly. She didn't get it.

"What is it? Is it me? Don't you like me?'

Then it bubbled out and Rowen sobbed, a train running through him "No! It's not you," he couldn't look at her, "Cass, my mother just died, what the fuck do you want from me?"

The air froze inside the van, and Cass leapt from the bed, pushed the door open, "I'm sorry! Ok!" she shouted.

Fucking A. Rowen gripped his head, fell into the bed, screamed into the pillow. He let her run off. Fuck this.

Chapter 104
Hettie

Hettie was looking out the front window when she saw Cass jump out of the van and run down the driveway. Jeez, she thought, these kids and their drama. What happened to my peace and my peace of mind. Hettie thought she also heard a sound from Rowen's van. Maybe he's finally letting go. Hettie hobbled back into the kitchen. Cups were strewn on the counter, dishes in the sink. She wasn't used to this company, but a part of her went back to when the boys were little. It was a constant battle. No wonder Jessie worked at a restaurant, cleaning and clearing and hauling plates. It was familiar to her, and at work she at least got paid. But now her daughter wouldn't have to work early mornings or late nights. Now her kin would have to clean up after themselves. She imagined Lou and Tate were sliding back into their usual ways. They were beyond Hettie, but Rowen, he could still get it together, whatever that meant. Hettie wanted him to start with doing something simple for her. A path to her outhouse, with a railing, so she didn't fear for herself every time she had to take a shit down the hill.

Hettie balanced on her good foot, and started the dishes, when Rowen walked in. His head was down, and he moved slowly. Hettie glanced at him. "Everything ok, black cat?"

"I don't know, Gran." Rowen came over to sit at the stool facing the kitchen. Hettie saw that his face was crumpled and wet. Her heart turned in her chest, and she set the dishes in the sink. "I'm so sorry I wasn't there for her," he said leaning his head into his hands.

Hettie hobbled towards him and got close enough to put her arms around him.

"Hush," she whispered, "don't you worry about that. There was nothing could be done. She was just finished, that's all." Rowen nestled into Hettie's shoulder and took a deep sighing breath. "That a boy. You can let it go." He nodded into her neck and Hettie felt she was useful, for the first time in decades. Her grandson, finally feeling. Life was going to be ok.

"Thanks Gran, you know I love you."

"I do." She leaned away and brushed her fingers under his eyes. "But that girl, I don't know if she knows."

Rowen shook his head slowly back and forth. "I can't. I just can't right now. I mean I do like her, but I know I shouldn't've left her here. I'm sorry."

"It's ok. Life can be messy. No one's hurt," Hettie said. Rowen nodded and went to the kitchen to finish up the dishes.

Hettie went to sit on the couch and relax herself. She liked him cleaning up. Maybe Percy's ghost didn't need to help him, maybe he could help himself, she thought. Hettie's great-grandaddy hadn't shown up since Cass and Rowen arrived. Although she missed him, and his fiddle playing just a little, she knew it was better to have living folk around her, if they didn't drive her too crazy. She wondered about Percy though. She hoped he was feeling less sore about his wife dying, she hoped things turned out ok for him in the end. Hettie gazed up at a stream of afternoon sunlight shining on the wall and making a streak right across the blue quilt. It was a diagonal streak and it sliced right through the middle of the quilt, lighting up the diamond patches, in sky, in black, in denim and in deep ocean. It was like heaven piercing across her cabin and straight through the eye of that bird, that traced open for her like a rainbow spark from a crystal. It was right there, and she could see its head following the light path to the top of the ceiling. "My, my," Hettie whispered and she looked out the far window, past the porch beams to the beauty of Crystal Mountain shining, too. She heard the water streaming from the sink and felt warm and comfortable resting on her couch. Hettie closed her eyes for a few minutes.

Chapter 105
Percy

As soon as it slowed, winding into the valley he knew well, Percy hopped off the train. The rough ground met him. He situated his satchel over his shoulder and started the walk to his home. Crickets buzzed, radiating the late summer heat and dogs barked in the distance. His feet steered him through the trees up a path his body knew like the back of his mind. He surveyed the ground, somewhat moist, darker in color, probably from a good recent rain. That was better than dry. As he climbed the inclining path, the breath drained from him. Molly wasn't walking behind him; she wasn't walking in front of him either. The hole her absence left was clear as day in his body, and Percy sighed, knowing that it was gonna be like that, every day.

Panic came in, too, hard like a rock he could slip on. He had to face everyone, his boys' tall frames that took after him, the dimples in the sides of their cheeks that stung of his Molly, and his little girl with eyes wide and curious like her, too. Percy continued on, forced a breath in and out, in and out, cradling his fiddle under his arm. He came out to the other road and walked to where he could see the outline of the house, roof sloping down like a face half sunk. The dog started his barking from that faraway place and the familiar sound perked Percy's heart. He walked on and saw his boys leaning against the porch poles. They were dressed in pants and long shirts. His daughter sitting on the porch in a skirt, legs swinging and tucking under the thin boards. Her hair was tied up pretty, he saw, coming closer, church. His sister had taken them to church. It must be Sunday.

He watched his sons raise their hands to shield their eyes and see him walking on up. His younger boy ducked into the house, and Percy stopped when the screen door slammed. His older boy just stood there, throwing little bits of something off the porch. He heard their voices, clamoring and shouting. And then his girl hopped off the porch and came running towards him.

"Papa, Papa!"

Percy knelt, put his things down, and captured her in his arms.

Chapter 106
Devon

They had turkey sandwiches for lunch. Emma told him exactly how to make them, a realization that she'd grown up fast bloomed in him like Spring tree buds.

"The mayo goes right up to the edge of the bread. Don't you know that, Daddy," she said, with her hands on her hips shaking her head dramatically play acting.

"Oh, you're absolutely right, Baby!"

She'd eaten a big sandwich in tiny bites and brought the dish to the sink. She was doing a remarkable job feeling comfortable in the cabin, Devon thought. Maybe it was too comfortable. Devon pretended they were on vacation, but also not on vacation. He knew little girls like her had to go to school. But people raised their children in all different ways. He could teach her there. They could live simply, like his grandparents probably did.

Devon looked around the cabin. He wanted to clean it up more. He wanted to plant a garden and get the wood stove scrubbed up for winter. He wanted to chop wood and sharpen the axe. He wanted to do an oil change on the new truck. He looked out the window and saw its hulking sandy colored shape. Panic zipped in for a moment when he remembered leaving his bike at that shop. The bike he'd ridden so many miles and roads on. It wasn't no more. He looked at Emma and blushed out any hard feelings for having let it go. Here was his daughter, snoozing on his couch, in New Mexico. Thank heavens for this.

"Caw, caw, cuckaw!" Devon heard muffled from outside, but right by the cabin. He looked out the front window and a big raven was waddling in front of the house. It called again. Devon shook his head slightly. No more, he thought. He was a father; he couldn't shift his body now. That was all over. And he felt a strange lift under his arms, inside his shirt, like the tug of a sore muscle. His eyes blinked quickly, and he could feel an odd twitch as his neck flicked from one side to another, a spasm. Devon blinked again and his breathing changed. Matching Emma's breath as she lay curled up on the couch. He saw her in a different light, without trying. Devon came close, so curious, perceiving the quiet and life that streamed through her. Through the window behind him, he heard the lift of wings flap high against the air and all his senses turned up: the clock ticking above the stove, the creak of wind through the wood cabin, a scuffle of tiny feet somewhere in the walls.

Chapter 107
Cass

The soles of her feet felt uneven on the forest path as Cass walked away from Rowen's grandmother's house. She sniffed loudly and wiped her sleeve under her nose, brushed wet cheeks with her fingers. She needed to pull herself together. Yes, Rowen had left to go to a show without her. Yes, he'd come back. Yes, her mom knew where she was. And, no, she wasn't high anymore. Her breathing steadied as she moved on the familiar path through pine trees, over needled grounds, amidst birdsong. Her mind came back to Rowen's words. She couldn't imagine what he must be feeling. She couldn't imagine her own mom dying, least not anytime soon. Rowen was hard to read. He always kept things so cool, that he seemed fine, but maybe he wasn't. Cass started to feel bad for pushing him about the two of them. To her, it was front and center in her mind—a man like him loving her, wanting to make some type of life with her. Even though Hillary had introduced her to The Dead, she didn't have the kind of drive or confidence or just money that she did. Rowen was her ticket out of Kansas life, but more so, she felt like she was in love with him.

Cass sniffed again and remembered her experiences on tour. Rowen was the biggest part of it, but she thought of Forrest, and Changa and Ollie and Jane. There were so many other cool people she liked meeting there. They were part of her Deadhead family, too. As the path narrowed, and then opened, she remembered being able to talk to anyone on tour: young, old, rich, poor, hippie or businessman. She liked that she could just chat with people on tour. The Steal Your Face on his cabin 300 feet in front of her was like a marker of welcome, a marker of community. Yeah, he had been kind of quick with her the other day, but he was a Deadhead, they had that in common.

Chapter 108
Devon

The telephone rang and rattled the inside of the cabin. It sent Devon's heart pounding in his ears. He didn't want it to wake Emma. He leapt to the kitchen counter and didn't dare to answer it but switched the little ringer button on the side. No one ever called. No one had this number. But it was also his only phone number, and everything he had to sign, all the papers, all the official papers, had it on there. Cora might have it, too. For one moment, Devon thought about Cora with something other than hate. Emma was her little girl, too, and even though she was a fucking bitch to him most of the time, he did love her at one point. She was probably terrified. She was probably out of her mind with worry over where Emma was.

Beads of sweat slid down behind his ears, and Devon found himself looking from the phone to Emma's little body on the couch, from the front window to the front door. It had been a little over 72 hours. What had he been thinking? Devon wanted to cry. He could hear and feel the metal slam of bars. He could hear the shouting of his old cell mates. Holy fuck. What had he done.

Just as he was about to pick Emma up off the couch, and rock her in his arms, there was a knock on the front door. He couldn't breathe. Shit. The knock came again, and then he heard "Hello? Devon?" It was Cass. He both did and didn't want to open the door. Something in him knew he would have to face the world. If it meant her, maybe that would be just fine. Get yourself together, man, he told himself. He opened the door. "Oh, hi, Cass," Devon said, stepping back and letting her inside.

"Shhh, Emma's just been napping."

"Oh, she's so sweet," Cass whispered.

Devon ran his hand through his hair, dampening the sweat down. Cass looked like she'd been crying. "Everything alright?"

"Yeah. How about for you?" Devon looked away so she couldn't study him too much, couldn't see the fear and worry and shame that he felt was seeping from all of his pores. They both heard a little whimper from the couch, and Emma turned on her side, and as she blinked her eyes open she cried a little, her face contorting until she took a sharp breath in. Devon rushed to the couch and scooped her in his arms. She was a baby bird. "Oh, what is it, Baby? Did you have a bad dream?'

"Mmm-hmm," she said nodding her head.

"It's ok now, honey, you're awake." She snuggled into Devon's shoulder sleepily. Then she looked up and saw Cass standing there quietly.

"Hi," she said to Cass.

"Hi, Emma." Cass walked to sit on the chair next to the couch. Emma rubbed her eyes and slid off Devon's lap. She walked over to the desk and got her bird coloring. She brought it over to Cass.

"Look what I did," she said to Cass, standing close to her.

Ok, Devon thought, maybe this was good. Emma could use a female around her. She might be confused about things. As Devon watched the two of them, he started feeling heat under his shirt collar again. He reverted to the sharpened senses, his vision changing and stinging his eyes. He went to stand and felt dizzy. His head was ringing, the remembrance of the telephone ringing, the buzz of crickets outside, the creak of the cabin. Devon put his hand out to hold onto the couch and walk around it.

"Are you ok?" Cass said quietly still engaged but looking up at him with concern in her eyes.

"Oh, yeah. Just stood up too fast," Devon lied. "I think I need some air. I'll be right back," he said and walked to the front door. Cass nodded and lightly put her arm around

Emma's shoulder, pointing to the picture and asking her questions. Before stepping outside, Devon looked back at the two of them, and he felt the softness of a pillow, of a blanket, of a quilt. His little girl. She was so precious, so young, so beautiful. He saw himself in the side of her cheek, in the slope of her tender jaw. His vision blurred to indigo, then to a whole combination of other colors. He stared up at the immense clear blue in the sky. Another raven call came, and then Devon saw the slow cloud of dust above the road. He heard the rush of car wheels on the dirt road. Instinctively, he walked around the cabin, lifted the metal trash can lid, and saw a glaring reflection, a red and blue flash. He pulled all of his clothes off, stuffed them in the trash can, clanged the lid back and walked behind the cabin into the woods. The sweat on his skin turned slick, and he became something else, just as two police cars pulled in the drive.

Chapter 109

Cass

Cass stood on Devon's lawn, one hand in her pocket, the other holding Emma's hand as she leaned closer to her, clearly afraid of what was happening. Three plain clothes cops were tromping in and out of the cabin, making notes, using walkie talkies, studying everything they could. What the fuck is happening, Cass thought. Why are they here? Where is Devon? She had answered one's probing questions as he took notes, a gun on his holster, handcuffs swinging on a clip. She'd told him she knew Devon from a concert, but she didn't know him that well, and she'd just met his daughter the other day. They didn't tell her why they were there, but Cass guessed it wasn't good.

Everything she'd been thinking about flew from her. She wasn't worried about her and Rowen; she wasn't thinking about the next Dead show. She had switched her perspective. She thought about Jack, just doing his job. She thought about selling beer in the parking lot. She thought about how she'd taken a lot of illegal drugs. And when she looked down at this little girl, scared and shaking, she thought about people who had done wrong to one another. It wasn't the free love, good all she knew on tour. This was something else. As the cops continued searching the property, Cass knelt down to talk to Emma. "Are you ok, sweetie?"

Emma shook her head, no. Cass squeezed Emma's hand and opened her arms when the little girl turned and reached for her. Tears slid down her face.

"Oh, honey, it's going to be ok. These men are just doing their job." Cass didn't know what else to say. She had seen, less than an hour ago, how much Devon loved this little girl. She had a feeling he'd run somewhere. What had he done? Cass hugged Emma and walked a little more around the yard, holding her and bouncing her like a baby. She did not go far. The cops wouldn't have let her yet. She tried to look like she was helping, taking care of this scared little girl. Cass looked around on the ground and saw little pebbles, nestled between the scrubby grass. She set Emma down and took her hand again. She reached for a little brown rock and handed it to Emma. She took it, turned it in her small fingers and dropped it. She took interest in others, picking up some and dropping them again. Then she spotted a larger one, white like the moon, and gripped it tight. She looked up at Cass, like a koala.

"What did you find, Emma?"

Emma kept her hand gripped and shook her head.

"Is it a pretty one?"

Emma nodded.

"Let's see, sweetie."

Emma looked around her, both ways, peering at the cops and back into the forest. Finally, she crouched near Cass and opened her hand. The rock she had there sparkled, little flecks alighting in the sun.

"Oh, that's a good one."

"I know," Emma whispered, "It's from Daddy."

Chapter 110
Hettie

Hettie limped to the front door, closing it securely and bolting it when the police folk had finally left. Having them in her cabin felt like an intrusion. She took charge of the conversations because she could feel Rowen's discomfort with their presence there. He'd spent the whole time sitting next to Cass on the couch, gripping her hand in plain sight.

So, Devon had taken that little girl. The one Hettie saw him walking in the field with. Even if he was her daddy, things didn't work that way anymore. Hettie only remembered hearing of Devon marrying someone out west but guessed it didn't last long. Not when he'd returned and started rumbling that motorcycle past her house. The cops had searched her whole place, too, inside and out, and she even watched them spend too much time tromping around her outhouse. They'd lifted and lowered just about everything sitting around Hettie's place. They'd shaken out all the quilts hanging on the walls, as if Devon could be standing behind them or something. So he'd disappeared. If he went anywhere, Hettie thought, it would be up Crystal Mountain. Jeez, now the whole valley was going to be crawling with these buffoons until they found him. Hettie was determined to help them as little as possible. Devon might be an outlaw, but she knew he wasn't a bad person.

"They just took her away with a female cop," Cass told them later, "apparently her mother was waiting in the next town." She shook her head and leaned into Rowen, playing with his long hair draped over her shoulder. People can get so messed up in love, Hettie thought. She said a silent prayer over Cass and Rowen, hoping they would be better at it than most. It seemed to Hettie that Rowen had softened, both when breaking down with her earlier, and being able to keep Cass close when the cops were there. Cass seemed like a token for him, some kind of good luck.

Hettie looked past them, and onto the wall with the blue quilt. She squinted, looking for that bird head, but it was gone. Instead the center lit up like wheel spokes, leaving a pure blue space in the middle. Hettie decided right there and then that it was time for it to go. Before their last day there, she would make Rowen and Cass take it off the wall, hang it over the porch railing to get some clearing nighttime air, and send it on the way with them. They might need whatever new blessing it held as they traveled all over the place. And it could be used to keep them warm. It was going to get cold soon enough.

The two of them stayed with her for a few more days, during which Marni's husband also came over and he and Rowen set to work making a solid wood railing, more proper steps and a path that Hettie could get down, even with her cast. She knew at some point she'd need more help from Rowen or somebody, but Hettie would be happy enough with small change.

In the late morning they were to leave, Hettie folded that blue quilt that was once dropped in her lap, making sure the corners were nicely lined up. She tucked it under her arm and made her way outside to her grandson's van. The kids were gathering their things from the cabin. When she opened the door, she heard a caw from up the mountain way and she smiled, laying the quilt on the back bench to travel on with them.

"You be good, black cat," she said to Rowen, "and take care of that girl, she's a good one." Hettie wrapped him in her arms and kissed his cheek. She did the same with Cass. When the rustle up of car wheels down the road faded, Hettie sighed, leaning back on her couch and enjoying her quiet space, finally, once again.

Chapter 111
Percy

The nighttime came and went and Percy huddled on the floor pallet in his house, listening to his boys tossing in their sleep across the room. He felt their tender selves readjusting to his presence there after many months. His disappearance to other places of coal, and coughs and quiet had kept him away from them. Percy's homecoming wasn't as welcomed as he'd hoped. Sure, in time, they might be glad to have another hand around to do things, but the fate of their place on that land that'd been in the family for six decades was unsure.

The stern lines set in his sister's face as she told him about selling the back few acres for mineral rights, had blame etched into them. "When someone dies, you don't up and quit the rest of yer family," she said. Percy hadn't said anything, he kept especially quiet around everyone except his daughter. Later he did see the two letters he'd written them on a side table, the edges ripped. There had been no money in them. The envelopes had arrived empty and torn open. How to find the way back to a life there with his children, and his sister who never seemed to like him his whole life, didn't feel clear. Molly was the sweet tree sap that made everything stand. Percy still couldn't imagine being there without her; a thought he knew others had no room for.

Early morning, Percy had gone out to the damp field and the drizzly path up towards the tracks that ran too close to his house. His legs felt weary and ached, his mind blank and heavy, his soul searching with reason and end. Percy replayed his day and night and the gone space of Molly. Yet, he felt this was here, too: the low bowl of hills, the empty morning, the sounds of Appalachia at dawn.

The tracks were nestled in rough, yellowing grasses, web strands crossing close through branches, too thin to mill. It was good to be back there, but a big part of him wanted to lay down and not get up. He imagined himself a field animal, so quiet and unmoving, the kind that doesn't see the descending trap, the soft ones that are taken quickly. Molly had a long battle, and she didn't want to die. She wanted to see her children grow and garden bloom and listen to her husband play good fiddle. Percy knew she loved him more than he loved her, and the stab of that seeped in as a soft rain came. Drops fled over his cheeks and coaxed the hurt out, too. He sat down by the heavy tracks and placed his palm on the iron. Warm and solid, it could pull him down, let him lie, and leave this place to join his love. His vision blurred as golden sun streaks ran across the ground, alighting all the dew drops suspended in the grass. The beauty of this, his home, softened him, and he reminded himself that he'd missed it here. He'd missed his family. And that there was plenty of them left. Percy's hand felt the tiny tremble, slick and coming. He stayed close, willing the power to wake him up.

The sound came like the baying of a mule and Percy stood to meet it. Pushing through this valley, carrying the coal, carrying the life away from it to the other parts of the country he'd now seen. He stretched out his arms, and met the sound, screeching like fiddle strings, a bow moved back and forth. Percy closed his eyes and saw his love, standing in the field close by, her long white gown fluttering and smile melding with the sunrise. Percy felt the power of her enter his heart, stretch his limbs, lift, lift him beyond—push out everything and leave him still as the train passed by him.

❂   ❂   ❂

The pop of warming trees, the barking of neighbors' dogs, the cock and doodle of roosters called him back to his home, back to the life he had yet to live. With each step of his worn-out shoes on the dirt road, Percy settled back into himself. The ache in his knees, in his elbows and lining the curve of his strong collar bone, he knew, would ache for days when he started building his house back up with the boys, when he pulled the mule along the field to plant something. There was a whole lot of work to be done if he wanted to redeem himself there, if he wanted to provide for his family in a present way.

Percy heard the shuffle of his feet and then that song from way across the country, "Going Down the Road Feeling Bad," entered his mind. The gentle guitar plucks moved in him like a worn wagon wheel, bumping over and over and over. The motion kept on in him. He wasn't gonna escape anymore, wasn't gonna hop on a train or crawl into a distant coal hole. He wasn't gonna run away from Molly's spirit, her ghost or the good memory of her there. Only on the small plot of land he knew he was lucky to have, would life build back up in him. As the sun lifted to the edge of the far mountainside, Percy gazed to it. Though he might feel bad walking down that road, he was determined to keep the tune going. He heard his fiddle's part in the song and knew, when a good day's work was done, he'd sit on the porch and play.

Acknowledgments

This book is a long time in the making. Back when I was a touring Deadhead skirting college, I had no more aspirations than getting to the next show. After Jerry Garcia died, my life changed and I went back to school and pursued many other things and traveled farther than the U.S. This novel followed me and changed several times. The inspiration remained and the many folks who supported me on the way.

First, I want to thank my Mom who always said I would take my own path, as has this book. I thank my whole family for accepting me for who I am. I am grateful to Dr. Valerie Ostarch who encouraged my love of writing starting in eighth grade and extending to present day.

I thank my original high school partners: Amy, Kate, Blakeley, Katie Mae, and Renee Prairie, and all the Deadheads, but specifically Adam, Mike, Nick, Indiana, and Merle.

I'm incredibly grateful to Elizabeth McKinley for many writing dates, endless encouragement and for designing the cover of this book. I'm thankful to developmental writing support from Linda Rodriguez, editorial guidance from Jane Friedman, and expertise from Deirdre Wait.

I couldn't have written this novel without the space given by the late Broom at Ocamora, The McClungs in Berkeley, S. Maine in Iowa, and Aimee Carrillo-Rowe near Lake MacBride. I am also grateful to my professors at The University of Iowa, including Eric Gidal and Nathaniel Minton, among others from The Writer's Workshop. I also valued the guidance at The Iowa Summer Writing Workshop and Big Sur Writing Conference.

I'm thankful to early readers Sherry Ruskin, Rebecca Lyon, Bert, Bryant, Rachel, Kathleen and Rob. I'm grateful to my cheerleaders Regan and the KC girls and my love, Padraic.

About the Author

As a teenager, Lindsay Rice traveled around the country following the Grateful Dead and integrated the music and Deadhead culture into her life. She studied creative writing at the University of Iowa. A Kansas City native, she was the president of Whispering Prairie Press, which publishes two Kansas City literary and art magazines. She is an academic and creative writing tutor and worked for a nonprofit adult education program. Lindsay lives in the Colorado mountains. *Birdenwheel* is her debut novel.